MINDS OF MEN

BOOK ONE OF THE PSYCHE OF WAR

Kacey Ezell

Theogony Books
Virginia Beach, VA

Chris Kennedy/Theogony Books
2052 Bierce Dr.
Virginia Beach, VA 23454
http://chriskennedypublishing.com/

Publisher's Note: This is a work of fiction. Names, characters, places, and incidents are a product of the author's imagination. Locales and public names are sometimes used for atmospheric purposes. Any resemblance to actual people, living or dead, or to businesses, companies, events, institutions, or locales is completely coincidental.

Ordering Information:
Quantity sales. Special discounts are available on quantity purchases by corporations, associations, and others. For details, contact the "Special Sales Department" at the address above.

Minds of Men/Kacey Ezell. -- 1st ed.
ISBN 978-1942936886

Like any book, this one was not written in a vacuum. I would never had been able to tell this story without the support and love of a whole host of people, and I beg your indulgence as I acknowledge them here. First, thanks go always to my husband, EZ, and my daughters, Coriel and Alicya. Thank you for letting mommy slip away to write. Seconds go to my wonder twin and aggressive muse, Christopher L. Smith, for all the pep talks and aggressive muse-ing. Thirdly, Nico, Speaker, Doc, Insectress, EP, Jeremy, Brian & Stephen, Griff, Bun-Bun, Jenny, Aaron, Bolger, Bridget, San, Jerry, Scary Uncle Joseph, Marisa, Massa, Jason, Sarah, Toni, and Brandy. You guys keep me sane…ish. Fourth, special thanks to Chris Kennedy, for believing in this story, and to Brenda Mihalko for the amazing cover. Fifth, thanks to Iowa State Senator Ken Rizer, Col (ret) USAF, for letting me Tuckerize him. Sixth (but never last!), thanks to Lt Col Marcus J. Jackson IV, USAF, for signing the paper allowing me to "get another job."

Researching this novel was a labor of love in and of itself. I would be remiss if I didn't recommend in the strongest of terms the following works: *Combat Crew: The Story of 25 Combat Missions Over Europe* by John Comer, *Silent Heroes: Downed Airmen and the French Underground* by Sherri Greene Otis, and *Little Cyclone* by Airey Neave.

To the coolest guy I'll ever meet.

Epigraph:

Minds of men fashioned a crate of thunder
Sent it high into the blue
Hands of men blasted the world a-sunder
How they lived, God only knew!
Souls of men dreaming of skies to conquer
Gave us wings, ever to soar!
With scouts before and bombers galore.
Nothing can stop the Army Air Corps!

Prologue
October 1943

"Go on in, Colonel," the general's secretary said softly as the London rain pattered against the office window. "He's ready for you."

Colonel Ken Rizer, Commander of the 381st Bombardment Group at RAF Ridgewell, gave the gray-haired woman a nod and walked through the general's door. Ordinarily, he would have thanked her or asked about her day. But this morning, he found he just couldn't stomach the thought of pleasantries.

Brigadier General Clarence Durant looked up from behind his wooden desk, then came slowly to his feet as his subordinate entered the room. Lines of sympathy and sorrow etched the strong features of his face. He opened his mouth to speak, then closed it and shook his head.

"You wanted to see me, sir?" Rizer asked.

"Yes, come in," the general said. "Please, have a seat."

"Yes, sir," the colonel replied and lowered himself to sit on the edge of one of the two chairs facing the general's desk.

"Ken," General Durant said, his tone softer as he, too, sat, "I want you to know that I am very, very sorry for your unit's losses. Yesterday was a tough day."

"Thank you, sir," Rizer replied. "That means a lot."

"I don't have the final numbers yet," the general went on. "But initial reports are the 381st was among the hardest hit of all our groups. What's your tally?"

"We lost seventeen of our thirty B-17s," Rizer said. "Ten were shot down by fighters or flak, their crews listed as missing in action. Three of the remaining seven are so badly damaged they'll be scrapped. We're pulling what parts we can cannibalize off those birds now. The other four will be repaired. Timelines on the repairs run from a day or two to three weeks at the outside."

General Durant blinked as he processed the numbers. Rizer waited a beat and then went on.

"One hundred twenty-one of my men are dead, General," the colonel said. "It was a very bad day."

"Ken, I know what you want me to say—"

"Sir, we need long-range fighter escort."

"I know."

"We can't go on without it. Our Forts are sitting ducks up there. If there's any weather at all, my pilots end up having to choose between a mid-air collision and being so far out of formation they can't cover each other with their guns. There's no way to win!"

"I know, Ken. I know. And you're right. Unfortunately, the long-range fighter is still a few months away."

Rizer froze, holding himself rigid so he wouldn't let the screaming profanity come out of his mouth. He'd been raised to be respectful, professional. He would maintain his military bearing, even though the world seemed to be collapsing around him.

"Sir—" he said, his voice low. General Durant held up a hand, and Rizer closed his mouth.

"Ken, I can't give you a long-range fighter escort until after the new year. Best guess. However, I may have another temporary solution."

"What's that, sir?" Rizer asked, careful to keep his tone even.

"Have you ever met my wife?"

"No sir," Rizer said. Where the hell was this going? "I haven't had the pleasure."

"Fascinating woman, my Ruth. Smart as a whip. Talented, too. She knows when the kids are misbehaving before they even act."

"Sir, that's wonderful, but I don't see what—"

"Ken, listen to me. When we were in garrison, Ruth used to tell me what to pick up at the market on the way home. While I was on my way home."

"How is that—?"

"She speaks to me," the general said, tapping his forefinger against his left temple. "In *here*. She can see through my eyes, make me see through hers. Two hundred years ago, she'd probably have been burned as a witch, but right now, women like her might just be our salvation."

Rizer leaned forward in his chair, interested despite himself.

"How do you mean, sir?" he asked.

"Ruth isn't alone, Ken. There aren't very many of them, but women with talent are out there. Psychics, some call them. Oh, I know that most who claim that title are charlatans, but there are ways to test a woman for the kind of talent Ruth has. She can detect it, if she's close enough. For the last several months, my wife has been part of a top secret mission to find and recruit enough talented women to help make a difference here."

"But...they're all women?"

"Unfortunately, yes. Seems men can't have psychic power. And most of the women who do aren't strong enough for our purposes. My last report from Ruth said that of the thousands of women she's tested, only a handful have anywhere near enough power to do what we will need them to do."

"And what is that, sir?" Rizer asked, his head spinning as he tried to keep up.

"They'll fly with our crews, communicate with one another. Help them fly tighter formation, help them have better communications. They'll help prevent the kind of fiasco your men experienced when the weather caused them to break formation yesterday. It's not a perfect solution, Ken; I know that. But damn it, it's all I've got until the long-range fighter arrives."

"Psychics," Rizer said. "Sir...I'll be honest. I'm skeptical. I mean, I've heard rumors of witches and such, but I just figured them for children's bedtime stories. But I have to admit, I am in no position to turn down anything that's going to help my men do their jobs, no matter how unorthodox. If you say this is a good idea, the 381st will give it a go."

General Durant smiled.

"That's the spirit, Ken," he said. "I've sent for the first class already. They're on a troop ship to Liverpool as we speak. You can probably expect them in a week. They're technically part of the Women's Army Corps, but they'll answer to you. I suggest you make arrangements for their billets and such right away."

Rizer could feel his eyes going wide as the logistical headache of billeting a group of women on a combat airfield began to present itself. He shook his head and chased that thought away. He would have to figure out the details once he returned to Ridgeway. He nodded and came to his feet.

"I'll look forward to their arrival, sir," he said.

General Durant stood and came around from behind the desk, his hand extended.

"Ken, I know this isn't what you wanted to hear. I give you my word, I'm working to get you those long-range fighter escorts. You just need to hang on until they arrive."

"Yes sir," Colonel Rizer said.

He only hoped it was possible.

* * * * *

Chapter One

The first thing she noticed was the chill. As a little girl, Evelyn Adamsen always thought of England as something like a fairy-tale land, where the sun shone down on airy stone castles, and lambs and horses frolicked in wildflower-bedecked meadows.

The reality was far colder and covered in mud. From the moment she'd stepped off the troop transport in Liverpool five days earlier, the sky had remained a solid gray sheet that leaked a fine drizzle. Damp seeped in everywhere, and even Evelyn's heavy woolen coat wasn't enough to keep the dreary mist from seeming to saturate her skin. She pulled her collar higher and hunched down into it, as she'd grown up doing during the brutal winters in the Black Hills of South Dakota. From behind, her friend and roommate Mary Lewis squeaked and let out a soft curse as she followed Evelyn off the bus from London.

"Mary," Evelyn said softly, reproof shading her tone. "The captain isn't going to like it if she hears you swearing. We're supposed to 'act like ladies at all times,' remember?"

Mary was a Southern California blonde with curves that made the men sit up and take notice. She smiled up at Evelyn impishly and rolled cornflower-blue eyes.

"What Captain Ledoux doesn't know won't hurt her," Mary said in her girlish voice as she threaded one arm through Evelyn's. Evelyn was thankful for the extra warmth, but she thought that surely they must look quite the pair: Mary's movie-star good looks next to her plain, skinny, too-tall brunette self provided a lot of contrast. That contrast was an echo of their personalities: the vivacious, charismatic flirt and the shy, awkward bookworm. Despite, or perhaps because of, their differences, they'd been inseparable since the first day of training.

Officially, they were Technician Fifth Class Adamsen and Technician Fifth Class Lewis, members of the Women's Army Corps. Captain Jeanne Ledoux, of Baton Rouge, Louisiana, was the commanding officer for their unit. Their only officer, in fact. Their small detachment, at only twenty members, was one of the smallest in the WACs. They'd only just arrived at RAF Ridgewell, home of the 381st Bombardment Group. Back when she'd first been recruited, Evelyn had thought it would all be one big, patriotic adventure.

So far, it was just a lot of mud.

"Girls!" Captain Ledoux called out, waving her hand imperiously. "This way!" The captain stood holding open the door to one of the thin metal "Quonset huts." These corrugated metal half-tube structures were everywhere, giving the airfield a temporary feel.

As usual, Captain Ledoux's face was set in lines of faint disapproval. Evelyn privately doubted the woman ever smiled.

She and Mary hustled into the shelter of the building, crowding in with the other women just as the rain started to come down in earnest. Evelyn grimaced as she felt the splashes of mud onto her stockings. She only had the one pair, and Ledoux was a stickler for dress and appearance. She would have a devil of a time getting them clean that night.

Inside the Quonset hut, rows of chairs faced a blank screen flanked by the flags of the U.S. and the UK. A man wearing the uniform of an Army Air Force colonel stood at the front, hands behind his back as he watched the women enter the room.

"Take a seat, ladies," he said as they piled inside, shaking the rain from their coats. Evelyn found his chiseled jaw and stiff military bearing intimidating, and that was before he looked at her. Once the piercing brown eyes seemed to fix them in place, every girl present hesitated.

Evelyn took a deep breath and walked forward.

"Sir," she said softly, nodding acknowledgment of the colonel as she took a seat in front. Mary followed closely behind her, and soon the entire group was seated. The thick scent of wet wool rose around them, and the rain beat loudly on the metal roof overhead.

"Ladies, my name is Colonel Rizer. I'm the commander of the 381st Bombardment Wing. Welcome to RAF Ridgewell." He stopped for a moment and looked around.

"I had hoped for more of you," he admitted, softly. "But I suppose we are fortunate to have so many. I will be honest with you, ladies. This is not some romantic adventure. This is war. The men here are rough. They're men who've seen their fellows die in front of them. Men who face the knowledge that every mission could be their last. There is a reason we don't send women to war...unless we have no other choice. It appears, in this case, we haven't.

"Ladies, your mission here is the brainchild of our commander, Brigadier General Clarence Durant. He seems to think that by leveraging your...abilities, you can help more of my men survive to complete their missions. I don't know how he came up with this idea. I never even knew that women could be...what do you call yourselves...psychics?"

"That is correct, sir," Ledoux answered, standing and coming to a crisp position of attention. "Each of these women is a highly trained psychic technician, capable of maintaining a telepathic net with multiple other minds. They have been extensively screened for talent and trained in—"

"Captain, I read the brief," Rizer said, interrupting Ledoux's boastful tone. "I know what your women are capable of. I have never seen anything like it, but if General Durant says it's so, then I trust it is so. I understand your women have all had aviation indoctrination training, is that correct?"

"They have, sir," Ledoux said. "I'm confident once they receive their theater indoctrination training flights here, they'll perform admirably for you."

Rizer shook his head.

"Captain, I don't know what you were promised, but we don't have time or resources for training flights here. Your women will meet their crews tonight and be listed on the combat roster as early as tomorrow morning."

"Sir! That won't work at all. The women must have an opportunity to work with their crews in order to ensure the integrity of the psychic net. Net work requires a familiarity with one's crew, otherwise—"

Rizer cut her off with a sharp gesture of his hand.

"Captain," he said, his voice cracking like a whip, "your women will meet their crews tonight. They will be listed on the combat roster in the morning. That is all."

Ledoux closed her mouth with an audible snap. Though her face was red, she nodded her understanding. Rizer returned her nod and handed her a piece of paper.

"Here are your crew assignments. Good luck to you all." And with that, he turned to leave the room.

Ledoux called a sharp "Ten-HUT," and the women scrambled to their feet to stand at attention. Rizer nodded once and left the room in a silence broken only by the steady tapping of rain on the metal roof. Evelyn swallowed hard against the nerves that gripped her throat.

"Well," Ledoux said, her voice crisp as she rustled the paper in her hand. "You ladies heard the colonel. There won't be any indoctrination flights. You must do your best to establish the needed rapport with your crews tonight. But remember, above all things, you are to act like ladies and represent the Women's Army Corps appropriately."

She looked around the room one more time, her face set in stern lines. In the back of Evelyn's mind, a tiny, irreverent thought pointed out that Ledoux looked like she was trying to ape Colonel Rizer's incredible presence. She didn't succeed.

"Right, then," Ledoux said. "Adamsen, you're assigned to Captain Carl Peters. Baker..."

* * *

When they walked back out into the rain, Evelyn was unsurprised to find Mary hot about the compressed timeline.

"I cannot *believe* this!" the feisty blonde said as she once again hooked her arm through Evelyn's. "How in the *hell* are we supposed to establish a psychic net with a crew in less than twenty-four hours? I mean, really? Do they expect us to *make whoopee* with all of them?"

Mary's indignant and inappropriate suggestion startled Evelyn into a giggle.

"Mary!" she said. "Keep your voice down! You know that's not what Ledoux meant. The colonel either. I'm sure he just doesn't know what all it takes to create a viable net. He didn't even know we *existed* until recently."

"My eye," Mary muttered, giving a delicate snort. "You know he was briefed on our capabilities before we got here, whether he knew about psychics beforehand or not. That man's not going to let an unknown up in the air with his boys. No, he knows exactly what he's asking of us. There's only one way to create a deep, solid connection in that short amount of time, but I'll be *damned* if I'm going to whore for the US Army Air Corps!"

"Mary!" Evelyn gasped. "Really, I know you're angry, but keep your voice down. Besides, even if he *was* briefed, I don't think the colonel realized what it sounded like he was suggesting. It's just...You've heard the gossip as much as I have. These crews are getting eaten up by those German fighters. They need a better way of doing things. We wouldn't be here if they had any choice. He said that, didn't he? So I just think—"

Evelyn broke off as a low, buzzing hum came through the mist. A shout went up from somewhere. Men emerged from buildings nearby and took off running toward the sound. Evelyn let her arm drop to grab Mary by the hand, and the two of them started running as well.

"I just think he's out of time," Evelyn finished in a breathless undertone as they splashed through puddles to join the crowd gathering near the flightline.

Off in the distance, the two girls could see a ragged line of aircraft heading toward them under the low ceiling of rainclouds. The first aircraft in the line trailed smoke from one of its inboard engines. As they got closer, Evelyn could pick out other signs of battle damage. Next to them, a man was counting softly.

"How many went out?" Mary asked him. The man looked at her, did a double-take, and then looked back at the incoming formation.

"Twenty-two," he said softly. Evelyn did a quick count of her own. There were fourteen aircraft starting their final approach. Mary gave a soft gasp, and her free hand came up to cover her mouth. The man looked at them again and gave a small, sad smile.

"Don't worry too much," he said, though his eyes were bleak. "If they got shot up pretty good, some of the birds might've set down at other airfields near the coast, or ditched in the Channel."

He looked the two of them up and down quickly. "What're you dames doing here, anyway? You gotta man on board one of 'em?" His tone was sympathetic.

"No, we're WACs assigned to the 381st," Evelyn said, shaking her head. "Just arrived. Ah...where will the crews go after they land?"

"Interrogation," the man answered, pointing to a large building marked "Operations." "They'll be in there about an hour and then come out to get some chow. What're WACs doing here? I thought they were keeping you all back home to free men to fight?"

"Thank you, we must go," Evelyn said quickly, and pulled Mary along toward the Operations building.

* * *

A s a little girl, Evelyn had been taught not to listen at doors. So, though she couldn't hear anything, it felt more than a little bit wrong to be lingering outside the Operations building's main briefing room whilst the crews finished their interrogation. She and Mary received their share of curious—and more than one blatantly interested—looks, but no one questioned their presence. Apparently the WAC uniforms were enough of an explanation.

When the doors finally opened, Evelyn had to hold back a gasp as soon as the men started filing out. Ever since she'd shown signs of psychic ability during early adolescence, she'd been trained to shield her mind from others' emotions and thoughts. It was the first skill any psychic learned, and she was confident in her ability to shut just about anyone out of her mind. But nothing could have prepared her for the men who exited that room.

A wave of tearing exhaustion overlaid with the absolute icy cold of futile grief made Evelyn's knees buckle. Mary's hand tightened in hers, and Evelyn knew that her friend was also fighting the overwhelming emotions that came pouring out of the briefing room. One by one, the men with the battered psyches came closer, exiting the room in twos and threes. Their proximity made the fraying pain worse, until Evelyn could no longer stand it. She turned and bodily shoved her way through them, pulling Mary after her out into the soggy chill of the English afternoon.

For once, Evelyn welcomed the cold, wet fingers of rain that managed to get inside her collar and up under her hair. She stopped a few yards outside the door and lifted her face to the rain, drawing in deep, ragged breaths. Mary's fingers slipped from her grasp, and a few moments later, Evelyn heard the sound of her friend retching behind the corner of the building.

"Is she okay?" a softly masculine, American voice asked. Evelyn took another deep, steadying breath and slowly opened her eyes. A man stood in front of her, wearing a creased uniform and a hat that had already begun to develop the characteristic "mission crush" that came from being worn under headphones. His brown eyes looked empty and haunted...but a wave of concern rippled out from him, smoothing over the rough edges of his exhaustion and pain. He reached out a hand, as if to take Evelyn's shoulder, but the young woman flinched away.

"No," she said softly. "Please don't touch me. It makes it worse."

The man froze, his expression going blank. Evelyn felt insult spike through the morass of his other emotions. She shook her head sharply, her eyes going unfocused as she fought to slam her mental barriers into place. They'd been overwhelmed by the sheer enormity of the aircrews' collective pain and fatigue, so it took some work, but no more than a heartbeat later, Evelyn's shoulders straightened, and she focused on the man's face again.

"I'm so sorry, sir," she said, noticing for the first time the captain's bars that glinted on his uniform. "It's just...Mary and I didn't know. We didn't realize how bad it would be in there. With all of you together, the pain...It was overwhelming, and we weren't ready for it."

The captain's eyes narrowed.

"I don't understand," he said. "What pain? Did someone in interrogation hurt you?"

"Yes, sir. I mean, no, sir. Not directly." Evelyn shook her head again, unable to find her balance and clearly articulate her thoughts.

With her full barriers so firmly in place, she felt cut off from the rest of the world, unable to communicate properly.

"We're psychics," she finished, sounding rather weak, even to herself. "Newly assigned to the 381st."

The captain's eyes widened, and the temptation to open up was just too much for Evelyn. She eased up on the mental pressure holding her barriers closed and allowed just a whisper of emotion through. Curiosity, incredulity, distrust. All of these swirled together in a dizzying rush and poured off of the captain, and Evelyn swayed under this new onslaught.

"I'm so sorry," Mary said, her sweet starlet's voice flat and empty as she rejoined Evelyn and slipped her fingers back into her friend's hand. With that touch, the blond woman offered her own strength, and Evelyn felt her silent plea to link up. It was a good idea. Together, they might be stronger. She allowed Mary's connection and felt a raw, ragged type of strength come flowing in. It wasn't full net link, but it was still connection enough for their emotional energy to bolster one another, and Evelyn felt her dizziness recede.

"Psychics? Like witches?" the captain asked, his eyes sharp. "I'm a little old for bedtime tales."

"We're to help the aircrews on their missions," Mary said, ignoring the insult. She, too, seemed to be feeling better with the addition of Evelyn's strength to her own. "We can link the crewmen's minds into a single net, which will allow for better communication and coordination while flying missions."

"But you said it was...difficult? Interrogation? Missions are a helluva lot harder than that, begging your pardon." His skepticism deepened, feeling like wet sand against the skin.

"We weren't ready," Mary replied, echoing Evelyn's earlier words. "But there are precautions we can take...It's complicated," she said, offering up a smile. True to form, the California girl was bouncing back with impressive rapidity. The thought made Evelyn smile her own smile. Her friend was a whole lot of toughness wrapped up in an adorably cute package. Evelyn envied Mary her easy charisma with strangers, and this was a perfect example of why.

"I'm Mary Lewis," she said, tucking a strand of her blond hair behind her ear. She offered her hand to the captain. "This is Evelyn Adamsen. And you are?"

The captain looked down at her outstretched hand with a bemused expression, but he took it briefly in greeting.

"Captain Carl Peters," he said. "I take it the two of you haven't been WACs long?"

"Oh!" Evelyn exclaimed as the name jarred her memory. "Um, no, sir, we haven't. But I'm, um, assigned to your crew. We were told we'd be meeting our crews tonight, but they gave us the names, and I got yours. Or so they said." She trailed off, feeling even more like an ungainly, awkward beanpole next to Mary's smiling prettiness. But Captain Peters didn't seem to mind, for he gave her a smile as well.

"So *that's* what the 1800 meeting is all about," he said. "They told us in Interrogation, but they didn't say anything else. Well enough...although, I'll be honest, I have no idea what you think you can do. Witches or not."

"Psychics, not witches. Let us show you," Mary said quickly, looking from Peters to Evelyn and back again. Evelyn felt a kind of mischievous eagerness from the other woman through their link.

Captain Peters' eyebrows raised up in amused condescension, but he nodded.

"All right," Evelyn said, taking a deep breath. She pushed the echoes of fear and fatigue back, imagined them dispelling through her skin. She gripped Mary's hand a bit harder as she opened their link wide enough to establish a full telepathic contact. Mary let her do so, keeping her own barriers open and welcoming Evelyn's thoughts into her own. It would have been much more difficult otherwise. Typically, it was harder to link with a woman, and near-impossible if the woman were trained to resist intrusion. Mary's instant welcoming spoke of her deep trust in Evelyn, a trust that the brunette woman returned.

All at once, Evelyn's vision took on a strange, doubled cast. She focused briefly, and two distinct images resolved in her mind: the image of Mary from her own eyes, and the image of herself through Mary's.

You're so good at this. The thought was Mary's, but it occurred in Evelyn's head as if the words had been her own. They accompanied a different flavor of the affectionate envy with which Evelyn had regarded Mary's social skill. Evelyn could have replied, simply by forming her own words in her head, and Mary would have instantly received them. However, instead she concentrated on how deeply she loved and admired the other woman and felt Mary's answering affection in return.

"Sir," Evelyn said out loud. "For this first time, it will be easier if I touch you. Would you please take my hand? I promise this won't hurt." Dimly, through Mary, Evelyn was aware that her own voice took on a quiet surety it normally lacked. She wasn't confident about much, but Evelyn knew very well that she was one of the best net builders alive.

Captain Peters reached out and took Evelyn's offered hand this time. As he did so, Evelyn reached her mind and emotions out to him, gently opening the natural barriers he had no idea existed. She couldn't have done so if he'd resisted, not without causing him serious harm. But the fact he'd acquiesced and reached out to make physical contact meant that Evelyn was able to slip inside the deliciously foreign landscape of his masculine mind.

Again, they felt that moment of visual disorientation until Evelyn resolved their vision into three separate images. She felt Carl tense up as he suddenly saw through her eyes and Mary's.

No, please relax, she thought. *I know it's strange, but you are safe. The strangeness you are feeling is the echo of our emotions. It's been an odd day.*

For...all...of...us? The words were halting and half-whispered as Carl stumbled toward communicating within the net. Evelyn sent him a burst of approval and encouragement that Mary echoed.

I can see me, Carl thought, his words shedding their tentative nature as he adjusted to the net. *This is incredible. I can see what we all three see. But it's...Oh! I just had to think that I wanted separate images, and I had them!*

The human brain is incredibly complex. It's extremely good at filtering out information we don't want and focusing on the information we do. And there's more, Evelyn said, easily falling into "teaching" mode. Before the Army had come looking for girls with psychic talent, she'd been studying to teach high school. With careful precision, she sent a quick thought to Mary, who reached out with her free hand and pinched Evelyn, hard, inside her elbow.

"Ouch!" Carl said out loud. He dropped Evelyn's hand and severed the three-way mental connection, taking a step back as he did so. "How did you do that?" he demanded, reaching up to rub the inside of his elbow.

"When we're in a net, what one of us feels, we all feel," Evelyn said softly. She gave him a little smile. "This can be helpful if a member of your crew is in distress and can't speak."

Captain Peters blinked, then nodded slowly in understanding. Then his brows came together.

"But if we have to be touching to create a net..."

"It only helps the first time. But now I know your mental landscape. With your permission, I can link with you whenever I want."

"Do it now," Captain Peters said.

"As you like," Evelyn said softly, and reached out once again. She blinked and once again felt his vision come to overlay hers, felt the strangeness of his mind and emotions.

What if...I don't want you in me? he asked, the edge of fear shading his mind.

Push me out, Evelyn invited. *Simply close yourself off. Perhaps, for you, it's a withdrawing...*

The tall brunette gasped and stumbled backward, nearly falling down in the mud.

"Evie!" Mary cried out, reaching out to steady her friend. The little blonde rounded on Captain Peters.

"Why did you have to go and do that?" she demanded, her eyes fierce. "Evelyn wouldn't have hurt you! She wouldn't hurt a fly! You didn't have to throw her out..."

"Mary, it's all right," Evelyn said, squeezing her friend's hand in reassurance. "I told him to. Please don't worry, sir, I'm all right. It's just that it can hurt, a little, to be forcibly ejected like that. But no lasting harm. It's akin to a...shove, or being bumped by a passerby."

"Oh. Well, I beg your pardon!" Captain Peters said, blinking rapidly. "I certainly wouldn't have done that if I'd known..."

"No, you needed to know," Evelyn said, quietly but firmly. Mary looked as if she were about to protest, but Evelyn squeezed her hand and shook her head.

"They need to know, Mary. If they're going to be opening themselves to us, they need to know how to protect their own privacy if needed. And not just from us. You know that as well as I do. I'll be teaching all of your crew to do the same, sir, just as soon as I have a chance to meet them."

Captain Peters looked as if he wanted to ask several more questions, but her words recalled him to himself, and he looked around at the now-deserted yard.

"Of course," he said. "They're likely all at chow or getting cleaned up. They'll be at the 1800 meeting, though. Or the officers, at least."

"We will see you there, sir," Evelyn said with a smile.

* * * * *

Chapter Two

The two WACs walked in silence back toward the Quonset hut that had been pointed out to them as their billet. Inside, the only two unclaimed bunks were the two nearest the door, but Evelyn didn't mind too much. She gave Mary the choice of bottom or top, since she had been the one to delay them so much.

"I still don't understand why you let him throw you out like that," Mary groused as she made up her bed. Despite her petite frame, she moved with quick assurance as she lifted the mattress of the top bunk to make passable hospital corners.

"Yes, you do," Evelyn said, her tone patient. She smoothed her own army-issued green wool blanket over her bunk and began tucking it under the mattress. The two of them had been having this discussion from nearly the first day of their training.

"All right, yes. They do need to be able to build barriers, I agree. But that could have waited, at least until you'd had an opportunity to teach them to be gentle. There's a reason men aren't psychics, Evie! They're too apt to go around manhandling everything in sight, and you don't need to be one of them!"

"No one knows why only women are born with psychic power," Evelyn shot back. "And you and I both know women who are a bit rough with their mental touch." A wry smile curved her lips as she thought of Captain Ledoux. The captain was a powerful psychic, but she lacked finesse in every sense of the word. She'd become their commanding officer simply because she'd been the first to come forward when Mrs. Ruth Durant had gone looking for women with abilities like her own.

"Don't change the subject," Mary said, shaking her head like a ferocious golden poodle. "You gave them the power to *hurt* you, Evie! Don't you see how dangerous that is? Didn't you hear the colonel? These are rough men!"

"They're *our* rough men, Mary! Or they will be, very shortly. Didn't you see those aircraft come limping back? Didn't you *feel* what they felt?" Evelyn felt a thread of anger pulse through her.

"You know I did!" Mary said, whipping her head up angrily, her own temper flashing in her beautiful blue eyes. "I was right there with you the whole time, Evie! I know everything you know about them...which, when you get right down to it, isn't very much! Yes, they were hurting, but damn it, you need to protect yourself as well! This is a war. You can't afford to be the trusting backwoods South Dakota rube here!"

Evelyn jerked backward, stung.

"Fine," she said, nearly spitting out the word. "Don't be late for the meeting." She turned and walked back out of the hut, ignoring Mary's calls to wait, to come back.

* * *

The 1800 Officer's Call meeting took place in Operations. Evelyn found her seat early and waited while the rest of her unit and the various crews filed in. Something twinged in her consciousness, and she looked up to see Captain Peters walk in. He, too, felt something because his eyes immediately found hers, and Evelyn felt the echo of the intimate net bond tug at her. She gave him a smile and a polite nod, and he did the same, but she could see it startled him. He turned, though, said something to the lieutenant next to him, and the two of them walked to their seats near the front.

Evelyn felt Mary walk in, too, of course, but she wouldn't have needed the experience of past bondings to tell her that the shapely blonde had arrived. The collective intake of breath from the men in the room would have done just as well. Still, Evelyn didn't look up until Mary had slipped into the seat beside her.

"Evie," Mary whispered softly. Evelyn shifted slightly but kept her head down. Mary's hand slipped into hers. "Evie, I'm sorry. Please forgive me. I didn't mean it."

"I know." She squeezed Mary's hand as she whispered back. "I'm sorry, too." She would have said more, something along the lines of agreeing to disagree, but Colonel Rizer chose that moment to walk into the room, and everyone came to their feet in a rush.

"Please be seated," he said. There was a general rumble of movement as everyone got settled, then turned expectant eyes up to him. The Wing Commander took a deep breath and beckoned to the side of the room. Captain Ledoux walked forward, saluted, and then came to parade rest next to him. Beside her, Evelyn heard Mary snort softly.

"Gentlemen...and ladies. This is Captain Jeanne Ledoux. She's the commanding officer of the Women's Army Corps unit that has recently joined us. Her presence here, and that of her WACs, is not classified, but who and what they are is." He took a deep breath and then plunged on.

"The truth is, boys, these ladies are psychic technicians. That means that they can establish a kind of link, mind to mind, with other people. Now, I know how that sounds. Bedtime stories and fairy tales, right? But these gals are the real deal. They can help us communicate faster and more completely than radios and can help us avoid some of the disasters that have plagued us in the past when bad weather crops up unexpectedly along the route."

Evelyn heard a rustle from somewhere in the back of the room, but she refused to turn around. She was very uncomfortably aware of the surreptitious looks coming their way from all of the men in the room. Some of them might have been interested...they *were* women, after all. But Evelyn knew that the vast majority of them were probably more distrustful than anything. Psychics were rare enough that few people really knew how they worked, or what they could do.

Not to mention, most people who claimed psychic power were frauds, which was a good thing, when one was trying to keep one's power hidden. It was much easier to scoff and pretend that someone was crazy when they accused you of reading their mind if you could claim that psychic abilities were a myth.

But she supposed that path to anonymity was closed to her now. Now and probably forever.

She hoped this venture would be worth it.

Despite her best efforts at maintaining a disciplined military bearing, Evelyn could feel her neck and cheeks heating up in a blush as a wave of cynical skepticism swept over her from the assembled crewmen. She heard Mary suck in a quiet breath next to her as they both reinforced their mental barriers and waited for the colonel to finish.

Captain Ledoux got up next.

"Gentlemen," she said, looking right past her girls to the men. Her demeanor was calm and cool as her Louisiana Bayou accent filled the space. Despite her appearance, however, Evelyn thought that if she reached out, she'd find the captain just as nervous as the rest of them. "The ladies have each been assigned to a pilot as an additional member of his crew. We were expecting a bit of time for spin-up, but Colonel Rizer informs me that won't be possible. So, the best thing would be for you to get together this evening and spend some time getting to know one another. That will allow for the most effective net in the limited time we have available."

One of the men in the back raised a hand. Captain Ledoux held up a hand of her own and inclined her head slightly in his direction.

"I know that you all have questions. Please believe me when I tell you that the best way for you to get them answered will be for you to ask your assigned psychic. The roster is posted at the back of the room. Thank you."

With that, Captain Ledoux took a step backward just as Colonel Rizer came to his feet. Somebody called a sharp "ten-HUT!" and everyone rumbled up to the position of attention.

"Gentlemen, ladies, you have your instructions. I will leave you to get acquainted. Carry on," Colonel Rizer said, and then gesturing for Captain Ledoux to precede him, left the room.

The noise level in the room rose as the occupants all let out a collective breath and relaxed, at least physically.

"Well," Mary said brightly but softly, "if this isn't cute. It's like a mixer! Though they could have at least provided some punch!"

"Mary," Evelyn said softly, giving her a quelling look. "Please, this isn't a social occasion."

"Someone should have told Ledoux that," the blonde shot back. Then she sighed. "I suppose I'd better find my own pilot. I'll bet a dollar that he's not nearly as handsome as yours, lucky girl."

"What does it matter if you're not going to *make whoopee* to strengthen the bond?" Evelyn asked in her own dry undertone. Mary responded with a brilliant smile.

"I'm not, but there isn't a thing wrong with a little eye candy now and again," she said with a wink. Then she leaned in and caught Evelyn in a hard hug.

"I'm sorry again," Mary whispered in her ear. "I'm so glad we're friends. I'm not sure I could handle all this without you."

"You won't have to," Evelyn promised as she hugged her friend back. Mary squeezed her one more time before stepping away. With a last smile, she turned toward the back of the room, only to come nose to chest with Captain Carl Peters.

"Oh!" the blonde said, giving a startled little laugh. "Captain Peters, pardon me. I didn't mean to...well..."

The pilot smiled and stepped back, letting Mary pass in front of him in the narrow aisle between the briefing room seats. She smiled up at him, flashing her California girl dimples, and Evelyn bit the inside of her cheek to keep her own smile from manifesting. Captain Peters wasn't quite poleaxed, but his eyes certainly followed Mary's retreating figure for a moment or two before he turned back to Evelyn and cleared his throat.

"Ah," he said. "Hello again, Technician Adamsen."

"Hello, Captain Peters," she said gravely. This close to him, the memory of their connection tugged at her, like a puppy eager for play. She deflected it easily enough, but the urge to reestablish the link was there.

"I...This is awkward," Captain Peters said, rubbing a hand on the back of his neck. "I'm happy to see you, but I feel...I want to..."

Evelyn nodded.

"That's the link. Once we've been connected, it's easier to link. The effect is intensified because you're a man. Our minds want to fit together. Have you ever known a married couple who have been together so long that they can finish each other's sentences?"

"My grandparents are like that," Captain Peters said with a little smile. "But my grandmother isn't a wi—psychic."

"No, but all humans have a bit of latent talent. Psychics just have ours more fully realized. In any case, close relationships will build an actual psychic link. It's just that most people don't have the ability to fully utilize it. But when you find yourself attracted to a woman, part of what attracts you is the fact that her mental landscape is compatible with yours. To a certain extent, we crave that connection."

"But what about..." Captain Peters said, then abruptly cut himself off and closed his mouth with a snap.

"I know what you were about to say," Evelyn said softly, her lips curving in a tiny smile. "My good friend back home...well, we are as close as siblings, but it was always harder to create a link with him. His mental landscape is too much like my own. It was a bit like two magnets turned the wrong way 'round so that they pushed apart."

"Hmm. Well, shall we go meet the crew?" Captain Peters asked and moved as if to offer his arm. Then he froze halfway through, as if realizing that she was a WAC in uniform, which rendered his gentlemanly gesture technically incorrect. Evelyn's smile grew, and with a soft, "Yes, please, sir," she fell in behind him.

* * *

Evelyn didn't have to go far to meet the copilot, navigator, and bombardier. All of the officers had been invited to the briefing, and the three of them stood in a tight knot against the side wall. The rest of the room echoed with chaos as crews and psychics tried to find one another and figure everything out all at once.

"Gentlemen," Captain Peters said as they approached. The three of them separated enough to allow first him and then, at his gesture, her into the circle of their conversation. "This is the WAC I was telling you about. Allow me to introduce Technician Evelyn Adamsen, our psychic. Technician Adamsen, this is First Lieutenant Bob Becket, copilot; First Lieutenant Abram Portman, navigator; and Second Lieutenant Paul Rutherford, bombardier."

The men all gave Evelyn a polite nod, though she could see varying levels of skepticism from them. She smiled back and murmured a soft "gentlemen" in acknowledgment.

Lieutenant Becket, the copilot, wasn't quite as tall as Captain Peters, but he had hair bleached blond from the sun and the remnants of a tan that spoke of life on a beach somewhere. His smile wasn't nearly as warm as his complexion, and he jerked his chin pugnaciously at her as he spoke.

"So you're gonna read our minds, huh?" he asked, sounding just this side of surly.

"Not exactly, sir," she said, pleased that her voice remained steady, though his tone set her nerves to quaking. "It's more that I'm going to link you all into a net so that you can read each other's minds."

Lieutenant Becket snorted and rolled his eyes, but then glanced at Captain Peters and declined to say more.

Lieutenant Portman, the navigator, was fully half a head shorter than Lieutenant Becket, but he was muscled all over, like a prize-fighter. He had a nose like a prizefighter's, too, Evelyn decided. He stuck his hand out immediately.

"Abram Portman," he said with a distinct Brooklyn accent. "This guy gives you any trouble, you let me know," he said, elbowing Becket.

"I doubt that will be necessary, sir," she said softly and with a mental sigh. Of course, it was only to be expected that there would be some among her crew who wouldn't welcome her presence...but that didn't make it any easier. She looked at the third officer, the bombardier, Lieutenant Rutherford. He refused to meet her eyes. For a moment, she thought perhaps he was another skeptic, but that wasn't what she got from him. In fact, she wasn't getting *anything* from him, which was telling in and of itself. Apparently, she wasn't the first psychic of Lieutenant Paul Rutherford's acquaintance.

"Technician Adamsen, do you want to start working here? Or..." Captain Peters was saying. Evelyn pulled herself from her reverie and looked up at him.

"Actually, sir, is there any way I could meet the rest of the crew? It would be good to build a full net as soon as possible," she said.

"We can get our regular guys," Captain Peters said, "but you should know that there are substitutions made on a pretty frequent basis."

"That will be all right, sir," she said. "It won't be hard to make adjustments once the basic net is built."

"All right," he said. "Then let's go find the boys."

* * *

The "boys" turned out to be a bit harder to find, perhaps, than Captain Peters had anticipated. They eventually tracked them down in one of the maintenance sheds not far from the flight line. Several of the enlisted crewmen had set up a little gambling hall there, complete with dice, cards, and booze they'd found somewhere.

When Captain Peters knocked on the door of the shed, the officers and Evelyn heard a mad scramble punctuated by multiple swear words coming from the inside. Eventually, the shed door opened, and a freckled kid with spiky red hair poked his head out.

"Yessir?" he asked, sounding slightly suspicious.

"I need to speak with the crew, please, Sergeant," Captain Peters said. Evelyn noticed that while his words were polite, his tone made it clear that this was not a request.

"One moment, sir," the redhead said, and ducked back inside. A moment later, he came back out, followed by five others. Captain Peters introduced them one by one. Evelyn felt as if the names went in one ear and out the other, so fast did they come. It wouldn't matter much, though. She would know their names and so much more about them in just a few minutes, anyway.

"It's nice to meet all of you," Evelyn said, after Captain Peters had told them her name and what she was doing there. Like the officers, the enlisted aircrewmen looked at her with varying levels of skepticism and suspicion. A flutter of nerves skittered over her skin, and she took a deep breath to calm herself before she began.

"I don't know how many of you have experience with psychics, but I'm happy to answer any questions or concerns you may have. However, as Captain Peters said, we have been asked to establish a connection tonight, as the leadership wants us to start flying as soon as possible. So, for now, I'll ask you to trust me and put your hands out in front of you."

Captain Peters was the first to comply, and his gimlet stare around the rough circle had the others following his lead, even Lieutenant Rutherford. Evelyn smiled and reached out to touch Captain Peters' hand, even though she didn't need to do so at this point. The connection snapped into place easily, and she blinked away Carl's vision before continuing. The redhead was next, and Evelyn reached out to touch her fingertips to the back of his knuckles.

Sean Carrol was younger than Carl. Younger, even, than Evelyn herself, and she sighed with pleasure at the sharp *zing* of youth that raced through her mind. She felt him start to stumble, reached out, caught at his hands before he could fall, and wrapped herself around his mind.

You're safe, Sean, she thought. *I have you. I will never hurt you.*

Sir? Sean asked, his mind voice halting and shaky.

Here, Sean, Carl replied. *It's weird at first. But you'll get used to it. Evelyn's good.*

Thank you, Evelyn said modestly. *Let me pull the others in,* she added, rather than face Carl's flustered realization that he hadn't meant to share that thought.

After a few moments, they were all tied in. There was the dizzying kaleidoscope of images seen through ten sets of eyes, but that was nothing compared to the confusing onslaught of emotions. It took Evelyn a few moments to sort through it all. The suspicion of her; the bored skepticism of this latest scheme of the leadership; the instant, instinctive awareness of her female body; the animal desire that went with that; the aching longing for sweethearts at home...and the fear.

Under it all, each of them had it. The cold, choking fear the next time they went up, they wouldn't be fast enough at spotting the fighters, they wouldn't shoot well enough to protect each other, they wouldn't be able to fly close enough formation to keep everyone safe, they'd get lost in the soupy weather over the Channel...

...the fears went on and on, reaching up with icy fingers to wrap around Evelyn's throat and squeeze, freezing her in place, unable to move, unable to act, unable to do anything but feel the scream building within...growing...

Breathe.

Evelyn never knew who said it. But she opened her eyes and separated out the images to see Sean, the redhead flight engineer/gunner standing in front of her with his fingertips on her face.

In fact, they were all touching her. Whether of their own volition or in response to her sudden need, the entire crew had drawn tightly around her. They'd reached out for the skin-to-skin contact that acted as an anchor to the real world. Her hands and wrists were held by four different men. Captain Peters had one hand on the back of her neck, his fingers buried in her hair.

Evelyn took a breath and let her barriers drop even further. The fear receded, replaced by all the various mechanisms that each man used to fight it back for himself. There was Carl's awareness of duty and Sean's laughing devil-may-care thrill-seeking. Bobby Fritsche, one of the waist gunners, had a deep trust in this group of men. Abram, the navigator, relied on his extensive training and a deep well of religious faith. Logan "Yum Yum" Ayala, the short, stocky ball turret gunner, felt his own youthful invulnerability and coupled that with a fatalistic sense that when it was his time, it was his time, and he'd meet death with both barrels blazing. Les Norton, the other waist gunner, prayed the Rosary daily and used his faith to push back the fear. Paul, the bombardier, pushed it back with thoughts of his family back home. Bob Becket, the copilot, also thought of home and a girl he'd left behind. She looked a lot like Evelyn, which would doubtless cause some embarrassment later, but in the net, it was just too intimate to be embarrassed. Rico Martinez, the tail gunner, had some of all of these devices at work, but mostly he just let the fear pass through him and concentrated on the here and now.

I...Evelyn said to them all, feeling a bit shaky. *I am sorry, I wasn't prepared...*

For war? Rico asked, humor leaking through, making several of them smile as they all felt his amusement. *Chica, none of us ever are.*

* * *

They worked quite late, only stopping for food when Evelyn began to exhibit signs of exhaustion. She'd managed to keep her hunger and fatigue from the men, due to her more developed shields, but the truth was that maintaining a net was hard, exhausting work. And the more inexperienced the members of the net, the harder the work on the focusing psychic. Evelyn knew she should have called a halt sooner, but she felt the desperate hope of each of the men that maybe, just maybe, she might be able to help them come home safely the next time. And so she pushed on.

Until her knees buckled, and her vision started to go bright gray around the edges. Captain Peters broke the net with a shove that had Evelyn crying out as she fell. Luckily, PFC Fritsche caught her and eased her down to the ground.

"Technician!" Captain Peters said, his voice anxious. Evelyn heard it as if it were coming through a long tunnel. She blinked away the sparkling grayness and pulled herself up to a sitting position. PFC Fritsche helped, steadying her and keeping hold of her shoulders, just in case.

"I'm all right, sir," Evelyn forced herself to say. Her voice was faint enough to make her feel a vast surge of self-directed irritation. She knew better than this! "I just...It's hard work, sometimes. Could...is there some water or something?"

"Ayala, give her your flask," Lieutenant Rutherford said, speaking for the first time during the proceedings. His tone was gruff and slightly uncomfortable. "She needs the kick. Oh, don't be coy, man! It's not like we don't all know you've got that rotgut hooch on you."

Private Ayala, the young ball turret gunner, ducked his head in a shamefaced manner and reached into his shirt to pull out a flat metal flask. He handed this over with a grin. Lieutenant Rutherford shook his head, but he took the flask and knelt beside Evelyn.

"Here," the lieutenant said. "Take a sip. A small one. This isn't good stuff."

Evelyn took the offered flask and tipped it up to her lips. Instantly, icy hot pain exploded over the inside of her mouth, like rubbing alcohol applied to a sunburn. She coughed, eyes watering, and doubled over.

But she was conscious.

Lieutenant Rutherford took the flask from her fingers and capped it, then handed it back to Private Ayala without a word. The bombardier then looked up at his pilot.

"She needs to eat, Cap," he said. "It's hard on them, especially when we're all new. Especially here," he added, but didn't elaborate.

Evelyn knew what he meant, though. He knew about the fear, and the fatigue, and the longing for home. For the second time since meeting him, Evelyn found herself thinking that Lieutenant Rutherford must have known a psychic rather intimately back home. As the lieutenant lifted her chin to check her pupils, Evelyn met his eyes.

"Who?" she asked, her voice barely a whisper. She was so tired.

"My twin sister," Lieutenant Rutherford said with a thin-lipped smile. "She died when we were twelve."

"I'm sorry," Evelyn said, and she meant it. The lieutenant didn't say anything else, just nodded and helped her to stand on shaky legs.

Eventually, and with the help of her crew, Evelyn made it to the chow hall. Lieutenant Portman and the three gunners commandeered a quiet corner for their use. The kitchen was just about to stop serving dinner, but Sergeant Carrol and Lieutenant Becket managed to talk the cooks into putting together a plate for Evelyn, and Captain Peters watched to make sure she ate every bite. In the meantime, he lectured her.

"I know, sir," she said finally, after she'd eaten the last bite of a pile of watery mashed potatoes. "And you're right. It was irresponsible of me, and I won't be so foolish again."

In truth, she'd considered the risks and judged them acceptable. There was every chance that they'd get called up to fly a mission tomorrow. Every chance and then some, now that Evelyn was with them. Colonel Rizer had to be wanting to know how his psychics were going to stack up against the hazards his crews faced every day. He'd said it himself: they didn't even have time for orientation flights. They absolutely *had* to create as comprehensive a net as possible in as short a time as possible. And since Evelyn was not about to, as Mary had said, "*sleep* with all of them," the emotional connection had to be made somehow. So she would work, work until she dropped, and let these men see that she would give them her absolute best.

"All right," Captain Peters finally said. "Let's get some shut-eye. The knock comes at 0430 if it's coming at all. So...everyone back to your billets. Sergeant, see to it, all right?"

Sergeant Carroll nodded, a ghost of a grim smile curving his lips. He might be the first one to suggest a few kicks, given nothing else in the offing, but he could read the cards as well as anyone. That knock was gonna come. He knew it.

They all knew it.

Lieutenant Rutherford and Captain Peters helped Evelyn to her feet and walked her back to her billet. She said goodnight at the door, pushing aside the ridiculous urge to kiss them both on the cheek. That was just an aftereffect of being in a net together. After such an intimate connection...well, it was natural to want to touch one another. The men felt it, too. She could tell by the way that Lieutenant Rutherford's hand twitched toward hers and by the way Captain Peters leaned his upper body toward her, just a bit, as she turned to go.

Evelyn slipped into the metal hut and pulled the door closed behind herself. Then she sagged against it and let out a deep sigh. The lights were out, but it looked like she was the last to come in. The darkness echoed with the sounds of sleeping women. Evelyn made her way by feel to her bunk and climbed into it with a sigh of relief.

"Evie?" Mary asked, her voice sleepy.

"I'm here, Mary," Evelyn said softly, not wanting to wake anyone else.

"Good," Mary said, and the bunk creaked as she rolled over and sank back into the deep sleep of exhaustion.

* * * * *

Chapter Three

Adalina Sucherin, Lina to her friends, settled herself in her seat and nodded to the guard that she was ready. He returned her nod and stepped out with his partner to collect the prisoner that Lina was scheduled to interrogate.

Lina was a graduate of the Reich's most prestigious academy for working women: the Reichsschule für SS Helferinnen Oberenheim. As a graduate of the Reichsschule, she was entitled to be addressed by her rank of SS-Oberhelfer. Reichsfuhruer-SS Himmler himself had established the Reichsschule. At its dedication, Lina had stood with the other applicants and listened with tears of pride as he spoke of the vital part that the SS Helferinnen would play in the Reich's future.

Everyone knew that a woman's proper place was in the home raising healthy, happy children. However, the fact was that the war was dragging on and on, and the Reich's enemies seemed endless. Every man was needed to fight. Therefore, the women had to step forward and do their part as communications specialists and in other non-combat roles.

And as psychics. Especially as psychics.

Lina didn't know how the Reich leaders had found out the great secret kept by so many women over the years. But they had, and they had sent letters of recruitment to every German family promising the protection and gratitude of the Reich for any women of talent who came forward to serve.

Lina had been part of the almost forty women drawn from every corner of the Reich that exhibited psychic power. They had ranged in age from Lina's seventeen (at the time) to their mid-thirties. Several were widows who had already given their husbands to the war. Now they had turned their children over to relatives and friends and stepped forward to give even more. Lina found them inspirational and vowed to be worthy of the same title they carried.

Despite being so young, she'd done very well at the Reichsschule. She'd always had a talent for learning quickly, and her psychic abilities were among the strongest of the group. She'd spent the last two years posted to Warsaw, assisting military intelligence in interrogating convicted criminals and other enemies of the Reich. Her psychic abilities yielded results. Much more reliable results than other interrogation means, and for her work, she'd recently been promoted to her current rank.

"Oberhelfer, we are ready," the guard said, leaning in the door.

"Please bring her in," Lina said. She composed her face and watched gravely as the guards did as she asked. The prisoner was an older woman, her eyes nearly lost in a web of lines. Her head had been shaved, and the stark contrast between her white scalp and her tanned, weather-beaten face stood out.

She shuffled in, slouching in her shapeless prisoner's smock. One of the guards shoved at her with the butt of his rifle, causing her to stumble forward.

"That is quite enough of that," Lina said sharply. She stared at the guard until he muttered an apology and stepped back.

"You may wait outside the door," she went on. "I will call for you to return."

"Oberhelfer, will you be safe?" the other guard asked. His SS rank insignia proclaimed him the more senior of the pair.

"I am quite certain of it. If you have doubt, I invite you to ask the commander of your detachment. He gave me this assignment himself." Lina gave the man a small smile as she spoke, making sure to keep her tone pleasant. She knew what they saw when they looked at her: a young slip of a girl, barely nineteen, with delicate features and wispy blond hair. It was natural for a young man, especially one of the Reich's elite soldiers, to feel protective, but it got to be a nuisance at times. She'd been fighting a version of that same battle since she'd arrived here in Warsaw.

Apparently, the prospect of speaking with his commander didn't appeal, for the guard desisted and urged his fellow out into the hallway. The heavy wooden door closed behind them with a soft *boom* against the stonework of the old building, and she turned her smile up at her guest.

"Men," she said, in near-perfect Polish. "Such silly creatures. I don't think they believe we can do anything without their help."

The prisoner looked startled, but her lips twisted in something like a small smile.

"Please," Lina invited. "Do sit down. I do not think we need to be overly formal. Would you like some tea?"

The woman lowered herself gingerly to a chair across the small table from Lina's. She was obviously skittish, expecting something terrible to happen. Her file said that she hadn't been in custody long, but that didn't mean much. The probability that she had been mistreated was, unfortunately, high.

Lina wished it were otherwise. Such things made her job so much more difficult.

"I'm not going to hurt you," she said as she began preparing to pour. The tea kettle was still warm to the touch, which was good. Lina hated tepid tea. "I just want to talk to you."

"I will not tell you anything about our group," the woman said, her voice roughened and hoarse. She sounded like someone who had screamed a lot recently.

"I am not going to ask you about that," Lina said. Steam rose as she poured first one cup, and then another. "I am interested in other things. I would like to know more about you, about your family, your culture. Who were you before the war?"

She put the tea kettle down and picked up one the cups by its saucer. She held it out with a smile, inviting the prisoner to take it.

The woman looked at her for a long moment and then slowly reached out. Her finger brushed Lina's, and the cup rattled in the saucer as she took it.

In that moment, Lina had what she needed. With exquisite precision, the SS-Oberhelfer reached out an infinitesimal tendril of thought, and as their fingers touched, she slipped inside the prisoner's outer mind.

"Wha—?"

"Merciful heavens!" Lina cried out in German as she brushed the hot kettle with the back of her arm. "Oh! What a clumsy dolt I am!"

The two guards burst in through the door at her cry, weapons at the ready.

"No! No!" Lina said, cradling her arm and surging to her feet. "I'm fine! I just burnt myself on the kettle. Please, go back in the hallway. The prisoner is extraordinarily well behaved and has offered me no threat."

"You are sure?" the senior guard asked.

"I am. Please. Go."

The guards left once again, and Lina sat back down, careful not to show her pleasure in the efficacy of her distraction.

"Are you all right?" the woman asked in Polish.

"Oh, I'm fine," Lina said with a smile. She could feel the slick, unfamiliar territory of the woman's psyche. It wasn't the easiest thing to penetrate, but she had been trained by the best psychic teachers the Reich could find. "I just feel stupid for being so clumsy!"

"The tea is very good," the woman said, taking a sip.

"Thank you. My mother taught me."

"Mothers know best," the woman said with a smile.

"Indeed. Do you have children?"

"Two daughters. Both grown and married now."

"How wonderful for you..."

* * *

"The prisoner is Rasia Boron. She is fifty-seven years old, has two married daughters. Her husband, Pawel Boron, died five years ago. She has significant ties to the underground rebel movement called the 'Armia Krajowa' through both of her sons-in-law, who were junior officers in the Polish Army," Lina said as she walked into the office of the detachment commander.

Kriminalkommisar Ardwin Bordstein looked up from his correspondence at Lina's abrupt entry. He set down his pen, his dark, handsome face giving her a brief smile.

"Oberhelfer," he said in his smooth, melodious voice. "I see you have made some progress with our inscrutable lady. Please, sit down and tell me about your interview."

"Your men made a mistake with her, Herr Kriminalkommisar," Lina said. She walked over to the chair he indicated and took a seat perched on the edge.

"Oh?" Bordstein asked, leaning back in his chair. "Why do you say that? My men are all very well trained."

"Yes, but they started off too aggressively," Lina said. "From the time she was brought in, she was subjected to strong, aggressive interrogations. It put her back up, made her suspicious. I had to spend over an hour with tea and small talk before even I got anywhere."

"Ah, yes. Your mental gifts. They were useful in this case?"

"They were essential, mein Herr. She is a very strong-willed individual. It was difficult for me to get her to relax enough to let her surface thoughts be unguarded."

"But you *were* able to do this?"

"After some time, yes," Lina said. "As I stated, she has ties to the old Polish army, as well as the current criminal Armia Krajowa organization. She has information about the perpetrators of the attacks on the rail lines last year. Several names came into her mind as we talked about that time. I have written them down for you, here."

She laid a piece of paper on the desk. Bordstein took it but did not look at it. Instead, he pursed his lips and studied Lina's face.

"Very good. Was there anything else?" he asked.

"Yes," Lina said. "I suspect, but cannot confirm, that when Boron was arrested last week, she was involved in the logistics and planning for another sabotage attack. This time on one of our supply depots outside of Warsaw. She seems to have been part of the financial backing in some capacity. A fundraiser, perhaps. I was unable to ask her directly without putting her on her guard. If I had more time with her, I think I could gather more information."

Another long moment and Bordstein idly tapped his fingers on the paper.

"Oberhelfer, this is excellent work."

"Thank you, mein Herr," she said.

"My predecessor, Herr Sendler, praised your performance and abilities before he left, and now I can see why."

"I am happy to serve the Reich, Herr Bordstein," Lina said.

"And you received training in more conventional methods of interrogation as well, yes?"

"Yes. Though it was mostly focused on how we could integrate our abilities with the accepted practices. Why do you ask, mein Herr?"

Bordstein tapped the paper again, pursed his lips, and then leaned forward in his chair.

"Do you know where Herr Sendler was assigned after he left Warsaw, Oberhelfer?"

"No, mein Herr."

"He was posted to Paris. Have you ever been there?"

"No, mein Herr." Lina wondered where he was going with this line of conversation that seemed to have little to do with her report. However, she had learned that it was better to be patient and impassive, especially when dealing with superior officers.

"It is a beautiful city. I think you will enjoy it very much."

Despite her determination, Lina felt her eyebrows rise in surprise. Bordstein gave her an easy, practiced smile.

"Herr Sendler has requested you, you see. And I don't see why such a lovely and useful asset such as yourself should be stuck here in miserable old Warsaw. Paris will be much more to your liking, I am sure of it."

"Thank you, Herr Bordstein," Lina said, choosing her words carefully. "But won't you still require my abilities here?"

"I will be honest with you, Oberhelfer. My orders indicate that our leaders are displeased with the continued resistance of this Polish criminal army. While your assistance has been invaluable, you have made no secret of the fact that you get better results when we apply a...gentler hand, shall we say?"

Lina pressed her lips together and nodded. While fear and pain were two of the classic tools of the interrogator's trade, they made for a difficult time penetrating a prisoner's psyche.

"Warsaw will not be experiencing a gentle hand in the future, Oberhelfer. Herr Sendler and I agreed that it would be better if you were spared from having to witness that."

Rasia Boron's tentative, genuine smile as she sipped her tea flashed through Lina's mind. She felt her stomach clench.

"I see," she said softly. "It is a war, after all."

"Just so," Bordstein said with that winning smile.

A tiny corner of Lina's mind wondered if he'd ever been an actor. He'd have been a good one, if he could smile like that while contemplating the harrowing of an entire city. She didn't know specifically what would be done, but she could imagine. The army had taken terrible losses from the criminals' attacks. They would require blood in return.

She came to her feet.

"Very well, Herr Bordstein," she said. "I serve the Reich. If I am required in Paris, I will go to Paris."

"Very good, Oberhelfer Sucherin," he said, standing as well. "I will have the arrangements made."

* * * * *

Chapter Four

As promised, the knock came at 0430.

Evelyn felt as if she'd only just fallen asleep. The banging on the outer door was, however, impossible to ignore, and she sat up amid the groans and protestations of the women around her. As soon as she had, the door slammed open, and Captain Ledoux walked in.

"On your feet, ladies!" she shouted in a voice that would have made a drill sergeant proud. "We've got a mission. You're to eat and report to your crews right away. They've already got the tail number assignments. Make sure you eat, mind! You'll do no one any good if you pass out from hunger and exhaustion halfway to France!"

The captain's voice held a high note of excitement. She had to be as tired as the rest of them, for she'd been working with her own crew late the night before, but her carriage was ramrod-straight as she strode down the aisle separating the bunks, and a gleeful light shone in her eyes.

Evelyn rolled out of her bunk just as Mary climbed down from the top. Evelyn gave her friend a little smile of commiseration as they both started to dress. Mary responded with a grunt. Evelyn was satisfied. That was typical for Mary before she'd had a drop of coffee.

Captain Ledoux walked down the full length of the hut, ensuring that every woman was awake and moving in a positive direction before she returned to the front. Before she exited, though, she turned back to look at all of them. Evelyn paused in the act of pulling on her utility boots.

"I want you all to know," Captain Ledoux said, her voice getting slightly thick. "That I am extremely proud of all of you. I know that you'll make a difference for those boys today. Good luck to all of you." With that astonishing speech, she turned and pushed out into the pre-dawn darkness.

Mary turned wide eyes to Evelyn.

"Well!" the blond girl said, startled into actual speech by the captain's actions. "Do you know, I believe the good captain nearly got a bit sentimental on us!"

"Don't tease, Mary," Evelyn said gently. "She's done her best, and she knows very well some of us may not make it back today."

"Hmph. That old battle axe!" Mary said, with a derisive sniff. "Well, I hope she's wrong about *that*, at least."

"So do I," Evelyn said. She finished tying up her boots and stood up. She ran her hands rather nervously down over her hips. This wasn't the first time she'd worn trousers. They'd worn them for their training flights, of course, but there hadn't been too many of those, and Evelyn still felt exposed with the shape of her legs so easily visible. Skirts were, however, simply not compatible with operating in aircraft. Women all over the country were wearing trousers to work back home. Evelyn told herself that this was no different.

It still wasn't comfortable.

"Are you ready?" Mary asked, her pre-coffee gruffness returning. Evelyn nodded, and they set out for the chow hall at a good clip. England was cold, after all. It couldn't hurt to get the blood moving.

* * *

E velyn might have worried about finding her aircraft and crew. The flightline was, after all, quite large, with hundreds of aircraft parked in clusters all along the outer edge. The rising sun gilded the wings and fuselages of the birds by the time Mary and Evelyn joined the stream of bodies headed out in that direction. Vehicles, too. Big trucks carrying the .50 caliber machine guns used by the waist gunners to keep the fighters at bay roared down the apron, belching clouds of diesel smoke into the air. Still, a fine mist rose from the grass infield, giving everything a silvery cast as the light caught the water droplets.

"These are my fellas," Mary said, breaking the silence that had fallen over the two women from the time they left the chow hall. Evelyn stopped and wrapped her arms around her friend in a hard hug.

"Good luck," she whispered. The blond girl tightened her arms in response.

"You too," Mary replied, her high, light voice trembling and devoid of her usual mischievous humor.

Evelyn gave her one more squeeze and let go, sniffing back her own tears. The two women shared a brave smile, and then Mary turned to greet the enlisted aircrewmen who had gathered at the nose of the plane, watching their interchange.

Mary's plane was the *Lucky Lou*. Her fuselage proudly bore a depiction of a woman lying on her back, her feet crossed in the air while playing cards laid scattered all around her. Though she was covered, the painted woman's posture showed her ample curves to advantage, and Evelyn felt her cheeks heat up every time she looked at the nose art.

However, Evelyn was pleased to see that Mary's crew reached out to her as she approached. That was a sign that their net was already strong. Mary might have envied Evelyn her finesse, but the truth was that she was a formidable psychic in her own right. Her strength of will and her natural charisma made for a powerful combination, and Evelyn knew Mary would do well. She kissed her fingertips and waved at her friend one more time, then turned to find her own crew.

As it turned out, she had no trouble. The net pulled at her, getting stronger the closer she got to her crew. Her instincts pushed at her to re-establish the connection; her mind longed to feel the minds of her men once more. Evelyn allowed the pull to guide her but shunted the worst of the urges off for the time being. She'd re-link everyone once they were airborne.

Corporal Martinez was the first to see her as she walked up, but the others weren't far behind. The net pulled at them, too. One by one, the four gunners climbed down out of the plane and approached Evelyn.

"Morning," Sergeant Carroll said, sounding uncharacteristically shy. Evelyn gave him a smile that she then gave to the rest of the group.

"Good morning," Evelyn said, feeling a bit shy herself. "I, ah, don't want to be in your way. Is there somewhere in particular I should stand?" She felt every bit of her small-town girl awkwardness come to the fore. To add to her mortification, she felt her face heating up in another blush. Sergeant Carroll ducked his head briefly and then let out a soft curse and reached for her hand. The moment he touched her skin, the net snapped into place between them, then leapt out and encompassed Rico, Les, Logan, and Bobby as well.

Evelyn reached out quickly to steady them all, sorting their vision and other inputs, helping them to make sense of the sudden quintupling of information flowing to their brains.

Whoa, that was fast, Les thought. *It wasn't that fast last night.*

Every connection strengthens the net, which makes connecting faster, Evelyn replied. *I wasn't fast enough to stop Sean from touching my hand. Physical touch makes it easier to connect, too, especially when the net wants to be built. Or, at least, that's how it seems. You all craved the connection this morning, so it was very easy...all of these things made it easy.*

Just at that moment, a Jeep roared up, and a lanky specialist with tousled blond hair and a mile-wide grin hopped out. Six pairs of eyes, including Evelyn's, turned to regard the newcomer.

John Gilmour, Sean thought. *Radio operator. Good man. Musta subbed in for Harry.*

Instantly, Evelyn felt flooded with the knowledge that their regular radio operator, Harry Richards, had gotten pneumonia and been taken to the nearest hospital to recover. The crew felt a collective pang of regret at not having their regular teammate there, but Evelyn noticed a certain cautious optimism. Everyone liked John.

Evelyn took a deep breath and shunted the men's thoughts off to a corner of her conscious brain.

"Specialist Gilmour," she said, hearing her voice echo through five other sets of ears. It never ceased to amaze her how much higher her voice sounded that way. "I am Technician Evelyn Adamsen. I've linked the crew into a psychic net for this mission. Do I have your permission to include you in this?"

Specialist Gilmour blinked several times, obviously taken aback. His cocky smile faded, and he flicked his eyes from her to the men ranged behind her. Evelyn felt Sean, Rico, Logan, and several of the others silently urge the man to accept. They wanted him on their crew. Evelyn smiled gently and pushed Sean to speak. He was the highest ranked of all of them, and as the flight engineer, the men naturally looked to him. He cleared his throat awkwardly and took a step forward.

"Look, John," he said. Evelyn could feel the disorientation that resulted from hearing his own words through other ears, and she gently did what she could to pull that away from the young sergeant so that he could concentrate. "This net thing, it's strange, but it's good. It lets us communicate instantly, so we can tell if someone's hurt or whatever...and it will help us see fighters, too, and fly closer formation, Evelyn says. Just, give it a try, will ya? She's good."

"All right," Specialist Gilmour said, his words coming slowly. "What do you need?"

"If you could take my hand," Evelyn said, "that would be good...and...have you anything on you? A token of some kind? Perhaps a lucky charm?" As soon as she said it, she knew she'd made a mistake. All of the men recoiled from her question. *You can't take his lucky charm!* Les thought fiercely. *It'll throw him off for the whole sortie! Ask for a dog tag or something instead.*

It was Evelyn's turn to blink rapidly.

"Oh! I am sorry. Not a lucky charm, I didn't know..." Well, of *course* these men pinned their hopes on something as small as a token. They had to have something to give them a sense of control over the completely uncontrollable fortunes of war. She felt sick at her own faux pas. She swallowed hard, making sure to shield the men from her dismay, and pressed on. "Perhaps, an identification tag? Something with your name on it, that you wear close to your skin?"

Specialist Gilmour eyed her with no little suspicion, but at Sean's nod, he reached into his collar and pulled out the chain that held his dog tags. A quick twist of his fingers detached one of the tags, and he held it out to Evelyn. She smiled again, trying to be encouraging.

"Thank you," she said, without reaching out to touch it. "I'm going to take your tag and your hand at the same time, all right? I just need you to relax." *Just relax and let me in,* she found herself thinking, and then for some reason she didn't want to examine too closely, found humor welling up from several of the crewmen. While her face flamed, Evelyn reached out and touched Specialist Gilmour's hand with her fingertips. At the same time, she reached out with her mind, seeking his psyche.

He was so cautious, and Evelyn didn't want to hurt him by forcing her way in (*another quickly stifled burst of amusement, like a silent snicker shushed by several disapproving voices*), so it was slow going. His mind seemed to simultaneously reach out for hers and shy away. Evelyn found herself murmuring soft reassurances. Her hand slid over his, her fingertips finding the rolled metal edge of the dog tag. She pushed slowly, just a bit harder, and reached across the slick surface of the metal to find the raised letters of his name. Her mind registered those letters, the pictures of the sounds that made up his name, and it was like a key turned in a lock. John's mind opened to her, and Evelyn gathered up all of his delicious maleness and wove it into the larger net.

What? John asked, startled as his vision fractured into multiple images. Evelyn hustled to separate his vision out and ease him in.

It's all right, John, Sean thought, reaching out and clapping the blond man on the shoulder. John's cockiness had completely disappeared, leaving only the same doubts that all of them had. *We're all here, Evelyn's got us, and she's good.*

I worked with them for some hours last night, Evelyn explained. *It will be easier for you to join the net the next time. You'd better have this back,* she said then, releasing the dog tag. *I don't need it anymore. Things with names on them make the net stronger, but you're required to wear two of them, and I am strong enough to hold the net without it.*

This is so weird, John thought, and the rest of the men in the net erupted into laughter. It was sympathetic laughter, but laughter nonetheless. Even Evelyn smiled at that.

We've still got a preflight to complete, Sean reminded them. *The officers will be here any minute. Evelyn, you can come with me. I'll show you your crew station and egress procedures.*

For the rest of the hour, Evelyn watched through separate pairs of eyes as they accomplished their various pre-flight tasks. Weapons had to be loaded, extra ammo stacked. She understood that they weren't exactly supposed to carry extra but that Logan had worked out a deal with the munitions guys. Normally, she didn't hold with working around the rules...but she felt their reasons, and their fear, and she knew that the extra ammo was a talisman as much as their various lucky charms. If they didn't have it, they'd be thrown off, and that couldn't happen. Plus, what if they needed it?

Don't worry, Sean thought to her, once he noticed her noticing their ammo load. *I've run the numbers on my own. We're still well under our max gross weight and well within our center of gravity limits. See how the cans are stacked there?* he asked her, looking at the load he meant, showing her through his own eyes. *They're stacked that way on purpose. That's so that they keep the CG where it should be.* Evelyn felt his self-satisfied smile and found her own lips curving in response. *We'll keep you as safe as we can, Evie, don't you worry.*

Mary calls me Evie, she thought in response, because that seemed the best thing to say at that moment.

I like it, Bobby replied, from his station in the right waist. *It suits you.* Evelyn felt the collective approval of the other men soaking through her, and she resigned herself to the nickname. All in all, it was a good sign. It meant that the men were feeling more and more comfortable with her presence and with being tied in together. Even John, who sat silently in his radio room and was preparing his radio equipment, was cautiously exploring the lines of the net. Evelyn could feel him tentatively looking through the other men's eyes as they loaded their guns and did whatever other tasks they needed to do.

Before too long, another Jeep pulled up, and the four officer members of the crew hopped out. Evelyn had been sitting in her crew station, next to the radio table. She heard Sean greet Captain Peters just as the net suddenly leapt and strained toward the four members it had been missing. Careful where she stepped, Evelyn climbed down out of the aircraft and walked toward her pilot and the others.

"*Pretty Cass,* today, hmm?" Captain Peters was saying. He had a smile on his face as he looked up at the nose art painted on the front fuselage. A dark haired girl in a striped bathing suit smiled back from where she lay on her stomach, her toes pointed up toward the sky. As nose art went, it wasn't the most risqué that Evelyn had seen, and the depiction was well done. She thought she recognized the picture out of an issue of *Esquire* magazine that had been tacked up on one of the walls in Operations.

Why do you paint pinup girls on the front of the aircraft? Evelyn found herself thinking.

The aircraft like it. They enjoy being treated like ladies, and then they're more likely to bring us home. That was Logan, and Evelyn could feel his grin as he thought about it. She smiled in response.

"Is that smile for us?" Lieutenant Becket asked, giving her a bit of a smirk. Evelyn schooled her face into more decorous lines and shunted the other men to the back of her head. Not all of them liked the copilot, she noticed. Some thought he was far too cocky for his level of skill. Most of them were just as happy that he was the copilot and that Captain Peters was in charge.

"If you like, sir," Evelyn said. "I try to be pleasant when I greet people for the first time in the morning." She turned her attention to Captain Peters. "The crew and I have re-linked the net already. I thought to wait until we were airborne, but the net had other ideas."

"You talk like it's a living thing," Captain Peters said. He shifted his weight toward her, and his hand sort of drifted out, as if it would take hold of Evelyn's. Evelyn sternly held her instincts back. She wouldn't incorporate him until he said to do so...no matter how much she yearned to make the connection complete.

"It feels that way sometimes, sir," she said. "Don't you feel it pulling at you even now?"

Captain Peters' brown eyes bored into hers, but he didn't say anything. Evelyn held her breath and held the clamoring minds of the enlisted crew at bay. Slowly, the captain reached out to take her hand.

He never got there. The moment Evelyn could see acquiescence in his eyes, the net leapt free of her constraints and embraced him like a lover. Evelyn felt Carl's consciousness flood into hers, followed quickly by Paul's, Bob's, and Abram's as the other officers naturally followed their pilot's lead. Evelyn worked quickly to sort everyone's senses, but she felt a giddy euphoria as the net sang through all of them. It was complete! They were a crew! It was time to fly!

* * *

Less than an hour later, Evelyn sat strapped into her seat, her mind rapidly cycling through the senses of each of the men. Running a net of this size wasn't new to Evelyn, but it could be a bit taxing, if she wasn't careful. Oddly enough, the best way to do it seemed to be to open herself wide and let all but her most necessary barriers drop. In this way, she became less of a conductress and more of a conduit. The men could sense each other nearly directly simply by casting their thoughts toward one of their fellows. In truth, Evelyn still facilitated things by routing attention and information streams to the desired recipient. It just happened fast, faster than conscious thought, as she welcomed the men into the landscape of her mind and let their consciousnesses mingle and flow.

Takeoff checks complete, Carl thought, and the back of Evelyn's mind registered the increased vibration all around her. Next came the sensation of motion, dizzyingly amplified through eleven other minds. Evelyn fought down nausea and worked to distill out the sensory inputs. She wanted to keep the channel wide open, so she couldn't just shunt them to the side as she'd done on the ground. But since the men were all experiencing the movement of the aircraft in different ways (some of them backward!) it made for a uniquely disorienting rush. Evelyn focused on her breathing while the plane pitched up, and with a shudder, they were airborne. The disorientation subsided somewhat, and she allowed herself to relax a bit. Upchucking would have been embarrassing, but it also would have represented a real danger to the crew. Last night had proven that she needed to fuel her body in order to do her job. She couldn't afford to be wasting calories by throwing up.

Their mission required them to fly over the English Channel into occupied France. The target was a factory complex that manufactured automobile parts. Parts that, according to the intelligence briefing that Carl and the other officers had received, the Nazis were adapting for their notorious Panzer tanks. The first part of the sortie was uneventful...which meant that it was dead dull. The aircraft (or "Fort" as the men called the B-17) thrummed with the vibration from the four massive Cyclone-9 radial engines. The rumble of the engines deafened speech, but with the net, they didn't need to speak, and the noise settled into a sort of subliminal roar. Evelyn tried to concentrate on relaxing and conserving her energy while keeping the net as open as possible to allow the men to get used to thinking at each other.

Evie, check your toes and fingers. Carl's thought cut through her sort of semi-conscious trance because it was directed specifically at her. Evelyn blinked and wiggled her fingers and toes obediently. Sure enough, her hands were numb and stiff with cold.

Sean, I think her gloves have gone out, the pilot thought. Evelyn felt a swift jolt of worried agreement from the red-headed flight engineer, and she blinked again, sleepily, as Sean turned and began to work his way back toward her. The formation was flying at 38,000 feet above the Channel. Evelyn didn't know how cold it was, but numbers like negative fifty floated around in some of the men's consciousnesses. The crew all wore electrically-heated suits with gloves and booties that fit inside their regular boots. They'd actually had to scramble a bit during the previous night in order to find gear small enough to work for Evelyn.

"Evie!" Sean called, out loud and mentally. Evelyn's eyelashes fluttered as she fought to focus on him. Perhaps it was a trick of the light, but he seemed a shadow figure, leeched of color. The edges of her vision started to sparkle.

Jolts of alarm came from all directions as each of the men began to realize what was happening to her.

Oxygen! Check her O2! Her tube must be frozen! Check her air!

Sean swore, but Evelyn couldn't have said whether or not she heard it with her ears or her mind. She felt a warm, contented kind of amusement at his colorful language. Didn't they know she was a lady?

She felt him tugging at the oxygen hose connected to the mask that covered her mouth and nose. More swearing, more mental alarm bells from the other men, and all she could do was smile. Her eyes drifted slowly closed, and for the first time since she'd landed in England, Evelyn felt a delicious, delicate sort of warmth steal over her.

Another jerk on her hose, and suddenly, a blast of air quite literally took her breath away. Evelyn's eyes popped back open, and the sparkling gray receded from center of her vision outward. A tight pain pierced her forehead right between her eyes as the forced O2 flowing from her mask reinvigorated her.

What happened? she asked. Her connection to the net felt ragged and worn, and she reached out with tentative mental fingers to repair it.

Hypoxia, Sean replied, grimly. *Your O2 hose froze over, musta got some water in there. Probably condensation. I switched you to an emergency bottle. Now let me see your hands.*

Her head continued to throb with pain as she obediently held out her gloved hands. Sean opened up the fur-lined collar of his jacket and felt the outside of her gloves against his exposed cheek. He swore again and stripped her gloves off. The frigid air felt as if it burned on her skin as he uncovered it. He unzipped her jacket and crossed her arms one over the other so that she could put her hands under her armpits.

Hold them there for just a moment, Sean said. *I've got a spare set of electric gloves. They'll be huge on you, but you're not doing anything with your hands anyway.*

Evelyn felt a quick surge of shame. Everyone else on the crew was using their hands, or would be. Was she just dead weight?

No! Carl's negative response slashed into her mind. *If not for your net, we never would have known you were in trouble until it was too late.*

Evelyn didn't respond right away, focusing instead on how Sean was chafing her hands before pulling the spare electric gloves over her frigid fingers. Feeling started to come back in painful prickles, and that gave her yet another excuse to not respond to Carl.

Because, of course, the truth was that if she hadn't been there, then she wouldn't have gotten ice in her O2 hose in the first place. And then Sean wouldn't have had to leave his crew position above the cockpit. He would still have been scanning for enemy fighters, or monitoring the engine gauges, or something else equally useful. Evelyn felt her own uselessness settle on her like a weight around her neck. But she couldn't let the men feel it, too. They couldn't doubt her, or the net would be further weakened. So she wrapped it up, shunted it away, and locked it behind barriers she hoped the men would never even sense, let alone wonder at.

A sudden tension flowed back to her from Carl and Bob in the cockpit. Sean caught it, too, because he straightened suddenly, gave her a thumbs-up and a pair of raised eyebrows as if to ask if she was all right. She gave him a smile and a pulse of wordless reassurance, and he turned to hustle back to his position.

Easy now, just tighten it up. Nice and slow, Carl thought to his copilot. Bob, the young lieutenant copilot, was flying. He was doing a fair enough job of holding formation, but as Evelyn looked through his eyes, she saw what had caused that increase in tension. White and gray wisps of cloud began to cut across their line of sight, cutting between their formation and the one ahead, now kissing the top or belly of the *Pretty Cass* herself.

Slowly, Bob pushed the four red-knobbed throttles forward, causing the engine noise to build slightly as the Cyclones took a deeper bite of the air, and *Pretty Cass* began to accelerate just a bit.

Back it off now, Carl thought then, nodding as his eyes stayed glued to their lead plane, flying ahead of them and to the left, at their eleven o'clock. *See how* Teacher's Pet *is getting larger in the wind screen? That's right, right there. Now just ride that line up on her...perfect.*

Bob followed Carl's mental nudges, and the Cyclones' whine changed again as the Fort's acceleration slowed. Evelyn felt a jolt of pleased surprise coming from the waist and ball turret gunners.

Nice hands, LT, Les thought, carefully articulating the thoughts. His wave of approval flowed down the link, and Evelyn caught a pulse of warm gratification from the copilot. He might not have wanted to admit it, but Lieutenant Bob Becket craved the approval and respect of his crew, and he desperately wanted to be looked up to, the way they looked up to Carl.

Evelyn caught that thought and quickly tried to squirrel it away so that the rest of the crew didn't catch hold of it. Things like that were often an awkward side effect of being in an extended net. It didn't help matters for after the job was done and the net dropped, so Evelyn did her best to mitigate such things and preserve what privacy she could.

Not that she could do much.

It's all right, Evie. It was Paul Rutherford, on an incredibly tight channel that spoke to her, once again, of his previous experience working in a net with his lost sister. *We all know already. Bob's a good sort, when he's not trying too hard. He works hard, and the men will all like him quite a bit once he calms down. A little bit of atta-boy will do him a world of good.*

Evelyn began to understand. These men were a crew, which meant something she'd only just now realized. Their relationship had already been tight and interdependent before she'd arrived on the scene. It hadn't been hard to build a net for them; in fact, the net had seemed to want to spring into existence with disconcerting eagerness. This was why, Evelyn realized. These men had flown together and fought together. They'd watched friends die together. Their very survival depended on knowing what each other was doing and thinking. They'd honed the ability to anticipate each other into something astonishing, and, truth be told, near psychic on its own. No wonder they had naturally clicked into her net.

We're fully IFR now, boys...and Evie, Carl announced. A quick look through his eyes told her what "IFR" meant: they were completely enveloped by the clouds. It was as if the formation of Forts existed in a sea of white and gray wisps. The formations ahead of theirs flickered in and out of sight like indecisive ghosts as the clouds played havoc with Carl's vision.

I can help, Evelyn said suddenly, as an idea occurred to her. *That's our lead aircraft, right? The one forward and to the left?*

At the eleven o'clock, Bob replied, his mind tight with concentration as he fought to maintain position.

Evelyn took a deep breath and reached out, seeking the mental signature of the lead bird's psychic. It wasn't easy, for they weren't really as close as they seemed, and there was a lot of distraction with the crew and the aircraft itself. Eventually, however, Evelyn made contact with the tightly wound threads of Alice McGee's mind.

Alice was young, only about seventeen, but she was tough as nails. She'd grown up on a farm in rural Georgia with seven brothers. She and Evelyn had bonded over being country girls thrown onto this wild ride, but where Evelyn was shy and demure, Alice was brash and cocky.

Only she didn't seem so cocky now, Evelyn realized as she touched her friend's mind in query.

Evelyn? Alice asked, her mind tone sounding near hysterical. *Oh, Evelyn...I don't...I'm not sure I can handle this...*

Alice, what's wrong?

The men, they're so scared, and we can't see where we're going, and I feel so disoriented...

Just then, Evelyn felt Carl's jolt of recognition.

"Roll out, Bob!" he said out loud, his voice urgent. Evelyn heard it through both Carl's ears and Bob's.

"Lead's in a bank," Bob replied. "If I roll out, I'll lose him in the cloud."

"Radio! Get ahold of lead!"

I've got it, Evelyn replied. *I'm in contact with lead's psychic. Carl, focus on the artificial horizon, please. I'm going to feed that to Alice in lead.* She took a deep breath and reached out again.

Alice, you have to calm down. Your panic is disorienting your crew. It was hard for me, too, but you've got to just open your channels and let them feel each other's minds. And then you have to control what sensations and emotions get through. Your pilot is in an inadvertent bank. Feed this image to him, Evelyn thought, passing along Carl's sensation and knowledge while Bob fought to keep position on lead. The clouds were getting denser and denser, and if they lost sight of the other aircraft in the formation, the risk of a midair collision increased.

Evelyn felt Alice's trembling acceptance of the image, and she felt the younger woman pass it along to her crew. The lead pilot recognized his error with a horror that echoed down the two joined links.

Alice! Suppress that! Evelyn snapped, on what she hoped was a tight channel. In any case, her whipcord order got through because she felt Alice grab on to her pilot's emotional response and dampen it, pull it out, away from the other men, and fine tune her crew's focus.

Lead rolled out of the bank, then transmitted a course correction over the radio.

Thank you, Evelyn, Alice thought to her. *How did you know I was in trouble?*

I didn't, Evelyn responded. *I just thought that in this dense weather, maybe we ought to link our nets together. I thought it might reinforce the integrity of the formation. Are you all right now?*

Yes, Alice thought, her mind firm and grim. *I am sorry about that. I let their emotions get away from me. It was just the flying in the weather...I let everyone's unease reinforce each other. It won't happen again.*

Evelyn hoped not, but she didn't say so, or even think it loudly enough for Alice to hear. That, then, was a vulnerability that they hadn't discussed in training. The negative emotions of the crew could get into a feedback loop that caused problems for everyone if their psychic wasn't on top of things.

Let's link up, Evelyn suggested again. *We should check on all the others and make sure they're not having problems, too.*

All right, Alice thought back at her. *My navigator says that we're over the Channel now, and that this weather should clear once we're "feet dry" again.*

Evelyn passed an acknowledgment to Alice, then reached out to link with the other psychics in the formation. None of them were in the same bad shape Alice had been in, but none of them were particularly comfortable. Their training hadn't prepared them for any of this...and they hadn't even entered hostile airspace yet.

Still, one did what one could. Evelyn passed along Alice's position report and her suggestion to maintain at least a light link with each other in the event that something went wrong. Maude Phillips, over on *Ginger Gal* on the other side of the formation, suggested that this might even help them keep some awareness, if and when they came up against Luftwaffe fighters. Deep inside, Evelyn quailed at the thought, but she appreciated the support to her suggestion.

Once the entire formation was linked in a loose net, they began to fly much tighter. Once again, Evelyn felt the way that this pleased her men. Close formation meant less vulnerability to enemy fighters. That could only be a good thing, as far as they were concerned.

The flight droned on. Evelyn began to feel a creeping sense of unreality to it all. The constant drone of the Cyclone engines, the numbing cold, the peculiar sensation of multiple perspectives...these things combined to leave Evelyn drifting along the streams of her own net.

* * *

"Look sharp, everyone," Carl said after a while. Evelyn couldn't have said whether they'd been droning for minutes or hours in the cold, dense white of the cloud cover. "We should be overhead the French coast in about thirty seconds."

The men all reacted to this announcement with varying degrees of excitement and terror. Sean got up from his seat and came back to her, holding an awkward looking arrangement of fabric and straps.

Put this on, he thought to her. *It's your flak jacket. And your parachute is just there*, he said, pointing. *If the captain gives the order to bail out, you go, clip this piece into your 'chute, and jump out the biggest hole you can find. Do you understand? You do, don't you. This psychic thing certainly makes explaining things easier*, he finished with a grin.

Evelyn gave him what she hoped was a brave smile and took the flak jacket from him. It was deceptively heavy, and she struggled a bit with getting it on. Sean gave her a smile and a thumbs up, and then headed back to his station.

The other men were checking in and charging their weapons. A short time later, Evelyn saw through Rico's eyes as the tail gunner watched their fighter escort waggle their wings at the formation and depart. They didn't have the long-range fuel capability to continue all the way to the target.

Someday, that long-range fighter escort we were promised will materialize, Carl thought. His mind felt determinedly positive, like he was trying to be strong for the crew and not let them see his fear. That, of course, was an impossibility, but the crew took it well. After all, they were afraid, too. Especially as the formation had begun its descent to the attack altitude of 20,000 feet. Evelyn became gradually aware of the way the men's collective tension ratcheted up with every hundred feet of descent. They were entering enemy fighter territory.

Yeah, and someday Veronica Lake will...ah. Never mind. Sorry, Evie. That was Les. Evelyn could feel the waist gunner's not-quite-repentant grin. She had to suppress a grin of her own, but Les' irreverence was the perfect tension breaker.

Boys will be boys, she sent, projecting a sense of tolerance. *But real men keep their private lives private.* She added this last with a bit of smug superiority and felt the rest of the crew's appreciative flare of humor at her jab. Even Les laughed, shaking his head. A warmth that had nothing to do with her electric suit enfolded Evelyn, and she started to feel like, maybe, she just might become part of the crew yet.

Fighters! Twelve o'clock high!

The call came from Alice. If she craned her neck to look around Sean's body, Evelyn could just see the terrifying rain of tracer fire coming from the dark, diving silhouette of an enemy fighter. She let the call echo down her own channels and felt her men respond, turning their own weapons to cover *Teacher's Pet*'s flanks. Adrenaline surges spiked through all of them, causing Evelyn's heart to race in turn. She took a deep breath and reached out to tie her crew in closer to the Forts around them.

She looked through Sean's eyes as he fired from the top turret, tracking his line of bullets just in front of the attacking aircraft. His mind was oddly calm and terribly focused...as, indeed, they all were. Even young Lieutenant Bob was zeroed in on his task of keeping a tight position and making it that much harder to penetrate the deadly crossing fire of the Flying Fortress.

Fighters! Three o'clock low!

That was Logan in the ball turret. Evelyn felt him as he spun his turret around and began to fire the twin Browning AN/M2 .50 caliber machine guns at the sinister dark shapes rising up to meet them with fire.

Got 'em, Bobby Fritsche replied, from his position in the right waist. He, too, opened up with his own .50 caliber machine gun, tracking the barrel forward of the nose of the fighter formation, in order to "lead" their flight and not shoot behind them.

Evelyn blinked, then hastily relayed the call to the other girls in the formation net. She felt their acknowledgement, though it was almost an absentminded thing as each of the girls were focusing mostly on the communication between the men in their individual crews.

Got you, you Kraut sonofabitch! Logan exulted. Evelyn looked through his eyes and couldn't help but feel a twist of pity for the pilot of the German fighter as he spiraled toward the ground, one wing completely gone. She carefully kept that emotion from Logan, however, as he was concentrating on trying to take out the other three fighters who'd been in the initial attacking wedge. One fell victim to Bobby's relentless fire as he threw out a curtain of lead that couldn't be avoided.

Two back to you, tail, Bobby said, his mind carrying an even calm, devoid of Logan's adrenaline-fueled exultation.

Yup, Rico Martinez answered as he visually acquired the two remaining targets and opened fire. He was aided by fire from the aircraft flying off their right wing, the *Nagging Natasha.* She fired from her left waist and tail, and the two remaining fighters faltered and tumbled through the resulting crossfire. Evelyn watched through Rico's eyes as the ugly black smoke trailed the wreckage down.

Fighters! Twelve high!

Fighters! Two high!

The calls were simultaneous, coming from Sean in his top turret and Les on the left side. Evelyn took a deep breath and did her best to split her attention between the two of them, keeping the net strong and open. Sean and Les opened fire, their respective weapons adding a cacophony of pops to the ever-present thrum of the engines.

Flak! That was Carl, up front. Evelyn felt him take hold of the controls, helping the lieutenant to maintain his position in the formation as the Nazi anti-aircraft guns began to send up 20mm shells that blossomed into dark clouds that pocked the sky. One exploded right in front of *Pretty Cass'* nose. Evelyn felt the bottom drop out of her stomach as the aircraft heaved first up and then down. She held on grimly and passed on the wordless knowledge the pilots had no choice but to fly through the debris and shrapnel that resulted.

In the meantime, the gunners continued their rapid fire response to the enemy fighters' attempt to break up the formation. Evelyn took that knowledge—that the Luftwaffe was trying to isolate one of the Forts, make her vulnerable—and passed it along the looser formation net.

Shit! They got Liberty Belle! Logan called out then, from his view in the ball turret. Evelyn looked through his angry eyes, feeling his sudden spike of despair as they watched the crippled Fort fall back, two of her four engines smoking. Instantly, the enemy fighters swarmed like so many insects, and Evelyn watched as the aircraft yawed over and began to spin down and out of control.

A few agonizing heartbeats later, first one, then three more parachutes fluttered open far below. Evelyn felt Logan's bitter knowledge that there had been six other men on board that aircraft. *Liberty Belle* was one of the few birds flying without a psychic on board, and Evelyn suppressed a small, wicked feeling of relief that she hadn't just lost one of her friends.

Fighters! Twelve o'clock level! Paul called out from his bombardier compartment in the nose. His smaller .30 caliber machine guns sang out, joining the chaos of lead and noise, and the acrid, burnt smell of flak and hot brass. Evelyn took a deep breath of her oxygen and tried to focus on her job: maintaining the net and keeping in touch with the other crews.

Stay tight on 'em, Carl thought to Bob. *Look, you can kinda feel what they're going to do, through Evie's net. See?*

Evelyn ignored the sounds of combat all around her, ignored the knowledge that another Fort in the formation had been shot out of the sky, and focused on the copilot. She fed him the inputs she got from Alice, who got them, in turn, from the pilot on the controls in *Teacher's Pet.*

Light ripped through her mind as shards of glass flew everywhere, little bee stings that faded into insignificance beside the piercing pain that raked across her (his?) chest. Evelyn screamed and heard Bob echoing the sound up front as he felt the bullets that ripped the *Pet's* pilots to shreds.

Fighters! Ten o'clock high! Twelve o'clock high! They got Lead!

That was Sean again, rocking backward as he worked the controls of his top turret. Evelyn tried to gather the scattered fragments of her attention. Her crew net had held, but she'd ripped herself out of the larger formation net, and now it felt like they were flying blind. She took another deep, steadying breath of the icy oxygen in her bottle and reached out tentatively, toward Alice.

Nothing.

Parachutes from the Pet, Logan reported, his voice still and calm but with that edge of angry despair she'd tasted earlier. *I count two.*

Yeah, two, Les echoed.

Alice wasn't one of them, Evelyn reported to the group, fighting down her internal trembles. She was gone. Just gone. *I tried to reach her...there was just nothing there.*

A long pause.

Sorry, Evie, Les said gently, even as he continued to scan for the deadly fighters. *It hurts, we know.*

Evelyn shook herself, physically, and ordered herself to get a grip. She took another icy breath and forced her head up, her shoulders down.

It does, but no more than losing any airman, she said. *Alice did her job to the end. I'll...try to do mine.*

* * *

I t was horrific. They lost five more Forts, two with psychics aboard, before they came close to the target. The whole time, enemy flak continued to pound them, rattling them about like pebbles in an old tin can. Evie came to hate the flak nearly as much as the dreaded fighters, though the chances of flak taking down a Fort were minuscule. The Luftwaffe fighters were much more deadly.

With *Teacher's Pet* gone, Carl took the controls and slid into the lead spot in the formation. That made Abram, their navigator, responsible for getting the entire group of Forts to the correct target coordinates. He'd been following along during the entire flight, just in case this exact scenario happened, and Evie felt him taking refuge in the familiar tasks he'd been trained to do.

Radio, need a fix, Abram thought to John, their substitute radio operator. John acknowledged with a wordless affirmative and set to work pinging the two nearest radio transmitters. From this transmission, he'd get a distance and bearing to the station, and Abram would use the intersection of those two bits of information to "fix" their position in space. Both John and Abram worked smoothly, and Evelyn was satisfied that they'd be fine, though she could feel the added sense of responsibility heavy on them both.

There seemed to be a lull in the fighter attacks, and Evelyn used the opportunity to check in with the other psychics in the formation. They were all a bit shaken up, some more than others. Because of the tenuous formation-wide net, each one of them had felt at least an echo of the trauma of Alice's death, as well as the deaths of the other two psychics who'd gone down with their aircraft. In each case, there had been a searing pain and then a violent ejection from that part of the net. In neither case had anyone been able to sense the psychic's mind once the parachutes started blossoming open. Evelyn didn't want to think about that too closely, as there was still the rest of the mission to get through, but it was definitely something they were going to have to consider back on the ground.

In any case, Evelyn took a moment to cast her mind around the formation and do, at least, a cursory check. Where she could, she tried to help the other psychics to smooth down their ragged edges. In all cases, she found a grim determination to see it out, to get *their* crews back safely. That was the net at work again, Evelyn reflected in the private corner of her mind. The bond always worked two ways.

Two minutes to the bomb run, Abram sent to the rest of the crew. A thread of excitement ran through the net. Evelyn felt the shudder of tension through her channels and drew in a deep breath of her oxygen to keep calm. From her connection to the men, she knew that as the lead bombardier, Paul's drop would signal all the rest of the formation to drop with them. In a very real sense, just as Abram was responsible for getting them there, Paul was responsible for getting the job done.

We're all responsible for getting the job done, Paul replied on that tight channel. Amusement flirted with the focus and tension in his mind. *Even you. Especially you. Are you linked with the other birds? You can help them drop simultaneously. This could be our tightest drop ever.*

Evelyn blinked, surprised that the idea hadn't occurred to her before now. *I can do that,* she replied to Paul. Then she reached out again to her fellow psychics.

Let's open these channels a bit wider, the fighters are mostly gone now anyway, she sent, just as another blast of flak rocked her hard against her seat. She grimly held on to her seat and focused on her message. *We're about to start the bomb run. When we do, bring up your bombardiers' channels. We're lead, so I'll pass my bombardier's thoughts on. If our channels are wide open, they should all drop in near unison.*

Starting the bomb run now, autopilot on. She's all yours, Paul, Carl thought as he made the appropriate control inputs. He kept his hands hovering near the yoke, however. Evelyn realized from the rest of the crew's response that this was typical of their pilot. He believed very deeply in the concept of an aircraft commander, and though he trusted his bombardier implicitly, he wasn't about to not be in position to save the crew if the situation demanded it. Keeping his hands close was Carl Peters' version of a lucky charm.

As they made their way through the flak and smoke to the target, the crew's tension ratcheted up higher and higher. The gunners continually checked and rechecked their weapons in between scanning out for more of the dreaded Luftwaffe fighters. Their earlier attacks had broken off as the fighters got low on fuel, but by now, enough time had passed for the Germans to get another group of the deadly little Me-109s into the air.

Bomb drop in thirty seconds, Paul relayed to everyone through Evelyn's net. She dutifully passed it on to the other crews.

Fighters! Twelve o'clock high! The call came from Sean, directly in front of Evie. She felt the adrenaline surge through the net as Sean and Abram both opened up with their respective guns. Carl's hands drifted closer to the controls, his gloved fingertips resting on the yoke as he yearned to take control back from the autopilot.

Down in the nose, behind Abram's furious fire, Paul bent over his bombsight and exhaled slowly. *Bomb bay doors opening,* he transmitted. The level of background noise suddenly grew from the vague background hum to a deafening roar as the bomb bay doors opened.

Drop in three...two...one...

Drop! Drop! Drop!

Fighters! Two o'clock! The fighter call came from Logan in the ball turret. He spun his turret around and opened fire on the enemy silhouettes. Evelyn simultaneously transmitted the drop call and watched the bombs fall past the Messerschmitts that Logan was fighting to destroy.

Behind and below, off to the side and above, all of the Forts in their combat box formation dropped their full payload of bombs. Thousands of pounds of destruction rained down through the sky to impact the machine factories down below.

Good drop! Good drop! Paul exulted as he watched through the bombsight. *Right in the bleeding pickle barrel! The whole formation dropped near simultaneously! Evie! You did it!*

Right, Carl thought, relief and satisfaction in his mind. He wrapped his hands around the yoke and toggled off the autopilot. *Let's turn around and get the hell out of here. Begging your pardon, Evie.*

Logan, Sean, and Abram were still firing, and enemy fighters still screamed through the sky at them. Far below, massive anti-aircraft guns continued to fire bursts of flak up at them, rocking them around in their flying tin can. But Evelyn was riding high on the backlash of exultation from Paul and the others in the formation. The job was done. It was time to go the hell home.

* * *

Unfortunately for them, no one told the fighters. The Luftwaffe Me-109s continued to arrow in at them, spitting deadly fire that raked across the formation of

Forts. Like wolves harrying a herd of deer, the fighters sought to separate the weak, isolate them, and move in for the kill.

Keep that formation tight! Evie, can you pull the psychics in tighter? Carl's mind delivered the order with the same crisp calm he had exhibited the entire time. Evelyn complied, reaching out toward the other girls with encouragement. They were tired, all of them, and it was showing. As the formation net frayed with fatigue, the Forts tended to slip out of the precise positioning they'd held on the way in. That left them vulnerable.

Come tighter, Evelyn sent to the other girls. *Rely on me if you have to. We just have to get them home, and these fighters can't beat us.*

Shit! That call came from Bobby Fritsche on the right waist gun. A fighter had come at them out of the sun, and he hadn't picked it up in time before the 109 was able to rake its fire across them. Shrapnel exploded along the fuselage, sending razor shards arrowing toward the right waist gunner.

Right?

*I'm okay...*Bobby thought to the crew, but Evelyn knew differently. It wasn't pain, so much as...well...she couldn't have said what. But he felt cold and not quite right. She felt her attention being pulled in several different directions as the other psychics drew from her in order to steady themselves and their crews, and Bobby...

Les! Check Bobby! Evelyn ordered, her mind voice ricocheting through the crew like the crack of a whip. *He's in shock and graying out.*

Shit! Sorry, Evie, just...shit! That was Les, busy firing his own gun at the fighters attacking from that side. Both Sean and Logan swiveled their turrets to back him up as Evelyn gave Bobby the mental equivalent of a slap. The pain hit him full force, like someone had taken a pair of sledgehammers to both legs.

Stay with us, Bobby! Evelyn ordered, holding his increasingly slippery mind in an ironclad lock. To the other girls, she sent a quick pulse of demand, followed by the visual from Carl's piloting up front. Then she disengaged from the formation net entirely. Bobby was going to require all of her attention for the moment. The formation tightened up obediently, and the crossfire from the other Forts' guns started to take some of the pressure off. Les fired a final burst and then whipped around to find Bobby slumped over his gun, blood soaking through the legs of his electric suit.

Bobby's hit in both legs! Les reported back, his mind voice savage with grief and anger. *I'm not sure why he's not dead already—*

I'm holding him, Les, Evie broke in. She knew some of the strain from her efforts was leaking into her tone, but she couldn't do anything about that. Bobby was in a lot of pain, and she was having to take some of it onto herself to keep him alive.

Evie! No! Paul called out, horror in his tone.

Left waist, get bandages on those legs! Evie, do what you can, but don't overexert yourself! We need you, too. That was Carl, imposing his icy calm.

I'll let him go fully unconscious once Les gets the bandages on, she promised them all, and herself. Bobby was feeling the pull of oblivion, but Evelyn was stronger. She wasn't going to let him go under until she knew he'd come back up. The effort was tremendous, but she wasn't the strongest psychic in her unit for nothing. She *would* keep him alive, she told herself. And him. And all of them.

Got it! Les announced, as he finished dumping sulfa powder in through the entrance wounds in Bobby's suit and wrapping pressure bandages tightly over the bleeds. The spreading stain of blood on Bobby's suit slowed, then stilled. Evelyn took a deep breath.

Go, she said to Bobby, and gave him a push toward delicious unconsciousness and shunted him to the back of the net. She really should disconnect him entirely, but she didn't want to take the risk of him starting to bleed out and her not knowing about it. Bobby slumped further into Les' arms, and his fellow waist gunner laid him down among the spent brass and empty ammo cans as gently as he could manage.

Evelyn took a deep breath and realized her entire body was trembling. Sean looked back at her with a look of concern, and she flashed him a "thumbs up" and a reassuring mental pulse. Then she reached back out to the formation net and concentrated on keeping their wingmen in position.

* * *

The flight home seemed to take longer than the flight out.

Evelyn didn't know whether it was the aching exhaustion, the worry for her injured crewman, her grief over the aircraft and crews they'd lost, or just a malignant headwind that genuinely slowed them down, but the minutes seemed to drag by with agonizing slowness.

Abram and John used the radio to update their position and navigate them back toward the English coast. Once again, they encountered a cloud deck over the Channel, and once again, they were forced to rely on instrument flight to cross through it. Midway through the crossing, they lost two of the formation's surviving Forts due to engine damage sustained on the bomb run. The wounded Forts couldn't keep up and were forced lower and slower. The hope was that they could limp all the way across the Channel. More realistically, however, they'd probably have to ditch in the water. The good news was that the day wasn't too far gone yet, so the British Air/Sea Rescue Service had a great chance of picking them up. Once it got dark, however, their chances plummeted.

Evelyn pushed that thought away and filed it under "things to be considered later, if ever." She did take comfort in the knowledge that that one of the birds, *One For The Money*, had Pearl Silvers on board. Pearl was a powerful psychic from Atlanta, Georgia. She was also one of the unit's three colored girls, which mattered not at all at this moment but stuck in Evelyn's mind for some reason. A racially-mixed unit was unorthodox, to be sure, but then, so was a unit of psychic women flying onboard combat aircraft. The Army needed their skills, and psychics were rare enough that the Army was willing to take those it could get, regardless of their skin color. Oddly enough, few of the white psychics minded. Privately, Evelyn thought it had to do with the fact that as psychics, they were used to "feeling" people as much as they "saw" them...and to a certain extent, all human beings "felt" the same. For that reason, skin color had never mattered much to her, nor had it seemed to matter much to the others. People just "felt" like people.

We're going in the water, Pearl passed to Evelyn and the rest of the formation. *We're still together. Y'all radio ahead and tell them Brit boys to come get us.*

You got it, Pearl, Evelyn said, and without her having to say a word, John sent out a ping to fix their location, then set about getting hold of the Air/Sea Rescue Service. To everyone's great delight, the Air/Sea Rescue Service radio operator answered back immediately, the transmission clear as a bell. John radioed the coordinates and description, and passed along Pearl's name and psychic status. The Brits radioed back that they'd launch immediately and see if they couldn't bring their own psychic along to help. That got an actual cheer from Logan, Rico, and Sean, all of whom had friends on *One For The Money* and *Tinsel Time*.

And that surge of joy got Evelyn through the last of the clouds until, without warning, they broke through into rare sunlight over the English coast. The last few minutes of the flight passed in a daze of John's radio calls, Carl's and Bob's checklists and responses, the rumbling of *Pretty Cass* as her landing gear came down, and the nerve-wracking jolt as her wheels touched down, and she taxied clear of the active runway.

Evelyn looked up at John as he turned back to her, his face creased with an exhausted, yet overjoyed, grin. "We made it, Evie," he said out loud. "You got us home!"

She made her lips curve in a smile, but then exhaustion reared up from the edges of her mind and spread its dark cloak of oblivion over everything.

* * * * *

Chapter Five

Evelyn woke in a room she hadn't seen before, but she immediately recognized the tell-tale arc of the Quonset hut ceiling. A woman in nurse's white held onto her wrist, counting pulse beats while looking at her wristwatch.

"Excellent," the nurse said, her crisp British accent sounding satisfied. She placed Evelyn's hand back down on the bed and turned away. "She's awake. You may come in now, only two at a time, mind you."

"Evie!" It was Mary's voice. Evelyn turned her head just in time to see the blonde launch herself toward Evelyn's hospital bed. Mary wrapped her arms hard around Evelyn's shoulders and hung on as if she had no plans to let go. The nurse made a disapproving sniff, and Mary rolled her eyes, but she did ease up and step back from the bed. Evelyn gave her a smile and slowly pushed herself up to a sitting position.

"Mary," Evelyn said softly. "It's good to see you."

"Oh, Evie!" Mary said again, giving a mighty sniff as her eyes welled up. "It's good to see you, too! I was so worried. I *knew* you'd overwork yourself as the lead bird, you stupid, brave, silly, ridiculous girl!"

"You gave us quite a scare, Technician," Captain Peters' calm voice cut through Mary's diatribe just as smoothly as it had cut through the chaos of aerial combat. Evelyn jerked her eyes to the face of her aircraft commander and struggled to sit a little straighter.

"Sir!" she said, finding herself feeling flustered and unprepared. Inside her mind, the net shoved at her like a tiger throwing itself against the bars of its cage. Her awareness *yearned* toward him, the instinct to connect made even stronger by the intense experiences they'd come through together.

Captain Peters took another step forward, but he moved as if he didn't realize it. Evelyn cut her eyes to Mary in a mute appeal for help, and the blond psychic quickly stepped in front of the captain. He seemed to recall himself and deliberately stepped back and put his hands behind his back. His eyes flicked up to Evelyn's and then darted away as if he were embarrassed. Mary gave him an understanding smile and patted his hand.

"Captain, you can see she's fine. Maybe you want to step out and tell your crew she's awake? Let us have a bit of girl time?" Mary said in her "sweet little girl" voice. Captain Peters swallowed hard and nodded, then turned and walked out of the room. Evelyn watched him go and tried to keep the net from reaching out and dragging him in by force.

When the door closed behind him, Mary let out a sigh and turned back to Evelyn.

"You're such a lucky girl," Mary said. "My pilot's balding and has a paunch. He's got the hands, though," she added, loyalty creeping into her tone.

"What happened to Bobby?" Evelyn asked, unable to wait any longer. Mary's dreamy expression disappeared, and she refocused on Evelyn's face with a piercing look in her eyes.

"Bobby? That would be your gunner, Private First Class Robert Fritsche? The one who took shrapnel to both legs on the egress? The one who *should have died*, except that *you held him back and risked your own life in the process?* That Bobby? He's fine. Recuperating in London. Evelyn. What in the sam hell were you *thinking?!*"

"He was going to die," she said, weakly. "I just helped slow the bleeding, kept him with us until the bandages and sulfa powder could do their jobs."

"OOH!" Mary said, stamping her delicate little foot and fisting her hands at her sides. "I swear, Evelyn Adamsen! I've never met *anyone* who makes me as mad as you do! If he was going to die, you should have *let him die!* It's a war! People die all the time. It's tragic, and sad, and we all think of them and cry, but *you could have followed him down!* And, you would have taken the rest of your crew with you, like as not. Didn't think of that, now, did you?"

She hadn't, but she wasn't about to tell Mary that. Mary crossed her arms over her chest and lifted an eyebrow at Evelyn.

"All right," Evelyn said. "You're right. I'm sorry. I shouldn't have done it."

"No," Mary said, "you shouldn't have." Then she sighed and uncrossed her arms, reaching out to grasp Evelyn's fingers with her own. "But I can't say I'm surprised you did. Just...oh hell. I'm not even going to ask you to promise not to try something like that ever again, because we both know you will."

"Mary, I—"

Mary shook her head. "No," she said, her lips smiling but her lovely eyes sad. "Leave it at that for now. How are you feeling?"

"Well enough. A bit tired, but like I've been lying around for too long," Evelyn said as she shifted in the bed again. "I'd like to get up, walk around." *See my crew*, she didn't add, but by the way Mary looked at her, the blonde had heard her anyway.

"You may, if you like," the nurse said, stepping forward. "I need this bed, in truth. If you're feeling up to it, you're free to go. Just be sure and drink plenty of water and get lots of rest for the next few days."

"I will, miss, thank you," Evelyn said, gingerly swinging her legs over the side of the bed. Mary helped her dress in her khaki uniform, and though she felt weak as a child, she felt immeasurably better afterward.

"Don't overdo it, mind," the nurse admonished as the two psychics headed toward the door. Mary answered with a breezy wave and ushered Evelyn out into the cold, misty damp of the English afternoon.

"How long was I out?" Evelyn asked after a moment's silent walking.

"A day and a half," Mary answered, her vibrant voice quiet. "You missed interrogation. Colonel Rizer was thrilled with the mission results. Target destroyed, he said. He was less thrilled to lose three psychics, but everyone agrees that your idea to tie the formation in closer was a good one. Your pilot, the dashing Captain Phillips, made sure that everyone knew that was one hundred percent your idea."

Evelyn felt her face heating up. She'd never been good with praise. Mary noticed and gave her a hint of her usual wicked smile.

"Of course, he was less pleased about that stunt you pulled with PFC Fritsche. Captain Peters defended you again, pointing out that Fritsche would have died without your intervention. I'll never forget Rizer's face as he told the captain that he only had twenty— seventeen now—psychics. It's like he was haunted by his own ruth- lessness." Mary shook her head sadly, took a breath, and went on.

"We lost Alice, Leona Wright, and Myrna Danners," she said. "Pearl's bird went down with another one in the Channel, but she and both crews got picked up within a few hours. Turns out the Brits have a psychic working with the Air/Sea Rescue Service."

"That's right," Evelyn murmured, as the memories of her harrowing flight home came back to her. "They mentioned something like that over the radio. It's a good idea."

"It's something we should have been doing a long time ago," Mary said firmly. "The number of small craft lost out of San Diego harbor every year...well...anyway." She shrugged and gestured for Evelyn to precede her through a metal door. Evelyn looked up, faintly surprised to see the entrance to the chow hall. She'd been so preoccupied with Mary's information that she hadn't really paid attention to where they were walking.

"Come on," Mary said. "You know you need to eat. Food will help you feel better faster than anything else. Except maybe a certain tall, dark, and handsome captain..."

"Mary!" Evelyn gasped, her face flaming up again. "He's an *officer!*"

Mary laughed and just gave Evelyn a little push. Evelyn shot back a dark look and pushed through the metal doors.

* * *

"Evie! Hey, fellas, Evie's here!"

It was Sean's voice. The red-headed, young flight engineer called out in jubilant tones. Immediately, Evelyn felt the press of male bodies as her crew seemed to envelop her, and Mary right along with her. Inside her mind, the net snapped out and caught each of the men before Evelyn could stop it.

What? Sean thought. *Oh man. Evie! We missed you!*

Mortified, Evelyn pulled back, both physically and mentally. The net resisted, clinging stubbornly to the minds of Sean, Les, Logan, Rico, and John. Only Bobby was missing, and the net didn't like that one bit. Evelyn took a deep breath and severed the connection with an audible gasp, feeling the reverb rock through her to her bones, causing Mary to reach out with a steadying grip.

"Evie?" Mary asked. "Are you all right?"

"The net," Evelyn whispered. "It manifested, uncommanded. I've never had that happen before."

Mary's lovely eyes grew wide with concern. Sean stepped up beside her, reaching out to take Evelyn's free hand with his own.

"Hey, Evie," he said softly. "You okay? I'm sorry, I didn't mean to scare you."

"No," Evelyn replied, slowly and reluctantly pulling her fingers from his grasp. "I'm the one who is sorry. I've never had a net connection get away from me like that. It's unpardonable to link like that without your permission. I am so..." To her further mortification, tears began to well in her eyes.

"Sean, hey man, why'd you have to go and make her cry?" Logan asked, aggrieved. He shouldered the flight engineer aside and reached out for Evie's hand himself. Evelyn sniffled mightily, all too aware of how unladylike she looked and sounded, and fought to get her emotions under control. She also placed her other hand on Mary's, mostly so none of the men could touch it. She wasn't entirely certain that the net wouldn't manifest uncommanded again. Touching any of them would make that more likely.

"Sean didn't make me cry," Evelyn said, squaring her shoulders and looking up. "I just...I am sorry. I'm weak still, and I wasn't able to control the bond well enough...that's why the net manifested. I am so very sorry to all of you."

"Hey, chica," Rico said, tilting his head to the side and giving her a half smile. "Did we complain? I don't know about the rest of these guys, but I missed you in here while you were out," he said, tapping the side of his temple.

"That's the bond," Mary said, her voice gentle. "It's a side effect of being connected in a psychic net for so long, and under such trying circumstances."

"But it doesn't mean we don't like it," Les said, and Logan and Sean nodded vigorous agreement.

"It doesn't matter if you like it," Evelyn said. "It's *wrong* for me to link you without your permission!"

"Then I give you permission," Sean said quickly. "We all do. Anytime you want, Evie. Anytime at all." Les, Logan, and Rico nodded agreement, John murmured his assent, and Evelyn couldn't help but smile at their earnestness.

"Thanks," she said. "But I've got it under control for the moment. I need to eat, though," she added, feeling her empty stomach churn at the scent of fried potatoes.

"We've got a table right over here," Sean said, taking charge again, as he was wont to do. He gestured with barely contained eagerness and then turned to Mary as if remembering his manners. "You'd be welcome, too, ma'am," he said formally.

Mary gave him her second-best smile. "Thank you," she said graciously. "But I promised my crew I'd meet them for chow. I just wanted to make sure Evie was settled."

"We've got her, ma'am," Sean said, reaching out to take Evie's hand again, and then remembering and letting his own hand drop.

Mary looked at Evelyn and reached out with a tendril of thought. *Will you be all right?* she asked.

I've got it under control, Evelyn assured her, adding another layer of will to the cage she'd slammed into place to contain the straining bond. *They're my crew. I'll be fine. I'll see you later.*

All right, Mary said and then slid her eyes to Sean's and gave her hair a little toss. "And it's Technician, Sergeant, not 'ma'am.' I work for a living," she said saucily, before turning her back and sashaying back to her own crew not far away.

Sean gaped. "Ah...s...sorry?" he stammered and then immediately received the rough ribbing and teasing of his crewmates. Evelyn looked on with a tiny, patient smile. Mary had that effect on men when she chose to do so. It never failed to entertain.

"Ah, sorry, Evie," Sean said, his face nearly as red as his hair. Les wouldn't stop laughing, and Sean gave him a shove. The waist gunner's guffaws subsided to an ongoing snicker, and Rico, Logan, and John all had wide grins. "Go get her something to eat, you pack of laughing hyenas," Sean said, and waved Evelyn toward a seat.

Evelyn took a look around the chow hall as she headed for her seat. The place was relatively full, with groups of men clustered around most of the trestle tables. Here and there, a female face smiled with them, as most of the psychics were eating with their crews. Not too far from the doorway, Pearl Silvers laughed at something one of her pilots said. Evelyn caught the dark-skinned woman's eyes and gave her a nod. Pearl flashed her a smile and a thumbs-up.

Though seeing Pearl and the other girls happy and well filled Evelyn with a warm joy, she couldn't help but wonder how Captain Ledoux would react to that development. During their training, the good captain had been very clear about her expectations. Interacting with the men in an inappropriate way would not be tolerated—she'd emphasized that point from the beginning. But from the looks of it, just about every one of the remaining girls was here, talking and eating surrounded by a cluster of airmen. The dull roar of hundreds of conversations under-laid the clatter of food trays and the bustle of the service line. Every once in a while, Evelyn could pick up a female laugh trilling over the rest of the noise. The scent of fried meat and old grease hung heavy in the air.

"Evie?" Rico asked, the faint lilt of his Puerto Rican accent lifting the end of her name. Evelyn blinked, then smiled at him and accepted his hand as he helped her take her seat on the trestle bench. "Are you all right, chica?"

"I'm fine, thank you," she said. "Just woolgathering." Behind Rico, John held a tray of standard soldiers' food that he put down in front of her. Logan followed with a glass of milk and one of juice. Evelyn smiled at them both and picked up the orange juice. It was watered down, reconstituted, and had too much sugar added. It tasted wonderful.

"Good," Sean said, sliding into the seat opposite her. "We could use some more wool. Damn English rain, begging your pardon, Evie."

"Ain't the rain, Sarge," Les said around a mouthful of over-cooked carrots. "It's the mist. It gets down inside your collar and everywhere." He shook his head mournfully and shoveled another huge fork load into his mouth.

Evelyn chuckled softly. "The snow is like that at home," she said, picking up her own fork and toying with the pile of instant mashed potatoes. "The wind drives it sideways, and it creeps into every seam."

"Where is home?" John asked. The blond-haired radio operator had clearly become a fully integrated part of the crew. He smiled his handsome smile at Evelyn, and she spared a passing thought for the sweetheart he'd no doubt left behind.

"Rapid City, South Dakota," Evelyn said, shrugging her shoulders up a bit. "Or just outside, really. In the Black Hills."

"You get lots of snow there?" John went on, clearly trying to draw her out. Evelyn gave him a tiny smile and nodded.

"Sometimes," she said, feeling unaccountably shy. It really didn't make much sense, considering that these men now knew her better than any other, thanks to the net bond that continually pushed at her.

"How did you go from Rapid City, South Dakota, to Merry Olde England?" John asked. Evelyn blinked and looked up at him, then shrugged. Their mission as psychics was classified, but these men certainly already knew. No one had said she couldn't talk about that part of it.

"I was studying at the teachers' college when Mrs. Durant and Captain Ledoux came to visit. They spoke at an assembly about our patriotic duty and helping to win the war. Mrs. Durant said that any of us with talent should come see her in the Dean's office the next day. You have to understand," she said then, looking around the table at each of them. "We *never* tell anyone about our talents. People don't understand. They think we're trying to read their thoughts or hurt them somehow. It wasn't really that long ago when women like me were burned at the stake...and then all of a sudden here come these glamorous women talking about patriotism and the ability to do something good, not just for our country, but for all psychics everywhere. 'If we can help win the war,' Mrs. Durant said, 'our sisters and daughters can finally come out of hiding.'"

"So what happened?" John asked. Logan, next to him, nodded eagerly. They all seemed rapt by her story.

"Well, I phoned my father and talked it over with my parents that night. Dad wasn't completely thrilled with the idea, what with my brother already having shipped off with the Marines and all, but Mother thought it was a good idea. I think she secretly hoped I could look after her baby boy," she said with a grin.

"Where is he?" Sean asked.

"Somewhere in the Pacific."

"Huh. So much for that plan."

"Yes. Anyway, so I went in the next afternoon and signed up. There were three of us who did, but the other two ladies didn't pass the qualifying battery."

"What's a 'qualifying battery'?" Logan wanted to know.

"A battery of tests. To see if we were psychically strong enough to do this mission. Basically, we had to withstand Captain Ledoux trying to force her way into our minds."

"Eeesh! And you did it, didn't you?" Logan said with a grin. "Atta girl, Evie!"

"I did, completely, and even counterattacked," Evelyn said softly. "And I don't think she's ever forgiven me for it. I think I embarrassed her."

Abruptly, Evelyn realized that she'd probably said too much. To cover her awkwardness, she looked down at her plate.

The instant potatoes were watery as usual, and the vegetables had had any semblance of flavor or texture boiled out of them, but it was food, and Evelyn knew better than to turn up her nose. Her family might not have suffered as much as some during the droughts that had plagued the farm communities during the thirties, but they'd all known what it felt like to go hungry, even if just for a meal or two. Mindful of her duty, she took a bite.

Though she hadn't felt much of an appetite, that one bite awakened a ravenous hunger in her, and she had to consciously slow down to keep herself from inhaling the entire meal like a starving barbarian. Her mother would have been mortified. The men didn't seem to mind too terribly much, however, and the conversation quieted as they all fell to the business of eating.

As they ate, Evelyn felt her eyes drift from her plate up to one of her crewmen, and then the next. They were all so different, she thought. And yet, there was a unifying element in their thoughts. Fear, bravado, and determination all tangled together into a thread that ran just under their conscious minds. Evelyn couldn't touch that thread without establishing a full net, and much as the bond pushed at her to do so, she still resisted. There wasn't a need for it here in the chow hall, and she felt uneasy about spending too much time linked together.

Well, that wasn't completely honest. The truth was, she felt really *good* about linking with them, but she'd always been taught that the bond had to be controlled, contained. Her earliest training had emphasized linking had to be done consensually and only for a specific purpose, for the bond was seductive and would lure the unwary into disaster. A psychic must be disciplined at all times, she'd been taught. That lesson had been underscored by the training the US Army saw fit to provide.

So Evelyn fought it down, denied her instinctive reaching toward the tantalizing landscape of their minds all around...

"Evelyn."

Captain Peters' voice startled her, but not nearly so much as the way all of the men sitting with her shot to their feet causing a racket of scraping benches and bumped, rattling dishes. Evelyn let out a cry that was half gasp and jumped to her own feet, bumping her knee painfully on the trestle table top. Without consciously deciding to do so, she reached out and snapped them all into a net, all of her senses pinging through them as she instinctively reacted to the unknown threat.

Evie! It's okay! It's just the captain!

Evelyn never knew who sent the thought, but she immediately broke the net connection as mortification surged over her. Once, perhaps, was forgivable, barely. But she should have better control than to snatch everyone into a net because one of their own people startled her! The strength of the bond and the urge to connect was nearly overwhelming, and she found that she was having to be constantly vigilant.

"Technician Adams? Are you all right?" Captain Peters asked, his dark brows creased as he looked at her with concern. She squared her shoulders and nodded.

"Yes, sir," she said. "I'm sorry, I didn't see you coming." Which was also odd. Ordinarily, she would have sensed the approach of any of her crew. But she was having to fight the bond so much, it was taking up all of her focus. This was a problem, but at present, she had no idea how to fix it.

"It's all right," he said with a smile. His eyes, however, were still dark with concern. "Colonel Rizer wants to see you."

"Of course," Evelyn said, putting her napkin down and extricating herself from the trestle table. It wasn't an easy thing to do in her uniform skirt, not and retain any semblance of modesty, but she managed. A *frisson* of anxiety skittered along her nerves. When one's wing commander desired to see one, it was rarely a good thing. She closed her eyes for just a moment and forced herself to concentrate on her breathing. Getting upset wasn't going to help her contain the bond. In fact, it made it harder.

Especially when one of them touched her. The net leapt again, and she shoved it down, hard, deep in her mind. Her eyes flew open, and she looked accusingly at Sean.

"Sorry, Evie," he said. "I just...link, will you? We all want it, and it's making you crazy to hold it back. That way we'll be with you, supporting you, whatever happens."

Her eyes went wide, then flitted to Captain Peters'. He pressed his lips in a thin line, then nodded his assent. Evelyn exhaled slowly and released her mental death grip on the bond. The net snapped instantly into place.

All right, boys, but keep anything you hear close hold, you understand? Carl thought, his mind firm with command authority.

What? What's going on? Evie? Did you link us in? Abram Portman asked, and Evelyn realized with mingled dismay and half-hysterical humor that that was exactly what she'd done. The net had gone out not just to the men in her immediate vicinity, as she'd intended, but to the *entire* crew. She got a glimpse through the navigator's eyes of a room filled with wall-mounted maps packed with minute detail. She blinked away Abram's vision and sent out a thought to all of them.

Yes, I initiated the net. I am sorry I didn't get your individual permissions first. I think I've been weakened, and the desire to link was too much for me to fight off right now. She tried hard to keep her words clinical, but some of her miserable self-recrimination must have soaked through.

No, Evie, this is good, Carl thought firmly. *We're your crew, and we're here to support you.*

No matter what, Paul Rutherford added staunchly. Evelyn blinked quickly as her eyes started to burn with tears. She could feel Paul's ironclad loyalty and the way she reminded him of his lost twin sister. The other men in the net echoed his sentiment, and Evelyn tried to discreetly dab the tears away.

Good, Sean thought in his typically irreverent manner. *Now I won't have to figure out how to let the other boys know what's going on without directly telling them. Sorry, boss. Wouldn't want to disobey your orders but...Evie's crew. And well...we all need to know what's going on with her.* Sean's thoughts behind his statement were starkly clear to the entire net. Evelyn was crew, but she was also enlisted. And since he was the senior enlisted aircrewman, that made her doubly his responsibility. In Sean's mind, he and the rest of the "boys," as they thought of themselves, would back Evie against all comers, and he wasn't willing to budge on that.

Carl Peters met Sean's eyes and with the wisdom of true leadership, nodded in acquiescence.

"All right then," Captain Peters said out loud. "Technician Adamsen, let's go."

* * *

Colonel Rizer's office wasn't exactly what Evelyn had expected. She supposed she'd been naive, but she'd imagined that such an august personage as a wing commander, a full colonel *must* have a spacious, plush office with deep carpets, cherry wood desks, and comfortable chairs.

It was large, which was about all she could say for it. Like the rest of the briefing rooms and offices she'd seen, Colonel Rizer's office was cold and drab. He did have a wide window that overlooked the flightline, but England's ever-present thick mist obscured the view.

Carl had knocked and reported in, and now he and Evelyn stood side by side at attention in front of the metal table that seemed to serve the function of a desk. The colonel was writing something when they came in. He finished, set down his pen, and leaned back in his chair as he looked at them.

"Technician Adamsen," he said. "I'm glad to see you're back among the living."

"Thank you, sir," she replied softly when it became clear he expected her to say something.

"I have heard the reports of your crew and your aircraft commander. Now I'd like to hear directly from you. What happened up there with PFC Fritsche?"

Evelyn drew in a deep breath and exhaled slowly.

"I became aware of PFC Fritsche's injury through our crew's psychic net, sir. I directed Les—Corporal Norton, that is, our left waist gunner, to try to render assistance, but Corporal Norton was busy engaging enemy fighters that threatened our aircraft, sir," she said.

The fighter fire was really heavy right then, Les supplied to her. *Tell him that. No one else could get to Bobby in time.*

"Through the net, I realized that PFC Fritsche's injuries were severe enough that he needed immediate attention, but no one could get to him right away, due to the heavy enemy fire. So I held on to his consciousness and refused to let him slip away," she said, unconsciously squaring her shoulders. It didn't take a psychic net to tell her that Colonel Rizer was skeptical.

"I didn't realize that psychics could do that," he said.

"I can," she replied softly.

"Captain Ledoux informs me that what you did was extremely dangerous. She told me there are stories of psychics trying to do exactly what you did. Apparently, it's happened before, but the psychic usually dies too. Why is that?"

Evelyn resisted the urge to squirm under his gaze and forced herself to speak calmly.

"The psychic bond works two ways, sir," she said. "When I took tighter hold of PFC Fritsche's consciousness, my consciousness also became more tightly wound with his as a result. An equal and opposite reaction, if you will. If his injuries had been so severe that his body shut down despite my hold on his consciousness...I might have died with him. When his consciousness died, it might have taken mine as well."

"I see," Colonel Rizer said, his voice flat. "And you judged that risk to be acceptable?"

Evelyn swallowed hard. "Yes, sir," she said, her voice soft and small, despite her best intentions.

"Technician Adamsen, are you aware of the results of yesterday's mission?"

"Yes, sir. I think so. I heard it was a success."

"An *unqualified* success," he said, leaning forward in his chair and pressing his index finger to the desk. "The target was 100% destroyed. Initial reports estimate it will take months, if not years, to rebuild up to its peak production capacity. This was a *phenomenal* success, and we only lost eight aircraft out of the entire formation. Eight! And two of their crews were recovered almost immediately because there was a psychic on board one of them."

"Yes, sir," she said again, not sure what else to say. He seemed angry, despite the good news he recounted.

"Technician Adamsen, I don't have to ask what you think made the difference, do I? Is it not clear? It was you ladies. You and your colleagues took a mission that had a sixty-three percent average casualty rate and made that a fourteen percent casualty rate. *And I have only seventeen of you!*"

Evelyn had to fight to keep from rocking back on her heels as Colonel Rizer came to his feet, leaning toward her over the desk and speaking with an intensity that echoed through the drab office.

"Yes, sir," she whispered.

"Losing one of you, even to save one of my men is *not* an acceptable risk. Do I make myself clear?"

"Yes, sir," she said again, a little louder.

Colonel Rizer stared at her for a moment longer, his eyes boring into hers with that intensity of command. Though she was tied up in her own psychic net, she couldn't help but feel his iron drive, his desperate need, and underneath it all, the anguish of knowing every order he gave meant more men would die. Evelyn's knees began to tremble, and her throat began to tighten up as tears threatened. Instantly, her crew was there, bolstering her, remembering their own episodes of reprimand for past incidents, supporting her. She swallowed hard and refused to let her eyes drop.

Colonel Rizer nodded sharply and sat back down.

"You are dismissed," he said, looking back down at the paperwork spread on the desk before him.

Evelyn made her facing movement toward the door as sharp as she could. Then she and Carl moved smartly out before she could lose her composure.

* * *

As they left the headquarters building, the quiet in Evelyn's head became conspicuous.

You agree with him, she sent to them all. It wasn't a question. It didn't have to be, after all. She could feel what they were thinking.

Evie, Sean thought slowly, after it became apparent that none of the officers were going to explain. *It's like this. The colonel is right. Bobby's a good guy, one of the best. But at the end of the day, he's...all of us...none of us is anybody special. There's a thousand guys in the training pipeline right now getting ready to come out here and do this job. None of us want to die, and none of us wants to see our friends die, either. And you girls...women. You psychic women keep more of us alive at the end of the day. So if you live,* we've all *got a better shot at living, see?*

Amidst her sadness and fatigue at the stark realities they all faced, Evelyn felt a tiny thread of amusement. Trust the baby-faced, redheaded sergeant to lay it all out there.

I do see, she sent quietly.

That's how my sister died, Evie. That was Paul, their bombardier. With a jolt, Evelyn realized that he was transmitting to the whole crew, not just herself. *We were twelve, and we'd been swinging on this old rope swing and jumping into the swimming hole near our house. I hit my head on a rock or something near the bottom. Lucy linked with me to try to keep me alive, but she couldn't. They got me out of the water, were able to revive me, but her heart just wouldn't start again.* His mental touch felt soaked with old sorrow, and Evelyn could feel the rest of the crew move, as she did, to offer wordless support. Her eyes burned, then filled and overflowed with emotion.

"It's a hard thing, Evie," Carl said softly, speaking out loud. He paused beside where she'd stopped. A group of enlisted men was walking toward them from the other direction. Carl stepped in front of Evelyn to shield her from their curious eyes as she fought to regain her composure. Carl returned their salute and watched for a moment to ensure they continued on their way before he reached down and wrapped Evelyn in a hard hug. "I'm sorry that you're having a hard time with this, but at the end of the day, the colonel is right, and Sean is right. You're too valuable."

Evelyn sniffed loudly, her cheeks red with embarrassment, and nodded. Carl gave her one more squeeze, then let go with a nod.

Thank you all, Evelyn sent across the net. *Your support means everything to me. I'm going to head back to my quarters now.*

Good idea, Carl said in the net. *That knock will probably come early tomorrow. You need your sleep because none of us want to go up without you.*

Wordless agreement echoed from all points on the net. She might have put herself at risk, but she'd convinced even the most skeptical of her crewmates. Evelyn took a deep breath, braced herself, and consciously severed the connection. She had to be rather firm about it because, of course, the bond didn't want to let go.

Captain Peters shivered slightly and blinked a few times.

"Wow," he said. "That's disconcerting. That felt even less comfortable than when you fainted."

Evelyn drew in another shaky breath and nodded.

"Every connection makes the bond stronger, which means it's harder on all of us to let it go. Especially ours. Ours seems...particularly strong."

"Are you sure it's not just because of what we've been through? You said that shared experiences make it stronger, right? You can't tell me you've ever been through anything like a bombing mission before."

"You know, you're right, sir," Evelyn said slowly. Her shoulders began to relax in relief. "That's a very good point."

The strength of the crew's bond had been worrying her. She absolutely did not want to fly with another crew, but she'd been afraid that she was going to have to, if only to keep the bond from growing out of control. But if the bond's strength was just a function of the missions themselves...well...then there was no reason she couldn't keep flying with her crew. Flying with any other crew would have the same effect.

"All right, I'll walk you back to your barracks," Captain Peters said. Evelyn would have protested that she didn't need him to trouble himself, but his tone told her he'd brook no argument on the matter.

They walked in silence back away from the flightline to the Quonset hut that held the WAC barracks. A few of the other girls were standing outside, and one raised a hand to wave at Evelyn before she recognized the officer standing next to her. The wave turned into a salute, which Captain Peters returned crisply before turning to Evelyn.

"I'll leave you here then, Technician Adamsen," he said, his tone formal and correct. Evelyn nodded and rendered her own salute. Captain Peters met her eyes and returned it, then dropped his hand and gestured for her to go on inside.

Before she could do so, however, Captain Ledoux came charging out of the barracks, fury all over her face.

"ADAMSEN!" she shouted. Evelyn jumped, then snapped to the position of attention. The other women ducked inside, leaving her alone under the captain's merciless stare.

"You stupid little girl! What in the hell were you thinking? Is your head so big that you think you can do what you want and don't need to listen to listen to nobody and forget all you been taught? Mais-la! I should ground you and send you home, but we need you too much. But don't think I'm not watching you all the time." Ledoux's face was red with fury, and her Arcadian roots became clear as she began to swear fluently in English, French, and the lyrical patois composed of both that characterized the dialects of southern Louisiana.

"Captain Ledoux," Captain Peters said, stepping up beside Evelyn. "Jeanne...really. Colonel Rizer already read her the riot act!"

Captain Ledoux rounded on Evelyn's pilot, her face red.

"Mind ya business, Captain Peters," she snapped. "Technician Adamsen is *my* responsibility."

"Then you ought to know better than to scream at her in public," he replied, his icy, clipped words cutting through the fire of her righteous indignation.

"How dare you?" Ledoux asked, her voice a hiss of fury.

Captain Peters shrugged one shoulder and looked supremely unconcerned.

"I dare because I was taught that leaders praise in public and reprimand in private. Not the other way around. Adamsen is a good psychic. She made a call, and Colonel Rizer judged it to be a bad one. He's already reprimanded her. He doesn't need you to underscore him and especially not out here in front of God and everyone."

Ledoux actually spluttered and opened her mouth as if she would say more, but Captain Peters spoke again in that same frigid tone.

"Colonel Rizer ordered her to get some rest. I suggest you let her do that. Unless you'd like to explain why you felt it necessary to countermand the wing commander's order? No? I didn't think so. Good night, Technician Adamsen. You're dismissed."

Evelyn's throat closed up, and fear spiked through her belly. Captain Ledoux looked at her with those hot, angry eyes, but she didn't say anything else. Evelyn swallowed hard and took a step backward on none-too-steady legs. She lifted her hand in a salute that she deliberately angled to include them both. Only Captain Peters returned it.

Evelyn dropped her hand to her side and fled to the safety of the barracks, leaving the two officers to work their differences out alone.

* * * * *

Chapter Six

So began a month that passed by in a blur for Evelyn. Ten missions in thirty days and nary a milk run in the bunch. With the success of the girls' first mission, Colonel Rizer and the powers that be decided to utilize their unique talents only for the most difficult, riskiest missions deep into the heart of Nazi-occupied Europe.

The nightmares started about two weeks in. They always began the same way: they were flying a mission, fighters were swarming the formation, and Evelyn and the other girls couldn't keep the net tight enough, and one by one they all went down...

It became a common thing in their barracks for the girls to wake screaming in the night. Unless it was you or your bunkmate, you just rolled over and went back to sleep. Anything else was too disruptive to the mission. They *had* to fly, and that meant that they had to sleep.

The grueling pace began to take its toll in other ways, too. None of the women could keep weight on, no matter how much they ate. Many of the crews, Evelyn's included, began to make it a personal mission at mealtimes to procure the best food for "their girls." When anyone in the unit would get a "care package" with treats from home, he could expect to be swarmed with enlisted aircrewmen willing to beg, borrow, and steal in order to procure some of the goodness for their psychics. Evelyn, at least, dutifully ate every bite they put in front of her, though most of the time she didn't want any of it. Her body needed the calories, as evidenced by the way she continued to lose weight. At night, she would drop, exhausted, into her bed and close her eyes, praying to whomever might be listening that she might get a few solid hours before either the dreams or the knock woke her.

On the days when they didn't fly, Evelyn and the others fought not to sleep all day. Captain Ledoux had announced in no uncertain terms that she would brook no laziness, so when they were allowed to sleep past 0400, they were up at 0630 for a uniform and barracks inspection. Privately, Evelyn thought that the captain would have been better off to allow the girls to get whatever rest they could, but she didn't want to cross the other woman. Especially not after the confrontation between Ledoux and Captain Peters. Captain Ledoux still glowered at Evelyn whenever she noticed her, so Evelyn tried to remain out of sight and beneath notice.

This, of course, infuriated Mary.

"Jeanne Ledoux wouldn't know leadership if it bit her on the hand!" she said disdainfully when Evelyn told her the story. They were sitting on Evelyn's bunk before going to bed one night. Several heads turned their way, despite Evelyn's frantic shushing.

"Oh, stop it," Mary said, tossing her blond hair with disdain. "It's not like we don't all know that anyway. She's only an officer because she was the first of us to sign up and because she's got a fancy college degree. She's not nearly as skilled as you...or even me, for that matter!"

"Mary, it's still not right to talk about her like that!" Evelyn protested. "Whatever you think, she's still an officer, and our commander, and she deserves our respect."

"Pffft," Mary said. "Respect is earned, Evie, you know that. When she's out there flying the line with us and our boys day in and day out, then she'll have mine. You know she's only gone on three missions. She might not be as skilled as most of us, but she's got plenty of power, and those boys could sure use it up there. You know I'm right!"

Evelyn did, indeed, know that Mary was correct. Still, rather than speak in such an inflammatory way about their commander, the dark-haired girl from Rapid City, South Dakota, kept her mouth shut. Captain Ledoux, like the rest of them, was handling the stress of flying in her own way. In the captain's case, her answer seemed to be not to fly, citing a need to handle the administrative responsibilities of commanding their small, unique unit. While Evelyn could appreciate the impulse to stay safely on the ground, she couldn't fault Mary for being harsh. Those men needed every one of them up there. Colonel Rizer had made that abundantly clear.

Not that there was anything either she or Mary could do about it. Captain Ledoux would do as she thought best unless and until an officer of higher rank took an interest and intervened. In the meantime, Evelyn and the rest of the girls would just have to keep doing what they could to keep their crews alive and get the bombs on target.

* * *

About five weeks after they'd arrived, Evelyn and the other girls received their first tiny break. There were no missions scheduled from Thanksgiving Thursday through the weekend, and anyone who wanted it was given a pass into nearby London. The British, of course, didn't officially celebrate the American holiday, but the pub owners and shopkeepers were more than thankful for the Yanks' business on these passes.

Mary and Evelyn and several of the other girls all made the trip into town, going to see a show at the theater, and then met up for dinner at a pub frequented by both British and American flyers on liberty. They wore their WAC uniforms, of course, which got them a round of free drinks and quite a few curious stares. But the overall mood was jovial and welcoming, and Evelyn found that she enjoyed herself immensely.

Mary, of course, fascinated the British men, and Evelyn found herself completely entertained by the way her friend flirted. It was almost like being at one of the dances she'd attended at the South Dakota School of Mines back home. The outgoing boys would approach her friend, and she found herself talking to, and even dancing with, the shyer, more introspective ones.

It wasn't until it was time to head back to the train that things got ugly.

They'd left the pub with a group, mostly WACs, but some of their crewmen joined them for the walk to the train station. Evelyn felt good, warmed by the good time and the excellent ale the pub had served. She looped her arm through Mary's, and the two of them walked together near the back of the group.

Mary sang in her high, clear soprano, belting out the lyrics to "That Old Black Magic." The hit song had been playing on the pub's ancient radio.

Evelyn joined in with her smoky contralto, singing about icy fingers running up and down her spine...

The hands weren't icy. They were hot and hard, and they reached out and wrapped around Evelyn's bicep so fast that she couldn't even blink before she found herself hauled up hard against a muscled chest. Another hand clamped iron-hard over her mouth and nose, cutting off her air. She heard Mary give a strangled scream that cut suddenly off in an entirely ominous way.

"Wait," Evelyn heard a voice from up ahead say. "Where's Evie and Mary?" It was Logan Ayala, her ball turret gunner. He'd joined them at the pub and had been walking just in front of the two women a few minutes earlier. Evelyn reached out with far more force than she intended, and the net snapped instantly into being between her and Logan...and the rest of her crew, miles away.

What? Evie? Carl asked, sitting up in his cot. *What's happened?*

Evelyn didn't bother to take the time to apologize for startling them. *At least two men grabbed us!* she said, throwing the thought at Logan. Her captor lifted her feet off the ground and began to haul her along with him into an alley between the brick buildings. She had no idea where Mary was.

Shit! Logan thought, not even bothering to excuse himself for his profanity.

"Oh, lookee at you. You're a right pretty bird, aintcha?" The man who held her spoke in a low, gravelly voice. His breath stank of tobacco and cheap liquor, and the rest of him stank of multiple days' worth of being unwashed. Evelyn struggled against his hold, but his arms only tightened, and he chuckled in a way that turned her insides to ice.

I'm coming, Evie! Logan thought. She could feel him running back the way he'd come, looking for them. She tried to send him clear images so that he could find the correct alley, but it was so dark, and her head felt fogged and slow from fear and alcohol.

From somewhere to her left, another man laughed, and Mary screamed again.

The sound snapped Evelyn out of her reverie. Her own captor's hand tore at the buttons on her blouse. Evelyn took a deep breath and forced herself to be calm.

I'm sorry, she said to her crew on the net. *You don't need to experience this.* And then she cut the connection.

"Evie!" Logan's voice rang out in desperation. He really wasn't that far away. But he didn't know where they were, and as far as Evelyn was concerned, she and Mary were out of time. So she fell back on her last resort, the one thing no psychic ever wanted to have to do.

She narrowed her focus down to a pinpoint and then slammed it home in the brain of the man holding onto her. He gasped as all of his natural psychic shields were ripped away as violently and painfully as he was ripping at Evelyn's clothes. His entire mind and emotional landscape lay suddenly bare to Evelyn's touch. She took hold of her fear and disgust and feelings of imminent violation and whipped them over that vulnerable surface, causing her captor to scream. His hold tightened on her, and then his arms abruptly fell away as she slashed at him again, opening him up, forcing her way down into his psyche where no one should ever be allowed to go. He convulsed, and she staggered away from him as he fell to the filthy cobblestones, writhing. Not far away, his friend held Mary up against a wall, one hand over her mouth, the other up under her skirt.

Evelyn turned from her downed assailant to Mary's. He turned to look at her as she struck, just as Logan rounded the corner between the two buildings. Once again, Evelyn rammed her way into the man's psyche, ripping and laying bare. Her rage became a weapon she thrust into his brain, causing him to jerk, and cough, and then double over, retching.

As for Mary, she took the opening that Evelyn's attack had given her and brought her knee up, hard into the man's face. The sickening crunch of bone echoed through the tight alley, and as the man went down, the California blonde followed, her lovely soprano voice screaming in fury as she beat on him with closed fists until both Evelyn and Logan had to pull her off of his half-dead form.

"Come on, Mary-girl," Logan said, half-lifting her. "Come on, there. You're all right; you're all right. He can't hurt you now. Let's get you two out of here. Let's get back where it's safe." His eyes cut to Evelyn's, but she steadfastly refused to reopen the net, no matter how badly it pushed at her. The feel of those men's minds clung to her like the scent of decay, and her stomach roiled with it. She wouldn't expose her crew to that, nor to the horror of what she'd done. Not in this lifetime. Not if she could help it.

* * *

The three of them stumbled out of the alley and into a halting half-run as they fought to catch up with the larger group. Evelyn spent the rest of the trip back to Ridgeway in silence. Logan and the rest of their group rallied around the two of them, but as Mary was more obviously distressed, she got the majority of the attention. That was fine by Evelyn. She sat quietly in her seat and slowly bit through her lower lip as she battled with what she'd felt and done.

Not until they disembarked did anyone notice anything. Evelyn waited until the others had gotten Mary off, then she followed. But she tripped, just a little, coming off the train. Logan reached out to grab her, and the second he touched her, the net slammed back into place. All of a sudden, the screaming horror of what she'd done rocketed through the gunner, as well as Carl and the others who were waiting for them outside.

Logan stumbled, his back slamming into the edge of the train car opening as he stared, wide-eyed, at Evelyn.

A commotion of shouting and protests heralded the arrival of Carl and the rest of the crew, who were apparently shoving their way in.

We're coming, Evie, Sean thought to her. His mind-tone felt shaken and sick, but underneath it was all steely determination to be there and support her. Tears filled Evelyn's eyes as blood from her lip filled her mouth.

I'm sorry, she sent to them all in a mental whisper. She didn't say it, but they all knew why she was apologizing. She knew she shouldn't have allowed the net to manifest. They didn't need to feel what she'd done. It was bad enough that she, herself, had to experience the utter violation she's visited upon her attackers. She didn't need to share it with the men she cared about most in this world. Once again, she moved to sever the net.

Logan reached out and caught her by the wrist. She looked up, startled, and met his eyes.

We're a crew, he said, his words bolstered by the determination of the others as they fought through the rest of the disembarking passengers to cluster around her. *You're ours, and you don't have to carry this alone.*

I can't...I...

Someone lifted her, nestled her head in the hollow of his shoulder. Other hands patted her back, smoothed her hair, held her close as the tears spilled over, and she began to cry deep, wracking sobs.

She didn't remember being carried. She didn't remember anything but the horror of the pain, humiliation, and violation she'd visited upon the two attackers. Somehow, though, she ended up in the little shed where she'd first met Sean and the gunners. Les held her cradled on his lap while Sean stroked her hair and murmured that she was all right, she was safe, and they wouldn't leave her alone again.

"Logan," Carl said out loud, though they were still linked in the net. He and the rest seemed to be concentrating on supporting Evelyn, helping her to deal with her reaction to what she'd done. "Suppose you tell us what happened?"

Logan nodded and opened his mouth, but Rico held out a hand first.

"Your flask," the Puerto Rican tail gunner said. "For Evie."

Logan nodded again, then reached into his shirt and produced the flask, which he handed off to Sean.

"We were walking back to the train from the pub," Logan said. Evelyn listened to his words and tried not to think, not to feel. She felt the onslaught of support from the rest of the crew, and Les' arms tightened around her.

"I heard the two girls, Evie and her friend Mary, singing behind us. I was talking to one of the guys from the 351st. I swear they were right behind me! Next thing I know, Evie's got me in the net and is screaming for me to come find her. Only I couldn't right away because I didn't know where those bastards—sorry, Evie—those thugs had taken them."

Evelyn closed her eyes and pressed her face into Les' shoulder. She wanted to breathe in the scent of him: clean sweat, aircraft engine exhaust, and the military spec oil used to lubricate the weapons. She wanted to obliterate the memory of the attacker's scent and replace it with the scent of home.

"Give her a drink," Rico said, nudging Sean. The redhead flight engineer jumped, then obligingly unscrewed the cap on the flask and held it up to Evelyn's lips. She obediently took a drink, welcoming the cleansing burn of the rotgut liquor. It tasted better than the memory of her dry-mouthed fear. She coughed as it seared its way down her throat. Sean nodded and re-capped it, but kept it close. They all figured she'd need more...they'd all need more...before this night was over.

Logan took up the story again.

"When I find them, I see one guy down, having some kind of seizure or something while Evie stands over him. She looked...Sweetheart, I'm sorry, but you looked like an avenging angel with a broken heart. I didn't know whether to cry or hit him for you."

Evelyn let out a tiny, soft bark of bitter laughter.

"Then I saw Mary, you know Mary, Evie's friend?" Carl nodded. Everyone knew the pretty Mary. "This other f...guy had her up against the wall. Evie turned to him, and then *he* flinched, started to retch, like he was going to throw up. He musta loosened his hold 'cause Mary hauls off and knees him in the face, really good like, and he goes down like a sack of potatoes. Then I'm pulling Mary off him and just trying to get the girls back to the damn train. Sorry, Evie."

"I didn't know, I swear, sir, I didn't know she was hurting so badly. She looked fine on the train, where poor Mary was a mess.

Guy had his hands all over her." Logan looked up at Carl, his aircraft commander. Through the net, they could all feel that Logan felt responsible, in so many ways. Not the least of which was that he hadn't recognized that Evie, too, was traumatized, maybe more so, even, than Mary.

I didn't want you to know, Evelyn whispered through the net to all of them. *What I did was monstrous. I can't...I couldn't let you see that.*

"Bullshit," a new voice spoke up, ringing loud and angry through the small space. It was Abram Portman, their navigator. He leaned forward, his round face looking remarkably bulldog-like with his heavy brows drawn downward in fury straight from the heart of Brooklyn.

"What *they* tried to do was monstrous. *You* defended yourself, Evie. And what I want to know is why in the hell aren't we tracking these pieces of human trash down?" He didn't say what he wanted to do once he'd tracked them down, but he didn't really need to. They could all feel the violence simmering in his intent.

"They won't survive long enough for you to find them," Evelyn said weakly. "That's part of what's so wrong with what I did. I didn't just penetrate their mental defenses. I stripped them. Permanently. They're wide open to every stimulus. They'll go mad in a few hours and be dead within days."

She closed her eyes, unwilling to see the looks of horror that she expected on her crew's faces.

Stop it, Evie. The thought came from Paul and whipped through the net, scathing her with its sharpness. *You're feeling sorry for yourself, and you're not giving us enough credit.*

*You don't understand...*she started to protest but found the net saturated with the combined denials of all of her crewmen.

We understand very well, Evie, Paul thought to her. His mind-tone took on a gentler feel, but she could sense the implacability behind his gentle touch. *We feel what you feel, sweetheart. Your net is that deep; you know that. We fully understand everything that you did in your own defense, and in defense of your friend. We understand, and we approve, don't we, boys?*

The wordless affirmative that came roaring into her mind struck her, made her physically flinch from its vehemence.

We just wish we could have been there to protect you. But we weren't. And so you protected yourself. You don't need to feel guilt over that. You did what you had to do. Paul reached out to take hold of one of her hands. One by one, the other members of the crew reached out, too, until every one of them was touching her. The contact reinforced the net, as it always did. The men poured their various flavors of support down those wide open channels.

Take this, Paul said, pressing something into her palm and curling her fingers around it. *It's not much, but in case you ever need it. We should have gotten you one before now.*

Evelyn opened her hand and looked down to see a folding knife. Tears filled her eyes again, but this time they were tears of healing and gratitude. She wept, safe in the arms of her crew, until she felt wrung out, hollow, and finally clean.

"There's going to be a mission the day after tomorrow," Carl said lowly, breaking the silence they'd held while Evelyn cried. "We're not supposed to know about it, but I do. Evelyn, can you fly? If we told Colonel Rizer that you'd been attacked..."

"No," Evelyn said. Her voice was soft, but resolute. "It happened, and it's over. We're at war, and I have a job to do. I can't feel sorry for myself any longer," she said with a glance at Paul. He smiled briefly and sent a pulse of approval down the net. "I think flying will actually probably be good for me," she said.

Carl nodded. He understood that. They all did. Flying was so all-encompassing that one had to focus entirely on one's job. Even during the drone out and back. By now, Evelyn had been flying long enough that she knew the moment one let one's mind wander, that's when things were going to start to go wrong in the air. Come what may on the ground, flying was a terrific distraction.

"Then we should all get to bed," he said. "Otherwise we *will* be answering questions about what we're all doing this late."

The men insisted on walking Evelyn all the way to the WAC barracks. Carl also made her promise to leave the net in place until she fell asleep so that they could help her if she suddenly needed it. She agreed, although her training nagged at her. Truth be told, she was too tired to resist. The net wanted to be in place. Let it.

Evelyn crept into the darkened barracks and eased into her bunk. She could hear Mary's even breathing above her. The sound reassured her since it was evidence Mary had calmed down and would eventually be all right. Evelyn let her own eyes drift closed and felt herself slip into sleep.

* * *

"Good morning, ladies! Get yourselves up and dressed! Inspection in ten minutes!"

Captain Ledoux's voice with its cheerful Louisiana lilt grated in Evelyn's ears. Her mouth felt as if it had recently been full of the sand that seemed to have migrated to her eyes. She ached all along her body, and the ever-present fatigue pulled at the edge of her psyche. Without a conscious decision to do so, Evelyn reached out and re-established the net that had gotten her through the night before.

She should have resisted. But she was too tired and mentally drained to care. The minds of her crewmen were just waking as well, for the most part. They, one and all, welcomed her touch in their own individual style.

"A fine morning, isn't it, Technician Adamsen?" Captain Ledoux asked in a sweetly venomous tone as she "accidentally" kicked the bottom of Evelyn's bunk. Above her, Mary muttered something likely quite profane under her breath.

She's a bitch. Sorry, Evie, Les thought, his thought sleepy.

Also an officer, Bob reminded the gunner. The copilot was obviously trying to emulate what he thought Carl would have said. The aircraft commander, however, was conspicuously silent on the matter.

"Yes, ma'am," Evelyn replied as she sat up and began to dress. A second or two later, Mary hopped down from her top bunk.

"Are you all right?" Evelyn whispered to her friend. Mary looked pale and drawn, but that could just have been lack of sleep. Evelyn was certain she looked no better.

"As I can be," Mary whispered back. Her blue eyes were troubled, but she had no problems throwing a scowl in the direction of Ledoux's retreating back. Evelyn felt a thread of relief. Mary's spitfire nature seemed to be reasserting itself. She'd be fine.

The inspection dragged painfully on, and Ledoux made a number of nasty comments about Evelyn's appearance not being quite up to her exacting standards. But it eventually came to an end, and the

WACs found themselves released to go get breakfast. Evelyn fell in beside Mary for the walk to the chow hall.

"I'm glad that's over," the brunette said to her friend.

"Ledoux gets more and more useless by the day. She'd do better to stop having so many 'inspections' and start flying more missions. Rizer's going to notice that she's not pulling her weight and replace her," Mary said with a derisive snort.

"With whom?" Evelyn asked in a dry tone. That got another snort out of Mary, this time one of acknowledgement. Evelyn smiled, just a little. Mary's snorts were very expressive.

"Are *you* all right?" Mary asked in a soft voice a few moments later. Evelyn felt her smile drop away.

"I wasn't," she admitted. "But my crew came and got me. They got me through it." *They're still getting me through it,* she thought, but didn't say. After a moment, though, Evelyn asked softly, "So...you know?"

"What you did? Yes. I know," Mary said. The sick tone of her voice said without words that she, too, was horrified by Evelyn's actions. "I know, and I can't believe you did it. But then, I can't believe I didn't."

Evelyn turned to Mary, tears filling her eyes.

"Evie, I'm so sorry! I should have done something..."

Evelyn wasn't much for initiating casual touch. Mary was usually the one to throw exuberant arms around someone, but in this case, the brunette couldn't think what else to do. She wrapped Mary up in a hug and held her tightly.

"What could you do? They took us both by surprise. I know what I did was horrible, but I couldn't...I didn't want them to hurt you. Or me, for that matter," she added, when her words sounded a little too self-sacrificing to her own ear.

"No," Mary said, laughing weakly through her tears. "I didn't want them to hurt either of us either. I'm just...I'm so sorry you had to do that, Evie. And I'm sorry I was such a mess I couldn't support you afterward."

"Mary, you'd just survived a violent attack. You had every right to fall apart."

"So did you, and you didn't!"

"Oh, yes I did," Evelyn said lowly. "I'm just quieter about it. But my crew knew, and they helped me understand it wasn't my fault any more than it was yours. I did only what I had to do to keep us safe."

Mary gave her a long, searching look. "I can't believe you're so calm about it," she said softly.

Evelyn let out a short, bitter bark of a laugh. "I'm not," she said. "Believe me, I'm not. But I will be. Eventually. Come on, let's get some food."

* * *

The next morning, the knock came early, as Evelyn had known it would. Once more, she and the other women rose and dressed in the pre-dawn gloom, and they shivered as they hustled to get to breakfast and then out to the flightline to meet their crews.

Evelyn linked with her crew again as soon as she woke. They'd spent all of the day prior linked in the net, and none of them wanted to even try and go without that connection. At this point, there didn't seem to be much sense in it. Especially not when it made their net tighter for the mission. Evelyn knew she should protest. Everything she'd been taught warned her against what she was doing, but she found that she felt a curious kind of defiance. She and her men *needed* the net. Who was anyone to tell them they couldn't have it? This was war, and they all did what they needed to do to survive.

The preflight inspection went smoothly, if a little more silently than usual, and before long, they were droning over the Channel. Once again, they flew the aircraft nicknamed *Pretty Cass*. Evelyn hoped that was a good sign. The roar of the Cyclone engines vibrated through Evelyn's body, making her teeth ache as she put her head back and concentrated on holding her net steady.

This mission was to attack a munitions factory in western Germany, near the Belgian border. As always, Evelyn linked their crew into a larger formation net, in order to facilitate communication between the aircraft and to allow the pilots to fly tighter formation. So when the fighter escort waggled their wings in the traditional gesture of "farewell, and good luck" and turned back for home, Evelyn once again felt the zing of anxiety as it ricocheted through the stacked layers of Flying Fortresses.

Once more unto the breach, dear friends, once more. The thought came from Abram as he bent over his navigator's table, double-checking their course.

The net was silent for a moment before Logan transmitted a sense of snickering mirth from his ball turret. *Begging your pardon, sir, but what the hell does that mean? For us uneducated, sweaty types?*

The laughter of the rest of the crew rippled down the lines of the net.

It's Shakespeare, you apes, Abram shot back through the net, and even his mental tone had a feel of Brooklyn about it. *Henry V. Look it up sometime. It means "here we go again." We're crossing into Germany.*

Fighters twelve o'clock! Sean called out. *Here comes the welcoming committee!* Evelyn felt the recoil as he rocked backward with each shot that flung a stream of lead into the face of the attacking Messerschmitts.

Evelyn reached out along her formation net, checking in with the other girls as they held their crews steady through the rain of oncoming metal.

Along with the fighters came the flak rising up from the ground below. No matter how many times someone told her, no matter how many times she looked at the statistics, flak always scared Evelyn far worse than the fighters ever did. At least one could shoot back at the fighters. Flak just bounced them around like so many sardines in their flying tin can.

The flight seemed endless, punctuated by the *pop-pop-pop* of the gunners' weapons and the rattling booms of the flak. Evelyn had learned not to think about the aircraft they lost. As long as they stayed tightly in formation, the Forts were mostly safely covered by the gunners' crossing fire. But sometimes a fighter would score a lucky hit on one of the mighty Cyclone engines, and the wounded Fort wouldn't be able to keep up. They'd drop back, and then the fighters would swarm them. Most of the time, at that point, it was just a battle to stay alive long enough for most of the crew to bail out. No one knew why none of the psychics ever made it out of the injured birds. No one liked to think about it.

Starting the bomb run, Paul. Autopilot on. You've got her, Carl said as he went through his ritual of toggling on the autopilot controls and resting his fingertips on the yoke.

Roger, Paul replied tersely. Evelyn reached out to the rest of the psychics in the formation and felt the links between them tighten. It had become routine to bring up the bombardier's channel so that they could make as near-simultaneous a drop as possible. Even the aircraft without psychics on board tended to drop more precisely. Evelyn supposed it made sense. It had to be hard to see and focus on the lead bird to the exclusion of all others. With more than one Fort dropping bombs at once, it had to be easier to see the signal and respond with one's own drop.

Bomb drop in thirty seconds. The call came from Pearl Silvers in lead, and her touch was reassuringly steady. Evelyn pushed the call down her net to Paul, who acknowledged with a pulse of awareness.

Fighters, twelve o'clock high, ten o'clock high! Sean called out, already firing. Abram echoed him with the .30 caliber machine guns in the nose compartment. As they pushed in closer, Les opened up with his left waist gun, followed moments later by Logan in the ball turret. Through it all, Paul stayed tightly focused on his Norden bombsight. Evelyn felt him slip into that zone of pinpoint intensity, where all other stimuli fell away, became irrelevant, and all that mattered was the target and his drop.

The gunners continued to fill the air with lead as the fighters kept coming. Paul opened the bomb bay doors in preparation for the drop, and Evelyn felt the change in pressure and sound that accompanied that action. A rumbling vibration sang through the airframe, followed by a whine she'd never heard before. Les, Logan, Sean, even Rico on the tail opened up for all they were worth as a trio of Messerschmitts zoomed by.

Shit! It was Carl, in the cockpit. *They got both engines on the left! We're on fire! Cutting fuel!*

Wait! Paul's thought whip-cracked through the net. *Ten seconds to drop, let 'em burn! We're still producing power enough to stay in formation. Shut 'em down after!*

I don't like it! Carl thought.

Five seconds! I don't care! Paul flung the thought back, savagely. *Better to crash without a bay full of ordnance!*

Drop, Drop, Drop! Pearl's call came down through the formation net, and Evelyn pushed it along to Paul. He released his bombs right on the third "Drop," and they fell in perfect concert with lead's bomb load. Once again, death and destruction fell on the buildings and inhabitants below.

We're hit! Evelyn sent back to Pearl as she felt Carl's hands flying over the switches in the cockpit. He worked feverishly to shut down the fuel flow to the two left engines. The thick black smoke that had been trailing off of their left wing thinned but didn't entirely dissipate. The props slowed, the pitch of their ever-present hum quieting, and Evelyn felt both Bob and Carl straining on the rudder pedals to keep the nose straight. Slowly, inexorably, their aircraft began to fall away from her sister ships as two engines proved inadequate to maintain the required altitude and airspeed.

Crew, prepare for bailout, Carl sent, his mind tone calm and devoid of the anxiety of moments before. He was back in control of the aircraft, Evelyn realized, and that meant he was back in control, period.

Carl, I'm sorry, Paul sent as he and Abram began to shrug into their parachutes.

I know. It was the right call, Carl said. *Bob and I will steer together until I get us over that patch of forest here to the west,* he continued. *I don't want to bail out over the town we just bombed if I can help it.*

A sick feeling pierced Evelyn's gut at that thought. They were going to bail out. Right over enemy territory. Enemy territory that they'd just attacked with several thousand pounds of bombs.

We'll keep you safe, Evie, Sean thought to her. *Just get your parachute on like I showed you. You and I will bailout together,* he said. Evelyn swallowed hard and nodded, then got up and started clipping into her harness. Her half-frozen hands shook, and it took several tries to get herself situated, but eventually, she was there.

That's a good idea, Carl said. The effort that he and Bob were having to expend in order to get the aircraft over the uninhabited forest was showing in his mind. *You guys stay linked with Evie. Then you can rally up on the ground and work to get safe. Go north from here. It's your best bet.*

No psychic has ever survived a bailout, Evelyn thought, her mind voice small and shaking at least as badly as her hands had done.

No psychic has ever had us, Evie, Les said with his trademark cocky grin. His eyes, though, were troubled, and she could feel his share of the fear they all felt.

Enough chatter, Carl said, as if they'd been talking on the aircraft's intercom system instead of through the psychic net. *We're losing altitude too fast. We're below ten thousand and just over the edge of the forest. Still closer to the target than I'd like, but those fighters aren't going to give us any quarter. You'd better bailout now.*

"*You?*" Evelyn questioned, suddenly realizing that Carl hadn't been including himself in the bailout plans.

Carl and I will stay to keep the bird stable and give you guys time, Bob thought. *We'll ride it in to the trees and hope for the best.* The young copilot's mind was calm and resolute as he pronounced his own probable death sentence. *Good luck to you all. It was a pleasure flying with you.*

You too, sir, Sean said as he grabbed Evelyn's arm and began taking her along the walkway to the open bomb bay. *Both of you.*

Wait...! Evelyn cried. But it was no use. Sean was too strong for her to get loose, and it wasn't as if she could do anything anyway. They entered the bomb bay, accompanied by Les and Logan. Abram and Paul weren't far behind, with John bringing up the rear. He'd stayed to make a mayday call. Rico was already there, waiting for them. Tears filled Evelyn's eyes and froze to her cheeks.

It's good, Evelyn. This is what we do, Carl thought. *Stay alive and keep my men safe.*

I— she thought. And then Sean lifted her off her feet and heaved her out through the bomb bay doors, and she fell.

* * * * *

Chapter Seven

Lina waited patiently in the outer office. She had been on the train bound for Paris when the conductor had informed her that she had an appointment here in Aachen, with the commander of the local Luftwaffe Gruppe.

"You can go in now."

The commander's secretary smiled at her from behind her desk. Lina gave her a tiny nod in return. Smiling made her look young, and Lina didn't want this woman thinking of her in a motherly fashion or any such nonsense. Civility was one thing, familiarity another, and when in doubt, Lina had always found it best to err to the formal side of things. Especially in such an irregular situation as this.

She entered the commander's office and stood tightly at the position of attention. The commander (whose name was Hauptmann Krieger, if his desk plaque was to be believed) greeted her rather absently.

"Please, Fraulein, be seated," he said, gesturing to one of the chairs that faced his desk.

"If you please, Herr Hauptmann, I prefer to be addressed by my rank," Lina said, remaining on her feet.

The Hauptmann's eyebrows climbed up his forehead, and he looked directly at her for the first time. Lina stood unflinching under his sharp gaze. She knew what he'd see: a slender woman, tall, but sleekly muscular in her immaculate uniform. Her strawberry-blonde hair cut short and curled sensibly away from her face, her green eyes clear and steady. She had earned her rank, and she wasn't wrong to insist upon it.

"Of course, SS-Oberhelfer, forgive me," he said, his tone stiff and offended. Lina felt a brief stab of regret at that. Perhaps she should have phrased her request a bit more diplomatically. However, to apologize would be to undermine her standing at this point, and so she simply gave him another of her small, formal nods and waited for him to tell her why she was there.

Hauptmann Krieger settled back in his seat and pressed his lips together. Then he drew in a deep breath and looked down at an open file on his desk.

"I see here that you've distinguished yourself in finding enemies of the Reich. Is that true?"

His tone was aggressive and slightly insulting. Lina decided that she didn't like this man. He seemed to be the kind who was overly impressed with his own importance, the type whose devotion to the Reich went only so far as his rhetoric. Lina was horribly tempted to sneak into his mind to see if she was correct, but she resisted. For one, it was wrong. For another, she really didn't need her talents. All show and no dedication, this one.

"Yes, Herr Hauptmann," she said calmly.

"Excellent. The Reich has need of your talents. During the bombing raid this morning, one of the enemy bombers made a forced landing nearby. At least four parachutes were spotted. You will retrieve the survivors and bring them to me."

"Herr Hauptmann..." Lina drew in a deep breath, preparing to explain that her abilities didn't work quite that way.

"What? Were my orders unclear? Or perhaps you feel that your vaunted talents are...inadequate to the task?"

Lina felt anger ignite under her skin.

"No, Herr Hauptman," she said, her voice cold. "My talents are more than adequate to any task."

"Good," Hauptmann Krieger said with a thin smile. "Now, I would certainly not send such a valuable asset as one of our precious SS-Helferinnen out to look for enemy combatants alone. You shall have an escort of six men: a group of Fallschirmjager detailed to me for light duty during convalescence. They should prove ample protection for you during your little adventures. I believe they await you outside my office. Good hunting, SS-Oberhelfer. Unless you have other questions?"

Lina kept her hands closed so that they didn't betray her anger by trembling.

"No, Herr Hauptmann," she said, somehow keeping her voice level. And then, very correctly, she raised her arm and rendered the appropriate salute. The Hauptmann returned it in a somewhat lackadaisical fashion, which only further cemented Lina's low opinion of the man. Lina then turned on her heel and walked out of the room with her head held high.

Sure enough, a young man in the uniform of a Luftwaffe Stabsfeldwebel stood outside. A diving eagle clutching a swastika glinted on his left breast pocket as he turned to face Lina.

"Guten Tag, Fraulein," he said. "I am Stabsfeldwebel Josef Wolffs. My men and I shall escort you on this mission," he said, his expression formal and correct. He was tall, of course, with sandy blond hair and blue eyes that assessed her even as she assessed him. Mindful of her misstep with the Hauptmann, she allowed her lips to curve in a small, not-quite-warm smile.

"Hello, Stabsfeldwebel Wolffs," she said. She tried to make her voice sound light and pleasant, but she feared she just sounded young and possibly flirty. That was *not* the impression she wanted to give. "My name is Adalina Sucherin. I am a graduate of the SS-Reichsschule at Oberenheim. I've earned the rank of SS-Oberhelfer."

Wolffs gave her a small nod and turned to gesture toward the doorway. His expression gave nothing away, so Lina was left wondering if she'd once again offended.

Such a stupid thing! she groused internally as she preceded him out of the office. *Trust a man to be angered by a woman who insists on being called by a title she earned! I don't imagine he'd have liked it if I refused to address him as "Herr Hauptman!" I just hope that the rest of these Fallschirmjager aren't so egotistical. This shall be quite the "little adventure" otherwise!*

"Where are we going, Stabsfeldwebel?" Lina asked. She'd exited the Hauptman's office into the hallway outside, but from there, she didn't know where to go.

"To meet the rest of my unit, Oberhelfer," Wolffs replied in that same formal tone. "They await us in a conference room down this hallway and to the left. I was told you would likely want to meet us all, and then I will brief you on the details of the mission so far. Does that suit?"

"Admirably, Stabsfeldwebel," she said, again trying to sound pleasant and competent. Again, she was afraid she'd failed. She stifled a sigh and opened the door to the conference room he'd indicated.

Five men in Luftwaffe uniforms with the Fallschirmjager Eagle on their breast pockets stood as she entered the room. They were, to a man, tall and athletic, with the upright carriage and broad shoulders touted as the German ideal. Stabsfeldwebel Wolffs followed her in and closed the door behind them.

"Men, this is SS-Oberhelfer Adalina Sucherin. She is detailed to us for this mission. Oberhelfer, would you like to be seated?" Wolffs asked as he walked around her to the front of the table. He spoke with clear confidence, and Lina swallowed hard against her sudden nerves. She nodded and reached for the nearest chair.

One of the Fallschirmjager beat her to it and pulled the chair out from under the table. She glanced up at him, startled by the sudden, silent courtesy, then nodded again and sat down. He gently helped push her chair in so that she could see the maps and documents spread over the table and then stepped away. All without a single word.

Once she was seated, Wolffs made a gesture, and the other Fallschirmjager seated themselves at the table. Lina glanced around, impressed at their cohesion and apparent discipline.

"Oberhelfer Sucherin, we've been ordered to find the crew of an American bomber that crashed in the forest to the northwest of here. Luftwaffe spotters counted between four and six parachutes, depending on whom you ask. We've narrowed down their probable landing areas to this section of the forest, here."

He slid a terrain map across the surface of the table. Lina leaned forward to see the section that had been outlined in red pencil. It was large, several kilometers across, and roughly wedge shaped. It was also, according to the map, heavily forested with several creeks twisting through the terrain. Anxiety began to skitter along Lina's nerves. The search area was huge. In her mind, she could imagine the Hauptman laughing at her.

"Where—" She stopped, cleared her throat, started again. "Where were the parachutes spotted?" she asked.

Wolffs stared at her for a moment, then a tiny smile curved his lips. Something that might have been approval flashed in his eyes. "Here," he motioned. "And here, here..." Then he looked up at her. "And a fireball was spotted here that very well may have been the aircraft crashing."

Lina nodded, then waited. Though she held a rank and a title that she'd earned, SS-Helferinnen did not give orders to men. She would do as her title suggested and help when called upon to do so. Wolffs met her eyes again and then nodded slightly.

"So, we will begin our search here," he said, pointing to the spot where he'd indicated the fireball. "Now, what are your capabilities? Why are you assigned to assist us in this?"

Lina drew in a deep breath. Time to come clean.

"In truth, Stabsfeldwebel Wolffs, I am not certain. I have had some success in interrogating criminals, but in this situation...I am not sure what assistance I can provide."

Wolffs nodded, and to Lina's relief, his expression did not change appreciably.

"But, you *are* psychic, yes?"

"I am."

"Very well. Perhaps you cannot act as an instant locator for our downed enemies, but I think, perhaps, you may be able to help us in another way. Can you make it possible for my men and I to communicate over distance with one another?"

Lina blinked, startled, then straightened slightly in her chair.

"I can," she said, her voice stronger. "Yes, of course I can."

"That will allow us to spread out and cover more ground," Wolffs said. "I had hoped that this would be the case. Excellent. Have you arrangements to make, then?"

Excitement replaced the anxiety that skittered along Lina's nerves.

"No, Stabsfeldwebel," she said. "I was leaving for Paris when I was ordered here. I am all ready to go."

"Then we shall leave immediately."

* * *

They made the first part of the journey via motorcar. Lina sat with Wolffs and one of the other Fallschirmjager, a young Unterfeldwebel by the name of Kristof Schmied. During the journey, Kristof had relaxed from the uniform formality of the conference room and had begun to try and draw Lina out. He did this by smiling at her, then asking her about herself. When her short answers proved uncommunicative, he bravely soldiered on, cheerfully telling her about himself and his family.

It seemed that his father, Herr Schmied, had been a pilot in the Luftstreitkrafte during the Great War and had been wounded when his Fokker E. I. was shot down by British fighters. Herr Schmied had managed to dead stick his bird to a crash landing near the German lines and had been given a hero's welcome and prompt medical attention. His injuries were bad enough that he'd missed the end of the war, but he'd raised his son on stories of Max Immelmann and Oswald Boelcke, and the legendary Manfred von Richthofen.

Post-war Germany was, however, a bleak place. With the military destroyed by the humiliating War Guilt clause of the Treaty of Versailles, young Kristof's dreams of following in his father's footsteps seemed out of reach. He apprenticed to a local brewer and had made something of a name for himself in adapting newly emerging technology for the preservation and serving of beer. Kristof never lost his deep patriotism, though, and when the opportunity arose to volunteer for the elite Fallschirmjager unit, he jumped on it.

"And so now you know everything about me," Unterfeldwebel Schmied said with a smile, as the motorcar bounced into the forest. Their well-maintained road had disappeared a half a kilometer ago, and Lina was afraid that she might bounce the fillings right out of her teeth. "So, since we are to be comrades in arms, will you not tell me something about yourself, Fraulein Oberhelfer?"

Lina shook her head with a small smile. Some men would never give up. This she'd learned early in her nineteen years.

"What would you know, Herr Unterfeldwebel?" she asked. She intended to sound tart, but she wasn't sure it came across.

"Where is your home, to start? Have you any family?"

Lina drew in a deep breath.

"I was born in Hamburg," she said. "And I have no family any longer. They died while I was at school."

"Ah, I am sorry," Schmied said. "How did they die?"

A spike of anger flashed through her. How dare he ask something so personal? She lifted her eyes to his and let him see the seething rage therein.

"Their house was bombed while they slept," she said, her voice icy. "My father and mother and my little sisters were sleeping. They never had a chance to get out."

Schmied sat back in his seat, his pleasant expression draining away.

"I see," he said. Then his lips stretched in a different smile. This one was less pleasant and more...feral. It also seemed more real.

"So you are one of us," he said softly.

Lina's eyebrows went up, and the ice in her expression remained.

"I told you," Wolffs put in. He'd been so silent up until then that Lina had almost forgotten his existence. She turned sharply to the Stabsfeldwebel.

"Told him what?" she asked, anger threading through her tone.

"That you were more than a pretty face in a uniform," Wolffs said, apparently unperturbed. "I read your file from the Reichsschule. Your instructors praised your dedication and drive."

"How did you...?"

Wolffs waved a hand as if to say that the "how" was immaterial, and that he wasn't going to tell her anyway.

"The important thing is that you are here with us, on this mission. As I requested."

"As *you* requested?" Lina asked, startled. Wolffs nodded.

"Again, *how* I know this is not important. But we've intelligence that the Americans are putting psychics on board their bomber crews. Why they would risk such a precious resource is beyond me, but Americans are crazy. So far, we've never found one of their psychics alive. However, due to the precision of the attack yesterday, I believe there *were* psychics on board those aircraft. This might be our best chance to find one. *That* is why we've requested your presence on this mission, Oberhelfer. And why it was granted. My superiors trust me. We're the best in the world at what we do, and what we do is find those who've bombed our families, and we bring them to justice."

A shiver that had nothing to do with cold ran through Lina's body. Her throat felt tight with pride and deep, angry longing. She cut her eyes from Wolffs to Schmied, who smiled that feral smile and nodded slowly.

"Yes," Lina said, and to her surprise, the word came out in a defiant hiss. She squared her shoulders and nodded. "Yes," she said again, letting the ferocity of her need for vengeance fill her up and bleed out of her pores. She clenched her fists together, and in the ancient way, gave her assent a third time to seal the pact. "Yes!"

Wolffs smiled, then tapped on the driver's shoulder. The man, another of the Fallschirmjager, braked as gently as possible on the rutted forest track, and the motorcar came to a stop.

Schmied opened the door, exited, and then extended a hand to help Lina out of the motorcar as well. Lina was grateful she'd worn sensible shoes, as the ground was rough and uneven. The other Fallschirmjager were also extricating themselves from the vehicles and coming to stand near her. The young man who'd been driving went around to the trunk of the motorcar and pulled a valise out of it. At Wolffs' gesture, he brought the valise over to Lina and handed it to her.

"I have some things for you," Wolffs said. He took the valise and opened it, then pulled out a sturdy-looking pair of ladies' ankle boots, a wool coat with a hood, and a strange-looking object that Lina didn't see clearly before he palmed it.

"Thank you," she said, feelingly, and immediately reached for the boots. Wolffs chuckled and pointed to the open car door. Lina seated herself sideways in the passenger seat so that she could still listen to him as she put on her new boots. They were slightly large, but they had warm, thick wool socks stuffed inside, and she was grateful to have them.

"I thought that you might need them," Wolffs said. "I anticipate that we might be living rough for a short time. My men all have packs, and I've a smaller one for you. Camping gear, mostly, and a weapon, if you want it. Though I suspect that you have your own defenses."

"You suspect?" Lina looked up at him, her expression sharp.

"I know," he confirmed, with another small smile. "My Oma had your talents. She taught us well. I have great respect for your prowess, as do my men. You need not fear untoward conduct from us, even without your defenses."

Lina straightened her spine. "Herr Stabsfeldwebel, I would not have thought so ill of soldiers of the Reich in any case."

"Then you are, perhaps, naive, Fraulein Oberhelfer." Wolffs smiled sadly. "But it does not matter. The point is that you are safe, and we have a mission. Have you ever seen one of these?" He showed her the object he'd been holding in his hands.

It looked like a pair of pilot's goggles with the glass fogged over. The head strap had been modified such that two earpieces dangled from the strap. A long cloth was attached to the back of the strap, and as she watched, Wolffs flipped this cloth over the rest. A memory tugged at Lina: during her early days at the Reichsschule, one young woman had learned of the death of her beloved at the front. In her grief, she'd gone mad and had broadcast her pain throughout the immediate area. The other psychics had been slammed by her rage and loss, and blinding headaches, ringing in the ears, and even seizures had resulted. Lina had been lucky. She'd been strong enough to block most of the onslaught, but even so, she'd been sensitive to light for days afterward. The cadre at the Reichsschule had consulted with some of the older psychics and had devised a device similar to what Wolffs now held. It was, in essence, a sensory deprivation hood. By removing external stimuli to the grieving girl's mind, the other psychics were able to slip inside her defenses and push her into healing sleep. They'd hindered her ability to transmit, providing much needed relief to the rest of the psychic students.

"I have seen such a thing," Lina said, her voice calm, though the sight of the device stirred a tremor of instinctive fear and loathing deep in her belly. "It can be used to shut down a psychic's transmission ability, but only if there is another psychic, or more, available to run it."

Wolffs nodded. "Yes. I believe there is a chance we may capture the American psychic alive. If we do, can you imagine the intelligence opportunities that interrogating her may provide? How many enemy minds has she linked to? How much has she seen through eyes other than her own? We must keep her alive and relatively intact. Your file said you were quite strong. Can you run one of these hoods?"

Lina swallowed hard against the ice in her belly. Using the combined power of several experienced psychics to gently shut down the transmission power of a grief-mad girl was one thing. Holding a forced psychic feedback loop against an enemy combatant was another. Lina didn't know this American psychic, but from all she'd ever heard about Americans, they were bitter, vicious adversaries who would fight until long past the point where all hope was lost. This girl would fight her; she had no doubt about it.

"Remember Hamburg," Schmied said softly. He stood with the others, ranged around her as she sat in the open motorcar. Lina looked up to him, and he gave her a gentle smile and a nod. His eyes, though, were hot and hard. They matched the fire of rage that burnt in Lina's heart. The fire that, even now, melted the icy fear in her belly and straightened her carriage.

"I can, and I will," she said, her voice quiet, but strong and cold as naked steel.

Schmied smiled, and Wolffs nodded again.

"So you will," the Stabsfeldwebel said, deep satisfaction in his voice. "So. Let us begin our hunt. You must meet the rest of my men."

"Kristof you know," he said, gesturing at Schmied. "May I now introduce Unteroffizier Hans Richter, Unteroffizier Werner Zimmermann, Hauptgefraiter Horst Fischer, and Obergefraiter Willi Mueller. I have briefed all of them on what we know of your capabilities. It seems that now would be a good time for us to build your psychic network."

Once again, Wolffs startled Lina with the abruptness of his manner. But he seemed almost...enthusiastic under his command demeanor, and she found that oddly disarming. So she nodded and reached out to him.

"It's easier if there's contact, the first time," she said. He smiled as if to say he'd known that and took her hands in his own. Lina closed her eyes and stretched her awareness out to him.

It was so different from an interrogation. Instead of a criminal mind desperate to hide its secrets, Josef's mind opened wide and welcoming. Lina shivered in pleasure as her consciousness slid over the landscape of his mind. He was all delicious male power. Strength, courage, determination...

You feel so good, he sent to her, his mind-touch almost tentative, then growing in confidence as he became more accustomed to her mind enveloping his.

As do you, she replied, almost shyly. It almost felt sinful.

How can this be sin? he responded. *You are as strong and powerful in your way. It is natural that we should...I had not thought to tell you this right away,* he admitted, a bit of rueful mortification coloring his consciousness for just a moment. *But I find I cannot hide from you, Lina. The blood of psychics runs in my veins. My grandmother was powerful and fierce, just like you. Imagine what we could create together, the two of us. I had thought to woo and wed you, so that we might together give rise to a line of powerful, talented children who would serve our thousand-year Reich.*

Surprise rocketed through Lina. Not at the concept. At school, they'd been very clear on this point: SS-Helferinnen were expected to pair off with brave soldiers of the Reich and be model couples, raising large broods of healthy, happy children. No one knew what caused psychic talent, but sometimes it did run in families, passing from mother to daughter, or grandmother to granddaughter. The Fuhrer himself had recognized that psychic talent was one that should be preserved and, if possible, cultivated. So it stood to reason that she would be expected to find a suitable mate and be about the process.

She just hadn't expected it to happen so suddenly.

I apologize, Lina, Josef thought, sounding flustered and frustrated for the first time since she'd met him. *I've handled this so badly. Please, do not think...I am not so cold and calculating as all that. Look...feel what I'm feeling! You must know how attractive I find you, how deeply I admire...well...everything about you.*

And she did know. Suddenly, she saw herself through his eyes, and what she saw was breathtaking: fragile beauty underlaid with solid, steely determination and bright confidence in her own strength. Lina had never considered herself to be particularly fragile, but she supposed that compared to your average Fallschirmjager, she qualified as downright dainty.

...and *that* thought was clearly an attempt to self-distract. Lina squared her shoulders and opened her channels wider so as to let Josef see further into her mind as well. Further than she'd allowed anyone to see before.

I thank you, she said. She instinctively couched her articulated reply into formal tones, but the formality stood at stark odds with the intimacy of the connection Lina allowed. She could feel his presence, almost like a physical being, sliding over the contours of her consciousness. Like silky mink fur against the underside of her skin. Her entire being hummed with the connection, and the way in which he seemed to so perfectly weave himself into the fabric of *her.*

Someone coughed, a booted foot shuffled on the rocky ground. Lina blinked, recalled to the present after who knew how long. Josef still held onto her hand, her fingertips resting lightly against his palm. She looked down at the place where her skin touched his, then back up into his eyes.

We must include the others, she sent softly, regretfully. *We have a mission.*

Yes, he replied, but made no move to release her hand. Confusion and desire warred with duty inside him. She felt it, reveled in it. *I want...I...*

I know, she sent, soothing his need with her own. *We will return to this...what we have found. But for now, the job.*

Yes, he sent again, and dropped her hand with a wrench. A brief flare of something very like pain flashed in his blue eyes and then disappeared.

Lina inhaled a shaky breath and lowered her hand to her lap. Her fingers trembled, just a bit, and she hoped that none of the other men noticed. Or, if they did, that they'd chalk it up to the chill in the air.

Focus, she reminded herself. *You must be calm for them, else they will not learn well how to be in a net.*

You will teach them well, Josef supplied. *I had faith in you before, but now that I have tasted the strength of your mind, I have no doubt. They could not be in better hands. Nor could I.* His confidence sang down the link of their connection and bolstered her own. She felt her spine straighten, her chin lift. Time to do the job.

"Gentlemen," she said. "I have created a psychic link with your Stabsfeldwebel. As you can see, he is taking no harm from the connection. In fact...well." She broke off, not wanting to allude to what she and Josef had shared. Not yet. With a pulse of regret, she pulled back from him just a bit and allowed her mental barriers back into place. She didn't need the intimacy of a full connection to build the net, and she wasn't about to share that much of herself with all of the men. She was a bit startled that she'd even shared it with Josef, but she hadn't seemed to be able to do anything else.

"I'll go next, then, with your permission?" Schmied said, stepping forward with his sunny, charming smile. He held out his hand in invitation, and Lina gave him a tiny smile as she reached out to put her fingertips on his.

Once again, she reached out and gently slipped inside the barriers that guarded the sandy-haired Unterfeldwebel's mind. Behind the easy charm, his mind was a roil of violence and anger. Kristof, it appeared, deeply felt the wounds inflicted upon his nation and countrymen.

I lost my family, as you lost yours, he thought, his words tentative at first, but growing in strength. *First they ground us into humiliation after my father's war, and when we have the temerity to try and rebuild our nation, they bomb us with fire and metal. I hate them for hating us so much.*

Lina didn't reply with words, merely wrapped her presence around him so that he could feel her there, know that she felt his pain and sympathized. So that he knew that he wasn't alone.

None of us are alone, Josef thought, pushing the silent words down the lines of Lina's net so that Kristof could hear them. *We are brothers in this, family forged by blood and fire.*

Kristof blinked as his vision tripled, then resolved into a single image as Lina sorted the optical inputs. Then he reached out his hand and clasped Josef's forearm, just as Josef clasped his.

Brothers, Kristof repeated. *Forever.*

Lina felt a great swell of pride building deep within her chest. What magnificent countrymen she had! Whether it was the influence of the two men's minds on hers or her own sentiment, she didn't know, nor did she care. For the first time, this mission felt like less of a duty and more of a passion.

One by one, she added the other four men to the net, learning something about each of them in the process. Werner, it turned out, had a wife and baby daughter back in Salzburg. Horst stuttered and, therefore, rarely spoke. But his thoughts were lightning quick, the quickest Lina had ever felt. Hans exuded a focused loyalty: he'd follow Josef to the ends of the Earth. Like Kristof, young Willi had grown up on stories of the Great War and felt a deep pride at being among such elite company at the age of nineteen. She wove each of them into the connection, teaching them how to communicate down the lines of her psychic connections, how to channel their thoughts and shield their innermost mind...and how to share what they sensed.

When she was done, the Fallschirmjager could look through one another's eyes, hear through one another's ears, and know instantly the thoughts of every man in the group...as well as her own. Josef's pleased response ran through her in a warm wave of affirmation.

This is how we will proceed, he said. *From here we will hike to the wreckage, which was spotted approximately eight kilometers to the northwest of here. We will see what we can learn from the site, and from there, we will begin our search. Lina, you can hike while maintaining the net, yes?*

Yes, Lina said, although doubt colored her mind. Maintaining a psychic net required a fair amount of concentration, and she would not be able to keep her full attention on their activity. She had a quick mental image of herself stumbling through the forest around them, tripping and falling behind.

A pulse of humor came down the net from Kristof's general direction. *We will not let you fall, Lina,* he sent gently.

No, for I will punish any man who does not treat you like the treasure you are, Josef said.

If we do not get to him first, Willi said, with all of the hotheaded pride of youth. Lina turned a bit of her attention his way and realized the boy looked at her with eyes full of worship. He found her beautiful and powerful and was well on his way to a full-blown infatuation.

Do not be concerned for Willi, Josef said to her on the private channel she'd instinctively held open with him. *He knows you are not for him. His affection will be from afar only and may, in fact, help to keep you safe.*

Lina responded without words, just by sending a pulse of awareness, of the sense of deep connection that had suddenly tied Josef into her being in an utterly unexpected (and still somewhat undiscovered) manner.

"Let us go," Josef said out loud, and the men dispersed from the rough semi-circle they'd made around Lina as she created the net. They spent the next few minutes hefting packs, settling gear, and just basically getting ready to start their hike through the woods. Lina ensured her new boots were tightly tied and the psychic damping hood was accessible in her small pack.

The Fallschirmjager were predictably efficient about their business, and within a few minutes, they were ready to go. Josef ordered that Lina would march in the center of the group, immediately preceded by Willi and followed by Kristof. The two of them would be primarily responsible for her safety as they marched. Werner would take point, followed by Horst. Hans and Josef himself would bring up the rear so that he might watch and ensure they were all moving well.

They started out slowly, taking an easy pace through the heavy forest. Thick pine and deciduous trees tangled one with another, hiding the fact that the terrain consisted of rolling hills and ridges. The few paths seemed to meander, more like game trails than actual human roads. At first, Lina felt a stab of guilt. She was certain they were going so slow in order to be solicitous.

Not at all. The reassurance came from an unexpected source. Their point man, Werner, sent back the mental equivalent of a smile.

It is good to start out slow, especially in heavy forest like this. We make less noise this way and prevent stupid injury while we get used to the terrain. Do not fear, we are not going to baby you, Lina. We will protect you, but we can all feel how strong you are. Weaker in body, perhaps, than us, you are clearly still every bit a soldier of the Reich.

Thank you, Lina sent to the man.

Of course, Werner replied. *I imagine you and my wife would get along. You two should meet when the war is over. She is strong like you, though not psychic. But she does her duty in other ways,* he said with quiet pride in his woman.

I would be honored to meet her, Lina said as she stepped over a fallen log. They appeared to be following one of the game paths that led along the side of the current ridge and over the far hill to the supposed crash site. As they hiked deeper into the forest, the broad leaves filtered the day's sunlight and turned it a lovely shade of green. Though the woods weren't silent, Lina felt a particular kind of hush settle over her as they hiked. The chittering of the birds and various small rodents that protested their intrusion just added to her sense of reverence. It felt like being in an emerald cathedral with choirs of small animals heralding their measured steps through the undergrowth.

Lina didn't believe in a god, per se, but she couldn't help but feel that the universe smiled on her and her team. Right was on her side, and for the first time since her family had died in fire and pain, Lina felt the dragging loneliness lift. She was no longer alone. Against all the odds, she'd found another family, here, with these Fallschirmjager.

* * *

Before long, night rose around them. When Josef finally called the halt, Lina stumbled to a stop, her whole body leaden with exhaustion. Still, a curious thread of exultation wound through the numbing fatigue. Whether it was the excitement of being on the hunt or the seductive kinship of the net itself, Lina didn't know.

"We make camp here," Josef ordered. Lina passed the message to Werner, their point man. He acknowledged and started back, passing along the thought he'd seen that clearing earlier and thought it would be a good campsite as well.

The Fallschirmjager obviously knew their various camp tasks well, for they went about them with a minimum of talking. Lina looked around, at a loss for what to do, and finally settled on shrugging out of her pack and setting it against a nearby tree.

"Oberhelfer," Josef said. He'd walked up behind her, though she'd known he was there. Of course. She had the feeling that she'd have known it was him, even if they hadn't been linked in a net. She straightened and turned to him, struggling to keep her face from showing the sudden joy she felt in his nearness.

"Yes?" she asked.

"You are still holding your net, yes? Perhaps you should let it down, in order to conserve your strength." *But stay with me*, he didn't say. She heard him anyway, on that incredibly private channel.

"Yes," she said, hearing the mind-dragging fatigue in her own voice. "All right."

I must rest now, she sent out to the men.

Of course you must! That was Kristof, over by the fire. He looked up at her with a smile, his sandy hair in disarray from his work splitting wood for their fire. She smiled back at him.

I will reestablish the net in the morning. Thank you for allowing me to link with you all today, she said, as she felt her brain's instinctive reluctance to sever the connection. Net work was so seductive, especially with men.

It was our pleasure, Oberhelfer, Josef said, smoothly taking over. She swayed, and he reached out to grip her shoulders, hold her steady. Lina let her eyes fall closed and concentrated on gently letting go of each connection, one by one, until only her link with Josef remained.

I cannot bear it, she whispered in her mind, as if it were some great, guilty admission. *I do not wish to be separated from you.*

Nor I, you, he admitted. His brown eyes searched hers. *I dreaded it all day. My Lina...*

Yes, she said. For suddenly, irrevocably, she was his Lina, and he had become her Josef. This thing between them that had hovered in the background of their connection all day burst over them both like a tidal wave. Lina felt her awareness expand to include his every nerve ending. She knew him, knew that he knew her more intimately than anyone had ever known her before. He knew her, and because of it, he had become part of her.

She felt him move, as if it were her own body. She felt his agonizing desire to touch her skin. She lifted one gloved hand and pressed it against his cheek, now roughened from the day's growth of stubble. His liquid brown eyes, full of nothing but her, drifted closed.

Somewhere a twig snapped, a fire crackled. The spell broke.

Lina dropped her hand, opened eyes that she hadn't realized she'd closed.

"I must go," she whispered, unsure where, exactly, she was supposed to go to. All she knew was that she felt terribly exposed.

"Lina," Josef whispered. "Do not withdraw from me, I beg you."

She shook her head. "No, I will not. But they will see, they will know..."

He smiled. "They know already. They have been feeling the electricity between us all day. Go, refresh yourself. Willi has your tent up, rest awhile, but do not, please, do not ever leave me."

Lina blinked. "I cannot," she said, only then realizing it was true. "You are part of me."

She felt his deep, swelling emotions surge down their link, rocked back on her heels from the force of it. He reached out to grab her again, and she steadied herself with a hand on his chest. Sudden need slammed into her, and she dropped her hand as if he'd been actually aflame, instead of just metaphorically on fire with desire for her.

"I..." she said. Then trailed off. What could she say? She ached for him, wanted to be his in every possible way, but the circumstances were what they were.

He smiled. "My Lina," he said. "Go. Rest. I will be here. Always."

It felt cowardly, and not really at all what she wanted to do, but Lina turned and fled into the solitude of her tent.

* * * * *

Chapter Eight

For the rest of her life, Evelyn would have nightmares about that fall.

Sky spun into ground spun into sky, in an impossibly violent whirl of aching blue and dark, threatening green. The wind tore the breath from her lips and slapped her face with stinging, acid cold. Her stomach rebelled as she spun, and spasms of nausea ripped through her as she heaved, helpless and hurtling to the ground. A throbbing roar echoed in her ears, overwhelming her senses.

She may have screamed. She never knew. The only thing she could think to do was to claw at her chest, where Sean had said the ripcord was.

Then something jerked at her, snapping her legs up over her head and then back down. She suddenly found herself hanging under a round canopy. The edges of the canopy dished in momentarily and then snapped out over and over again. The straps of her harness dug into the soft flesh between her thighs, and it was all that Evelyn could do to force her lungs to breathe again.

Focus, take stock, she told herself. The world seemed drowned in noise as the wind whipped past, even if it was slower than the freight-train roar of the wind in free fall. Despite this, however, the trees beneath seemed to be rising up at an alarming rate to meet her. A burst of memory from the one, pitifully inadequate lecture she'd had on this subject surfaced.

"Feet and knees together, eyes on the horizon," she whispered to herself. "Cover face and jugular in trees, and...and..."

The dappled green of the top layer of leaves seemed to reach up at her, and Evelyn flung her hands up to cover her face. Some instinct helped her to keep her elbows tucked in, close to her body. A crashing, ripping sound greeted her. Something ragged and sharp sliced up the inside of her leg, and she let out a pained gasp. She'd forgotten to cross her legs for the landing in trees. A tiny, detached corner of her mind pointed out dryly that her mother would be disappointed in her. The rest of her fought to belatedly interlock her ankles. Those same jagged wooden claws sliced up her forearms and hands, and Evelyn couldn't help but scream. Her head bounced back and knocked against something hard enough to jar the teeth in her skull, but she kept her palms pressed tight against her face until she came to a stop. Her right hip and shoulder pressed against something solid, but her feet dangled in the air. Her head throbbed, and as she hung there, her body began to twist slowly to the left.

For a moment, all Evelyn could do was tremble, braced against some other wracking pain that she was certain was about to hit. Her chest heaved, first with panicked breaths, and then with full blown sobs as all of the lacerations and contusions made themselves known. She slowly lowered her hands from her face, feeling her spin continue as her risers and lines twisted in the branches overhead.

Look down, she told herself, willing her body to obey. Her eyes blurred in the dim green light, and she blinked rapidly and forced them to focus on the forest floor below. The ground looked to be only about five feet under her boots, and she breathed a sigh of thanksgiving. Her shaking fingers fumbled at her harness releases, and they opened before she was really ready.

Evelyn dropped and landed badly. As she came down, her right foot folded underneath her, rolling to the side and a sickening *snap* shot up through her leg and straight into the rest of her. She dropped to her hands and knees as the pain ripped a scream from her. Her eyes filled, and she stuffed one gloved fist into her mouth to quiet the sobs that started all over again. Unable to do anything else, Evelyn collapsed onto the leaf-covered forest floor and sobbed out her fear and pain (so much pain!) and grief all at once.

She must have lost consciousness at one point. Eventually, however, the rest of the world once again asserted itself into her awareness. Her face was cold. Actually, all of her was cold, but her face was also wet, both from her tears and from being pressed against the moist, snow-pocketed ground of the forest floor.

Evelyn put her trembling hands against the slick ground and pushed, trying to lever herself up. As she moved her right foot, that tearing, shooting pain lanced through her again, eclipsing what she felt before. She let out another scream, followed by a series of whimpers. Jagged blades of agony stabbed into her with every movement. She sucked in great mouthfuls of air, feeling her face buzz from the overload of oxygen, but she couldn't seem to stop. Eventually, she forced herself to half-roll, half-push herself to a seated position up against the trunk of the tree.

Sure enough, her right foot sat at an odd angle. Maybe it was shock, or the cold, or just more pain, but at first, Evelyn couldn't quite wrap her mind around what she was seeing. She tried to bend forward to touch her boot, but her flight gear was too restrictive to let her fold herself down that far. And when she tried to bend her knee to bring the ankle closer, agony shot through her and caused bright flashes to appear in her vision. She held herself very still after that and concentrated on just breathing enough to make the pain sparkles go away.

"Okay," she said out loud. Her voice sounded disturbingly high and shocky. She took another deep breath to try and calm down. Sudden nausea churned in her stomach, intensified by the throbbing pain that radiated from her ankle and lower leg. She closed her eyes and leaned her head back against the rough tree bark and focused on not throwing up. Not that there was anything left in her stomach. She'd lost it all on the way down.

Where had Sean and the others gone? The thought suddenly occurred to her. She hadn't been the only one to make it out of the doomed Fort, had she? Her fall itself had been so violent and terrifying that she'd lost track, but surely at least one or two of her men had survived as well. After all, *she* was alive, and she had been given much less training than any of them.

"Okay," she whispered again to herself, trying to calm her mind. "Okay, Evie-girl. They're out here somewhere. You're hurt, so you can't go find them physically, but they can't be that far. In London, I could reach Carl...Captain Peters..." She stopped as grief crushed her chest with a pain that was almost physical. Once again, she closed her eyes against the threatening flood of tears and tried to focus on making herself breathe.

"He might be alive, too," she whispered, knowing it was almost certainly a lie. A tear slipped from the corner of her eye and ran in a warm, wet line down her clammy cheek. "He's such a good pilot. Maybe he and the lieutenant survived the crash. Maybe I can find them."

It wasn't much, but it was the best chance she had. After all, what option did she have? She was alone, injured, untrained, and terrified.

She couldn't even move without screaming from the pain. If she could find even one of her crew, then she could guide him to her. Any of them would be glad to help. John would smile his handsome smile. Sweet young Logan would offer her a nip from his flask and help her to stand. Rico would likely just pick her up with his Latin gallantry. Les might do the same, but he'd make some kind of off-color joke to lighten the mood. Evelyn's lips curved in a smile at the thought. Sean...Sean would probably do all three and then find a way to splint her ankle so that she could walk on it.

Actually, Evelyn reflected, that was an excellent idea. Thanks to her breathing exercises and her thoughts of the crew, her panic had started to recede. She took one more deep breath and opened her eyes, determined to take stock and come up with a plan before reaching out for help. That way, when she reached them, the men wouldn't be sucker-punched by her uncontrolled fear and pain. She nodded firmly. Yes. That was what a responsible psychic should do. She had to be a member of the crew, not a helpless drain on their resources. It was bad enough that she'd gotten herself hurt.

"So," she said, still speaking out loud. The sound of her own voice helped her to feel less alone, and if one of the men heard her...so much the better. "What is my situation?"

She put her hands to her head and carefully began to pat herself down. She winced as her fingers caught several burgeoning bruises on her head, and she could feel a few gashes on her face where her hands hadn't protected her. Her torso was mostly unharmed, as it had been protected by her bulky flying gear, but the long scrape up the inside of her leg stung fiercely. And then, of course, there was the ankle. In the time she'd been sitting there, Evelyn could see that it had begun to swell. Her leather boot felt tight and uncomfortable.

She was tempted to take it off, but the thought that she wouldn't get it back on again stopped her. Plus, who knew if she could even get it off. Just moving the joint was enough to make her vision start to sparkle. She really didn't want to pass out from pain.

So, her situation could definitely be better. So what were her assets? What could she use?

"Well," she said, answering her own silent questions. "I have my flying clothing. I have my knife," she said, reaching into the inner pocket of her jacket. Sure enough, the folding knife that they had given her rested there, hard against her ribs. Sean had told her that she should always carry it because who knew when it would come in handy? She also had a small flask, like the one Logan had. Hers, however, held water rather than the rotgut hooch the ball turret gunner always carried.

"I have water," she said, her tone taking on a note of wonder as she pulled it out. She'd forgotten all about the little flask. Her hands still trembled, though not as badly as they had. She was able to get the flask uncapped without spilling too much of the water inside and lifted it to her lips. The cold, metallic taste of it filled her mouth. She took it in, swished it around to clear out the taste of bile and panic, then spat it out. Then she took another deep mouthful and swallowed. Her eyes closed in bliss. It tasted wonderful. It tasted like hope. Like maybe, for the first time, she might actually be able to get out of this predicament.

She took another long drink and then resolutely capped the flask and put it back into her jacket. Who knew when she would be able to get more water?

Right, so. Splinting the ankle. Evelyn wasn't a nurse or anything like that, but she had grown up on and around farms. In rural South

Dakota, first aid was a way of life, especially because the closest doctor might be a hundred miles away. Once they'd lost the farm and
moved to Rapid City, things had changed, but her family had always
insisted on being as self-sufficient as possible. Evelyn had splinted
her little brother's wrist once, after he broke it jumping out of a tree.
The basic concept was to immobilize the joint and ensure as much
stability as possible. So...for that...she needed some sticks.

Luckily for her, Evelyn sat under a tree. And as it was the tree
that she'd recently come crashing down into, the snowy ground
around her lay littered with branches and the like she'd broken off.
She reached out and pulled one or two close enough for her to work
with. The one she ended up choosing had roughly the same girth as
her wrist. It was about three feet long and reasonably straight. Evelyn
figured that if she could break it in half, it would work admirably as a
splint, if she could tie it to her boot or something.

The problem was that the wood was green and springy and didn't
appear likely to break anytime soon. She gave the limb a few tentative whacks against the ground and got the expected result: nothing.
From her seated position, there was no way she was going to get the
power needed to snap this young, thick branch.

She huffed out a breath in frustration. If she weren't hurt, she
would simply stand up and step on the branch in order to snap it. Of
course, if she weren't hurt, she wouldn't need to break it in half. She
shifted slightly and thought about trying to bring her uninjured foot
up to try and snap it, but the prospect of whacking her injured side
with a suddenly broken length of wood dissuaded her from that idea.

Evelyn slumped back against the tree trunk with the offending
length of wood in her lap. She could always try to find another couple of pieces that wouldn't be as big, but there wasn't anything in

reach that seemed like it would work. And moving too much wasn't really an option. She lifted her hands to scrub at her face and felt her folded knife poke her in the ribs.

Wait. The knife.

Evelyn sat up quickly, and immediately regretted doing so, as her right foot shifted, sending pain shooting from the ankle throughout her body. She hissed at the renewed onslaught but kept herself from screaming, barely. She reached inside her jacket and pulled out the knife. Unfolded, it was longer than her hand and might even have qualified as something her daddy would have called a "pig sticker."

She snapped the knife open and turned it to catch the green-filtered light. Sure enough, the back edge of the blade was serrated. It would take a long time, but she just might be able to saw through this blasted branch in order to make a serviceable splint.

Evelyn carefully arranged herself, moving slowly and carefully to avoid disturbing her ankle. She propped the branch on her left thigh and eyeballed the midpoint as best she could. Then she took the knife and started sawing.

At first, it didn't appear to have any effect at all. Despair started to rise within her, but she fought it and pushed it back down. She just needed to have patience, she told herself. Patience and an unwillingness to quit. She renewed her efforts and sawed back and forth faster, pressing down into the wood.

Slowly, slowly, the knife started to do its job. Its serrated teeth bit into the tough, green wood of the branch, carving out a fragrant trench bit by bit. Eventually, the teeth got gummed up with chewed-up wood and sap, and Evelyn had to try and clean it out. She did this by wiping the knife on her jacket and by carefully using her fingers to pull the wood pulp out from between the teeth. Then she was back at it.

By the time she was halfway through the branch, her arms ached, she had blisters forming on her hands, her neck throbbed, and her ankle was on fire. She took a break to stretch and get some more water, and then she re-attacked. She must have worked for a number of hours, for the light under the forest canopy changed subtly, casting longer shadows that melded with the growing green darkness.

When she had cut three-quarters of the way through, she picked up the branch again and attempted to snap it. This time, it gave with relative ease and a loud *snap*. Evelyn gasped in relief and felt her eyes fill all over again. She'd done it! She'd seen a problem and found a solution! She wasn't helpless after all!

Moving as quickly as she dared, Evelyn took the two lengths of wood and placed them alongside her swollen right ankle. Then she fumbled at her neck for the scarf she wore to protect her throat from the icy cold while flying. It came free, and she gritted her teeth and managed to use it to wrap under and around her boot and the makeshift splint. Once again, pain stabbed through her, and her vision threatened to recede under a sparkling gray nothingness. She bit her lip, took shallow breaths, and hung doggedly onto the shreds of her consciousness. Eventually, she managed to tie a knot just above her kneecap. It wasn't comfortable, not by any stretch of imagination, but it was the best she had.

She sat back again, gasping for breath, but this time triumph rose within her rather than despair or panic. She treated herself to another drink of water and considered her next move. When she found her crew, she'd likely have to move, so maybe she ought to find some kind of crutch that she could use. However, she still really kind of hoped that they'd be nearby enough to come get her, so she decided not to delay any longer. Plus, it was getting dark. She'd vastly prefer not to be alone in this forest in the night. Who knew what kind of wild animals lived in German forests?

That thought decided it. Evelyn took another drink from her flask, (once she found the men, refilling that would be her next order of business) and started in on the exercises she'd learned as a young girl. They served to clear the mind before strenuous psychic work. She hadn't needed them in years, but at this point, she figured they couldn't hurt.

She closed her eyes once again. This time, instead of forcing her rapid breaths to calm, she focused on drawing them out, picturing the rapidly cooling air filling her lungs, gathering up the pain in her body, then pushing it out again. She did this for a count of twenty and then opened her eyes.

The sun had begun to set in earnest, and the light slanted gold and gray through the conifer needles and trunks of the forest that surrounded her. She focused on the light, paying attention to the way it struck her skin, the way it gleamed on the old snow. A breeze rustled through the branches overhead and caressed her cheek. Her arms and torso were comfortably warm, though the bulk of her clothing felt binding. Her legs felt heavy and leaden, and her ankle throbbed with pain. Another deep breath, and just as if she were separating out the sensory streams from two members of a net, Evelyn isolated and compartmentalized the pain. It was still there, pulsing angrily at her, but she had pushed it to the side. She couldn't ignore it, but at least she could work around it.

With the clean, sharp scent of snow in her nostrils and the sounds of the wind in the branches, Evelyn cleared her mind and reached *out*.

It was harder than it should have been. The pain in her leg pulled at her attention, like an animal throwing itself against the bars of her compartmentalization cage. But Evelyn persevered, pushing her consciousness outward, reaching, seeking...

You.

A female mind, powerful, foreign. A flash of shocked triumph...and a grasping, fighting to get a grip on the slippery landscape of a psyche too similar...

Evelyn gasped and broke the contact. Her head slammed backward against the tree trunk from the effort and the surprise. *Who had that been?*

A psychic, clearly, for she had reached out to try and hold onto Evelyn, even as Evelyn fought to wiggle away. A German psychic?

Fear lanced through Evelyn, icy and cold. Psychic girls, though rare, were born all over the world. It stood to reason the Germans would have some of their own. If the US Army could find a use for psychic talents in war, the Nazis probably could as well. Could this girl be out looking for her? And her crewmen?

"Well, if she wasn't before, she is now," Evelyn said out loud, self-disgust joining the fear roiling in her belly. How could she have been so stupid? Reaching out as she had done in the middle of enemy territory was akin to lighting a bonfire and hiring a full orchestra to herald her arrival. Plus, that brief contact would have told the other girl that she wasn't a German since language shaped human thought so much. Psychics didn't necessarily need words to communicate, per se, but the structure of the psychic's language always lingered in the way she formed her thoughts. And if the German psychic spoke English, there was a good chance she would have recognized its flavor in Evelyn's mind. She felt another stab of self-recrimination. What had she been thinking?

"One thing's certain," she muttered to herself again as another terrifying thought iced through her. "I don't want to be here when she arrives." Evelyn had no idea how strong the other girl was. Most psychics didn't have the power to track an individual's location just based on a momentary contact.

But the other girl *had* reached out to hold the connection, and that spoke of training. And when Evelyn retreated, she'd followed, at least for a little ways. So if nothing else, she had a direction. That decided the issue in Evelyn's mind. She had to move.

Of course, there was still the small matter of her injured ankle. Splinting it hadn't made it hurt any less. Though, with the joint stabilized, Evelyn reasoned that she should be able to, at least, move on it, even if it couldn't bear any weight. Maybe if she had a crutch...

She looked around herself, reaching out for more of the tree limbs that had come crashing down with her arrival. Most were twisted or too small to serve. There was one that looked like it might be promising, but it was out of her reach. Evelyn gritted her teeth.

No help for it. She couldn't just sit there and wait for the German psychic to show up with who knows how many of her compatriots. Evelyn took a deep breath and closed her eyes for a moment, praying for strength to anyone who might be listening. Then she opened her eyes, and reaching out with her hands, she began to drag herself through the leaves and detritus toward the larger stick she'd seen.

It wasn't far, all told, but Evelyn had had a bit of a rough day up to that point, and so it was more difficult going than she'd expected. At one point, her hip caught a sharp stone or bit of tree root buried under the snow, and she bit her lip to keep from crying out. This was, of course, in addition to the waves of nauseating pain that pulsed from her ankle with every movement. She tried to tense her leg muscles in order to keep from jouncing the joint too much, but it was no use. Her breathing started to come in ragged gasps as she fought to keep from screaming.

The branch couldn't have been more than fifty feet away, but it felt like an eternity of agony before she was close enough to touch it. Small whimpers of pain issued forth as tears and mucus streamed down her face. She stretched her hand out and just barely grazed the rough bark with her fingertips. With a sob, she tried again. This time, Evelyn managed to hook her fingers into the bark and inch the limb close enough to get her hand around it.

Finally. She could feel the urgency beating against the inside of her skull. How long? How long until that other psychic traced her direction back and found her?

Not long. Not long enough, anyway. So, with much cursing and crying, Evelyn managed to get herself rolled back onto her hands and knees. Her hands shook, worse than before, but she was out of time, so she maneuvered the heavy tree limb up and jammed the end of it into the snow in front of her. It didn't go in very deep, but it was enough for her to hold onto and get her healthy foot underneath herself. Then, with a mighty heave, she pushed herself up.

And nearly fell down again. The concept of balance seemed to have completely fled, along with any calmness. In order to keep from toppling over, Evelyn instinctively put her injured foot down, and the pain lanced up her leg with renewed fire. Bright, sparking spots danced before her eyes, and she was forced to cling to her walking-stick and pant for a few moments before her vision cleared.

But she was up. And that meant she could move.

After a moment's surprise that she'd managed that much, Evelyn squinted at the sky and wished she'd looked at Abram's charts before they'd flown. In any case, west seemed a better option than east, and so she decided to set off in the direction of the afternoon sun that slanted through the leaves.

She reached out with her walking-stick and then followed that up with an experimental hop-step. She didn't fall. It was slow and awkward, but it was progress. Hills would be a challenge, but perhaps she could stay in the low ground.

With one tentative, halting step after another, Evelyn began to move.

* * *

They hadn't been hiking for long when Lina felt her.

It wasn't a pull, per se. It was more of a reaching out, a searching. At first, Lina was so shocked by the suddenness of it that she could barely respond. It was her! The American psychic! And she was reaching out? For what? For her crew? For help?

Lina reached back, pushing her own awareness out, back along the tenuous line that the American girl had extended. A jolt of recognition, a sudden realization of *otherness*, and the American's thought retreated as quickly as it had come.

Lina gasped out loud and reached out her hands as if she would physically hold the connection intact. Her view of the Fallschirmjager in front of her faded as she focused all of her attention and senses on holding on to that fleeting, slippery touch...

Gone.

Like that, the American girl was gone, and Lina cried out in frustration. Strong, warm fingers gently interlaced with her own, and the psychic opened the eyes she hadn't remembered closing.

"Was that her?" Josef asked softly. *We felt your shock, and then you seemed to go elsewhere very quickly, my darling. Are you all right?*

Lina nodded. For no reason that made sense, she felt breathless.

"I couldn't hold the connection," she said, sounding winded. "I am sorry."

"No! Do not be sorry, my dear!" Josef said as he squeezed her hands. "You have proven my theory correct! She *is here*, and now we know that! This is more than I had hoped for. How magnificent you are!"

Heat crept up Lina's face at Wolffs' effulgent praise. But she couldn't help the smile that softly curved her lips, so she squeezed his fingers back in thanks. Kristof, too, gave her a smile and a nod, and the other Fallschirmjager gave her approving looks.

He is right, Kristof said, using the net. *Already, you give us a better lead. Can you tell her direction from here?*

Lina started to say no, but stopped. The American psychic had fled, surely enough, and Lina hadn't been able to hold on to her mind-touch. But she *had* been able to reach after her, and she'd reached in...

Lina closed her eyes and pointed. When she opened them, her finger indicated the same general direction they'd been following.

"This is not precise," she warned them. "But her position lies in that general direction."

"So, we keep moving west, toward the wreckage," Josef said. "We will either find it first, or we will find her. Both cases offer a victory of sorts. Let us continue. Oberhelfer, continue to try and find her."

"I cannot do much," Lina said. "But I will do my best, Herr Stabsfeldwebel." *My abilities do not work like those of a tracking hound,* she added along their private channel. *As much as I want to do what you ask, it may not be possible.*

I understand, Josef replied the same way. *But I have the utmost faith in you, my...Lina.*

As they started off again, Lina couldn't help but wonder what Josef had started to call her. He'd addressed her as "my dear" in his initial enthusiasm, but Lina didn't think that any of the men had thought much about it. Such a mode of address was apparently consistent with Josef's personality, particularly when speaking to a woman who had performed a service for him. None of them had felt the surge of...what was it? Desire, certainly, but also a feeling of pride and belonging that had rocketed down the private link the two of them held. Lina felt her own emotions tangling in response. Something was clearly happening here, between them. The question was, what?

* * *

The sun set far more quickly than Evelyn had anticipated. She was moving slowly. That much she had expected. What she hadn't expected was the terrible, searing pain of her injured ankle. With every halting, hopping step, agony stabbed up through her leg, until her eyes were blind with tears and it was all she could do to keep moving forward.

Evelyn found herself dropping into a kind of focused trance state. She couldn't move far or fast, so she had to move steadily. Nothing mattered but the progress. Her awareness narrowed down to a pinpoint as she moved through a sequence of endless actions.

First, the stick. Push it into the snowy ground. Then, wrap her hands around it, feeling the roughness of the bark through her gloves. Then inhale, hold it. Close eyes, grit teeth, and hop forward on the good leg. Gasp at the pain. Repeat. And repeat again.

Her concentration wavered when her body began to tremble with the evening's chill, preventing her from stabilizing the butt end of her walking stick forward where she wanted to step. She drove it into the icy ground beside her instead and blinked, then looked around.

A soft, purple gloom had risen from the east and wrapped itself around the forest and what she could see of the sky. She was shaking and out of breath. As she stood there, a cutting wind knifed through the branches overhead, rattling them like bones. Evelyn's shivers intensified, and she realized with a sudden horror that she had been sweating inside her heavy flying gear. The sheer effort of pushing herself along, coupled with having to fight through the pain of her injury had made her sweat right through her inner layer.

And now, for the life of her, Evelyn couldn't get warm. Moreover, she didn't have anything with which to start a fire, and if she did, she was afraid that it would only bring the German psychic running. Her breath came faster, steaming in the rapidly cooling air, as panic started to wrap its claws around her throat.

No, she told herself. *Stop, think. You're still alive. Breathe slowly. What do you need? Warmth, rest.*

She looked around again, noticing the configuration of the trees and terrain. Not far away, a deadfall had created a surface for snow to drift upon. A story from her childhood came back to her, and with it, an idea.

South Dakota winters could be brutal. Every year, some unwary soul got lost in a blizzard and died, their bodies missing until the spring thaw. Evelyn's father had told her that once, when he was a boy, he and his uncle had been out feeding livestock when a deadly spring storm kicked up. The day had gone from beautiful and sunny to a complete, zero-visibility whiteout within thirty minutes.

The two men had been forced to shelter beneath a feeding lean-to for a day and a half, until the snow abated. Evelyn's father had told her how they'd used the snow itself as insulation and how by scraping down to the surface of the dirt, they'd been able to keep themselves alive.

Though he had lost the little toes on both feet.

Evelyn pushed that thought away and hobbled toward the dead-fall. The detritus itself had built up around a sheltered area, and then the snow had drifted on top of that. With a silent prayer that she would be able to get back up again, she lowered herself to her seat and began scraping the snow out of the sheltered spot.

When she had cleared out the area under the deadfall (and assured herself that there weren't any wildlife occupants present!), Evelyn thought that she could just fit under there. She spent the rest of the light packing snow up along the sides of her shelter, leaving only a hole large enough to crawl into. She disguised her walking stick as part of the deadfall itself and then gathered up a few arms-length sticks to disguise her entrance.

Her shivering had intensified. She had to get her wet underclothes off. She couldn't do anything about her trousers, of course, thanks to her splint. But she could and did strip off her outer jacket and sweatshirt. Her teeth chattered together as the cold air wrapped around her wet torso. She tried to clamp them together but just succeeded in giving herself a headache. Or more of one, anyway. With hands that shook so badly that she could barely accomplish the task, Evelyn stripped off her sodden undershirt and brassiere. Then she nearly dove back into her heavy outer flying clothing. The cold bit at her exposed skin, and she couldn't seem to get covered up fast enough, but eventually she was wrapped up in warmth again. The shakes continued while she crawled (weeping, gasping at the pain of her ankle) into the makeshift shelter and then placed the sticks over her doorway to disguise its shape. The cold air still flowed in, but Evelyn didn't see any way around that. She curled herself into as small a ball as she could manage and put her exhausted head down on her arms. Despite the cold and the pain of her injury, she was fast asleep within seconds.

* * *

Water dripped all around her. Icy fire pierced her neck just below the ear and ran in a line of agony down the curve of her neck. She radiated heat, and pain wrapped itself all around her. A tiny corner of her mind told her that she needed to get up, needed to move, but it wasn't loud enough to drown out the screaming anguish of her abused nerve endings.

Her skin felt aflame and wrapped in ice, and the shaking wouldn't, couldn't stop.

"Evie."

Light seared into her, through her closed eyelids. She tried to scream, but all that came out of her mouth was a whimpering croak.

"Oh, Evie! Okay, come on. Come on now."

The words didn't make sense. Hands lifted her, jarred her feverish body. Again, she tried to scream. Again, she couldn't. She felt herself gathered close, like a child in its father's arms. But her father wasn't here. He was an ocean away, mourning a lost farm, fearing for a daughter he sent to war.

War. The war. England. *Pretty Cass.* Her crew. The fighters. The fall...

Memory came flooding back, and Evie opened her eyes. The ravaged face of her navigator, Lieutenant Abram Portman, stared down at her. He looked like hell. A long gash ran across his forehead, and blood and dirt mingled all over his unshaven face.

Of course, I can't look all that fresh, either, she realized with the type of hyper-clarity that told her that she was feverish. Every bit of her ached. Except for the leg she'd broken. "Ached" wasn't the right word for how much that hurt. There really wasn't a word for it. She knew, she'd spent most of yesterday trying to find it.

"Evie?" Lieutenant Portman said, his voice ragged and filled with a terrible hope. "Evie, are you all right?"

She tried to shake her head, but the way he had her cradled in his arms prevented this. Plus, she felt an overwhelming lassitude that made moving anything at all incredibly difficult. At least the uncontrollable shaking had stopped. That was something.

"No," she finally whispered. "But I'm glad you're here, sir."

For a second, nothing happened. Evie felt her eyes begin to close again of their own volition. The last thing she remembered seeing was a slow, wide grin splitting the face of Lieutenant Abram Portman. Right before the big, burly navigator from New York City bent his head over her and cried.

* * *

Lina awoke to the cold, clear light of sunrise slanting across her face. Her overlapping tent flaps rattled with the morning breeze as she blinked away the last of an unremembered dream. With a sigh, she sat up inside the crowded space of the one-man tent and tugged her clothing straight as best she could.

You're awake, Josef said into her mind on a mental caress. Joy and desire flooded into her from him and spoke eloquently of how impatiently he'd waited for her.

I am. Did I oversleep? Lina asked, moving aside the tent flap to peek out. The sun was just rising through the trees, and the snow around them gleamed bluish in the first rays of daylight.

No, you needed the rest. We agreed that it would be best to let you sleep.

Annoyance spiked through her mind. She did not need them to coddle her.

No, but we need you sharp, Josef answered her wordless accusation. *You worked harder than any of us yesterday, and we cannot afford to miss any opportunity that may arise. We know our quarry is out here now. Today, you must be ready to catch her if you can.*

I am ready, Lina said mildly. She still felt annoyed, but she told herself sternly to put it away. Josef was right. She wasn't as strong as the *Fallschirmjager*, so she needed to do what was necessary to keep up. With that thought pushing at her, she tidied up her hair and emerged into the camp.

"Good morning, Oberhelfer." Kristof greeted her with a smile. He held out a steaming mug. "Would you like some coffee? It's a bit on the watery side, but it's not bad."

"Thank you," Lina said with a smile as she accepted the mug. Its warmth stung against her cold fingers, but she cradled it close and inhaled the fragrant steam anyway. Kristof nodded and then slowly stepped away, as if reluctant to do so.

In fact, all of the men seemed to be casually drawing near to her. It took her a moment to realize it, but it definitely seemed to be the case. First young Willi brought her water for washing, then Horst, strong and silent, drifted near enough to start taking down her tent. Willi joined him, joking playfully with the older man. Kristof walked past her with a smile and went to confer over the map with Josef, and Werner began to pack up her pack.

"I can do that," she protested softly.

"I don't mind," Werner replied with a smile and shifted his weight closer to her in the snow.

It was the bond, she realized. Their minds craved her net, just as she felt herself wanting to reach toward them all and wrap her consciousness around them again. The only one who didn't seem affected was Josef. She raised her eyes to look at him.

And found him staring back at her with such heat and desire that it brought a blush to her cheeks.

You want to form the net again. That is good. I want it, too, for it serves our mission, and yet, Josef sent over their channel. Once again, his mind felt like the silken touch of a lover inside her skin. She shivered inside her coat. *And yet, I find I do not wish to share you.*

It is not the same, she assured him. *I do not share everything with them, not the way that I do with you.* Her blush deepened as she made this admission. *They are like brothers. You...are something else.*

They yearn to be near you. Are you certain that they view you as a sister? Josef asked, with a bit of arch amusement coloring his thought. Amusement laid in a thin layer over something darker, possessive.

It is only the bond, Lina assured him. She felt certain that her own mind touch carried the impatient asperity she felt. *Being connected mind to mind builds a closeness, even if it is not as all-encompassing as our...connection.*

What word were you going to use? Josef asked, his eyes intense across the smoky campfire where Willi knelt to prepare their breakfast rations.

What?

You changed your thought. I felt it. You would have said a different word. Tell me, my Lina, what should we call what lies between us?

Lina hesitated. It seemed so strange to her. She had always been a rational girl. Exposure to the wild storms of others' emotions had taught her that it was always best to lead with one's intellect. But Josef's mind was so powerful, so compelling, and had been so from the first touch. She couldn't deny that they'd become intertwined over the short time of their acquaintance, and the thought of severing their psychic connection caused her an actual, physical pang. He had become essential to her, and it had happened all at once.

Love, she whispered in the silence of her mind.

Yes, he whispered back.

Joy and terror surged through her, tangling in her mind and threatening to leak out as tears. She swiftly ducked her head over her coffee mug and fell back on her training. She must remain calm, else she could not form a strong net.

"Oberhelfer? Are you well?" It was Willi, looking up at her over the sausages he was frying. She threw him a smile and a nod, not trusting her voice yet.

I love you, Josef sent. *I cannot imagine breathing without you. When this is over, we will find a party official, and we will wed.*

I will marry you, Lina sent, as joy gained ascendance over panic in her mind. *I will marry you, and we will continue this work together.*

She felt his mind start to protest this thought. Of course, he would want her to remain safely at home, to raise their children. But she had a gift, and the Reich had need of her talents. That was why she'd gone to the *Reichsschule* in the first place.

You are right, of course, Josef said. Reluctance soaked his words, but Lina could feel his admission reverberate with sincerity. She witnessed him fight between his loyalty to the Reich's cause and his need to protect her and see her safe. Her own love for him swelled through her.

I will be with you, he said, after a moment. *You are right, we will be together. When we bring back the Ami psychic, the high command will give us anything we want. I will be your escort and your husband, and I will see you safe. My Lina, I will never let anything hurt you.*

I know, she replied, and she blinked rapidly as her eyes threatened to overfill. *But now, we have a job to do. I must link with the rest of the men.*

Lina felt his wordless acquiescence and the brute force of his love for her. She allowed her own love to flow down the link for just a moment longer and then stood up. The eyes of the other Fall-schirmjager turned to her. She gave them a smile.

"Let us re-link," she said, "so that we may be about our business today."

To a man, the Fallschirmjager smiled.

* * *

Lieutenant Portman had carried her somewhere. It couldn't have been far, Evelyn reasoned. She wasn't a small woman. The lieutenant was a burly, stocky guy, but he'd been banged up, too, and he was carrying all their gear besides. He'd brought her to a sheltered spot under a thicket of thorns. Evelyn wasn't certain how he'd found it, but it seemed a better place to hide than her little deadfall. She didn't remember much about the journey there, nor his care of her once they'd slid under the camouflaging thorns. She did remember finally feeling warm.

When she opened her eyes again, the sun was in the process of setting. She pushed herself up to a half-seated position. She felt weak as a newborn kitten.

"How did you find me?" she asked. Her words came out as a raspy whisper. The lieutenant looked up from where he seemed to be digging a hole in the dirt with his knife. A smile creased his dirty face.

"Hey, Evie," he said. He laid down the knife and scooted close enough to put the back of his hand against her forehead. It was an oddly maternal gesture, and it made Evie want to laugh. All she could manage was a weak cough, however.

"Whoa, take it easy there, Evie-girl," Lieutenant Portman said. He reached inside his jacket and pulled out a flask like hers, then tilted it carefully at her lips. She drank greedily, as the water rehydrated her fever-baked tissues.

Lieutenant Portman lowered the flask slowly, then smiled at her as he capped it. "How are you feeling?" he asked.

"Weak," she replied. "But clearheaded. I had a fever?"

"Yeah," he said. "I found you huddled up under a snow-packed deadfall. I never would have seen you if you hadn't left your shirt and...ah...brassiere out in the snow beside the entrance." Evelyn could have sworn she saw him blush swarthily under the dirt and stubble.

"I did?" she asked, feeling a fair amount of mortification color her own cheeks. "That is embarrassing. I remember feeling like I needed to hide, but I couldn't go on any farther. I think...I think I knew I was ill."

"I'm not happy you were ill, but I'm happy it made you leave a sign. I would never have found you otherwise," the lieutenant said. "You did a good job of hiding...except for that."

"I didn't want her to find me," Evelyn said softly, idly.

"Who?"

"What?"

"You didn't want who to find you?" Lieutenant Portman asked, his voice intensifying. He scooted closer. "Evie, did you see Nazis out here? Are they looking for us?"

"No, I didn't see them," she said. "But yes, they're out here. And they're looking for us. Well...they're looking for me." She slumped slightly. Lieutenant Portman reached out and helped her lie back down.

"I was so stupid," she whispered, tears coming to her eyes. She blinked angrily, infuriated at her own weakness, but the tears just kept coming. She drew in a deep, shaky breath and plunged on.

"I was alone, and hurt, and scared. I thought, if I could just find the crew, I couldn't have been the only one who survived. So I reached out. Only I didn't find you, or anyone else. I found *her.*"

"Her?"

"Her. A German psychic. She tried to hold me, to follow me back, but I was able to break contact. I think...I think I surprised her. But she definitely knows I'm here, and she's definitely looking for me. And I very much doubt she's alone."

Lieutenant Portman took a deep breath.

"All right," he said. "Well, that complicates our situation a bit."

More tears flooded her eyes. She couldn't see.

"I know, I'm so sorry," she whispered.

"Evie, no," he said, brushing a hand across her hair. "Shhhh, it's not your fault. You didn't know. How could you know they had a psychic nearby? It's nobody's fault. It just is. Now we have to figure out how to deal with it, all right?"

Evelyn nodded, sniffled mightily, and then nodded again.

"Atta-girl," Lieutenant Portman said as he patted her shoulder. "All right, so here's the question, you made it down, and I made it down. I gotta think there's a chance some of the other guys did too, you know?"

"I hope so," Evelyn said. "I would like to think so."

"Right. So if it were me, I'd be trying to make my way toward the wreckage of the *Cass.* I gotta think that's what they'd try to do, too. Though if there are Nazis out there, they might do the same. But then, that's all the more reason to go."

"What? Why?" Evelyn couldn't imagine anything that would make going toward the German psychic palatable.

"To warn them. If they're heading for the *Cass*, and the Nazis are out looking for us, then it's a trap. We know that, so we have to warn them."

Evelyn was certain there was a flaw in this logic somewhere, but in her fatigued, weakened state, she couldn't find it for the life of her. So, she simply nodded and laid back on the makeshift pillow that the lieutenant had fashioned for her.

"We'll wait the rest of today, stay here the night," the lieutenant said as he shifted across the ground back to the hole he'd been digging. "Then we'll start out early tomorrow. I have a fair idea of where they might have ended up. We're not far. I think we can get there before nightfall and then hole up, watch for a while, see who shows up."

"That sounds reasonable," Evelyn said. Her eyes felt heavy, and a quite lassitude stole over her. She realized that she should be ravenous, but all she felt was the aching need for sleep. Her eyes drifted closed.

A sharp, stinging slap to her cheek recalled her to herself. She forced her eyelids open and stared at the lieutenant with as much anger as she could summon.

"Evie!" he said, sounding panicky. "Evie, stay with me! Don't go to sleep, Evie."

"Why not?" she asked, her voice sounding high and querulous, even to her own ears.

"Because, you're cold and in shock, and hypothermia could kill you before I can build a fire!" he said. "C'mon, Evie-girl, just sit up for me again. You were doing so well! I'm sorry, I shoulda gotten this fire built..."

He pulled her up rather roughly and propped his own pack behind her. Then he went back to frantically digging in the dirt. Evelyn giggled, sound burbling up like bubbles from a soda fountain.

"That's not a fire; that's a hole in the ground," she said. This time, she could hear her words slurring. She blinked and tried to make her eyes focus in the fading light.

"Digging down so that if the Nazis are nearby, they won't see it," Lieutenant Portman said. He scratched at the dirt a few more times and then wiped his knife on his trouser leg and sheathed it. He went to work with his hands next, scooping out handfuls of sandy earth until he had a hole approximately the size of his head.

"You're gonna build a fire in there?" she asked.

"Yep," he said. "I figure it's gotta be better than doing it out in the open."

"How's a Brooklyn boy know so much about stuff like this?"

He grinned at her and reached for a small pile of twigs she hadn't noticed before.

"I used to spend summers with my cousins on my uncle's farm upstate," he said. "He didn't like it when we killed his ducks, so we'd have to cook and eat them out in the field."

"Duck is good," she said. "Pheasant is better," she added, feeling a pang of homesickness that may have actually been hunger.

"I'd settle for squirrel right now," the lieutenant muttered. "But we'll work with what we have."

"What do we have?" Evelyn asked, interest sharpening her voice. He had food?

"Not much," he admitted. "But I do have a tin of sardines I threw in my pocket. And we have water. We can boil down the sardines and make some broth and soup. Best idea I've got."

"Sounds wonderful," she said bravely. He looked up at her with a grin and a chuckle, and then for no reason at all, they both started to laugh. A little bit at first, but then the laughter grew into belly-holding, gasping gales of mirth. Neither of them could stop until their eyes were streaming with tears. Evelyn swiped at her running nose with her sleeve and huffed a last few chuckles. Lieutenant Portman wiped his eyes and let out a long sigh as he returned to arranging his kindling and tinder in the pit he'd dug.

"Tell me something, Evie," he said as the echoes of their laughing fit faded. Evie smiled and opened her stubbornly-closing eyes again.

"Mmmhmm?"

"How come you haven't linked us yet?"

Evelyn blinked. The truth was that she hadn't thought about it. She'd been too preoccupied with staying alive and not losing her mind from the pain of her leg. That was one part of it, of course. She didn't want to expose the lieutenant to her agony. She could *probably* compartmentalize it such that he wouldn't feel it too badly...but then, maybe not. She really was weak. That fever had done a number on her. Even now, fatigue dragged at the edges of her mind, whispering to her to close her eyes...relax...sleep...

"Evie?"

Her eyes snapped open, and she shifted slightly, pressing her lips together against the pain that rocketed through her body with each movement.

"I'm awake," she said, blinking rapidly.

Lieutenant Portman looked narrowly at her for a moment, but then turned back to his fire. Evelyn watched as he finished laying in the kindling and tinder just so. He then pulled a flip-top lighter from inside his coat and began striking it. He angled his body to hold the tiny flame into the kindling, and Evelyn found herself holding her breath while she watched and hoped that that tiny flame would catch.

It did. Slowly at first, but then with growing strength, the lieutenant's fire licked up along the twigs he'd so carefully placed. A thin, barely-there wisp of smoke began to curl upward toward the tangled branches of their thicket shelter.

"I want to," she said softly, her eyes never leaving the nascent fire. "The bond *is* pushing at me, but I'm afraid. I don't know how strong I am right now, and I don't want to transmit the pain of my injury to you."

"What?" The lieutenant looked up, anger writ large on his features. "Evie, are you kidding me? I can help you, and you're not letting me? What is wrong with you? Link us!"

"No, you don't understand..." she said, shaking her head in frustration.

"I understand you're a woman, and you're hurt! You're maybe the bravest woman I've ever met, but that doesn't change the fact that as a man, I'm supposed to help you however I can! Damnit, Evie, don't be stubborn with me on this. Just do it."

"I don't think..."

Lieutenant Portman had apparently heard enough because he cursed softly under his breath and reached out to take her hand. The moment skin touched skin, the bond within Evelyn leapt at him, and the psychic connection snapped into place between them.

Evelyn reeled, falling back onto the makeshift pillow. Abram's consciousness flowed into hers like water into a desiccated husk. Her whole body shuddered with the sensory overload of it as the longed-for connection re-established itself.

"Sonofa...sorry Evie," Abram breathed. "Motherf...That does hurt."

I'm sorry, Evie thought to him, relishing the feel of his mental landscape, and the way it fit with hers. For the first time since being thrown out of the *Pretty Cass,* she felt almost good. Still, she couldn't let Abram carry her pain. She began to gather it back in to herself, to wall it away from him.

"No," he said sharply, his voice rough. He gripped her hand tighter, pulled himself closer to her. "Don't pull that back from me. I can handle it."

I know, she assured him, even as she continued to compartmentalize the pain. *But you have to keep your strength up, or else neither of us is moving anywhere.*

I can handle it, Abram insisted and pushed at her barricade. *It'll be easier if we share the load.*

Evelyn could have held him off. He was only a man, and despite the practice he'd had on their many missions together, he was no match for a trained psychic. But the truth was, she was simply exhausted. From the injury and the fever that followed. From the fear and the cold. From the relief of finally finding one of her crew, at no longer being completely alone in the dark of the German forest. All of these factors had taken a terrible toll on her, and so, in the end, she acquiesced and let Abram share her pain.

"All right," she breathed, and she squeezed his hand once in thanks. He returned the squeeze and then turned back to the fire as she let her eyes drift closed. The tiny fire was starting to warm their little thicket, and it was almost cozy.

Don't sleep, he reminded her.

I won't, she promised. *But with the link in place, I can rest more than I did. I will keep my alertness with you. Tell me what you're doing?*

Can't you see?

I can, but this will help me stay awake. And it's good practice, honestly, she said. *Just keep up a running narration for me. That will help build the strength of the link, which we'll need if we're going to be traveling linked like that.*

All right, he thought. *I'm getting out the sardines, and then I'll...Shit. Ah. Sorry, Evie...*

Sir, she sent on a pulse of humor, *at this point, I think it's all right if we indulge in a little swearing. This is a hell of a fucking predicament, after all.*

Evie! he said, looking over at her with his dark eyes full of surprised mirth as he snorted a laugh through his nose. *Where did you learn to swear like that?*

Evelyn giggled out loud, even while her face flamed up in a blush. *Ugh,* she thought, *I hate it when I giggle. I sound like I'm twelve years old. I learned from ranch hand friends of my father. After we lost our farm in '32, we moved in nearer to the city. My father sought work on some of the local cattle ranches nearby. Sometimes my brothers and I would go out with him and do odd jobs. It was good money, while it lasted.*

Abram, too, was chuckling. *You sound like a Brooklyn harridan. I love it. Now, we have one problem. I don't have anything in which to boil water to make our broth. We're just going to have to eat these sardines as is.*

I'm hungry enough to, Evelyn said, though she couldn't disguise her distaste at the thought. Fish, unless it was fresh caught mountain trout, preferably from her own hook, had never been her favorite. Canned, salted fish, packed in oil seemed...unsavory.

But hunger, as they say, is the best sauce. There were five of them, little silvery bodies packed in tight, glistening in the light from their fire. Abram insisted that Evelyn take three, and he swallowed the remaining two seemingly whole.

Though it was probably the height of silliness, Evelyn felt obliged to try and eat like a lady. She propped herself up as best she could, using Abram's assistance when he offered it. As they had no utensils, she was reduced to pinching one of the slippery fish between her fingers and lifting it to her mouth.

It tasted like an explosion of salt under a thin slick of oil. Evelyn gave an experimental chew and found it to have a meaty, smoky taste. Of course, it was fishy and oily, too, but in that moment, she enjoyed it as much as if it *had* been a rainbow trout fresh off her own hook.

Good? Abram asked, grinning at her as he sucked the last of the oil off his fingers.

Delicious, Evelyn confirmed.

Good. Eat them all. You need the strength, he thought. Evelyn would have liked to protest, but the combination of grinding fatigue and pain-laced hunger made her hesitate. Plus, one look at the pugnacious set of Abram's jaw told her clearly he would hear no argument. So she ate, chewing slowly so as to make the two remaining sardines last as long as possible.

"When I was a kid," Abram said out loud, speaking softly, "my dad lost his job for a while. After the crash of '29. That was the first time us kids moved out to my uncle's farm. First time I was ever in the country, just a scared city kid who'd never been hungry before. I learned what it felt like that summer, though. My uncle didn't like us much. Didn't approve of his baby sister marrying a Jew, I guess."

Evelyn looked up at Abram, but his eyes remained fixed on the tiny fire he'd made. She sent him a pulse of affection and support though the bond, but he seemed too lost in his thoughts to notice.

"Anyway, he didn't give us much to eat. I was the oldest, so it was up to me to take care of the little ones. I used to sneak them whatever I could squirrel away. My cousins helped, some. They're good people. They didn't like their mean old man much, either." At that, he looked over at Evelyn with a grin that came nowhere near his eyes. Evelyn felt the deep sadness welling up inside him.

"He sounds terrible," Evelyn murmured.

"He did his best," Abram shrugged. "Ma said he was never the same after the war. He got shot up in Belleau Wood, came home, and started drinking. Never quit. He took us in when it counted."

It's not your fault he didn't like you, she thought to him. She never would have presumed to say something so personal out loud, but the intimacy of the psychic bond allowed for much more personal communications.

I know, Abram said. *It wasn't his fault. It was just a hard thing. I tried so very hard, but I was just a kid. Just another mouth to feed.*

So how'd you get here? Evelyn asked, trying to change the subject.

Abram shrugged. *I was good in school. Especially math. I got a scholarship to NYU, studying cartography. When the war broke out, the recruiter said that with my background, I'd be a natural as a navigator, since I liked maps so much. So here I am. What about you?*

I was at the teachers' college, Evelyn said. *Captain Ledoux came by one afternoon and asked if any of us with talent would join up. "Do my part." I talked to my parents, and we all agreed that it was only right that I go. I think my mother secretly hoped I'd be able to look after my little brother. He's in the Marines.*

Where?

The Pacific somewhere. I don't know exactly. My parents got letters for a while...

Doesn't mean anything. You know how sporadic mail can be, and that's assuming he's got time to write. Those boys over there have a big job. I'm sure he's fine. No news is good news, Abram thought, staunchly.

I know, she said. *Thank you.*

They finished their meager meal in silence, both physical and mental. After a while, Abram stirred himself from his contemplation of their little fire.

"We'd better sleep," he said, speaking out loud in order to break the spell of lassitude that had come over them both. "I'll bank these coals so we'll have heat all night. You should be warm enough that it'll be safe. Tomorrow's going to be a long day. We'll head out at first light. I don't think the crash site is far, so we'll find a place nearby where we can hole up, get the lay of the land. See if any of our boys are around with the same idea we had."

We should have decided on a meet up plan before we bailed out, Evelyn thought, her eyes already closing. *I'm sorry. I should have seen to it.*

We all had bigger problems on our minds at the time, Abram thought back. *No use beating your head about it now. That will be good information for when we get back to Ridgeway, though.*

*When we get back...*she thought. And on that thought, sleep finally reared up and claimed her mind.

* * * * *

Chapter Nine

L ina was frustrated. Another day down, tramping about this benighted forest with no sign of the psychic or any of the downed airmen. She knew Josef and the others weren't bothered by their lack of progress, but she was. Deep inside, Lina felt a great drive to succeed, to find the Ami psychic, to interrogate her, and to gain the intelligence her countrymen so desperately needed to win this war.

Patience, my Lina, Josef said into her mind for the thousandth time. *This is the way of the hunt. We stalk our quarry, let her run herself out, and then we move in for the kill. Our ancestors did the same, felling great herds of ancient deer and mammoths across this primeval land. Now we follow in their traditions. Though our quarry is weaker, she is craftier, but in the end, patience wins out over all. It is the hunter's greatest weapon. No one can escape time.*

Lina smiled down at her boots as she stepped over yet another tree root. *Poetic, my love, but what if time decides to ally with the Ami girl instead of with us? What if she uses this time to heal and escape?* She'd been hurt. Lina knew that. It had taken her a while to realize it, but she had definitely felt the sear of pain, ragged and raw around the edges of the mysterious woman's mind.

Doubtful, he said. *Wounded prey is easy prey. She will be slowed by whatever it is that you felt. We are healthy and quick. It will not be long before we find something.*

Lina had always heard that wounded prey was the deadliest, but she decided not to push any further. Josef sounded so splendidly confident in the essential truths of his argument, and she had no desire to create needless discord between them. Besides, if the Ami girl was going to be dangerous, it was likely going to be through her psychic powers, and Lina was more than prepared to deal with trouble of that kind.

Up ahead, Werner came to a sudden stop. *Halt*, he thought, the order crisp through the lines of Lina's net. *Make no sound.*

Lina held her breath, her body quivering with tension. Slowly, so slowly, she pushed her mind outward, using Werner's awareness as a springboard, and with the lightest of touches, scanned the area immediately in front of them. Through Werner's eyes she could see a break in the trees ahead. A clearing, though it didn't smell like a meadow. It smelled like hell and burnt metal.

Werner crept closer, moving slowly and quietly between the pine trunks. The ground underfoot changed from soft, snow-wet leaf-fall to crisp, dry ash. Something had burned here. Something large.

A moment later, he saw it. A twisted, scorched shape of metal that may have once been something magnificent. It had impacted near the treeline ahead, shearing off the tops of the pines on the other side of the clearing before gouging deep furrows in the earth as it came skidding to a halt.

The cockpit was gone, buried in the earth and compressed beyond survivability by the impact. The entire wreck reeked of smoke, and black char lines ran along the entirety of the shape. Werner squinted, and he could barely make out the shape of a woman's body painted on the side. Beneath that, he could see the letters P-R-E-T-T-Y C-A-S-S.

He started to form the shape of the sounds, reaching back to the English he'd studied in grade school when something else caught his attention. Movement, there in the grass by the wreck.

We have reached the wreckage of the American bomber, Werner thought back through the net. *I can see the scorch marks through the trees.*

Someone is alive there, Lina reported, *not the psychic. A man. I dare not probe deeper. If he has been working with the psychic, he may feel me should I try.*

Can you get a location? Josef asked, all trace of affection gone from his tone. This was the hunt. This was what they'd come for.

Directly ahead, Lina said. *About a hundred meters from Werner's position.*

Fan out, the stabsfeldwebel ordered. *Let us take him alive, my brothers. But we need not be overly gentle in doing so.*

* * *

The journey wasn't pleasant, but it was infinitely better than struggling along on her own. At first, Abram wanted to carry her, but Evelyn convinced him that they'd be better off if he didn't completely exhaust himself. So he walked ahead, scouting their route, while she hobbled along behind with the aid of her stick. They stopped frequently. Abram said it was so that they could look and listen, be prepared for what lay ahead. Evelyn didn't need the psychic link to know it was so she could rest.

I can go farther, she protested at one such stop.

Certainly, and so can I, but I'd rather not blunder into your group of Nazis, Abram replied breezily.

They're hardly my *Nazis,* she shot back, allowing her mind touch to carry a sting of asperity. His humor came back at her in a wave that washed over her. She gave him the mental equivalent of a shove in return. She was hot and sweaty from her exertions, and her leg ached abominably, and while she appreciated the rest, she didn't need him coddling her. His good-natured response just served to ratchet her annoyance factor up higher. Evelyn had been taught to be sweet and to control her emotions, but the events of the past few days had served to fray her patience into oblivion. She just wanted to find the rest of her crew and go home.

If any of them lived.

And if she could escape the Nazis. *Her* Nazis. The ones she'd alerted just as surely as if she'd flown a banner over the forest. Perhaps, she realized, it wasn't really Abram with whom she was angry.

She started to say something along those lines when he started moving again. So Evelyn settled for reaching out down the psychic link with a feeling of apology. She felt his acceptance and reassurance. In much better spirits, they moved on.

Abram had found a game trail that wound westward through the forest. It was far easier for them both than cutting through the trees. For one thing, Abram could see farther, and for another, there was less in the way of obstacles for Evelyn to negotiate. The trail took them up to the top of a ridge and then followed along the crest of it. Here and there, Evelyn could look out and see the forest spreading along the valleys on either side. It really was beautiful country. So very different from her own Black Hills. She was used to craggy granite mountains and forests of green-black pine. Here, the hills seemed rounder and the trees greener.

Stop! Abram's command whip cracked down the lines of her link, and Evelyn stumbled to a halt in response. He stood perhaps fifty feet in front of her, and slowly, as she watched, he sank to his knees and then flattened himself to his belly. Fear skittered along her nerves, tightening low in her belly. Abram inched forward in his prone position and then looked back and waved her forward.

She moved slowly, hoping that by doing so, she would minimize the noise of her clumsy, hobbling steps. When she came up to where Abram's feet lay, he motioned to her to get down as well. It hurt, pain stabbing through her ankle and up her whole leg as she first knelt, then carefully lowered her body down to lay beside his. When she did so, he handed her the miniature field glasses he'd found in his parachute survival pouch.

There, do you see? he asked her silently. *Through the trees, down into the valley. A line of smoke...*

The Cass! Evelyn said, her mind both exultant and horrified. The fuselage of the ruined Flying Fortress was recognizable, but only just. Her form had been grotesquely twisted and torn by the impact with the trees and the ground, and all that was left of her cockpit was a crumpled ruin. If the pilots had been in that space when they hit, Evelyn didn't see how it could be possible that they survived.

Yes, Abram thought back, his mind echoing her sadness. *Now look aft, toward the tail. Do you see?*

Evelyn obeyed his instructions, scanning the glasses back toward the mostly intact tail section. As she did so, her eyes caught it, a tiny movement in the long grass of the field and a shape...

A human, a man, lying on his side, facing away from them. He wore a leather jacket, much like the one on Evelyn's own shoulders, and what looked like it might have been the remains of a parachute harness. It was hard to see at first, but when he moved his head, Evelyn caught sight of a red curl.

Sean.

Her breath caught, and only Abram's hand heavy on her shoulder kept her prone. She wanted to struggle up to her feet and push her way through the rest of the ragged fringe of trees. The bond pushed at her, urged her to reach her consciousness out toward the man sleeping beside the embers of a fire.

It may be a trap, Abram told her.

It's Sean! Evelyn's mind wailed at him.

You don't know that, he said, repressively. *It could be one of them dressed in his clothes. They could be lying in wait nearby. I don't like it. It looks too neat. And Sean would know better than to light a fire in a clearing that could be seen for miles away.*

He could be hurt! He could be feverish, like me. I know it's him, Abram! The bond is pulling at me so hard, it can't be anyone but him! We can't just leave him!

No, we won't leave him. But neither will we go blundering in there like a bunch of fools. Link with him, tell him we're here, see what he can tell us. If it's a trap, he'll know.

That made sense. Evelyn pulled in a breath of relief. Abram wasn't going to suggest that they back away, leaving Sean alone and scared. Having felt the hell of that fear-soaked loneliness, Evelyn couldn't imagine sentencing anyone, let alone one of her crew, to that.

The instant she let her control relax, the bond leapt from her, as if it were some sort of invisible predator. Her awareness stretched out, arrowing through the trees and across the tall grass toward the twisted metal and the man who lay beside it.

Sean! Evelyn exulted as the link, now a true net, clicked into place. The familiar contours of the flight engineer's mental landscape filled her awareness, sending pleasure flooding through her brain and down the net to include Abram as well. In the snow beneath the trees, Evelyn shivered in near-ecstasy.

Evie? Sean's thought was weak and thready, as if he were in tremendous pain. *Evie, no! Go, run!* And then, with all the force she'd taught him to use, he shoved her out. She gasped out loud, unable to stop herself as his unexpected push broke her concentration, and with it, her link to the lieutenant as well.

"Evie?" Abram murmured, alarm in his tone. Nearby, snow crunched under a footfall.

A single man stepped into the clearing. He was tall and fair and dressed in the green of the Luftwaffe's winter uniforms. On his chest, he wore the badge of an eagle clutching a swastika. He held his empty hands out from his sides.

"Miss Psychic," he called in accented English. "We know that you are out there. I give you my word that if you reveal yourself, no further harm will come to this American airman."

Shaken, Evelyn reached out and re-established the link with the lieutenant. *Sean shoved me out. Told me to run. What do we do?*

"On the other hand, Miss Psychic, if you do not reveal yourself, you will be forced to watch as we break all of the bones in your friend's hands and feet. And then we will find you anyway. You see, we are not without psychic resources of our own."

The German psychic! Evelyn thought, her heart sinking. *That must be why I didn't sense him here. She must be shielding him.*

Them, Abram corrected her, his own mind voice sounding strange and strained. Evelyn turned her attention to him and realized that he was focused on a single, pinpoint sensation: the barrel of a 7.92mm Mauser pressed against the nape of his neck.

"Do not try," another accented voice said softly. "If you try to touch me, your friend here will lose his head, and we will still hurt your other friend very badly. I am not alone in these woods."

Evie...Abram started to say. She could feel his mulish determination rising within him. He was a scrapper from Brooklyn. He thought this Nazi prick was bluffing. He could move his leg, just so, sweep the other guy's stance, make him fall...

"No," Evelyn said, both mentally and physically. "Do nothing! I am here." She put her hands against the cold ground and pushed herself up to her knees. Though she tried her best, she was unable to suppress a grunt of pain as she did so.

Instantly, two other Germans materialized out of the trees and reached under her arms, helping her to her feet. The one who had spoken grinned, reached down, and roughly pulled Abram up as well.

"We will join your friend in the clearing," he said. "Willi, Werner, help her walk. You, my good friend," he added to Abram, "will walk in front of me, with your hands in the air like a good boy."

Evelyn could feel Abram's anger radiating down the lines of their link. She shrank back from it, severed the connection. What had she done? What was she supposed to have done? She could no more let them torture Sean and shoot the lieutenant than she could do it herself. She knew she had done the only thing she could...

So why did she feel like such a traitor?

The Germans brought them through the trees and out into the open clearing. The tall blond one smiled at their approach and beckoned them forward. "Put that one here, next to this one," he directed in English, nudging Sean with his boot. The flight engineer began to thrash, and the blond German kicked him in the stomach without even looking down. Evelyn let out a little cry of protest.

The blond German smiled.

"Ah, you do not like that, do you, miss? Well, let us understand one another, then. Your friends' treatment will be directly correlated to the level of cooperation you provide to me and my specialist. Do we understand one another?"

"You should address me, not her," the lieutenant said, his voice rough and angry. "I'm senior here."

The blond German raised an eyebrow and spoke quickly in German. One of the men holding Evelyn let go of her and stepped over to grab roughly at the lieutenant's hands. Evelyn watched as he wrenched Lieutenant Portman's hand down and forced him to spin around. While the lieutenant faced their smiling German captor over the barrel of his rifle, the other one tied his wrists together behind his back. Then he grabbed the lieutenant by the collar and kicked at his legs, throwing him down on the ground next to Sean, who rolled to try and see what was happening.

Misery flooded Evelyn. What had she done?

"I will speak with you presently, Lieutenant," the blond German said, once the navigator was down on the ground. "Right now, I am interested in this young lady." He turned his head and looked at Evelyn again. Lieutenant Portman started to say something else, but the soldier that had found them in the woods kicked him, hard, in the face. Evelyn cried out again and reached out toward him, only to find herself restrained by the iron-hard arms of the blond German.

"I am a reasonable man, Miss," he said, his slight accent growing just a touch thicker. "I do not wish to treat anyone in a rough manner, let alone a lady. But I require cooperation, and I will have it. It is your choice as to whether I must treat you ill to get it or not."

For just a moment, Evelyn considered fighting back. She could strip his mind bare, the way she'd done with the men who'd assaulted her and Mary in London. She could even, eventually, probably do the same to all...five of the German soldiers she counted now in the clearing. But judging by the way the soldiers held their rifles pointed at both Sean and the lieutenant, she didn't think that either of her men would survive the battle.

"You are right. It is not a good idea," the blond German said.

Evelyn looked up at him, startled. He chuckled and let his hands drop.

"No," he said. "I am a man and, therefore, not favored with your gifts. I am, however, conversant with them, and I know that you have your own defenses. You wear a warrior's uniform. A warrior would at least consider using her abilities to try and escape. So I have planned for this. We are not without defenses of our own. Any attempt to psychically harm me and mine will result in failure for you and the deaths of your men. Do you understand?"

Evelyn felt the blood leave her face. Of course. The German psychic who had shielded them from her senses earlier. She would be protecting them now. Her mouth felt suddenly dry with fear as she looked into the blond German's pale eyes. Slowly, unwilling to trust her voice, she nodded.

"Good. Now that we understand one another, let us repair to a more comfortable location?"

Someone shoved a cloth hood down over Evelyn's face. The last thing she heard was Sean screaming her name, and then her mind exploded in pain.

* * *

L ina gasped as the psychic hood took effect. By all the heavens, this Ami psychic was *strong!* She could feel her attention and consciousness being pulled by the device, which required psychic energy commensurate with its victim's power. She reached out with one hand and steadied herself on the frame of the wrecked bomber and sent out a pulse of message to her Fallschirmjager.

The hood on the Ami girl requires most of my energy. I must drop our connection, she sent on a pulse of need as she screwed her eyes shut in concentration. Without waiting to hear any sort of acknowledgement, she dropped the link...except for that with Josef. That link had become like air to her and severing it never even crossed her mind. Everything else that she had, though, she channeled into the device that Willi had just thrown over the American girl's head.

"Oberh-h-helfer?" Horst asked, his tone worried. He reached out one hand but didn't quite touch her. "Are y-y-you w-w-well?"

Lina breathed in slowly through her nose, then exhaled and nodded with a tiny smile. "Yes," she said. "Thank you. It's just...she is very strong. I thought I was prepared, but it seems that I will have to focus almost entirely on maintaining the feedback loop the hood creates."

"She is down on her kn-kn-knees," Horst said, as he peered around the twisted metal that had shielded them from the dramatic interactions between their commander and the Americans. "I can signal the stabsfeldwebel. Perhaps we m-m-may a-a-approach."

Josef hadn't wanted Lina to be visible, just in case the Americans had someone nearby with a rifle. Lina had told him that she sensed no one, but he would permit no argument. Her safety was paramount. Since Lina was confident that she could run the device from a short distance away, she'd agreed. But now, having felt the way that the hood demanded so much of her, Lina thought that a little more proximity might make things worlds easier.

"Yes, please," she said softly. And then, before he could move, she laid a hand on Horst's arm.

"I am sorry," she said, "that I had to drop the connection. I know you don't enjoy speaking...but your mind is among the fastest I have ever known. That is why you stutter. Please don't feel self-conscious around me, my friend."

A slow flush crept up the hauptgefraiter's face, and he gave her a quick nod. Then he turned and stepped out away from the wreckage and into Josef's eyeline.

Lina could have asked Josef directly, of course, but she still wasn't certain she wanted everyone to know of the depth of connection between them. She felt his assent, however, as soon as he saw Horst's hand signals asking the question. As soon as the hauptgefraiter turned toward her with a nod, she reached out for his steadying arm and allowed him to help her pick her way through the twisted metal and back toward her beloved and his prisoners.

"Oberhelfer," Josef said as they approached. His smile was carefully professional, but his mental caress made her shiver. "Congratulations! Your bluff worked phenomenally well, judging by the Ami girl's reaction when Willi hooded her."

"What have you done to her?"

Lina looked down, startled, at the man who'd asked the English question in ugly, furious tones. One of the prisoners, the one with red hair. The one she'd found when they first approached the wreckage. The one who'd been subdued and functioned as bait for the psychic girl now lying in a heap nearby.

"She is unharmed," Lina said, carefully articulating the English words. She hadn't used the language much since leaving school. "She is wearing a hood to control her psychic abilities..." She gasped, then, as Josef charged forward and booted the captive squarely in the face.

Blood fountained from his nose, and the other American prisoner started to struggle against his own bonds. He got a kick for his efforts, too, from Kristof. Josef backed up a step and took Lina by the elbow, turning her away from the two prisoners as the other men moved in to continue the beating.

"You need not answer questions from such as they," Josef said softly. "They will not address you again."

"I do not mind—" Lina started to say. Josef cut her off with a raised hand.

"I do," he said, his voice harsh. "They are killers, Lina. They are the evil that bombs our cities. They rain fire and death down on the ones we love. They have no right to address you. Do not concern yourself with them. You must concentrate on the girl."

Lina nodded, slowly, and allowed herself to be led slightly away.

"I wanted to tell you. She is much stronger than I had anticipated. I will need to remain in close proximity to her."

"How close?" Josef asked.

"A few meters. Within the same room. I just...it is tiring because the hood draws from *my* energy."

"Of course, whatever you need, my dear," the stabsfeldwebel reached out and stroked her upper arm lightly. "I do not recommend that you touch her because we do not yet know whether she is capable of physical violence, and I will not risk you."

"I am safe enough," Lina assured him as she leaned ever so slightly into the caress. "Especially with you near."

I will always be near, my love, he promised her. Lina smiled and despite everything, felt as if she might just drown in the blue of his eyes.

* * * * *

Chapter Ten

Josef decided they would make camp there in the trees that ringed the clearing. Lina knew he didn't realistically think any other surviving members of the bomber crew would turn up, but he figured it didn't hurt to be close, just in case. And Lina also knew he didn't want to take the American psychic back until she'd had a chance to be thoroughly interrogated by Lina herself. His fear was that if they brought the girl back and turned her over to the party leadership, or even to the Luftwaffe command, she would be lobotomized before he'd had a chance to show how useful she could be as a source of intelligence.

But for that, he needed Lina to get inside the Ami girl's head. And that was proving difficult. Lina still couldn't believe how much of her attention the damping hood required. She hadn't even been able to help with setting up the camp. Rather, she'd simply watched as the American girl was tied hand and foot (which, apparently, was painful. She'd been badly injured, enough that the pain spiked through the damping hood to Lina), then carried over to the spot Josef had selected for a camp. Lina had followed closely, her eyes only half-focused on the world around her, as the majority of her consciousness was engaged within.

The psychic damping hood worked by enforcing a sensory feedback loop on its victim. However, it required another psychic to double the psychic sensing inputs back on to the victim so she couldn't break her consciousness loose. It prevented the victim from transmitting or receiving from everyone except she who held the loop. It also overwhelmed her with her own psychic power. It was effective, but it was a lot of work for Lina.

By the time the sun had started to set, the men had a camp set up, complete with a tent for Lina and her captive. The other American prisoners found themselves blindfolded and tied to separate trees so that they could not communicate with one another. Horst stood silent guard over them both.

"Let us take the American psychic into the tent," Josef said out loud to Lina, startling her into a little jump.

"All right," Lina said, her voice weak. Josef nodded to young Willi, and he lifted the American girl in his arms. Josef gestured to Lina to go first, Willi and the Ami girl next, and then he followed them into the largest canvas tent they'd brought.

Inside, Lina could see they'd set up a camp bed, a table, and several chairs. Willi set the girl down on a rug near the bed and took the precaution of tying her bound hands to the bedpost. Then he gave both Josef and Lina a respectful nod and left, letting the tent flap fall closed behind him.

Lina turned to Josef, and for the first time, she let the despair she felt show on her face.

"She is so *strong,*" she breathed, sinking down to a seat on the camp bed. Josef pulled off his leather gloves and sat beside her. The mattress dipped under his weight, and it forced Lina to lean toward him. He wrapped one arm tenderly around her shoulders and kissed the top of her head.

"So are you, my love," he whispered into her hair. "It will take time, perhaps, but you can break into her mind. I know you can do it. What do you need? I will give everything I have to aid you in this task."

Lina drew a ragged breath.

"I don't...I don't know. Sleep, perhaps. And food. I cannot keep the hood on her all the time because it requires so much of my strength."

"Would unconsciousness work?" Josef asked. "We have chloroform."

Lina wanted to ask why on Earth they were carrying a powerful anesthetic, but she was too relieved at the prospect to do much more than nod. Josef smiled, kissed her head one more time, and then stood.

"I will return shortly," he said. "Do what you can in the meantime."

Lina nodded again and lay back on the bed. She closed her eyes, the better to focus her consciousness on the mind she held captive. Slowly, carefully, she let a tendril of awareness snake out along the lines of her link to the hood and the American girl held in its thrall. Almost immediately, she felt the sickening maelstrom of the feedback loop. Scent blurred into sight, tangled with sound and touch and taste. The overwhelming power of it crashed over her like an ocean wave. Lina gripped the rough wool blanket that lay under her, feeling its scratchy warmth bunching beneath her fingers. That one sensation grounded her to her own body, which gave her an anchor in the storm.

With her body's reference point established, Lina let more of her awareness play out as she attempted to ride the waves of the American's mental hurricane. Sensations battered at her, but she dove on, seeking a way in, past the noise and the violence of it all. She could feel herself getting closer with every smashing wave of input...

Lina! Come back, my love! Come back to me! From impossibly far away, Josef's anguish filtered down the tattered, stretched lines of their link and pulled Lina slowly back, out of the storm.

She gasped and shuddered as she opened her eyes to find herself still on the camp bed, but cradled in Josef's arms, which tightened convulsively around her.

"Lina!" he gasped. He used one hand to brush the hair out of her eyes and cup her face. "My Lina, come back!"

"I'm here," she said. Or tried to say, anyway. Her voice came out as barely a whisper. She was so tired from fighting the waves, she found she could hardly speak. Her eyelashes fluttered as she forced her eyes to remain open and focus.

"*Mein Gott!*" Josef swore, and hugged her tightly to him. "My Lina, you cannot ever do that again. Promise me!"

"I can't," she whispered. "I have to. It's my task. I'm so tired."

"Knock the Ami girl out!" Josef said harshly, using one arm to wave someone forward. Lina thought she could see Werner carrying a cloth and a small bottle. He bent in front of the captive psychic and put the cloth over her mouth and nose, under the hood. Almost immediately, the scent of sweet, cloying decay rose in the tent. Lina felt a distant cold, and then an easing of the demand on her consciousness. The drain lessened as the Ami girl slipped into oblivion, only the tiniest pull remaining to let Lina know that she still lived. Lina let out a relieved sigh and felt her body relax into Josef's embrace.

"What happened?" he asked her, after Kristof had slipped noiselessly out of the tent.

"I hardly know," Lina said as he helped her to a sitting position. "I tried to infiltrate her mind. The magnitude of her power is...unprecedented. But I was almost there. I think, next time, I will reach my goal."

"Lina..." Josef started to say. But she held up a hand to cut him off.

"No," she said sharply. "I know you will not risk me, but this is my task. This is why you brought me out here. I *can* get inside her mind and interrogate her. I wasn't prepared, this first time. The next time, I will be."

"All right," Josef said slowly, pursing his lips. Clearly he didn't like the idea, but he nodded anyway. "But you will not try alone again. I will be in here with you. With the chloroform ready."

"As you like," Lina said, giving him a smile and raising one hand to caress his cheek. "And thank you."

Josef nodded again, his expression softening slightly. He leaned forward and brushed his lips across hers.

"Now rest," he said. "I will have one of the men bring you food in a little while. Sleep, and prepare."

"I love you," Lina whispered, her eyes already starting to close.

"And I, you."

* * *

Evelyn woke with the stale, acid taste of vomit in her mouth. Her head pounded as if her skull were about to explode into a thousand tiny pieces, but she found that a welcome change. The dizzying maelstrom of pain and guilt and loss had subsided, at least for a moment. She still couldn't see, but she could feel individual sensations again, and that was an improvement.

So. Her wrists were tied, her hands numb behind her back. She could feel the constriction, but not the actual rope or whatever it was that kept her bound. She twisted one hand, uncomfortably aware that she was probably tearing her skin, but unable to do anything about it. Something held her eyes shut, and she couldn't hear any sound other than her own harsh breathing. She could smell, though, she realized. She drew in an experimental breath, trying to get past the sour stench of whatever it was she'd thrown up at some point. She detected a hint of wood smoke, and the scent of thick, heavy canvas with just a touch of mildew.

A tent? Were they still in the forest?

Evelyn had no idea how long she'd been out. But if they hadn't moved far, then surely too much time couldn't have passed. That was another welcome thought. If not too much time had passed, then perhaps she could still reach Sean and the lieutenant. They hadn't been happy with her, but perhaps...perhaps they would forgive her.

Hands gripped her shoulders, lifted her so she was no longer lying on her right side. She felt her equilibrium tilt, and nausea rose within her again momentarily before she found her backside plunked down on something hard. Someone ripped the hood away. Sunlight stabbed into her brain. She recoiled, then forced her eyed to open to at least a squint.

She blinked hard to try and clear the resultant tears and focus on the figure in front of her. The blond German sat on a short log, facing her, a slight smile on his face. Another figure moved next to him.

As Evelyn's vision adjusted, she saw a woman, younger than herself, but absolutely beautiful. She had fine, aristocratic features, with large, wide-set eyes that assessed Evelyn coolly. She wore some kind of uniform, but it was something Evelyn hadn't seen before.

This, then, would be the German psychic.

"Miss...what is your name?" the blond soldier said. Evelyn reluctantly tore her attention away from his companion and focused on his face.

"My...Adamsen. Evelyn Adamsen," she said. The question itself startled her. She hadn't expected niceties. *Where were her men?* She considered reaching out with a tendril of thought, but the measuring gaze of the German psychic stopped her. If she tried, this slip of a girl would surely try to block her. Evelyn might be able to overpower her; in fact, she probably could, given enough time. But that was time in which the girl's soldier friends could hurt or kill Evelyn's men.

Brute force, it seemed, might not be the way to go.

"Miss Adamsen," the blond soldier said. "I am Stabsfeldwebel Josef Wolffs. I was sent to recover the crew of the downed American bomber. Am I right in assuming that you were, also, on board?"

Evelyn licked her lips and stopped herself from nodding, barely. This was an enemy interrogation. That sudden, stark thought impacted her like a freight train. This was an interrogation, and she was a prisoner of war.

"Sir," she whispered. "May I have some water?"

This served two purposes. One, she really was thirsty, and the taste of old vomit in her mouth made her stomach roil all over again. But two, it was a ploy for time and space in which to think, to figure out what she was going to do.

Wolffs leaned back, gave a small smile. "Of course," he said. He snapped his fingers, and another one of the Germans came forward with a canteen. The German psychic took this canteen while the much younger soldier knelt to untie Evelyn's hands. Fire erupted within her wrists as the restricted blood flow opened up again. She gasped, unable to help herself, and hunched forward over her hands.

"Shake them," Wolffs said. "It will help the circulation to return. When you are ready, I will give you a drink."

Evelyn did as he said, shaking her limp, floppy hands until the feeling crept back into them, and her fingers once again obeyed her commands. When she was able to curl both hands into fists, the German girl stepped forward and handed Evelyn the canteen. She took a good, long drink, trying to rid her mouth of the sour taste of vomit and the sickly sweet taste that underlaid it. The water helped, even eased the pounding in her head. Her foot still hurt like seven kinds of hell, and fear raced along her nerves, but small mercies were still mercies. She thanked the blond man with a nod when she handed the canteen back.

"Now," Wolffs said as he screwed the cap on. "I believe I asked you a question, Miss Adamsen."

Evelyn swallowed hard. "You did, Stab—"

Wolffs smiled slightly. "Stabsfeldwebel," he supplied for her.

"Stabsfeldwebel Wolffs," Evelyn finished. Her head may have eased in its pounding, but her heart more than made up for it in her chest. "You did. Thank you for the water, but I regret that I must decline to answer any more questions."

Wolffs nodded, as if he'd expected that answer. "I see. I will not pretend that I am not disappointed, Miss Adamsen. Even if I knew that you would say this. I confess I had hoped we could be civilized about things."

"I am prepared to be as civilized as you like, sir," Evelyn replied, with just an edge of tartness in her voice. As soon as she spoke, she wished she hadn't. She didn't want to antagonize this man. "I don't mean to be troublesome. I just cannot answer any questions. I do apologize," she added, in a rather more conciliatory tone.

Wolffs stared at her for a moment and then nodded again. He raised a hand and beckoned to someone behind her. Evelyn turned to look, just in time to see two of the other German soldiers untying Sean from a tree and dragging him forward. A great pit opened up in her stomach, and fear shot through her. Sean looked to be barely conscious and completely unable to support his own weight. They'd really worked him over.

The soldiers dragged him over to where Wolffs sat facing her and tossed him to the ground. Evelyn pressed her lips together to keep from crying out, but she couldn't keep her hands from clenching into fists.

"As you can see, your man is still alive," Wolffs said. "I told you before that his well-being is directly tied to your cooperation. This remains the case. So I will ask you again, Miss Adamsen. Why were you on that bomber?"

Evelyn tore her eyes from Sean's battered form and met Wolffs' icy blue gaze.

"I am truly sorry, Stabsfeldwebel Wolffs," she said, her voice trembling slightly. "But I cannot answer your question."

Wolffs pursed his lips and then gestured with his right hand. One of the two soldiers knelt beside Sean and pulled out a pocket knife. Evelyn bit her lip hard as the German flipped the blade open and took hold of Sean's right hand. With neat, economical movements, the German placed the blade of the knife against the skin of Sean's little finger, just above the knuckle, and began to saw back and forth.

Sean's eyes shot open, and his scream ripped through Evelyn. Her hands came up over her mouth, and without thinking, her mind reached out. The link snapped into place between them, and agony seared through her own finger as she felt his pain. That wasn't even the worst part, though. This was just the latest in one long series of excruciating hurts. Nothing on his body wasn't bruised or bleeding. Pain permeated his being and flowed back through the link to her.

Oh Sean, her mind whispered. *I'm so sorry, I'll make him stop. I will! He already knows that I was on board, surely there's no harm...*

No. Sean's mind voice was weak, but adamant. *Don't tell them anything.*

But they'll hurt you. They might kill you! I can't let them do that...

You aren't letting them do anything, Evie, Sean said. *They are doing this to me. This is a war, and they are the enemy. Don't let them in your head like that. You aren't making them do anything. Now go, I don't want you to feel any of this,* he said, and cast her out once again. Evelyn rocked backward on her log, nearly toppling off of it from the force of his shove and the sudden absence of the all-consuming pain. She tried to link again, but Sean had thrown up a barrier that she daren't breach. Helpless frustration surged through her. If only she had some kind of focus...

Oh. Now that was an idea.

Slowly, so as not to draw anyone's attention, Evelyn placed her hands on the rim of her log seat. Then, as carefully and casually as she could manage, she started to pull at a sliver that had splintered off when the log had been cut.

"As you can see, Miss Adamsen, I am very serious," Wolffs was saying over the sound of Sean's screams. Evelyn forced herself to look up at him, and this time, she was unable to keep the naked hatred from her eyes. Next to Wolffs, the German psychic had gone pale, but she still said nothing.

"So am I, Stabsfeldwebel Wolffs," Evelyn said, her voice cold, her nerve steeled. If Sean could handle it, then so could she. She wouldn't let his hurts be in vain. "I cannot stop you from murdering my crewman, but I *will not* answer your questions."

"Yes," Wolffs said softly. "You will..." He stopped suddenly as the German psychic reached out and laid a hand on his arm. He looked up at her, and though Evelyn wasn't linked in with them, it became suddenly very obvious to her that the two of them were linked with each other. They had the unmistakable look of a pair of people having an intimate, silent conversation. In fact...unless Evelyn missed her mark, there was something beyond the professional between these two. She took advantage of their momentary distraction to break off the splinter she'd been working at and quickly palmed it. Then she brought her hands back to her lap.

"Very well," Wolffs said suddenly, making her jump. For the first time during the whole exchange, he sounded angry. With a shrug, he flipped the German psychic's hand off of his arm, and leaned forward.

"Oberhelfer Sucherin has persuaded me that this method of getting what I want out of you will take too long. I had hoped not to have to use the hood again," he said, and horror swept over Evelyn as she realized what was about to happen. "But I am reminded we do not have the luxury of unlimited time. Take him back to his tree."

They did as he asked, the taller of the two snapping the pocket knife shut before the pair of them lifted the groaning Sean between them. As they carried him away, Evelyn began to wring her hands, feeling the bite of the wooden sliver that she now concealed between two fingers. She needed more time.

"No, please," she said, hoping to stall him. "Give me, give me a moment..."

"You have had all the moments I have to give," Wolffs said. "There are none left for you now, Miss Adamsen."

And with that, he stood and put the hood over her face again. And once again, Evelyn plummeted into the madness of her own mental maelstrom.

* * *

Lina stumbled as the hood went down over the American psychic's face. Instantly, the younger girl felt the intense drain as the feedback loop demanded her attention to maintain it. Josef rounded on her, his face livid.

"Do you see?" he asked. "This is why I wanted to interrogate her using more traditional means!" he spat. "Look what this is doing to you!"

Please, my love, not out here, she pled silently. "You need not fear for me, Stabsfeldwebel," she said evenly. The fact that she kept any sign of strain out of her voice pleased her immensely. "I am perfectly in control of the feedback loop."

Josef glared at her for a moment longer, his nostrils flaring as he stood with his hands on the shoulders of the Ami girl, keeping her from falling over. Lina gave him a slow smile. He was so infinitely dear like this: all high dudgeon and passionate desire to protect her from anything that might harm her.

I am well, my love, she sent silently. *Let us go into the tent, and I shall show you how well.*

Josef blinked, astonishment erasing the anger on his face. Lina caught the edge of his thought through the bond, and it was all she could do not to burst out laughing.

That is not what I meant, sadly, Lina sent on a caress. *I meant only that I would infiltrate the Ami girl's mind. I think I know how to do it, now.*

Oh, Josef thought, and though he fought not to let his disappointment show on his face, Lina felt it anyway, through their everpresent link. He wanted her so very much, craved the closeness of being mentally and physically entwined in every way. Lina understood, she wanted it too...but just now, there was work to do.

Soon, she promised him. *After we know what we need to know from the Ami girl.*

Josef nodded and then bent to pick the American psychic up. He lifted her as if she weighed nothing, and Lina spared a moment to admire his muscular strength before she followed him into the tent.

As before, Josef laid the girl down on the floor. Lina took a deep breath and laid herself down on the bed.

"Do nothing until I say, please," Josef said softly out loud. "I wish to be ready with the chloroform, in case I feel any distress coming from you. If our link is severed, I will knock the Ami girl out again."

"Yes, please," Lina said, closing her eyes as she gripped the wool coverlet as before. "Let me know when you are ready."

She heard the clinking of a bottle on something hard, a few other rustling sounds, and then felt Josef's hand cover her right one on the bed. With a soft smile, Lina turned her wrist so that their fingers could twine together.

As an anchor, I couldn't do better than your loving touch, she thought to him.

That is my hope. You must come back to me, my Lina.

Always, she promised.

Then go. I am ready, he replied, and squeezed her fingers lightly. She returned the squeeze and then turned all of her mind toward the violent cyclone of thought that held the Ami girl in a prison of her own mind.

As before, Lina stretched out her awareness, as if she were seeking a link. For that was exactly what she was doing: seeking a link with this powerful prisoner of hers. But in order to get there, she had to make her way through the storm. The force of Evelyn Adamsen's power battered at her, swept her along like a piece of driftwood in a hurricane. Lina felt her mental shields taking a pounding as she tumbled out of control...

No. The blanket was scratchy in her left hand, Josef's hand was warm in her right. Instantly, Lina was back in her body, her bond with Josef as strong as ever. She took a deep breath, steadied herself, and then tried again.

This time, though, rather than fight to withstand the punishing waves of the Ami girl's power, Lina wondered what would happen if she just let them carry her where they willed. It was a feedback loop into the girl's mind, after all. Eventually, it almost had to take Lina where she wanted to go.

It was difficult, tremendously difficult not to push back, not to fight against the crashing, brutal force of the girl's mind whipped into a frenzy. But Lina held herself still, held the feeling of Josef's warm fingers in her own mind. And this time, after a few terrifying moments of feeling lost beneath the waves of power...Lina began to ride them.

Their path was anything but predictable, anything but safe. Fear and anger and loss tangled and howled through her like a gale, but Lina let it blow through her and over her, and she merely floated on, letting the girl's consciousness take her where it willed.

* * * * *

Chapter Eleven

The sun set, and darkness rose from among the trees to envelop the camp. One by one, bright, icy stars stabbed their way into being, piercing the inky silk of the night sky.

Horst felt the soft, wet crunch of leaves and twigs under his boots as he walked the camp perimeter. He passed Werner, circling in the opposite direction, and acknowledged him with a nod before continuing. Not far away, Willi bent over their campfire, stirring something in a pot. The scent of some kind of stew drifted out under the trees to the gloom where Horst walked.

As a matter of discipline, he kept his eyes trained away from the lit campsite. It was better for his night vision. Plus, chances were that if there was a threat, it wasn't going to come from within the camp itself. Lina's power had reduced the American psychic to a pathetic, whimpering thing unable to move, and Hans had the two Ami airmen well in hand. Though their eyes still glared with defiance, they'd been well subdued. A few stout lengths of rope secured them to a tree just inside the circle of firelight, and Hans stood vigilant over them with his rifle at the ready.

Horst started to move on under the trees, but by then, it was too late. A hand clamped over his mouth, pressing his lips against his teeth hard enough to bruise. Agony shot from his lower back throughout his body. He tried to open his mouth to scream, to call out a warning, but only a muffled grunt escaped.

Blackness closed in around him, like a lover denied for too long.

* * *

After he'd passed Horst, Werner angled his path farther away from the lit center of the camp. The moon wasn't up yet, and the darkness under the forest canopy was near complete, but Werner had grown up in mountainous Bavaria. He'd always had relatively good night vision. For the next half hour, he moved slowly, quietly, more for practice than anything. It was good discipline to post two guards, especially with the value of the quarry they'd captured...but he seriously doubted anything stalked through the forest this night. At least, not anything that presented a threat to *him*.

He was wrong.

A hand like iron closed over the lower half of his face and wrenched his head backward, throwing him off balance. Hans fought through the disorientation to try and bring his rifle up, but there was no time left. Reflected firelight glinted off the blade that swung in from the side to stab down between this throat and his collarbone, opening his carotid artery. Liquid fountained up into his mouth and eyes. The last sensation he ever registered was that his blood tasted warm and salty, like the Italian sea he'd visited as a child.

* * *

The trees where Hans had tied the prisoners sat at the edge of the small camp clearing. The Amis were faced in toward the camp but away from each other so they couldn't communicate. They each had a rag shoved into their mouths and tied around their heads as a further barrier to speech. They looked exactly like what they were: battered, pathetic, beaten men. Even if they didn't know it yet.

In order to stave off boredom and complacency, Hans had developed a routine in watching these two. He'd sit for about ten minutes staring at the younger one, then get up and look closely at the older...the officer. Of the two of them, the officer was in worse shape, but that bothered Hans not at all. He deserved it. They both did, for who knew how many innocents were dead because of their bombs?

After looking closely at the two of them, Hans would circle slowly around the pair of trees to which they were tied, checking their bindings to ensure that they hadn't been able to work loose. Not that he expected they would. Hans had tied the knots himself, and he knew what he was about.

Once that was finished, usually either Werner or Horst would be passing nearby on their own perimeter circuits. So, he would usually look up and exchange the professional nod that indicated all was well.

Only this time, there was no one to return his nod.

Hans frowned and looked back over his shoulder. He could just see Willi heading for the command tent, obviously in response to a summons from within. Kristof was nowhere in sight. Hans looked down at his prisoners again. They appeared to be dozing against their bonds, their heads hanging limply forward.

For fun, he kicked them each awake.

"No sleeping," he barked in heavily-accented English. The officer cleared his throat and spat a disgusting pink-tinged wad in

Hans' general direction. Hans grinned and slapped the man, hard, with the back of his hand. The lieutenant's head jerked back and bounced against the rough bark of the tree.

"No spitting," Hans added and then straightened, looking once more into the gloom under the nearby trees. The light from the campfire was making it difficult to see, so he stepped away from the prisoners, under the darkened forest canopy.

He was still blinking, trying to bring his dark vision into play when something fell down from above him and knocked him to the ground. Hans suddenly felt his face being smashed into the leaves and dirt of the forest floor. He heaved his body, trying to roll over, and something grabbed him and flipped him to his back while he spat the dirt from his mouth.

A hand grabbed his hair, yanked his head back. A face he didn't recognize leaned down close to his ear. Something cold pricked the skin just below the hinge of his jaw.

"No spitting," the voice was a low growl, and it spoke in American-accented English. Hans writhed and tried to shout, but to no avail. The pinprick had become a tearing pain as the mysterious assailant opened his throat from ear to ear.

* * *

Evelyn screamed, but no one heard.

As before, the moment the hood covered her face, her mind erupted into a violent, whirling cyclone of psychic energy. Her thoughts doubled back over and over again, drowning her with their vehemence. All of her sensations echoed and re-echoed through her mind at once, until they blended together into a terrifyingly synesthetic blur of agony. She was lost, trapped, caught in perpetual motion and unceasing pain that sickened and never slowed. Nothing was still, all was that horrid, cycling movement...

Except there.

Right there. One tiny speck of calm in the drowning, lashing sea of her own mind. Evelyn fastened on to that speck as if it were a lifeline, clinging to it as if her sanity depended upon it, because it did.

Too late, she realized her mistake. Just as she fastened her consciousness to this improbable lifeline drifting in the feedback storm, a sense of triumph not her own rocked through her, and she realized that she'd fallen into the German girl's trap.

Despair joined the rain of emotions that drove against her mental being. The German girl's mind was slick and unfamiliar, and she couldn't find purchase without fully opening herself up. If she did that, though, the girl would know everything she knew, see everything she'd seen. That couldn't happen, but she couldn't face casting herself back out into the storm to drown in her own amplified pain and fear...

Wait. Something...

Like a crack in a cliff face that opens onto a cave system, Evelyn discovered a psychic channel leading...somewhere. With no other choice, she flung her awareness headlong down that channel, not caring where or with whom she ended up...

She blinked and saw her own body lying curled on the floor, the ugly hood contraption draped over her head, down to her shoulders. She knelt beside some kind of bed, her hand gripping tightly to someone's...Lina's?

She was Wolffs, who loved Lina, the German girl. She was Evelyn, hiding from the violence of her own mind, somehow inhabiting Wolffs' thoughts. Somehow, in the connection between the hood and Lina and Wolffs, Evelyn had found her way into the Nazi leader's head.

Quickly, without thinking about what she did, Evelyn acted before Wolffs could detect her presence. It helped he was so tightly focused on his ladylove. It allowed Evelyn to reach out her consciousness and take hold of the picture in front of him...

And twist it. Lina became Evelyn, lying on the floor, curled in pain. Evelyn became Lina, hands warm and free.

Evelyn felt Wolffs lurch to his feet, stumble backward, disbelieving. On the bed, Evelyn-Lina opened her eyes, her expression questioning.

She overpowered Lina! Evelyn shouted into Wolffs' head. *Do not let her escape! Grab her!*

Wolffs lunged forward reached out and wrapped his hands around the seeming American's slender neck. "No...Josef! What are you..." she gasped.

Save Lina! Evelyn countered, throwing the considerable weight of her power behind the thought. Somewhere behind her, the maelstrom howled, clawing at her, but she had found an improbable way out, and she had no intention of going back. Evelyn-Lina's fists began to frantically pound on Wolffs' arms. She tried to scream down their psychic link, but the real Evelyn was already there. She shunted Evelyn-Lina's cry back into the maelstrom of the hood's feedback loop and silently urged Wolffs to squeeze harder.

He flexed his hands, shaking her as her blows weakened. She began to claw at his fingers, trying to get him to loosen, to *listen* to her.

Nothing worked, for in his head, Evelyn subtly ramped up his anger and aggression, until Evelyn-Lina's eyes began to bulge from her sockets, and her lips turned blue.

Somewhere, the maelstrom slackened, the winds calmed as the will that keep the feedback loop going slipped into unconsciousness. Outside, a commotion sounded. Wolffs panted softly from his exertions as he dropped the limp girl back down on the bed. Someone fumbled at the tent flap.

One of the German soldiers stepped through, then froze. He gaped in horror at the girl on the bed with the livid bruises ringing her throat and then at his commander, who stood in the tent with a look of vicious satisfaction on his face. Wolffs glanced at his subordinate and then did a double take as Evelyn layered the features of Lieutenant Abram Portman over the German's face and body.

Wolffs stumbled backward, fumbling for the Luger pistol he carried holstered on his belt. *Shoot him,* Evelyn whispered into his mind. *The American killers are trying to escape!*

Hands shaking, Wolffs finally got his pistol free and raised it. The German soldier looked at him with disbelief in his eyes. A tiny corner of Evelyn's mind whispered he was the youngest one, hardly more than a baby. The rest of her mind didn't listen. It was too focused on remembering the way that "baby" had beaten and kicked Sean and Abram. She held Abram's features steady and pushed at Wolffs again.

"Stab..." the German started to say. He never finished because Wolffs pulled the trigger. The Luger's report blasted through the air, making Wolffs' ears hurt. Voices shouted outside.

"Stabsfeldwebel! Willi! Are you all right?" a voice shouted. Evelyn recognized it from the forest. It was the voice of the soldier who had captured her and Abram. Wolffs' mind supplied a name: Kristof. Kristof burst into the tent, flinging the tent flap aside, letting the late afternoon sunlight come pouring in. Wolffs (and perforce, Evelyn) was momentarily blinded, and blinked rapidly.

"Horst and Werner have completely disappeared!" Kristof said in German. "We found Hans with his throat cut, and the two Amis gone...Oh my god!" He stared down at the body at his feet. "You shot him!"

"Yes," Wolffs said, still blinking. His mind fought Evelyn as she tried to superimpose Sean's features onto those of this Kristof. Wolffs knew Kristof's voice. But then, why would Kristof be reaching for his own weapon? Why would he be so aghast at the sight of the dead American?

Kill him! Evelyn pushed, hard. With Lina unconscious, the feedback loop had quieted, and Evelyn was able to put quite a bit of power behind the demand. Once again, Wolffs raised his weapon and fired. Sean-Kristof staggered backward as a red stain began to spread over his belly. He tripped over the dead soldier's leg and fell. His own pistol fell to the ground as he clutched at his gut.

"Josef," he whispered. "Why?" The agony and betrayal in that one question undid Evelyn's illusion. Wolffs' mind righted itself as what he *knew* to be true took precedence over her whispers. Sean's face faded away, and he beheld the face of his best friend and second in command.

"Kristof?" Wolffs asked. Evelyn felt the nausea that rippled through the stabsfeldwebel. He dropped to his knees as Kristof coughed. Blood sprayed from Kristof's mouth in a tiny fountain. Willi's body lay twisted, the top half of his head gone. Wolffs turned his head and saw Lina laying half on and half off the camp bed.

"What have I done?" he whispered. For just a moment, Evelyn reveled in his pain. The knowledge he'd strangled the woman he loved felt like a noose around his own neck. That was bad enough, but the knowledge he'd shot his own men rocked through him like heat and nausea and cold, icy despair all at once. He couldn't breathe; a part of his brain started to scream long, howling keens of grief and guilt. He couldn't feel his legs and feet, and he tasted blood in his mouth. With shaking hands, he raised the Luger one more time and put the barrel between his lips.

No! Evelyn shouted, as his intention stiffened into a crystalline resolve. She threw every bit of her power at him. Not to save him, but to set her free. Even without Lina conscious to run it, the sensory deprivation hood still kept her head-blind and vulnerable. She needed Wolffs. Too late, Evelyn realized what he was going to do...what she'd done to him.

He pulled the trigger, and Evelyn instantly found herself trapped inside her own head. Like before, she couldn't stretch her consciousness out beyond her own head. The storm had quieted. That was all.

Or not quite all. Evelyn became suddenly aware of the scent of blood and foul things. Like an outhouse...or a slaughterhouse. She could smell, and just like that, she could feel and hear.

Like that sound? That was the sound of a pistol being cocked.

"American girl," she heard. It was Kristof's voice, though it was weak and ragged with pain. "I do not know if you can hear me, but if you can, know that I am still alive. If you move, I will shoot you in the head. Understand that."

Evelyn's breath accelerated as she froze.

"Oberhelfer!" Kristof called. "Oberhelfer! I know you live, I saw your hair fluttering over your mouth when you exhaled. Please, Lina...Wake up!"

Evelyn's mind raced. She had to do something before Lina awoke and brought back the storm...or just killed her outright. But what? If only she could reach out to her men. Kristof had said that they escaped. Maybe they weren't far...

Of course, the splinter that still lay in her hand. The focus. With a focus, and with the hood weakened by Lina's unconsciousness, maybe she was strong enough to break through...

With excruciating care, Evelyn slowly moved her fingers until the sharp end of the wooden splinter stuck out. Then she placed that point against the tender flesh on the inside of her forearm and pressed down. She prayed to whoever might be listening that Kristof was too busy trying to wake Lina to notice her slight movements, and she began to scratch an "S" into her skin.

Slowly, agonizingly slowly, Evelyn etched the letters of Sean's and Abram's names in her skin. Every stroke of every letter burned like fire, but that was all to the good. It made it that much easier to focus on the shape of the sounds that made up their names.

About midway through, she realized Kristof had fallen silent. Dead, unconscious, or resting she didn't know. Later, perhaps, she would care, but right now, her every effort zeroed in on forming the names of her crewmates.

When she'd finished, she drew in a slow breath, and tried to force her mind to calm. She could almost feel the German's pistol trained on the back of her head, but she shunted that image to the back of her consciousness. From deep within, she focused on the affection, the trust, the love she had for these men. They'd flown through hell time and again together, and they had made it out. This was just another type of hell...but they would make it through this, too. When her mind was as calm as it was going to get, Evelyn focused all of that emotion, all of that love, and fueled it with every bit of her considerable power. She had yet to meet a psychic who could best her, because there was no one. She was the most powerful psychic in the U.S. Army, and she channeled all of this power into the focus of her men's names.

There was a momentary resistance, like trying to walk through water up to the waist, and then Evelyn's consciousness *exploded* through the hood's feedback inducing mechanism. She smelled acridly sweet smoke, but it didn't matter. For her mind was *free*, and it flew like a bullet from a gun straight into the minds of Sean and Abram.

Sean lay hidden in the deepening shadows beneath the trees not far away. He carried a knife in one hand and a German rifle in the other. Every part of him hurt, but a fierce satisfaction rode over all of the aching pain. He blinked, astonished, as the link sprang into being, and his mind filled with the delicious silkiness of her consciousness.

Abram, too, lay hidden. Someone had wrapped a bandage around his arm. He, too, ached all over, but the stabbing pain in his midsection told her he'd taken a worse beating than Sean had. Still, he looked up at the touch of her mind. "Evie?" he whispered out loud.

"Evie's here?" someone asked. Evelyn recognized the voice. Abram looked up and smiled at the mud-streaked face of their bombardier, Paul Rutherford.

Instantly, Evie reached out again, skipping from Abram's mind to Paul's, and just like that, the net sprang into being.

Come get me! she wailed to them. *Get this thing off me before she wakes up!*

Where are you, Evie? Paul asked. *We didn't know. We would have come...*

In a tent. The door flap is open. The one with the bodies, she added, with a touch of hysterical giggle to her thought. *Two, maybe three bodies. I don't know if Kristof is dead. He wasn't; he said he'd shoot me in the head if I moved. But we shot him in the gut, and he stopped calling her, trying to get her to wake up...But if she wakes up, she'll bring the storm back, and I don't know if I can survive that again...*

We're coming, Evie, Sean said. His mind tasted of steely determination. *We know where you are now. We can feel the bond pulling at us...Just stay with us, Evie-girl and don't move until we know that asshole's dead.* A pause. Then. *Sorry, Evie,* he added, as if he couldn't help it.

The hysterical laughter built in her mind, spilled over, and flooded down the lines of the connection. On the floor of the tent, she clenched her body tight to keep the giggles from pouring out of her and ricocheting through her body. She couldn't move. Not until they knew the asshole was dead. Sorry, Evie.

The sun had set, but Evelyn could feel the three of them running over the dark, snow-covered ground. They ducked from tree to tree toward the camp and remained out of sight as long as possible. She could feel Abram doing a mental calculation as he ran. Of the Germans they'd seen so far, they could account for all of them. Paul had gotten two of them earlier, then killed their sentry when he set them free. Evie had said that there were three bodies in her tent, plus the German psychic. Abram hadn't seen any more than that, but that doesn't mean they weren't out there.

Paul had been out there. The Germans had never known. Abram's mind reeled at the implications of this, so much so that he stumbled as they sprinted toward the cluster of tents. He'd been out there, had evaded capture, and as far as they knew, detection, and had apparently begun to stalk and eliminate the German soldiers one by one. Abram couldn't help but glance over at his buddy, his bunkmate, his best friend throughout this whole godforsaken war. He realized, best friend or not, he hadn't really known Paul Rutherford, or of what terror and bravery he was capable.

But hell, had anyone? Had Paul? Had Evie?

Evie.

Hurryhurryhurry, her mind sing-songed at them as she felt Abram's every footfall. She felt the sweat and the stinging cold in his lungs as they burned. She felt the sharp, piercing pain that stabbed into the navigator's side with every step. Something was broken, or at the very least, badly bruised. He shouldn't be running. She shouldn't be urging him to run, but she couldn't help it. Terror raced through her thoughts, edging everything in white. *Hurry*, she urged them. *Hurry. Hurry, hurry, please hurry!*

We're coming, Evie. That was Sean, dogged and tough, and scared through. *You just hang on. We're almost there, I can see your tent...*

Hold here, Paul commanded them, his mind strangely calm and empty. *We can't just go barreling in there. If that kraut is still alive, he might shoot Evie.*

Please, Evelyn sobbed silently. *Please hurry! I can't...if she wakes...I can't face the storm again!*

We're coming, Paul said, his tone like steel. *Just hold tight.*

Just a bit longer, Evie-girl, Sean added gently. *We won't let them hurt you anymore.*

Evelyn felt the ragged edges of her mind fraying away into inco-
herent sobs of fear and desperation. The net she'd created with the
three men faltered briefly, then stabilized as she startled herself out
of her panic spiral. She had a net; she wasn't alone. Her men were
coming, and she had broken out of the hood once with the aid of
their names carved into her living flesh. With a focus that intimate,
and the bond that resulted, there was no way that anyone, not even
the talented German girl, was going to overpower her.

She forced herself to breathe in and out slowly, hating the way
the sensory deprivation hood trapped her hot breath against her face.
Her arm burned, the fire forming the shapes of Abram's and Sean's
names. Evelyn focused on that burn, her mind clinging to it like a
lifeline. She had the men, and they had her. They were connected.
They were coming. She just had to hold on, just for a little bit longer.

Not far from her, someone stirred.

He's alive, she's alive, someone's alive and moving in here! Evelyn
screamed down the lines of her link. *Oh please, please, please hurry!*

She heard a groan and huddled down into herself in response.
The stream of information flowing from Abram, Sean, and Paul narrowed as she closed herself off in terror.

Evie? Sean asked. *Evie, stay with us.* He and the others had slowed
at her panicked cry. Evelyn felt him flex his hands on the grip of the
German rifle he'd picked up. Her breath came hot and fast under the
cloth hood. She watched through Abram's eyes as Paul stepped forward. She watched through Paul's as he gently, slowly, moved the
tent flap with the barrel of his weapon.

Light spilled across the floor from the camp lantern that hung
from the center tent pole. A tangled pile of limbs lay sprawled across
the ground. Paul blinked, unable at first to make out who was whom.

The dark stain of blood spread slowly out from under the pile. A sound like a groan came from the topmost body, who shifted and lifted his head. His eyes went first wide with surprise at the sight of Paul (and presumably Paul's rifle) and then narrow with pain and resignation. Abram shouldered in beside Paul and trained his own weapon on the gut-shot German.

Get Evie, Abram sent to Paul through the net. *Sean's covering outside. I've got this one.*

Without any further prompting, Paul stepped carefully over the legs of the man without half of his head and around as much of the blood as he could. He saw Evelyn on the floor, curled into the fetal position, as small as her broken limb would allow.

Evelyn felt her breathing accelerate, the fire in her arms nearly pulsed as she felt him draw nearer and nearer. Until finally, someone ripped the accursed hood away, and the cold night air flowed over her face. She drew in a great, gasping sob of a breath and began to cry like a lost baby.

I've got you, Paul said, his mind tone smooth and gentle as always. Of all of her men, Paul had the most practiced psychic touch, thanks to his childhood with his psychic sister. He slipped one arm under Evelyn's knees and another around her shoulders, and lifted. Evelyn felt him cradle her close, like a child. His heart beat fast, and anger lurked beneath the surface gentleness of his mind. Paul Rutherford was livid at what had been done to her, to all of them.

"Let's get her out of here," he said, his voice rumbling through his chest. She sagged against him, letting him be her strength for the moment while she drank in the deliciously cool air outside the hood. She felt the sensation of movement, followed by Paul bending slightly over her, and then they were out of the tent.

Cold air assaulted her raw senses. She gave an involuntary shiver, and Paul responded by holding her closer. Through her net, Evelyn could feel Sean and Abram moving around, covering her and Paul and now and then grabbing something from the camp as they passed through it and out into the trees. Sean got two of their hiking packs and another weapon. Abram had snatched up the pot that had been set over the fire with their dinner. Evelyn felt something cold and wet brush against her forehead and then her cheek. It had begun to snow.

This is good, Abram thought to everyone. *Snow is good. It will hide our tracks away from this place.*

It could also kill us, Paul thought, darkly. *Evie's weak, and you guys aren't much better off. Hypothermia isn't going to help that any.*

Not that we got much vote in the matter, Sean pointed out as they reached the treeline. *We should probably just focus on putting as much distance between us and the camp as we can before dawn....sirs.* He added the last bit belatedly, as if only just remembering that he was an enlisted man in the company of two officers. Evelyn snorted a laugh through her nose, surprising herself. She felt Paul shift as he bent his head to look at her.

I'm all right, she thought to him in response. She could feel the giggles bubbling up from within, tinged with hysteria. The tiny, dry corner of her mind observed she was getting rather used to the feeling of hysterical laughter. She'd certainly felt it often enough in the last few days. *It was just funny. Though I can't really say why...*

It's all right, Evie, Sean replied. *They wouldn't understand the humor anyway. They're both officers.*

Hey! Abram protested as he pushed a tree branch back to allow Paul to pass with Evelyn in his arms. *That's not fair, Sean. I have a terrific sense of humor!*

Sure you do, sir, Sean thought back as he pressed forward, leading their way. Evelyn knew he hoped he was taking them west. He'd headed roughly in the same direction as the late sunset, reasoning that if nothing else, they could get some terrain between them and the camp before figuring out a more robust plan.

I do! Ask Paul. Everyone says I do, Abram continued to insist. Evelyn continued to swallow hard against the overwhelming desire to giggle. So much so that she felt her entire body spasm in a quick jerk that nearly had Paul dropping her to the forest floor. She'd managed to give herself the hiccups.

I'm sorry! Evelyn wailed down the net, and the dam broke. Unable to choose between laughing and crying, she did both. Punctuated, every few minutes, by a jerking hiccup spasm. Paul's arms shook as he, also, fought back laughter. Soon, Sean joined in, and Abram was left staring at the three of them, frustration pinching his features. He snorted softly. Then the corners of his mouth turned up.

See? he asked, as if their current state of laughter-induced incapacitation had been the result of his joke, rather than a hysterical reaction to what they'd just seen and been through. That, of course, made everyone only laugh harder, until the four of them ended up huddled down in a low spot, behind a fallen log, clutching each other while the laughter turned to tears, and they expunged the fear and anger and adrenaline in one great cathartic blast.

All around them, snow drifted down through the darkness.

* * *

Consciousness came slowly to Lina. She felt as if her awareness was trying to swim through thick, cloying mud up to the forefront of her mind. It was cold, and her throat hurt. And something...wasn't right.

She blinked, then tried to breathe in, and it set off an attack of coughing. A necklace of knives stabbed at her as she spasmed, rolling onto her side and fighting to drag in the tiniest of breaths. Tears streamed from her eyes. She brought one hand up to clutch at her throat and immediately regretted it. The necklace of knives stabbed at the outside of her throat, too.

Slowly, painfully, Lina was able to force herself to calm and take tiny little sips of air. Her chest ached, screamed for more, but she couldn't chance breathing deeply again. She opened her eyes one more time to see the lamp-lit canvas of the tent wall.

She was lying on the camp cot. She was cold. Something was wrong, though she still couldn't put her finger on it.

Her muscles protested any attempt at movement, and she set off another coughing fit, but eventually she was able to push herself up to a seated position.

Blood. So much blood, running in half-congealed rivulets over the floor of the tent. Pooled around a tangle of something that her mind refused to identify for the moment. The air itself felt tainted with the metallic tang of blood, edged in the crystalline iciness of snow. The wind rattled the tent canvas, blew in through the open flap of a door, made the lantern swing from where it hung beneath the center pole. Wild shadows careened across the space, mingling with the blood and the pile of whatever-it-was that she wasn't seeing right now.

"Lina."

Barely a whisper. Nearly impossible to hear over the whistle of the wind through the trees all around. Lina couldn't have said if she heard it with her ears or with her psychic mind. But it was there. It was a voice she knew.

"Kristof?"

"Yes. Thank the gods, whoever they are. I had hoped...well. Never mind. I think I'm too close. You have to get out of here, Lina. Hike back to the trucks. Drive yourself to safety."

"Kristof," Lina said. Or tried to say. Speaking resulted in ragged agony. She could barely manage a harsh whisper. "I don't...understand. What happened?"

"The Americans," Kristof replied. The lantern slowed in its wild swinging, and Lina could see his legs move slightly. Part of the shape she refused to see resolved itself into Kristof's form. He was sitting on the floor, leaning back against...something. His hands were red, pressed to his belly. A dark stain soaked his clothing from chest to knees. Josef wouldn't be happy about that. Her beloved held his men to a high standard of dress and appearance.

"What do you mean?" Lina asked, forcing her mind to focus. It was more difficult than it should have been, especially for someone with her training. Every little distraction seemed to sing its siren song to her, luring her attention away from Kristof and whatever it was he had to tell her. And her mind was more than willing to be led down the rosy path of distraction...but she was no child at play. She was who she was, and there was work to do here. Even if she couldn't quite wrap her mind around what, exactly, she was supposed to be doing...

Damn, but her throat hurt!

"The Americans," Kristof said again. "They've escaped. I don't know how. They must have had a third one following us. One we never saw. Somebody cut Hans' throat, and the two airmen were gone. I came in here to find...Lina. What happened? Why was Josef strangling you? Why did he shoot me?"

Josef? Strangling her? Lina wanted to laugh. What a ridiculous thought. Josef loved her. He would never...

She wheezed and coughed as shards of agony ripped through her throat, cutting off any air, any hope. Memory slammed back into her mind as, finally, her eyes saw clearly the inside of the tent.

Josef, jerking away from her, fear and loathing in his eyes.

Josef's hands wrapped around her throat, tightening mercilessly as air and light faded together.

Josef's body, sprawled on the ground, his legs tangled with poor Willi's; both of their skulls replaced by a bloody ruin.

And Kristof, gut-shot, bleeding to death in front of her.

"*No!*" she screamed, her torn voice ripping through the night. She lurched forward, stumbled, tripped over somebody's leg and ended up on her knees in the blood beside Kristof. She grabbed one of his hands. It was icy cold.

"No!" she repeated. "You will not die on me, Kristof! I refuse to let it happen, do you hear me?" She reached out with her mind, intent on capturing his consciousness, on forcing it to stay, to steady, to not leave her alone here in the dark and the cold and the blood.

Too late.

His fingers curled around hers as the light left his eyes. Right there, funny, witty, passionate Kristof became just another body in that charnel house of a tent.

Lina was alone.

She wanted to weep, to scream. She wanted to find the Americans and rip them apart with her bare, bloodied hands. She wanted to know what, exactly, had happened to make Josef turn on her like that.

The wind whipped at the tent flap door again, blowing snow inside. Tiny white pinpricks landed on the darkly slick red stain. Her throat hurt. The lantern swung again.

SS-Oberhelfer Adalina Sucherin got to her feet. She reached across the body of her beloved and two men who'd been like brothers and removed the lantern from its hook on the center pole of the tent. She couldn't, perhaps, go far in this storm, but she would not stay in this tent any longer. She would gather up supplies from the camp. Make up a pack, rest in another tent until the storm abated. Then she would do as Kristof had said. She would hike back to their trucks and drive one back into the city. She would report what had happened here, and then she would return. She would bring soldiers and tanks and whatever else she needed. She would find those American bastards.

And she would make them pay.

* * * *

Chapter Twelve

By the time dawn reached them, Evelyn and her three surviving aircrewmen had managed to put a scant few miles between them and the site of the camp. It was slow going between their injuries, the unfamiliar terrain, the cold, and the snow.

As Paul carried her through the darkness, Evelyn struggled to put herself back together, and mostly failed. She wavered between hysteria-induced laughter and terrified catatonia. The only thing that anchored her to reality was her psychic connection to each of the men. She clung to their consciousnesses, drawing strength from the knowledge she was no longer alone in her own head.

"We should stop soon," Paul said, as the first rosy fingers of sunrise began to reach through the trees behind them. "Find a place to hole up for the day. Eat, rest. We all need it."

"Good idea," Abram said. "Let's push on along this ridge until we find something that will suit."

Paul did find something, about five minutes later. It was a stone house, or the remains of one anyway. The roof had long since fallen in, and a tree had grown up within the three walls that remained. It looked as if it had been untouched for centuries. It would do nicely as a hiding place for the day.

They tucked themselves inside the walls, between the spreading roots of the tree. Abram dug another one of his fire pits, and Sean set about making something out of the supplies they'd stolen from the Nazi camp. They'd long since eaten what had been in the pot that Abram had grabbed, but the pot itself was more than useful as a cooking utensil.

"At least it will be more than a few oily sardines today, huh, Evie?" Abram joked as he knelt down beside her. He and Paul had fixed a nice little nest for her. She lay snug in the junction between two of the larger roots, cushioned by one of the bedrolls from the Nazi packs. She looked up at him with a wan smile. His face looked terrible, all purple and green from the beatings he'd received. At least one of his teeth was missing, having been knocked loose at one point or another. He still favored his right side as he moved; he probably had a cracked rib that had to be ridiculously painful. Still, despite all of this, the navigator smiled with his own brand of irrepressible optimism and humor. And that caused Evie to smile back.

"Those were the most delicious sardines I'd ever tasted," she said softly, her voice sounding rusty and disused to her own ears. She shifted just a bit, pulled the bedroll blanket up a bit higher as she spoke. She didn't want him to see...

"Evie! What in the hell?" Paul and Sean looked up sharply at Abram's cry. The navigator grabbed the blanket under which she'd been trying to hide and ripped it down, exposing her bloodied forearms. Abram's eyes went dark and narrow with anger.

They did this to you? he asked her through the net.

No! No. I...I did it, she admitted. He grabbed her wrist and turned her arm over so he could see better. The bloody, angular letters stood out in stark relief against the white flesh of her arms. *That was how I broke through the hood's feedback loop,* she said to all of them. *I needed a focus, something that would resonate with all of you. Names provide a pow-*

erful focus, as they represent what we think of as ourselves. By putting your names on my skin, I was able to create a connection powerful enough to blow the hood's electric amplifiers. They were causing the feedback that was keeping me discon-nected from all of you.

But then why is my name there? Paul put in from across the fire. He'd seen her arms through Abram's eyes. Sure enough, there were three names etched into her skin. *You didn't know I was alive until after you broke through and reached out to Abram and Sean. Why would you have put my name there?*

I just added it, Evelyn admitted, somewhat shamefacedly. *Just a few minutes ago. I-I was...am...afraid. If they catch us again, or...or if something else happens. I won't be severed from you again.* She felt a kind of mad ferocity swell within her at this statement and spill out down the lines to touch each of their consciousnesses.

We won't ever let that happen, Evie, Sean said. The two officers nod-ded, bolstering his words with their own agreement.

I know, but...I just needed it. Please. Don't be angry.

What did you use? Abram asked. Evelyn blinked, then handed him the wooden sliver that she had kept in her hand throughout the en-tire ordeal. Abram hissed between his teeth.

All right, Evie, he said. *I can see the necessity, but let me at least clean these out. The last thing we need is for you to get another infection.*

All right, she agreed in a mental whisper. Relief flooded through her. They knew. They knew about her focuses, and they weren't an-gry at her. Her men supported her still. That was important in a way she couldn't think about right then.

Sean came forward and helped Abram as they cleaned and band-aged her arms. Then they re-splinted her leg. Each of them had plen-ty of wounds to be cleaned and bandaged as well, and by the time they were done, the food was ready and the sun had risen above the level of the trees.

Let's eat, Abram said. *Give Evie the majority of it. Then we'll make a plan and get some rest.*

* * *

Evelyn woke to the feeling of a rifle barrel being pressed to her chest. Her mouth went dry, and her consciousness instantly snapped out to Paul, Sean, and Abram. The men were waking in similar circumstances, and Evelyn could feel the instinctive violence that surged through them as they reached surreptitiously for their weapons...

Wait, she said. *They're not speaking German!*

It was true, they weren't. She didn't recognize the language, per se, but it wasn't German. It was similar, but the speakers had more of a round throatiness to their diction, and the words weren't the same. They weren't soldiers, either, these people. There were five of them, all armed, though only three held what looked like hunting rifles. The other two carried a pitchfork and a stout cudgel, respectively. Their clothes were rough and well-worn, and the grim set of their faces didn't do much to reassure her...

...but they weren't speaking German.

"Ben jij Engels?" the man with the rifle said lowly. "Amerikaan?"

Evelyn stiffened slightly.

"American. Yes. We're American," Abram said, from off to the side.

"Naam?" the man said, speaking slowly. "Bommenwerper?"

Evelyn licked her lips and glanced over to Abram.

Can you tell what they want? Abram asked her. *Who are they?*

I can't link with him without him noticing, Evelyn answered. *And If I reach out, there might be a psychic nearby who would feel it...*

Gotta take that risk, Paul said. Through the net, Evelyn could feel him wrap his long-fingered hands around the German Mauser he'd hidden under his coat. She swallowed hard against her dry-mouthed fear and lifted her hand slowly from the blankets. The man holding the rifle gaped at the blood-spotted bandages that covered her forearm, then narrowed his eyes as he saw her fine-boned hand. He spoke another sharp word over his shoulder, and one of the other men came forward.

Not a man, Evelyn realized, and passed through the net. For although the figure was clothed in a drab, figure-hiding coat, she could see the thin face and pointed chin as the other woman came forward and set her pitchfork on the ground within easy reach. Then she reached out and took hold of Evelyn's wrist.

Evelyn started to reach out, to draw her into the net, but then stopped. If this was a trap, if this woman was another enemy psychic, she didn't want to expose her men. Better that she drop the net connection entirely first...

The memory of the storm rose up within Evelyn, howling behind her eyes, engulfing her senses until she cried out in an unmistakably female voice and collapsed backward against the roots of the tree. A sharp pain in the back of her skull told her she'd hit her head. That, as much as anything else, hauled her back to reality.

The net connection was still strong. She could feel her men's concern pouring down the lines toward her.

I can't, she whispered to them, shame trembling in her thoughts. *I can't let go of the net, and I won't risk bringing her in. It could be a trap. But if I let go...*

No, Evie, it's all right, Sean said stalwartly. *I don't think they're going to hurt us. Look.*

Indeed, through his eyes, she could see that out the door, another person approached. This one was wearing a hat, a long, dark overcoat and carrying a distinctively shaped bag with a caduceus painted on the side. A doctor.

*It could still be a trap...*Evelyn replied, fear building within her chest.

"Dokter," the woman said, welcome in her tone. "Deze is een vrouw, en ze is gekwetst. Ik denk dat ze allemaal zijn. Kun je ze helpen? Ze zeggen dat ze zijn Amerikaans."

"American?" the doctor said, his accent clipped and British. "And a woman? Yes, of course." He removed his hat and looked around at them with blue eyes wreathed with smile lines. He was tall, thin, and completely bald, this doctor. Evelyn had the irreverent thought that she would have left the hat on.

"Doctor?" Abram asked, his voice somehow managing to be both harsh and tentative. "Who...ah...who are you? They?"

"Doctor Frederic van Duren, at your service," he said with a wintry smile. "You and your friends are very lucky. Please forgive my companions their caution. We have learned hard lessons of late. However, your injuries lend credence to your claims. As does the presence of the young lady. I cannot imagine the Nazis would plant a woman in with men wearing the uniforms of downed aircrew. What would be the point? No, I think you must be genuine."

"We are," Abram said. "But why are we lucky? We haven't felt all that lucky lately."

"Ah, my new friend, but God smiles upon you even so," Doctor van Duren said. "You see, we are with the Belgian Resistance."

* * *

The woman identified herself as Deedee, and it turned out that she was one of the nurses who worked with Doctor van Duren at the hospital in Brussels. Despite her apparent youth, her hands were gentle and competent as she and the doctor examined each of them. Evelyn's ankle and Abram's ribs occasioned the most concern.

"This was not set properly," the doctor said, his voice soft and grave. He looked up and said something to Deedee, who nodded with sober brown eyes and pushed a tendril of curly brown hair back under her stocking cap. She got to her feet and said something in the language the doctor had identified as Flemish Dutch. Two of the other men stood and followed her out of the ruined farmhouse.

"What does that mean?" Sean asked. All three of Evie's men were sitting or standing nearby as the doctor performed her examination. Or as much of it as he could in this setting. Evelyn was thankful he hadn't asked her to undress.

"It means that if she is to walk again, I shall have to re-break it and set it properly. Even so, she will likely limp for the rest of her life. But I cannot perform such a procedure here. We must take you in to Brussels, where I have the facilities and tools I need."

"Brussels?" Paul asked. "That seems dangerous. Brussels is under Nazi occupation."

The doctor looked up at him with a grim smile. "All of Europe is under Nazi occupation, or near enough as makes no difference. If you are to survive this, you must trust me. We have helpers who can keep you safe. But you must do exactly as we say."

Paul looked at Abram, then Sean, then Evelyn.

Do we trust them? he asked.

They haven't killed us yet, Abram pointed out. *And he's a doctor...and we're all in pretty bad shape.* For the first time, the navigator let a bit of the pain he was feeling slip across the lines of the net to the others. Evelyn gasped and tried to take more from him, but he quickly shut her down. He didn't need to say it as his intent was clear: she was as bad off or worse than him.

I...I think we can trust them, Evelyn said. *I can't read any of them right now, but...my instincts say we can.*

And it's not like we have much choice anyway, Sean said. *The lieutenant's right. Evie's bad hurt and so is he. And I'm not exactly on the beam myself.*

Paul looked at each one of them one more time and then turned to the doctor and nodded.

"Fine," he said. "Don't see as we have much choice in the matter."

"None at all," the doctor said, almost cheerfully. "So I am pleased you are willing to listen to reason. Now, I must have your weapons. Those are a death sentence if you are caught...for both you and your helpers. This is an absolute condition of our help. Give me the rifles, and we will dispose of them discreetly."

Paul let out a soft curse, then pulled his rifle out from under the blanket where it had been hidden. Abram and Sean followed suit, and the doctor took each of them without another word.

"How did you know?" Paul asked.

"You did not have both hands over your head," Doctor van Duren replied. "Even though our men were pointing their weapons at you. You each kept one hand buried under the blanket. It stands to reason that you had something under there. I will not ask where you acquired Nazi weapons, for it is far better I do not know."

"Ain't that the truth," Sean murmured.

"It is, indeed," the doctor replied. One of the other men returned to their rude shelter and said something else, and the doctor nodded, then handed him the weapons. He took them outside, and another, larger man took his place beside the doctor.

"The truck has arrived," Doctor van Duren said. "There is a road just on the other side of this small hill out here. Can you men walk that far? I will have Lucas here carry this young lady."

"We can walk," Paul said shortly, getting to his feet and then offering a hand to Sean and Abram. "And I can carry Evie," the bombardier added.

"I have no doubt, but you have been weakened by your ordeal as well. Lucas has three daughters of his own. He will be a perfect gentleman, I assure you," the doctor said, and gestured to the big man beside him.

Lucas pulled off his cap, revealing a weathered, craggy face that looked to be in his late thirties or so. He nodded at Evelyn and bent to pick her up. His touch was surprisingly gentle. She suppressed a cry as he jostled her, but then she found herself cradled in his arms like a small child. His jacket smelled of wood smoke and rain and felt incredibly soft under her cheek. It was impossibly difficult not to nestle against this stranger's chest, and after a moment, she stopped trying.

Paul, Sean, and Abram followed as Lucas carried Evelyn out of the ruined structure and then up and over the hill the doctor had indicated. About a hundred yards beyond that, a small, heavily rutted track cut through the trees.

Calling this a "road" might be a bit optimistic, Paul thought dryly. *Riding in that truck is like to jostle the teeth right out of our heads!*

Better than trying to walk, Evelyn thought, trying to keep her bitterness out of her words. *I've been slowing everyone down. This will be much better.*

We're all slow, Abram said. *No need to feel special about it.*

That caused Evelyn to snort with laughter, and Lucas looked down at her with a smile that softened his forbidding features. This close, she could feel his gentleness and almost paternal concern for her emanating from his psyche. Evelyn smiled tremulously back and thought Lucas must be a good man.

They arrived at the truck, and the doctor translated while Lucas and Paul worked together to get Evelyn arranged in the back. The truck itself looked as if it had been an abandoned piece of military equipment. It had a flat bed and a metal frame, over which was strung some kind of canvas material. She sat on a pile of what looked like empty feed bags, with her injured leg elevated on another pile of the same. The three airmen piled in around her, checking her over once again, reaching out with shaking hands to touch her. Almost like they needed to reassure themselves she was still whole, after being in the care of someone else.

Lucas watched until they were all settled, then nodded and closed the back flap of canvas, leaving them sitting in the dark. The truck's engine rumbled, then roared to life, and they lurched forward.

The ride was, to say the least, painful. Evelyn's bottom and legs felt like so much tenderized meat by the time they turned off the rutted forest track and onto a smoother road. Though her backside felt an instant relief, anxiety flooded through her, echoing through the minds of her men and doubling back along the lines of the net.

A road, Abram thought grimly as the truck picked up speed. *A real one.*

Let's hope these guys know a way around patrols and entry points, Paul replied, nodding. Evelyn felt him move, although the darkness in the back of the truck was so complete they could hardly see one another.

Despite the fear, Evelyn felt herself drifting as the road noise and sensation of movement lulled her into a light doze. She couldn't have said how long they drove, though it was long enough for her to slump over onto Sean's shoulder. Paul sat with her injured leg in his lap, helping to stabilize and cushion it, and Abram reached out to cradle her right hand in his. The bond thus reinforced by physical contact, the three airmen soon followed Evelyn into sleep.

All of which disappeared in a flash of adrenaline when the truck slowed to a stop. Evelyn sat up straight and then hissed as she inadvertently jolted her injured leg. Sean gently placed his palm over her mouth, and Paul ran his hands over her ankle, checking for further injury. It hurt, but Evelyn managed not to make any more sounds.

The back flap of canvas flipped open, revealing the dim outline of a man, and the doctor's voice floated in to them.

"You must be very quiet now. We are entering the town."

"How are you gonna—?" Abram started to ask in a pugnacious whisper, but the doctor forestalled him with an outstretched hand.

"Please. You must trust me and be absolutely quiet and still."

Evelyn felt Abram's fear rising throughout the channels of the net.

This could be a trap, he thought bitterly, *and we've walked—or ridden—right into it.*

I don't think so, Evelyn said, amidst the answering fear of the other men. *That man, Lucas, when he carried me, he felt so protective. I don't think they're going to be selling us out.*

Are you sure, Evie? Sean asked. He'd dropped his fingers from her mouth and taken possession of her left hand instead. His hand tightened almost convulsively around hers. *I don't know if we'd survive being captured again...*

As sure as I can be, she answered. *I'm so...our link is so strong, but I feel almost cut off from the rest of the world. I can't get all the information I'm used to getting. But Lucas held me, so I could feel his surface emotions. He genuinely wanted to help.*

Of course, it did occur to her that she should probably try to sever their net in order to be able to better sense the world around them...but even the thought of doing so brought the screaming terror too close. And so she locked the thought away before even fully acknowledging it. Severing the net wasn't an option for her. Not right now. The men could feel it, and so they didn't ask.

Just then, Evelyn started to notice the faint strains of music. It sounded like some kind of jazz piece and was accompanied by the high sort of engine whine she'd never heard before.

What is that? she asked the men through the net. *Do you hear it?*

Duke Ellington, Sean replied, and she could feel his grin. *And what sounds like a motorcycle.*

I've never seen a motorcycle, Evelyn replied. Not that it mattered. It didn't look like she'd be seeing this one, either.

As the music and the motorcycle's engine got louder, the truck under them began to roll forward once more. They crept along at a pace just above idle. Pretty soon, Evelyn could hear that someone was singing along with the swinging jazz piece. None of them could understand the words, but the singer certainly sounded as if he was having a good time. Eventually, a few exasperated shouts in German joined the cacophony. For an idle moment, Evelyn wondered if anyone nearby was trying to sleep. It had to be really quite late.

The truck never paused but continued its slow creeping motion through what turned out to be some very twisty streets. Eventually, the sound of the shouting German, singing Belgian, and blasting jazz started to fade, and the truck began to pick up a little speed again. They made a few more turns, bumping over streets that must have been made of cobblestone. Evelyn reached down and pulled Sean's hand back up over her mouth, just in case they still needed silence.

Before too long, they rolled to a stop again, and Evelyn heard the sound of a roll-up door being opened behind them. Then the front doors of the truck cab slammed and the back flap flipped open once again. This time, a gentle lantern light greeted them, along with the doctor's smiling face.

"We made it, my friends! Thanks to Gerritsen," the doctor said, shaking his head. "Come, we must get you inside."

Her airmen helped Evelyn to slide toward the back of the truck where Lucas lifted her into his arms once more. The big Belgian then carried her close to his chest as he walked under a short awning, up a few steps, and in through a large wooden door.

Once they were inside, Evelyn head the soft *boom* of the door closing, and she lifted her head and looked around. They stood in a large, echoing empty hall made of stone. If she craned her neck backward, Evelyn could just barely make out the great stone arches that supported the vaulted ceiling.

"Is this a church?" she asked softly as Lucas started walking forward.

"A seminary," Doctor van Duren said. "Or it was, before the occupation. Now we use it as a local hospital and orphanage, since our hospital was destroyed during the invasion. You should be quite safe here, as the Nazis have their own facility. Follow me, please. The clinic is in the cellar."

He led them through the vast, echoing room that had been stripped of any sort of religious finery.

Sad, she thought idly. The pain and the exhaustion were combining to make her rather limp in Lucas' arms.

What's that, Evie? Sean asked. His mind felt just as fatigued and scattered as her own.

This place, with all the trappings gone. It must have been beautiful...

I'm sure it was Evie. Evie? Evie...

The darkness at the edge of her mind swelled, drowning out Sean's frantic calls, erasing the feel of Lucas' chest as he started to jostle her, blanking out the pain and the fear and everything as she finally went dark.

* * * *

Chapter Thirteen

"Well...Fraulein Sucherin! What a surprise to see you returned so quickly!"

Hauptman Krieger hadn't improved since their last meeting, Lina reflected. She stood motionless in front of his desk, just as she'd done when she'd first reported to his office...days ago? Weeks? She couldn't say for sure. Time had blurred together since...

No. She must not think of it. She must not fall apart here. Get through this interview, receive her assignment, and then move forward. Once she was free of this odious man, she could begin planning her next task.

She could resume her hunt.

"Very tragic, too. Who knew that such a decorated group of the Reich's Fallschirmjager would be so incompetent as to get themselves into a motorcar accident! You were lucky that you weren't harmed, my dear," Krieger said, his voice an insincere sneer.

Lina couldn't help it. Her fists clenched at her sides, and for just a moment, her anger and hatred flashed in her eyes as she stared at the pig of the man behind the desk.

Krieger merely grinned at her, enjoying her discomfort.

"Well, fortunate that you, at least, were saved. It would have been a pity, indeed, for the Reich to lose such a lovely vessel as yourself." Krieger got slowly to his feet and walked around the desk toward her. Lina fought to stand her ground, even when he came close enough to touch her cheek.

"Have you orders for me, Herr Hauptman?" Lina said quietly as the man stroked her face.

"No," he said, his voice soft. "You are to remain attached to my command for the time being."

Fear and anger clenched in Lina's gut. That couldn't be true! As a trained psychic, she was far too valuable to the Reich to be sidelined here! Not to mention, Krieger's inappropriate manner was leaving little doubt of what he envisioned as her role here.

With great care, Lina steeled her stomach and reached out a feather-light touch toward the Hauptman's surface mind: salacious desire coated his outward thoughts, along with a cruel glee and satisfaction that he'd managed to put her defiant self into his power.

She wanted to scream and blast him with her own power.

She wanted to cry Josef's name out to the heavens.

She wanted to weep until she was sick.

She did none of those things. For none of them would help her reach her ultimate goal of revenge. Instead, she took a crisp step backward, rendered her salute, and turned on her heel to leave Krieger's office.

The sound of his chuckles followed her out.

"I will see you tomorrow morning, Fraulein," he called after her. "First thing."

Lina said nothing, simply let the door close behind her. She gave a polite nod to Krieger's secretary. The woman sat behind her desk, looking at Lina with something that may have been sympathy or pity. Lina didn't know. Moreover, she didn't care.

For a plan had just emerged fully formed in her mind, as if put there by the shade of her lost beloved. She could imagine Josef's smile as he told her the details. It wouldn't be terribly hard, even. As the war dragged on, certain departments were more often in disarray than not. She would use this to her advantage.

But there was no time to waste. With firm steps, she strode out of Krieger's headquarters toward the lodgings she'd taken when she'd first arrived in this town. Fortunately for her, she'd never fully unpacked.

Two hours later, Lina boarded a train for Paris. In her handbag, she carried her original orders to Paris, where she was to assist in interrogating enemies of the Reich. Though the date on her orders was now several weeks old, the stationmaster hadn't blinked an eye when she'd presented them in lieu of a ticket.

She allowed herself a sigh of relief when she finally sank into her seat in a quiet corner of the car. It had been a close thing for her to make this train. It hadn't taken her long to gather her belongings, but she'd made an extra stop between her lodgings and the train station. She'd had to post a note she'd written to her old intelligence colleagues in Poland.

I realize this is somewhat unorthodox, she'd written, *but I haven't time to search out the proper channels, and they might be compromised, anyway. I fear this sector is in bad shape, chiefly because of the mismanagement of Hauptman Krieger. You know I hesitate to make accusations, as my word is considered proof enough, but I would not be doing my duty to the Reich if I failed to report this. His behavior appears so deliberate, so malicious, it seems to me to go beyond mere incompetence and enter the realm of deliberate sabotage. I believe my own orders were tampered with, so I attempted a covert scan of his surface thoughts. What I found there supports that hypothesis. I am forced to conclude, then, that Haupt-*

man Krieger is, at best, an uncommitted fool unsuited for command at his level. At worst, I believe he may actually be a dissident enemy of the Reich. I implore you to investigate the matter further, as I must now proceed to my next assignment in all haste, thanks to the Hauptman's mucking about and delaying my progress.

Damning. It might not seem so on the surface, but her record with the intelligence service was such that those lines from her would entirely destroy Krieger's career, if not cast him into prison for the rest of his miserable life. Lina knew this, and once it might have fazed her. But not now. Not after Josef and his men. Not after what Krieger had done to their memory, and not after the way he'd stood in her way.

For Lina had a mission, and it was one she would accomplish, regardless of who or what stood in her way. She *would* find that Ami psychic, Evelyn Adamsen, and she would destroy her. Utterly.

Then, only then, would Lina weep for what she had lost.

* * *

"There, now she comes back to us."

Evelyn blinked at the sound of the voice that she didn't immediately recognize. Or, at least, she tried to blink. Her eyelids felt stiff and heavy and coated in sand. Her mouth, too, felt as if it had been stuffed full of cotton. She exhaled a bit in frustration and tried again.

This time she got her eyelids open, and the face of Doctor van Duren smiled down at her.

"Hello Evie," he said softly. "Welcome back. Your friends have been very worried about you. Are you up to seeing them?"

Evelyn nodded, feeling like she was missing something. Why would her friends be worried? Her mind felt excruciatingly slow, like she was trying to swim upstream against a current of pudding.

"Could I have some water?" she whispered. The doctor smiled and nodded.

"Of course," the doctor said. "That would be the morphine, my dear. It makes the mouth dry. Here you are."

He reached a hand behind her shoulder and helped her up to a half-seated position before holding a small cup to her lips. Evelyn drank as deeply as she could, not caring in the least that she spilled a fair amount down her chin and onto the bedclothes that surrounded her. In fact, she found she didn't care much at all. About anything.

The doctor settled her back down to the pillows behind her, then waved to someone out of her line of vision. Still feeling like she was moving underwater, Evelyn turned her head to the side to see three men walk in through the narrow doorway.

Memory came swimming back through the fog in her brain. Evelyn reached out a hand, only to find that it was rather inconveniently tethered by a tube that ran from the back of her hand to a bottle hanging above her head. She frowned at this nuisance, then looked at her men.

For that was who they were, of course. Abram, Sean, and Paul. Her crew, or what was left of them. She felt a flicker of surprise the net hadn't snapped into place immediately upon seeing them...

Panic reared up from nowhere and overwhelmed the disconnected lassitude she felt in her mind. Without the net, she was adrift and vulnerable. The storm would take her again! It would...

"Evie!" Sean shouted, and she felt Paul grab for her fingers.

The minute his skin touched hers, the net snapped back into place, banishing the lassitude entirely. Pain came roaring back, stabbing up her leg enough to make her gasp out loud...which made her realize she'd been screaming.

"Evie, Evie, it's all right. We've got you," Paul murmured as he threaded his fingers through hers. Sean and Abram came forward as well, and both of them reached out to touch her. Abram took her other hand while Sean stroked her hair.

We're here, Evie, Sean said down the lines of the net. *You're safe. We've got you.*

Why did you leave me? Evelyn asked, pain and fear making her feel panicky. She closed her eyes and focused on the sensation of their male consciousnesses weaving in with hers. The slide of their minds was cool like the water had been, yet paradoxically warm and safe as the blankets around her. She shivered with pleasure at their return, and she slowly fought back the panic and opened her eyes.

"We didn't leave you, Evie," Abram said out loud. "You fainted downstairs, and the net broke. We would never leave you."

"But why couldn't I link with you?" Evelyn asked. Her voice sounded high and tear-soaked and edged with lingering fear.

"It was probably the morphine," Doctor van Duren said. Evelyn hadn't noticed he'd returned, though she supposed he'd probably come running when his patient started screaming. "It depresses the central nervous system. When your friends told me you were psychic, I wondered if the morphine would interfere with your gifts. It seems so. Pity, for I imagine you won't want any more, and it is the best painkiller we have."

"What did you do to me?" she asked.

"I set your leg properly. You have a fracture low above your ankle, and it was beginning to heal badly. It's going to hurt like the devil for the next few days, I'm afraid. Are you sure you won't take more morphine?"

Evelyn shook her head as vehemently as she could manage.

"Evie," Sean said. "It's okay, you can trust the doc. You've been out for a whole day, and all he did was fix us up."

"No," she gasped. "That isn't it. I need...without the net...I cannot..."

Doctor van Duren nodded.

"As I suspected," he said. "I am not extremely familiar with psychic phenomena, given the secretive nature of most psychics and the relative novelty of their...shall we say...open existence? But the literature I have read would indicate that for a psychic, the net itself can be nearly as addictive as opiates themselves. Fascinating. I wonder, Evie, if after the war, you would mind if I published a paper on you..."

"Not right now, Doc," Paul said softly, his eyes on Evelyn's face. "Evie needs to rest."

"Isn't that my decision to make?" the doctor asked a bit dryly, raising his eyebrows above the wire rims of his glasses. Paul turned and gave him a look, and the Belgian lifted his hands in surrender.

"Peace," he said, chuckling. "Worse than mothers or husbands, the three of you! Very well, I will leave my scientific curiosity for another day. And yes, Evie, you should rest. It is imperative you heal as quickly as possible, for we cannot keep you here indefinitely. It is not safe for the helpers, nor for you three. As soon as you are able, we must see about moving you along."

"Moving us along where, Doctor?" Evelyn asked.

"Why, to France, child. To France and then, God willing, home."

* * *

If Evelyn had thought she experienced pain before, the next day disabused her of that notion. Without the buffering of the painkilling drugs, her leg savaged at her in pulsing waves of agony. It was worse than it had been in the woods, by far.

The men helped, some. They bullied her into letting them take some of her pain, reasoning her body would heal faster if she didn't hurt so much. Doctor van Duren seemed fascinated by this hypothesis and watched her closely. It seemed as if he were taking her temperature and examining her every five minutes, though she knew it wasn't that frequently.

What didn't help was the complete lack of activity. Early that morning, Doctor Van Duren had moved them from her room in the basement clinic of the main chapel to an abandoned storage room under the empty dormitory wing of the seminary. It would be safer for them there, he said, since the Nazis and everyone knew he operated the clinic for the townsfolk.

Their new quarters were spartan as could be, but clean. Each of the Americans had a pallet on the floor with several warm blankets and pillows. A nearby cleaning closet had been converted into a washroom with a working pump, so they at least had plenty of water when they needed it. Though Evelyn, at least, couldn't walk and was forced to use the indignity of a bedpan to relieve herself. She would have been mortified if it hadn't hurt so much.

Other than that, though, there was simply nothing to do. So she was bored. And in agony. And the two together were maddening.

Once again, the men came to her rescue, talking about their lives before the war, about the girls they'd left at home, about what they hoped and planned for the future when they got back...anything at all to try and take their minds off of Evelyn's pain and their own healing injuries.

"How'd you first know you were psychic?" Sean asked, late that night as they huddled close together in their darkened room. They didn't want to risk any lights, for fear someone might come and investigate.

"I don't remember not knowing," Evelyn replied. Try as she might, she couldn't keep the pain from tightening her voice. She felt Sean stir next to her, and his arm went around her shoulders.

"Here, lean back on me," he said. *We're here, Evie. Let us take more of it.*

With a sigh of surrender, she acquiesced, and loosened her mental barriers enough that more of the pain could flow down the lines of the channel towards the men. She felt Sean's quick intake of breath, could hear rustling as Abram and Paul shifted uncomfortably on their pallets. She started to close it down, regret spilling into her.

No, Abram said. *We're all right. Keep talking. How did you first learn?*

"I...my mother knew," she said softly, her voice less tight, but now soaked with guilt and worry for the three of them. "I don't know how. I suppose it ran in our family. I'm told it usually does, but I don't know of anyone else with talent, for sure. But Mother knew I had it and taught me to keep it a secret."

"Why?" Sean asked. "I mean, it's amazing, the things you can do. Why did you have to keep it a secret?"

"Did you ever hear of a place called Salem, Mass?" Paul asked.

"Massachusetts? Sure. The witch trials."

"Exactly, the witch trials. That was only two hundred and fifty years ago, bud. But twenty people were killed because of accusations of witchcraft," the bombardier said, his voice bitter. "My sister was so careful, but people called her a witch anyway, even when we were just little kids."

"You defended her," Evelyn said, certain it was true. She didn't even need to touch on his memories to know.

"Yeah, I did," Paul said. "Someone had to. Anyway, I got real good at fighting. Too good, really. Then when she died, trying to save me...well...I guess I went a little crazy fighting everyone and everything. I fell in with a bad crowd, did some bad things for some bad men. I'd probably be in prison if not for my grandmother."

"What did she do?" Abram asked. "Knock your block off and set you straight?"

"Not quite," Paul said. "It was the damnedest thing. There was this guy in my hometown, a real heavy hitter type. I was working for him, you know. Roughing guys up...sometimes more. Sometimes...well. Sometimes, in that business, people gotta be silenced, you know. I got real good at keeping them silenced. I ain't proud of it, but it's what I did. Anyway, Granny, one day, she up and rolls up to my employer's business and goes in and sits down with him, like a regular appointment. When she comes out, she gives me a hug and a kiss and leaves. He calls me in and tells me that I ain't working for him no more, and he's sending me to college. I got no idea what she said to him."

As he told the story, Paul's usually very careful, correct diction thickened and roughened. Evelyn could hear the echo of the scared, lost young man he must have been.

"That's how come you were able to kill those Nazi guards so quietly the way you did," Abram said softly into the silence that followed.

"Yeah," Paul said.

In the darkness, Evelyn reached out her hand and found his. His fingers jerked a little, then closed tightly around hers.

"But the point is, it wasn't safe for a woman to let on she had psychic talent," Paul said. "I don't imagine it's safe now. I'm surprised your family let you join up. I wouldn't have let my sister."

Evelyn shrugged.

"I wanted to do my part," she said. "And with the sanction of the U.S. Army, who's going to burn me at the stake for witchcraft anyway? Besides, it's 1943. People have changed."

"Not that much," Paul said gloomily. "But don't you worry, Evie. We'll keep you safe."

"Damn straight," Sean said. "Sir."

That got a chuckle out of them, even in spite of the pulsing ache that pulled at all of them through Evelyn. The silence stretched comfortingly between them all. Safe in the feel of their minds on hers, Evelyn slept.

* * * * *

Chapter Fourteen

A few days later, Doctor Van Duren pronounced Evelyn well enough to travel.

"There has been a change of plans," the doctor said, excitement lighting up his eyes behind his spectacles. "One which, I hope, will get you home much sooner. We had thought to send you through Paris and south to Mme. Ballasdens in Bayonne, but that is a long trip, with much risk at every step."

"We're not afraid," Abram started to say, but the doctor waved a hand for him to be still.

"Of course you aren't, but it isn't you for whom I worry. Rather, the greater risk is for those helpers who risk themselves to clothe, feed, hide, and transport you. This risk is magnified every day you remain on occupied soil. So the quicker we can get you off occupied soil, the better."

"What do you mean, Doc?" Paul asked. Through the ever present psychic net, Evelyn could feel his dark caution. "We won't risk harm to Evie."

"Silly man," the doctor said, with a little laugh that dispelled any rancor in his words. "She is already at risk. This is why we must get you out as soon as possible. And that, my friends, means going to sea."

"To sea?" Abram asked, startled.

"Yes, indeed. For I have been informed that a most audacious scheme has been attempted and achieved great success. You see, my friends, instead of going south to the mountains, you shall go west to *la mer*, and from thence into the arms of the Royal British Navy."

A soft cough sounded from behind the doctor, and he turned with a smile to let the newcomer step past him into their storage closet.

"Deedee shall accompany you for the first part of your journey," the doctor said, holding out his hand to Paul first, and then Abram and Sean. When Evelyn's turn came, Doctor van Duren helped her to her feet, then embraced her and kissed both of her cheeks.

"I cannot thank you enough," Evelyn said, feeling her voice suddenly thick with tears. After so much inactivity, everything seemed to suddenly be hurtling forward. Twin threads of excitement and fear tangled inside her mind, ricocheting back and reflecting the similar emotions of the men.

"Survive and thrive," the doctor said with a smile. "Get home to safety. That will be thanks enough. Now go! There isn't much time. Listen to Deedee and follow her instructions exactly. There is no one better suited to guide you."

Evelyn blinked back sudden tears and gave the doctor a nod, then stepped away and turned to face the solemn-faced nurse they'd met in the ruined farmhouse so many days ago.

"None of you speak French, yes?" Deedee asked. Her English was passable, if accented.

"Yes," Paul said. "I speak a little Italian, that is all."

"I have some French," Evelyn said. "Enough to teach it to schoolchildren back at home."

"That may be helpful, a little," Deedee said, frowning. She turned to walk out into the basement hallway of the seminary, gesturing for them to follow her.

Though her ankle twinged as expected, Evelyn was pleased with how she moved. Apparently all those hours of alternate rest and exercise had done some good. She stepped past Deedee, who watched her closely and nodded.

"Good enough," the Belgian girl said. "If the doctor says you are fit, you are fit. I wouldn't want to take you over the Pyrenees for another few weeks, but if the sea rescue is working well, that is not an issue."

If? Evelyn heard Abram ask down the lines of the net. But he didn't say anything. They all knew that nothing was certain, least of all a rescue or escape.

"So, we shall travel together, the five of us. Evelyn, which of these men is your lover?" Deedee asked briskly.

Evelyn first paled, then flushed red. It was too dark in the dim hallway to see, but she felt certain that her face glowed hot with embarrassment. It certainly felt warm enough.

"Listen," Sean said rapidly, as Paul and Abram both growled in angry protest. "Evie's a good girl! Don't you dare..."

"Stupid man," Deedee said, impatience coloring her tone. "I'm not trying to stain her honor! I'm trying to save her life. We will be much less noticeable if we appear to be two married couples traveling with an extra man, rather than three suspiciously silent men and two women. She will be more natural if she is paired with the one she likes best anyway. So which..."

"I am equally close with all of them," Evelyn said quickly. "I will be fine pretending to be married to any of them."

"Fine," Deedee said. She flicked an impatient gesture toward Sean. "Take this one, then. And I shall be married to Paul. Abram can be your brother or cousin. The two of you look enough alike to pull that off. Our papers are being produced as we speak. We will collect them on our way to the train station. But for now, follow me. We must get you some other clothing."

* * *

Three hours later, Evelyn leaned back into the hard wooden seat as the train lurched forward and began to move. Her hands, palms damp with sweat, lay curled in her lap, and she held herself very still, careful to keep her eyes on the toes of the shiny brown boots Deedee had given her.

Sean reached over and pulled one of her hands into his own. She turned to give him a wan smile.

Are you all right? he asked her, his concern flowing down the lines of the net.

I'm fine, she replied. *Just nervous. I'm supposed to be looking ill, right?*

Deedee had decided that the easiest way to avoid being questioned was for Evelyn to pretend to be ill and sleep most of the time. The train was to take them all the way into Paris, with a stop at the French border. In a small valise at her feet, Evelyn had the precious forged papers that Deedee had handed her an hour ago. From what Evelyn could tell, they seemed to be very good forgeries. They didn't look new at all.

Across the aisle, Deedee herself sat with Paul, her head leaning on his shoulder as she, too, pretended to sleep. Or perhaps she really slept. Who knew? Her unrelenting calm collectedness made Evelyn feel even more like a ball of nerves. How many times had the Belgian nurse carried out this particular ruse? Was it possible she'd gotten used to the risks?

She's not as calm as she looks, Paul said with a trace of humor. *I can feel her pulse thudding in her wrist. I don't think she's asleep, either.*

I should have linked with her, Evelyn said, feeling a stab of regret. She also felt a surge of trepidation at the thought of allowing another woman, psychic or not, into her mind. She shoved that away, though, and refused to acknowledge it. *I suppose it might be useful to be able to communicate.*

We can do that later, if need be, Paul said. *I don't think you need to worry about it right now.*

The train accelerated steadily ahead, sending a rhythmic, rocking motion through the train car. Evelyn closed her eyes and followed Deedee's example by resting her head on her "husband's" shoulder. After a moment, she felt Sean's hand stroking her hair.

She didn't really sleep, but the motion of the train lulled Evelyn into a kind of semi-consciousness. She remained peripherally aware of her surroundings through the senses of her three companions and let her own mind drift. It wasn't sleep per se, but it was better than nothing.

Some time later, she felt Abram's attention sharpen.

We're slowing, he said. *We must be approaching the border.*

Sure enough, Evelyn felt it too: a building force that dragged at the train around them, forcing her weight gradually forward in her seat as they slowed. She blinked and lifted her head to find Sean looking down at her.

I'm all right, she said with a smile, and reached down for her bag. Just as she pulled out her traveling papers, the door at the far end of the railroad car opened up, and a man wearing the uniform of a customs inspector stepped inside.

Be calm, Paul advised them as he, too, sat up straighter in his seat. *Remember, we want to blend in.*

Doing my best, but I don't have a pretty Belgian to cuddle with, Abram shot back with a bit of humor. Evelyn fought the urge to smile and looked down at her papers.

The inspector was quick, but thorough. Before long, he stepped up to stand beside Evelyn's seat and reached out a hand.

"Bonjour. Your papers, please?" he said in French.

"Bonjour," Evelyn whispered, and handed her papers over. Sean did the same.

"You are bound for Paris?" the man asked. Evelyn transmitted his question over the net, and Sean nodded.

"What is your reason for traveling?"

"My sister is ill," Deedee supplied from her seat across the aisle. "We are taking her to see a Parisian doctor. Please forgive my brother-in-law, monsieur, he does not hear so well."

"Ill, on a train? There is no risk of contagion, then?" the inspector asked sternly.

"Oh, no, monsieur," Deedee said. "It is a female complaint."

"Ah," the inspector said, nodding. He handed the papers back to Sean and gave them all a nod. "Best of luck with the doctor then, madame."

"Merci," Evelyn whispered again, and the inspector moved on. Once he'd made his way around the car, he exited, and Evelyn felt each of the men take a breath of relief. Without further incident, the train slid jerkily back into motion, and they continued toward Paris.

* * *

L ina had heard Paris called the "City of Lights," but she didn't see it that way. The sky, the light, and the buildings were gray and old, the streets crowded and dirty. Perhaps before the war, people had been friendly and welcoming, but that was not the case now. Or at least, that was not the reception she received.

With a deep breath, Lina squared her shoulders and stepped away from the train platform. The uniformed police officer gave her a perfunctory nod as she walked past him and out onto the rain-slick streets. The drizzle had stopped for the moment, but the gloom remained.

Fortunately for Lina, she didn't have far to go. The Paris office of the intelligence service was about a kilometer from the train station. As the day was chilly, Lina welcomed the exertion, especially after sitting so long on the train with nothing but her dark thoughts for company.

She couldn't have said why, but all of her instincts drew her here, to Paris. If she was going to track the Ami psychic and her butchers down, she had to start here. The hand of the Reich had been much lighter here than in Warsaw, she knew. Perhaps that would encourage the fugitives to make a careless mistake? She could only hope so. One thing, however, was certain. The Ami bitch *would* make a mistake eventually.

And when she did, Lina would be there.

"Lina! As I live and breathe!" a jovial voice called out her name, and despite everything, Lina felt her lips curve in a smile. "You made it! I was thrilled to get your note and learn you'd been posted here."

A moment later, Lina found herself enveloped in a crushing bear hug. She let out a little laugh and patted the wide shoulders that held her.

"Herr Sendler! Some air, please!" she said softly and dryly. The big man let out a booming laugh and immediately let go.

"My apologies. My enthusiasm overcomes my better sense," Neils Sendler said, giving her the disarming grin she'd seen so many times before. As ever, his red hair looked slightly disheveled, and his blue eyes twinkled in merriment. One of the qualities that made him so effective as an intelligence operative was that Neils Sendler was the best she'd ever seen at disarming people. He played up his cuddly, harmless image and used it to get people to open up to him, to trust him. Next to Lina herself, he'd had the best record of successful interrogations during their time in Warsaw. And, as he was a man, he did it all without psychic abilities.

"I see you've been promoted," Lina said then, glancing around at the interior of the office. It was sparsely furnished, but clean, and what furnishings there were looked well-made and expensive. "Congratulations."

"And to you, Oberhelfer," he said with a smile. "You certainly deserve it. Shall we step back into my office and have some tea? I'm afraid it's going to rain again soon, from the looks of the damned gray sky."

"I would like that, thank you," she said. He patted her hand and gestured for her to precede him down the hallway.

"Just here, on the left. The tea is already on its way," he said as she stepped into the small room. It, too, held a minimum of good quality pieces: a fine wooden desk faced two cushioned chairs. Behind the desk, a window opened onto the Parisian street. As she watched, a few fat drops of rain began to patter down and splash against the glass. She let out a little sigh and sank into one of the chairs. Perhaps she should have waited for an invitation, but Neils was, after all, an old friend.

"You are well, then?" he asked as he gently closed the door. "I was somewhat alarmed at the tone of your note."

"I am," she replied, smiling up at him as he seated himself at the desk. "As well as I can be."

"Krieger did not hurt you? We have taken steps already, of course, but if he dared to outrage you..."

"No," she said. "I have no doubt that was his intent, but I got out of there quickly enough. And I thank you for your actions on my behalf."

Neils waved a hand as if to say that it was of no moment. Just then, the door opened and a young Frenchwoman brought in the tray of tea.

"Ah, thank you, Sophie," Neils said. The woman gave him a smile and let herself back out. Though the door closed silently behind her, Lina could hear the creaking of the floorboards as she walked away. The psychic raised an eyebrow at Neils, who smiled back.

"Elegant," Lina said.

"Thank you," Neils said modestly. "I am relatively certain that Sophie can be trusted, but in Paris, who knows?"

"That was what I wished to speak to you about," Lina said. "Has there been much in the way of resistance to our occupation?"

Neils shrugged and tilted his head to the left, then to the right.

"Some," he said. "Nothing we cannot handle, of course, but some. Why?"

"Specifically, I am interested in knowing if the people here are sheltering enemy airmen."

"It happens," Neils said, leaning forward and putting his elbows on his desk. "We have caught some. I am certain there are more. Again, Lina, I ask. Why?"

Icy hatred gripped Lina's throat; she found herself unable to speak for a moment. She swallowed hard and forced the words past teeth that wanted to clench.

"My last assignment, we found four of them. They were prisoners, but they killed my men and escaped. I want them captured. I want them to pay."

She hadn't meant to add that last bit. In truth, even revealing the personal nature of her quest was a risk. Revenge was all well and good, but there were some who would argue it did not serve the needs of the Reich. Lina herself had been one such, only a few short weeks ago.

A few short weeks...but a lifetime ago.

"I see," Neils said softly. He looked at her for a long moment, his blue eyes grave. "You cared about these men."

"Yes," Lina said, her mind flinching away from the thought of one in particular.

"Well," he said slowly. "As it happens, I do have orders to look into that very thing, though it's not the top priority. But Lina, I need to know...can you do this? As a professional? I know that this is personal with you, and I do not object...so long as you are able to do the job properly."

"I am," she said, her voice devoid of emotion. "I give you my word. If I find otherwise, I will tell you. I will follow procedure and provide appropriate documentation and updates."

"I know that you will, Lina, my friend," he said, his blue eyes soft and sad. "And...I am very sorry for your loss."

"So am I, Herr Sendler. So am I."

* * *

They made it to Paris. Evelyn felt as if she were on edge the whole time. Her nerves echoed back through the net, ricocheting off of the men and magnifying their own anxiety. She should have disconnected the net for all of their sakes...but she couldn't. She couldn't even entertain the idea without the specter of the howling storm rearing up in the back of her mind.

So she didn't think about it. Besides, there were significant benefits to remaining in a constant net with the men. She knew when one of them was asleep; she could see through their eyes; she could tell when they were angry, or nervous, or in pain. They could communicate without words. She could even, after a fashion, teach them a few words of French.

This was a game that they played on the train. None of them could really sleep, so they practiced thinking of simple words and phrases. Evelyn found them to be quick studies, but she worried about their pronunciation.

You must make your consonants softer, rounder, she said at one point, when Sean was trying to say "good morning" in his head. *French is a romance language. You must speak it like...like...*

Like kissing a girl? Abram said slyly. Evelyn felt her face blush and looked to where he sat, leaning against the opposite window, eyes closed. A bit of a smile curved his lips. *Soft and round and gentle-like?*

I suppose so, Evelyn said, rather primly. *I've not kissed many girls, so I'll defer to your greater experience.*

Sean snorted softly and squeezed Evelyn's hand in acknowledgment of her hit. Across the aisle, Paul coughed softly into his hand to cover a bit of laughter.

Evelyn would have cautioned him, but just then the train's horn blasted through the air. She felt her body jerk forward and shudder as the engineer began to brake. A look out the window showed that the winter countryside had faded away, leaving cold-looking old buildings stacked cheek-by-jowl next to one another. The conductor opened the door at the end of the car and made a short announcement: they had arrived in Paris.

The train pulled to a stop, and in the bustle of gathering up their things, Deedee managed to whisper instructions to Paul.

"Stay close, and don't say anything," she said. "Have your papers out so that you needn't speak."

Paul nodded, and Evelyn bent to retrieve her traveling papers from her bag. She could feel her tension ratchet up again as the passengers began to file off the train. In order to keep her hands from shaking, she wrapped her arm through Sean's.

It's all right, Evie, the redhead said, patting her arm and giving her a smile. *We're all here. We'll be all right.*

I hope so, she said. She smile and put a brave face on, even though her insides roiled with fear. What if someone tried to speak to them as they got off of the train? What if they were caught? What if...?

No. That way lay madness. Evelyn forced herself to focus on the here and now. She pulled strength from Paul, Abram, and Sean. Each of them acted as a pillar of steadiness in completely different ways. Sean focused on her, allowing himself to sink into his role as solicitous husband. Abram adopted a pleasant expression and glanced around like a country boy visiting the big city for the first time. Paul remained stony-faced and stoic, much as he must have once done as a mob enforcer.

Evelyn felt her shoulders straighten, and she forced herself to smile tremulously at Sean. Her men were here, with her. They would keep her safe. She would be all right.

With this litany running through her mind, Evelyn and Sean followed Paul and Deedee off the train. Abram brought up the rear of their little group, his bumpkin-like gawping serving as an excuse to look for police or anyone who might give them trouble. The only potential problem was a bored-looking sergeant waiting as they disembarked. He barely glanced at their papers before waving them through.

"This way," Deedee said in French, as she led them from the train platform into the large, bustling terminal. "Back toward the back. There is a washroom where we may freshen up." People crowded close all around them, hurrying to and fro. The air seemed filled with a dull roar of conversation and movement. The noise and jostling seemed to crowd in on Evelyn. She'd never been in such a large train station before.

We've got you, Sean reminded her. Evelyn forced herself to take a deep breath and keep walking. It helped if she focused on the pleat at the back of Deedee's coat, she found.

Eventually, the noise dimmed and began to sound like it was coming through a kind of echoing tunnel. Evelyn raised her eyes to see they'd entered a hallway off the main open terminal space. Two doors stood alongside the right wall, each bearing a picture of a vaguely human silhouette.

Deedee stopped suddenly and turned to Paul. She put her hands on either side of his face and lifted herself up on tiptoe so that she could press her lips hard against his.

Evelyn felt Paul's shock zing through him. Something hard and warm pressed against his lower lip, and the abrupt realization that she was passing him something reverberated through the net. Both Sean and Abram jumped slightly, and Paul finally raised his hands to cup Deedee's face as he pulled the metal object into his mouth.

"We won't be long," Deedee said with a smile, and reached out to take Evelyn's hand.

Paul nodded and tried to look as if he wasn't holding something in his mouth. Deedee gestured to the washroom door bearing the sign of a figure wearing trousers and then pulled Evelyn through the other door.

"What did you give him?" Evelyn whispered as soon as she realized that they were alone in the women's room.

"A key," Deedee said. "It opens the door that they will find on the back wall of the washroom. I told Paul about it on the train. How did you know?"

"I...just guessed," Evelyn said. It wasn't that she didn't trust Deedee. Indeed, the woman held their lives in her hands. It was just that she didn't know whether *Deedee* would trust a psychic. "So someone is waiting for them on the other side?"

"Yes, one of our people."

"Who is it?"

"What?"

"Who is waiting for them? What do they look like?"

Deedee narrowed her eyes and looked at Evelyn closely.

"Mademoiselle Garreau," she said slowly, "Why? Will you tell them?"

"What?" Evelyn asked, startled. She took a step back from the intense young woman in front of her. "I—I don't know what you mean."

"Please, I have eyes, do I not? The doctor told me that you have a habit of...linking with your companions. Are you linked with them now? You must trust me, Evelyn. This could become a matter of life or death."

It already is, Evelyn thought, and then to the men, *Deedee knows about the net. She says that someone, one of her people, is waiting for you on the other side of that door.*

What about you? Abram asked.

I don't know yet.

We're not leaving without you.

I know.

"They say," Evelyn whispered, "they're not leaving without me."

Deedee's lips may have curved in a tiny smile just a bit, Evelyn wasn't sure, but her nod was all business.

"Of course not. Nor should they. They will wait in a café across the street with my contact. We will exit out of a neighboring shop. Buy a trinket, that kind of thing. What tourists do in Paris."

"All right," Evelyn said, and relayed the plan to the men. Paul objected to having Evelyn out of sight for too long but was mollified by the information the "shop" was really an open-air booth next to the terminal exit. They'd be able to see her the whole time.

And it's not as if we need line of sight like this, she added.

No, but if we can see you, we can get to you faster, Paul responded grimly, and Evelyn had to concede that his point was valid. In any case, this plan, too, worked like clockwork, and a few moments later, the two women walked across the wet-slick cobblestones of the Paris street to join the men at the café. In the shop, Deedee had purchased a lovely scarf of pale blue, which she had given to Evelyn with instructions to put it on.

"So if you need to change your look suddenly, you remove the scarf from your hair. Voilà, you are much harder to find," the Belgian woman had said, matter-of-factly.

"Thank you," Evelyn had said, but inwardly, she'd wondered how many times Deedee and her ilk had done this. She seemed to be almost frighteningly good at it.

I hope she's that good, for our sakes, Paul said. *Her attention to the details could be our salvation or our downfall. I suppose I'm happy she thinks the way she does.*

As am I, Evelyn said. Besides, it really was a lovely scarf.

After the café, they boarded a streetcar that took them to an established, but apparently well-to-do neighborhood. Their guide, Mademoiselle Garreau, led them down one side street after another until they eventually entered a home through a small gate in a wildly overgrown hedge. Had Mademoiselle Garreau not been there, Evelyn would never have known the gate existed.

Beyond the gate, a small, neatly laid out garden sat at its winter's rest. Stepping stones laid out a curving path that led to a back door in an unassuming white house with gray shutters.

"Inside, quickly," Mademoiselle Garreau said, gesturing for them to hurry. The sun had set, and under the cover of the deepening twilight, they slipped one by one into the Paris safe house.

* * *

Thanks to all the walking they'd done, Evelyn's leg had begun to throb in agony. She limped across the threshold of the door and nearly ran directly into someone who was standing on the other side.

"Come in! Come in! Ugh, this winter weather. Come in, child, sit by the fire and get warm!"

The man's voice was deep and melodious, like that of someone who sang well and often. Evelyn looked up to see the flash of a white smile before someone gently took her elbow and guided her through a narrow hallway into the room beyond.

It was a kitchen...but *such* a kitchen! The room was large and sunken so Evelyn had to navigate about three steps on her healing ankle. The person holding her elbow helped, but before she could utter her thanks, she found herself whisked over to a large, cushioned armchair by the massive stone fireplace. The thing looked as if it were big enough to roast an entire cow, and a corner of Evelyn's mind wondered if it hadn't done just that at some point or another in the past.

Several more chairs ringed the hearth, their mismatched upholstery painted in an orange glow from the flames. Evelyn heard the voices of her men and then Mademoiselle Garreau's soft murmur.

"Any trouble?" the man asked.

"Non," Mademoiselle Garreau said in French before switching to English. "Papa, Deedee you already know. These are Paul, Abram, Sean, and the lady is Mademoiselle Evelyn."

"Enchanté" Monsieur Garreau said, smiling over at Evelyn. "Welcome to our home. I am Marc Garreau, and you've already met Nicole. We have been expecting you. Will you have some wine? Food? Tea?"

Garreau and his daughter began to bustle about, slicing bread from the huge loaf that sat on the equally impressive wooden table that dominated the room. They poured warmed, spiced wine into tumblers and handed them out. Evelyn took a sip of hers and felt it burn a delicious trail all the way to her stomach. With the wine, the bread, some cheese, and a few slices of beef from a roast the Garreaus kept in their icebox, they made a merry, if exhausted, meal.

"So the plan," Deedee said, "is you will rest here tonight and board the train for St. Brieuc in the morning. It will be early."

"We will be ready," Abram said.

"Good. Gentlemen, you will sleep downstairs in the cellar. Evelyn, you and I will share Nicole's room," Deedee said.

Paul looked like he wanted to protest, but Evelyn pushed him to be silent through the link. While they were eating, she'd noticed that the Garreaus' decor carried a definite religious tone.

I think Garreau is a devout Catholic, Evelyn said. *I know that war is war, but he's been so kind to us. I don't wish to upset him. And...I don't think we're in danger from them.*

I don't like it, Paul said.

I don't, either, Abram put in, *but Evie's right. We need to respect the man's beliefs in his own house. And if they wanted to hurt us...*

We'd already be in a Nazi prison. You're right. I just...

I know, Evelyn said, and sent a pulse of soothing affection down the lines of the net to all of them. *I don't like being far from any of you, either. But we'll be linked. I think it will be all right.*

And so it was. Evelyn found herself lying in a large bed between Deedee and Nicole Garreau, who made a quiet remark that it was almost like having her elder sisters home again. Evelyn smiled and wished for a moment that she'd met the quiet, dark beauty under other circumstances. She rather thought that she and Nicole would have gotten along well in the normal world.

Her last thought as she drifted off to sleep was of Mary, the closest thing she had to a sister of her own. How was her friend doing? Evelyn wondered. And would she really see her again soon?

* * * * *

Chapter Fifteen

Despite the early hour, Evelyn actually felt pretty good as they boarded the train the following morning. Deedee had stayed at the Garreaus' house, and only Nicole accompanied them to the train station.

"Keep your wits about you and blend in," Deedee had admonished Evelyn when they left the house. "Your tickets are to Guingamp, where you will meet with my contact. Look for a girl in a blue coat at the central market. She will be selling pears. Ask her if she's got any work. She will help you backtrack to Plouha. Beyond that, it is better I do not know your route."

"I understand," Evelyn had said, and she did. Having been at the mercy of Adalina Sucherin, she knew very well the Nazi Reich had powerful interrogation assets. Deedee was clever and tough, but these were not true guarantees of safety. If she were to be taken, too much knowledge could cause the entire line to collapse.

"Good luck," Deedee had said and then surprised Evelyn with a quick, hard embrace before turning to leave.

Unlike the previous day, this winter morning in Paris dawned bright and almost warm. This unexpected cheer contributed to Evelyn's good mood as they made their way to the train. It wasn't the huge, bustling terminal of the day before, but rather a smaller station with rail lines to several outlying provinces. As before, the police checked their documents as they boarded, but judging by the yawns, their particular officer was more concerned with his lack of sleep

297

than with spotting fugitives. They settled in to a half-empty car and waited for the train to jerk into motion.

Everyone all right? Abram asked down the lines of the net once they started to move. *I feel more rested than I have in a while.*

Me too, Evelyn said. *My ankle even hurts a little less, finally.*

That's terrific, Evie! Sean said. *But...*

I know, Paul said. He'd closed his eyes and was pretending to sleep, but Evelyn could feel the roil of his all-too-active mind. *It makes me nervous, too. I feel like everything is going too smoothly. Like the other shoe is about to drop.*

We just have to keep our wits about us and blend in, Evelyn said, thinking of Deedee. *If we can do that, we'll be all right.*

Plus, Abram added, *we have you, Evie.*

I don't know how much help I am, she said, feeling a jolt of self-deprecation.

Stop! Sean said, from where he sat next to Evelyn. His emotion cracked across the lines of the net like a whip. *Just stop it, Evie!*

What—? I—

No. You think we don't feel how you devalue yourself? Just stop it! I wouldn't be here. None of us would be here if it weren't for you. We'd be in some Nazi camp, getting the sh—snot beaten out of us!

Paul rescued you, not me, Evelyn protested, mostly because she didn't know what else to say.

Bullshit, Paul said, and for once, no one apologized for the profanity. *The only reason I was able to do what I did was because you had that Nazi psychic's attention all locked up. If it hadn't been for you, she would have felt me as soon as I took out the first guard. I never would have attacked if I'd known they had a psychic. So you kept me safe. And I'm betting that it's not a coincidence that the Nazi commander just decided to up and shoot his men and then himself, after strangling his psychic. I don't know what you did, but it's the reason we're not all dead right now. Sean's right. Stop devaluing yourself. It weakens all of us.*

Evelyn felt as if she'd been slapped. She turned her face to the window and blinked to keep her sudden tears from falling.

Evie, Sean said, his tone less angry, but no less vehement. *Don't take it like that! It's just. Damnit, Evelyn. We love you. Can't you see that? You're closer to us than...anyone. It just kills me...all of us...to feel how you don't know your own worth.*

I know I'm powerful, Evelyn said slowly, miserably. Her fingers sat woodenly in Sean's, and she kept looking out the window. They'd left the outskirts of Paris behind, and sun-drenched, winter brown hills rolled past. *I've always known that.*

That's not what we're talking about, Evie, Sean said. He sighed quietly and let the matter drop, but he didn't let go of her hand. Nor did she withdraw it. Even angry as she was, his touch helped to push back the memory of bloody bodies sprawled in a tent.

The silence stretched on for several miles. As the train wound its way west, the sun rose higher in the sky, and the long shadows of the track-side telegraph poles shortened to nothing.

After a while, Abram shifted slightly in his seat and put down the book he'd been pretending to read. He turned to look out the window and reached out along the net.

We're going to St. Brieuc, right? Anyone know why we're continuing on for two stops beyond that one? he asked.

Deedee told me, Evelyn said, trying not to sound tentative. *They used to go to St. Brieuc and then take a local to Plouha, but the Germans closed that route down. There were arrests, apparently.*

What does that mean? Abram asked, pushing.

She didn't fully say, Evelyn said. *I got the feeling she didn't really want to talk about it. All I got was that one of the escapees blew their cover. Spoke too loudly in English, I think she said. Anyway, there was a German officer nearby, and that particular group got caught, along with their helper. They haven't heard from him since. They know he was shipped to a prison camp in Germany, but that's it. She fears he is dead.*

Sobering, Paul said, in his laconic way.

Yes, Evelyn said. *So now we take the train to Guingamp and backtrack to Plouha. She said we were to look for a girl in a blue coat selling pears at the market.*

There had better be only one girl who fits that description.

I think it's a small market.

Let's hope so.

* * *

The market in Guingamp was, indeed, small. Really, it was nothing more than a few stalls lining the street that led to an impressive church. Though she wasn't Catholic, Evelyn could appreciate the grandeur of the buildings belonging to the Church of Rome. France was a predominantly Catholic nation, and even though the Nazi Reich officially frowned upon the practice of traditional religions, Evelyn could see the people of Guingamp flowing into and out of the beautiful old stone building in a steady stream.

Pears, she said? Abram asked, breaking Evelyn out of her reverie. *There doesn't seem to be a single piece of fruit for sale at this market. There doesn't seem to be much of anything for sale, for that matter.*

Times are hard, Paul put in. *There's a war on. Maybe you've heard?*

Thanks, wise guy.

There's a girl in a blue coat, Sean said, interrupting the mental bickering. *Perhaps she's the one?*

I don't know, Evelyn said, doubt shading her mind. *What if it isn't? We could be in big trouble if we approach the wrong person.*

We could be in just as much trouble if we approach no one, Abram pointed out. *I say we ask her. I don't see anyone else in blue, so it's worth a shot, at least.*

You're the boss, Boss, Sean said. *Evie and I will go, and maybe Evie can tell if she's going to turn on us.*

I can try, Evelyn said, and shoved down the sudden geyser of fear that erupted deep within her mind. She hid it away quickly, hoping that none of the men would feel that treacherous bit of doubt. It had been plaguing her ever since the ruined farmhouse in the wilds of Belgium. She'd avoided thinking about it, but the truth was getting harder and harder to ignore: Evelyn wasn't sure she could do that anymore. The thought of linking with another woman made her mouth go dry and her pulse accelerate with fear. And then there was the issue of disconnecting from the men...no. She couldn't even think about doing that. Even if it meant she had to risk exposing the net to another person. She couldn't disconnect. The storm would swallow her again.

You can do it, Evie. We all believe in you, Sean said firmly, as he laced his hand in hers once again. He lifted a hand to the others, as if he was telling them that he'd be right back, and then strode over to the girl in the blue coat as she worked to disassemble one of the booths.

"Excuse me, Mademoiselle," Evelyn said in French. "My husband and I are wondering if you might have any work?"

The girl's head came up sharply, and she looked narrowly at them.

"No. I have none, as you can see. Who told you to ask?"

"A Mademoiselle Deedee, in Paris?"

Her face shuttered, and she turned away.

"I don't know anyone by that name."

Reach out, Sean urged Evelyn, squeezing her hand lightly. *Try!*

Evelyn pulled in a deep breath and tentatively began to push her awareness out toward the girl. It was harder than it should have been, likely because she was out of practice, but she judged she was gentle enough as she touched the girl's public mind. It also took much more of her concentration to keep that particular line of connection isolated from her net with the men, but she managed.

Suspicion. Fear. The sinking knowledge that if she were taken, others would likely lose their lives. The girl in the blue coat didn't think she could withstand the torture she'd heard the Nazis used to elicit information.

You can trust us, Evelyn said. *We're American airmen, and we were sent here by Deedee. Please, we're not going to betray you. We can't!*

The girl's eyes got very wide, and she looked up at Evelyn.

What...you?

Yes, Evelyn said. *Please, will you help us?*

How are you doing this? It is like I can hear you in my mind!

It is a talent I have. It is why you feel my sincerity when I tell you that we will not harm you.

You and your husband?

And two other men. There, by the fountain.

Yes, you are right. I can feel your sincerity. I am sorry I was suspicious at first. Others have been taken not far from here. But...there is an escape planned soon.

We are to be part of it, according to Deedee. She said to look for a girl in a blue coat selling pears.

Yes, well, the Nazis have taken them all. I have none to sell. But I will help you.

"Perhaps you can help me, after all," the girl said. "My name is Nanette. And I need this booth torn down. Do you and your husband have any friends you can call? I would like it if we could tear it down this afternoon. My uncle will come with a truck, and he can help us haul the pieces away."

"Yes, of course," Evelyn said, and gave Nanette a tremulous smile. Sean nodded at the girl and turned to walk back to where Paul and Abram waited by the fountain. The three men spoke in hushed tones, in case anyone might be watching, and then came back to the booth.

"Nanette, Sean, my husband. And these are our friends Paul and Abram."

"Good. You can begin by disassembling this table and these boards. I must go send a message to my uncle. If you are interested, he may have further work for you, but only if you are efficient and do not waste time socializing." The Frenchwoman spoke briskly, as if to someone she neither knew nor truly trusted. Through her connection, Evelyn could tell that Nanette worried a great deal about being overheard.

"Oui, Mademoiselle," Abram said, and touched the brim of the cap he'd been given by Monsieur Garreau. Nanette gave him a nod and an impatient gesture that said "get to it," then turned to Evelyn.

"You can sweep," she said, using that same tone. She reached behind the soon-to-be disassembled booth and pulled out a broom. *And if anyone approaches, speak for the men. You seem to have some French, yes?*

"Thank you," Evelyn said, taking the broom by the handle. *I do, yes. It is not perfect, though.*

It is better than nothing. It is well you are with them. The group looks far less suspicious with a woman. I will go see my uncle and ask him to hurry. The faster we get you out of here, the better. Nanette gave her one more nod, then turned her back and continued to gather up the remaining small items she had at the booth. A few moments later, she turned and left them without another word. Evelyn let the connection drop with a sigh of relief.

Do we trust her? Paul asked down the net as he used a clawed hammer to pry nails from boards.

I think we must, Evelyn said. *In any case, she felt genuine to me. She is very, very frightened, however. I think the Gestapo has been pushing hard in this area.*

Hopefully we won't have to worry about it much longer, Abram said. Evelyn could feel a note of determined optimism in his mind. Abram was their senior officer, and he seemed to feel it necessary to keep them from descending into a gloom of negative thought. In truth, it balanced well with Paul's often bleak realism and tendency towards suspicion. Perhaps, with their individual temperaments complementing one another, the four of them might make it out of this alive, after all.

They worked steadily for an hour or two. By the time Nanette returned, the men had the booth completely disassembled and the lumber stacked in neat piles, ready for pickup. Evelyn was just sweeping out the last of the detritus that had accumulated under the structure when a truck roared up and the Frenchwoman hopped out of the front seat.

"Hmm," she said, in a non-committal tone, and rattled off instructions to the truck's driver in a stream of rapid-fire French. He grunted a response that Evelyn didn't hear and climbed down out of his seat in the truck.

This is your uncle? Evelyn asked, as she reached out to Nanette's mind once more. Though her psyche was slippery, and not at all as delicious and comfortable as the minds of her men, it was easier to establish contact this second time. The thought gave Evelyn a tiny spike of hope. Perhaps she wasn't completely damaged, after all.

Yes. His name is Ned Cosca. He will take you all to Plouha. Your friends work quickly and well. I cannot say so out loud, but please relay my thanks when you can.

I will.

I thank you. Good luck to you all, Evelyn.

Thank you, Nanette, for everything.

With that, Evelyn severed the connection again, and they got to work loading the boards and things up onto the back of Monsieur Cosca's truck. It didn't take a terribly long time. Once they were done, Monsieur Cosca grunted and waved his hand at the bed and then opened the passenger side door and gave a little half-bow in Evelyn's direction.

I suppose we're ready to go, Evelyn said to the men on the net. She gave Cosca a small smile and climbed into the cab of the truck while the men clambered into the bed and situated themselves amidst the piles of booth debris.

Cosca shut the door of the truck and walked around to enter on the driver's side. As he started up the engine, Evelyn ventured another smile in his direction.

"Thank you, Monsieur," she said quietly.

He grunted and gave her a nod, then put the truck in gear with a slight grinding noise. Evelyn felt her teeth start to rattle as they pulled out onto the cobblestone streets, and she sent a wave of sympathy back to the men riding in the truck bed.

Thankfully, they didn't have far to go, at least not at first. Cosca brought them to a slightly dilapidated barn outfitted with a number of mechanical contraptions. Evelyn didn't know what they were for, but she recognized them as the tools of a mechanic's trade and realized that Cosca had brought them to his business.

"We will unload the truck, wait for dark," the older man said abruptly. "Easier to move about then."

"Even with the curfew?" Evelyn asked softly. Cosca grunted a vague affirmative.

"I carry supplies for the Boches," he said. "Special pass. They let me drive at night. Less cart traffic on the roads."

"All right," Evelyn said.

Evie, any idea why we're stopping? Abram asked as Cosca cut the engine and opened the door.

Monsieur Cosca says that we're going to unload the truck and wait until after curfew. Apparently he's got a special pass to move around at night.

How did he manage that?

He runs supplies for the German army.

Abram's only reply was a startled burst of mental laughter, echoed by a foreboding feeling from Paul. Sean said nothing, merely radiated support for Evelyn and the officers.

Well, let's get this stuff unloaded, then, Abram said after a minute. Evelyn opened up her door and followed Cosca out, but when she tried to lift a hand to help, he frowned at her and made a shooing gesture.

"This is men's work, Mademoiselle," he said in French. "Go inside and rest. There is bread and cheese, a little wine. We will join you shortly."

Evelyn shot a look toward Abram and relayed Cosca's instructions. Abram gave her a nod.

But be careful, Evie, he cautioned her. *If anything feels wrong, get out of there or call us immediately!*

I will, she promised.

But nothing did. As Cosca had said, there was a bottle of wine and half a round of a sharp, orange cheese sitting on the table next to two wide loaves. They looked freshly baked, but Evelyn could see no sign of anyone who might have baked them. When her quick, exploratory "hello" went unanswered, she shrugged and seated herself at the table. Once again, she had cause to be grateful to the men for giving her the knife she carried, as it came in quite handy for slicing the bread and the cheese.

About thirty minutes later, the sun slanted in through the grimy windows, and Evelyn felt the men finishing up their task. A quick look around the kitchen area where she sat showed her a rack of small but clean glass tumblers and a few mismatched plates. She took these items and arranged four simple meals of bread and cheese around the table.

Cosca was the first one in. He took a look at the table, and his face flushed. He nodded wordlessly to her and took his seat. Abram, Paul, and Sean followed. While the men ate, Evelyn busied herself by tidying up the kitchen as best she could. No need not to be a good houseguest, as far as she was concerned.

In truth, she wished she could do more. These people—Cosca, his niece Nanette, Nicole Garreau and her father Marc...and especially Deedee and Doctor van Duren—were doing so much for them. Evelyn thought of the medical care, the food, and clothing they'd provided. She thought of Nanette and the looming dread she'd be caught...but also her courage in helping them anyway. Evelyn's eyes filled with tears, and she ducked her head to keep them as secret as possible.

Not that it was very possible. Sean, of course, was the first to notice her emotionally charged state. He sat up straight in his chair and looked over at her, not caring if Cosca noticed.

Evie! What's wrong? Did he say something to you?

No! No, nothing like that, Evelyn hastily sent over the net. *He's been so kind. They've all been so kind...*

And that thought did it. Her breath broke out of her on an audible sob that had all of the men, including Cosca, looking up at her with alarm.

"I'm s-sorry," Evelyn said, her voice cracking and tears overflowing her eyes. "I'm so sorry! You've been so kind, Monsieur. So kind...all of you have. We owe you so much, and I fear we shall never be able to repay any of you..."

Another sob shook her thin frame, and she slapped her hand over her mouth to keep from making too much noise. Sean got up from the table and wrapped Evelyn in an embrace. She put her head on his shoulder and let herself cry.

Cosca looked at her for a long moment, then turned and looked at all of them.

"Yes," he said in thickly accented English. "You will. Go home. Return to fight. Kill the Boches. That will repay us all. *That* is what you owe to France."

"Monsieur," Abram said slowly. "You have my word."

"And mine," Paul added.

"All of ours," Sean said, as Evelyn nodded into his chest. She forced herself to take several deep breaths and drew upon the seemingly endless strength of her men. It helped, as it always did, and she began to calm.

"Good," Cosca said, switching back to French. "Then no more tears, yes? We leave as soon as it is dark."

* * *

The heels of Lina's boots made a satisfyingly aggressive clatter as she strode across the street toward Herr Sendler's office. She hadn't had to read the emotions of the messenger he'd sent to know something dramatic had occurred. Whether for good or ill, she didn't know, but when Neils Sendler told her to "come right away," Lina knew things were about to get interesting.

She pushed through the doorway, only to see the pale oval face of the French girl, Sophie. She gave Lina the smallest of nods and gestured for the Oberhelfer to go on in to Sendler's office. Lina gave her a nod back, reminded herself that Neils trusted Sophie, and went on in.

"Lina! I'm glad you're here," Neils said with a wide smile that went all the way to his eyes. He got up out of his chair so quickly a few of his papers fluttered from desk to floor. "We have had a breakthrough."

"Tell me," she urged, as he strode toward the door, reaching for his hat and overcoat. She hadn't even bothered to remove hers, so she turned and fell into step beside him.

"Last night, two of our agents posed as American airmen and were able to infiltrate one of the houses that serves to shelter fugitives. I had realized there must be one of their 'safe houses' in one particular neighborhood in Paris, and finally, we were able to pinpoint which."

"That is incredible! How did you make that happen?" Lina asked.

"Surveillance, mostly. I've had men in the neighborhood, in plain clothes, you understand, for weeks now, just watching for something...out of the ordinary. Strange visitors, things like that. Do you have any idea how often Parisians visit one another? Even in the middle of a war! It must be all the wine," he said, turning to her with his wide, excited grin. They'd come to the front door of the office, and he held it open and gestured for Lina to precede him through. A driver and a sleek black car awaited them outside.

"But they found something?" Lina asked, anxious to get on with the story. The driver saw her emerge from the office with Neils and moved to open the car door. She could feel her impatience mounting as she paused long enough to climb into the back seat. Neils followed suit, folding his big body into the space such that he didn't crowd her. Even in the midst of this exciting moment, she appreciated that he considered things like that. He was a gentleman, was Neils Sendler. She imagined Josef would have had great respect for him.

"Indeed. Last week, a woman was seen leaving the house in the late morning after a slightly larger group had left shortly after dawn.

My agents had noticed that same woman, though her hair and clothing were different, traveling through Paris with various other groups in the past months. She's rarely, if ever, with the same people. It was enough to go on. Since we'd spotted her leaving that house, we sent our 'Americans' there and had them seek shelter. Sure enough, they received it."

"And the woman?"

"Nothing yet, but we have her description. We'll have her soon."

"So you've arrested the family?"

"Yes, a man and his daughter. Butcher, Marc Garreau, and the daughter is Nicole. We're holding them here at the police station. I should like your expertise during the interrogation, Lina."

Lina felt her lips curve in something like a smile.

"I am happy to serve, Herr Sendler."

* * *

The police station in this section of Paris was very new and modern. A small, dispassionate corner of Lina's mind admired the clean lines of the architecture as their car pulled up to one of the rear entrances. She and Neils climbed out of the car and walked up the short flight of concrete stairs, then in through the large metal door.

"Herr Sendler, they're expecting you." The uniformed man spoke from behind a desk and gestured to a hallway opening to his left. "And your...assistant?"

"Oberhelfer Adalina Sucherin," Neils said briskly. "Oberhelfer Sucherin is an interrogation specialist. She alone may be able to break this discovery wide open. Somehow, fugitives are slipping through our fingers, and I mean to put an end to that. Place her name on the cleared list, please. Thank you."

"At once," the man said, nodding respectfully in Lina's direction. Once, she would have been pleased at his deference. Now she just wished he'd get on with it so she could do the same. Relief flooded through her when Neils started down the hallway. She fell into step behind him.

The hallway echoed with their footsteps as they approached the locked doors that held the prisoners. Neils came to a stop beside the first one.

"This will be Marc Garreau," he said. "I know you have attended interrogations before, so I hope you will not be shocked at his condition. We have found that we must be, unfortunately, *most* coercive when dealing with the members of these treasonous networks. I assure you every action taken was done so with the utmost of care to ensure no permanent damage..."

"Herr Sendler," Lina said softy, her smile a little more real. "I appreciate your solicitousness, but really, I am fine. As you say, I have seen interrogations before...and worse since we worked Warsaw."

"Yes, indeed. You still haven't told me about that."

"No, I haven't."

He looked at her for a long moment, then shrugged as if to say it had been worth a try, and opened the door.

The prisoner lay inside the small room, his wrists chained to an iron loop in the wall. His clothing had been stripped from the upper half of his body, and the bloody stripes on his back bore mute testimony of the beating he'd received. Several of the welts had broken the skin, and blood seeped down to stain the bare wood of the cot upon which he lay.

Lina took a deep breath, steeled herself, and reached out.

The man on the cot jumped as he felt Lina's intrusive probe into his psyche. She staggered a little bit under the searing weight of his pain, but a hand on the wall kept her from falling.

"What is his name?" Neils asked in a steady voice.

"Marc Garreau," Lina whispered. "He is a butcher by trade. His wife is dead, and he hopes he will be, soon. Nicole is his only daughter. She is what he values most in the world."

"No!" Garreau screamed and ducked his head down to cover it with his manacled hands. A few of the barely-formed scabs on his back broke with his movement, and more blood began to stream down his pale, abused flesh.

"What does he do with the enemy airmen he shelters?"

Lina bit her lip to keep her mind focused. It was difficult, as his psyche resonated with pain. More of Garreau's agony oozed through the connection toward her. She felt her hands and knees start to shake.

"Feeds them," she said, pulling the images from the prisoner's memories as they floated to the fore in response to Neils' questioning. "Shelters them for a day or more. They come in through the back garden so they can't be seen, and they leave the same way. That's why it took us so long to find the house."

"Where do they go?"

"The train station, mostly. He does not know where after that," Lina said after a long minute.

"Who is the girl? The one who comes back to his house multiple times?"

Lina closed her eyes and steeled herself against Garreau's pain as she tried to align her thoughts with his. A face flickered before her mental eyes, but then a tearing burn ripped through her as Garreau deliberately rolled onto his mangled back and writhed on the rough wooden boards.

"Stop!" Lina gasped. "Neils, stop him!"

Her knees buckled, and she fell to the cold hardness of the floor. She withdrew into the sensations of her own body, fleeing from the pain with which the prisoner fought her.

"Lina?" Neils asked, his voice thick with concern. "Lina? What has happened?"

"Outside," she said, holding out a hand for assistance. She felt Neils' large hand envelop hers as he drew her gently to her feet. On the cot, Garreau lay limp and panting, as if his exertions and resistance had drained him of all energy. Lina's head began to throb as they exited the prisoner's cell.

"Could you bring me some water, please?" Lina said to the officer standing outside Garreau's cell. The man glanced at Neils for permission and received an annoyed hand wave to get on with it.

"Lina, what happened?" Neils asked, pitching his voice low. Lina was grateful, for while she really did need the water, she also wanted some privacy.

"Your men were too rough with him," Lina said softly. "I understand this is procedure, but he was able to block my questioning by focusing on his own pain...and by making it worse. I've never seen anyone do something like that. I tried to stay with him, but..."

"Did he throw you out? Does he have training? His wife, perhaps? The daughter?"

"No, I don't think so. This wasn't the standard block we've encountered before, nor did he know how to eject me from his psyche. It was more that once he heard me articulating his conscious thoughts, he determined to make his conscious thoughts about nothing but pain. It was remarkably brave, to be honest."

"Brave for a traitor, you mean."

"Just so," Lina said, pinching the bridge of her nose. "If the daughter has been similarly treated, I must ask that such things discontinue, Herr Sendler. Especially if liberties have been taken with her. It is incredibly difficult to work with someone who has been broken in this way and will take far more time than we have."

"No, I can see that," Neils said, frowning as he considered this problem. "Perhaps...perhaps the time has come to soften them up with some kindness. I do not think the girl has been handled roughly, and I left specific orders she should not be...outraged. You know how I feel about such things."

"I do," Lina said, and smiled at her old friend and colleague. "And I appreciate your sensibilities and honor."

"Well," he said. "Let us leave this for now. I will give orders for Garreau to be cleaned up and given medical attention. We can return tomorrow. After you've eaten and rested."

"Thank you, Herr Sendler."

"Of course, my dear. Whatever you need. You will be key to breaking this web of traitors, and I will ensure you can do it."

* * *

Though it was wintertime, dusk seemed to take forever. Finally, the sun dipped far enough below the western horizon for the sky to darken to Cosca's satisfaction. He got to his feet, peered out one of the windows, and grunted softly.

"Time," he said in French. "Let's go."

Evelyn had already made a point of washing and putting away the dishes they'd used for their small meal, so there wasn't much else to do. The four Americans filed back outside. Cosca pointed to a pile of hay, then gestured at the truck.

"Tell them to pile that in the bed, then hide themselves underneath. You will ride with me. The Boches will think I have a young mistress," he said dryly. Evelyn glanced at him, startled, only to see his small smile. She smiled back, touched he'd thought to make a joke, even as awkward a one as that. He may have blushed a bit in response, but it was hard to tell on his darkly weathered face.

In order to avoid shouting in English, and because it still seemed like a good idea to be circumspect about their link, Evelyn walked over to the men and gestured for them to come close.

Cosca says that the plan is for you all to load that hay into the truck, then hide yourselves under it. I am to ride up front once again.

And pretend to be his mistress? Abram asked, lightheartedly. Sean glowered a bit at this, while Paul gave a wintry smile.

I suppose so, if we are questioned, Evelyn said. *I do not think he will take any liberties, though. He seems a good man.*

I'm sure you're right, Evie, Abram said. *I was just playing with you. We'll get moving right away with this hay.*

Within a few minutes, the mound of hay (sadly, mostly moldy and damp) lay piled in the bed of Cosca's truck, and Evelyn could feel her men's discomfort as they lay burrowed beneath it.

Perhaps the smell will discourage investigation? she offered.

It's certainly discouraging me, Abram said.

"You are ready, Mademoiselle?" Cosca asked, as he walked up behind Evelyn.

"Yes, Monsieur," she said, and turned to get back into the passenger seat of the truck. She supposed she should be grateful it was marginally more comfortable than the bed. Especially as *she* wasn't covered in moldy hay.

Once again, the truck's engine roared to life, and once again, Evelyn's teeth rattled together as Cosca steered them away from his garage and out onto the gravel of the nearby road.

He took an indirect route, Evelyn realized. No doubt this was to avoid notice, but it didn't make things any easier for the airmen hidden in the back. She tried to warn them when a turn was coming, but the moon had waned down to nearly nothing, and there wasn't much light from the headlamps on Cosca's truck. At least he appeared to know the roads extremely well, as his overall demeanor radiated relaxed confidence.

Which is why when he started swearing under his breath, Evelyn experienced a quick spike of alarm that she couldn't suppress. The men felt it, of course, and immediately went on the alert.

What's happening? Abram asked, as Cosca started to decelerate.

*I don't know, we're stopping. I think...*Evelyn squinted into the darkness. *Oh no. It's a checkpoint.*

Shit, Abram said.

Everyone lay still, Sean put in. *Maybe...maybe they won't find us.*

Cosca coasted the truck to a stop, and at a sharp gesture from the French uniformed policeman, cut the engine.

"Good evening," Cosca said as the two men came close enough to speak through the driver's side window. The taller of the two nodded in response, and Evelyn got the impression he knew the old man sitting next to her.

"You have permission to travel after curfew?" the shorter one asked, all brusque business.

"I do," Cosca said, and produced a folded piece of paper from inside his jacket. The taller officer took it, read it, and then handed it back with a nod.

"What are you hauling?" the shorter one asked.

"Old hay. I don't want it stinking up my property anymore."

"Why so late?"

"The army has me working all day and evening. This is the only time I can carry out my own necessary chores. I *am* still trying to run a business."

The shorter officer grunted, then took a step back and looked down the length of the truck. He squinted, frowned, then walked back alongside the wooden slats that bordered the truck bed on three sides and peered through. Evelyn saw Cosca inhale slowly and heard a soft clinking noise. She looked down to see his right hand reaching for the links of a chain as he slowly gathered it into his big, weather-roughened fingers.

They're searching! Evelyn sent. *Don't move!*

"Cosca..." the taller officer said slowly, in an undertone. "Cosca, stop. You've known me my whole life. Put the chain down and step out of the truck. What's going on?"

The old man froze, then opened his fingers and let the links of the chain drop back down to the floorboard. He let out a sigh and opened the door.

They know something, Evelyn said. A terrible calm seemed to come over her as she realized what would probably happen next. *We may have to kill them. Be ready. I will do what I can.*

She would have to touch the officers in order to attack them with her gifts, so she slid across the bench seat and followed Cosca out of the truck. The taller officer gave her a long look, but then turned back to Cosca. The shorter one continued looking through the slats of the truck. He even went so far as to pick up a stick from the road and begin to prod the mound of hay.

Oh shit. The bastard just poked me in the side, Abram said, just as the shorter officer let out a soft cry of triumph.

"Be honest, Cosca. You are smuggling contraband, are you not?" the taller one said.

"Not exactly," the old man replied. He took a deep breath. "They are airmen. American airmen."

He told them! Evelyn said, her tone throbbing with warning.

What? Do we attack? Paul asked.

Yes...wait! I don't know, Evelyn said. She knew the men could see through her eyes if they chose, so she opened that channel as wide as she could. *They're not doing anything.*

In fact, the two officers just looked at one another for a long moment. The shorter one gave a slight shrug, and the taller nodded.

"Carry on, Cosca," the taller said, as the two of them stepped back. "Vive la France."

"Vive la France," Cosca replied, with a nod to the two of them. He then turned and gave Evelyn a slight smile and gestured for her to precede him back into the truck.

Evie! What's happening?

They're letting us go, she said, feeling the unreality of the situation as she climbed back in and slid across the bench seat. Never in a million years would she have expected that. *Apparently they're patriots.*

Cosca followed her in and shut the door with a heavy thump before firing the engine back up. The two policemen lifted their hands in farewell. Cosca did the same, and Evelyn, moved by some impulse she couldn't name, rendered a salute as she'd been taught to do so long ago. The taller policeman met her eyes and smiled.

"Your debt," Cosca said roughly, his voice sounding like the gravel over which they drove. "Do not forget."

"We will not," Evelyn promised. "We will never forget it."

* * *

"Mademoiselle Garreau," Neils said with a smile as they entered the prisoner's room. "May I present Fraulein Lina Sucherin? Lina is a university student. She is doing a project on...what was it, Fraulein Sucherin?"

"A treatise on effective methods of interrogation, Herr Sendler. I aim to show the futility of brutal interrogation techniques, as they frequently increase the prisoner's determination to resist." Lina entered the room as she spoke and noted Nicole Garreau had been afforded some basic furnishings and comforts, just as she'd requested. Excellent.

"Ah, yes," Neils said. He gave Nicole a knowing look, as if he expected her to share in his amusement at Lina's answer. "Our Fraulein here is extremely passionate about her work, as you can plainly see."

Nicole didn't answer. She sat at the small table, unmanacled hands folded in front of her. Her hair was still slightly damp from the wash she'd given it that morning when Lina'd had the guards offer a bath. Her dark brown eyes flitted warily from Neils to Lina and back again as she attempted to figure out what, exactly, was going on.

Lina gave the girl the best smile she could summon and sat down, uninvited. Oh, so casually, she reached out and touched the back of the girl's hand. At the same time, she sent a spike of her consciousness arrowing into the girl's psyche.

It was so much harder with a woman. Her mind felt so slick and uninviting. There seemed to be nothing solid, nowhere for Lina to anchor the connection she sought to establish. The girl jumped, startled, and looked hard at Lina. The psychic held her breath, for if Nicole Garreau had any psychic talent or training, things were about to get very uncomfortable. Being forcibly ejected from someone's mind *hurt*.

For once, however, the fates smiled on Lina. At that moment, Neils cleared his throat and sat down as well.

"Would you like some tea?" he asked Nicole. "Or some bread and cheese? I can have them fetch something if you are hungry?"

"Yes, Monsieur," Nicole whispered. Lina exhaled slowly. She was in. Hanging precariously on to the girl's psyche, perhaps, but in. And Nicole had been well distracted.

"Very well," Neils said. "Then perhaps we should begin, yes? I wish to inquire about your treatment here. The guards and officers...they have been courteous?"

"Mostly," Nicole said, still in that barely-there tone of voice.

"I must ask you to be more specific, Mademoiselle Garreau. When you say 'mostly,' what do you mean? Was there one incident of discourtesy? Two? Ten?"

"No, Monsieur," she replied. "Nothing like that. They were...not nice, exactly, but no one was rude or mean."

"Ah. I see. Good. And were you treated roughly? Physically?"

"No, Monsieur."

"Did they touch you at all?"

"Yes, Monsieur."

"How did they touch you?"

"On my wrists and arms, Monsieur. When they chained me and brought me here. My knees buckled, and they helped me to stand."

"Ah. I see," he said again, and gave her a smile. "Nicole, you're doing very well. Now, a few more questions, if you please."

Nicole said nothing.

"When you were brought here, were you offered any kind of...insult?"

"Monsieur?"

"Did any of the men try to touch you...inappropriately? Did anyone try to take liberties?"

Nicole's eyes widened in shock, and a pink blush stained her cheeks. She really was a lovely girl, Lina thought, careful to keep the observation confined to her own mind.

"Oh, no, Monsieur," she said quickly. "Nothing like that."

"Excellent. I am pleased to hear this, Nicole, for I believe such crimes to be unnatural and unfitting of a true man. So would you say, then, that your treatment here while in our custody has been...gentle?"

"I suppose...yes, Monsieur."

"Good, and now, does that dispose you to cooperate with us?"

Lina felt the girl's guard go up. For just a moment, she wished she were linked with Neils so she could have warned him to tread lightly here.

"In what way, Monsieur?"

"In the easiest of ways, my dear. I am curious about a few things. Why a girl such as yourself would engage in such dangerous pastimes as hiding fugitive enemies, for one. Did your father force you to?"

"No!" Nicole cried out. Lina felt fear for her father flood the girl's mind. "He had nothing to do with it. *I* brought *him* in!"

And it was true, Lina realized, feeling the resonance of it echo through Nicole's mind. Her father had been her willing accomplice, but *she* was the true prize. She glanced over at Neils and gave him the slightest of nods to indicate truth.

"Ah, I see. This must be very hard for you, then, Mademoiselle," Neils said, his voice full of sympathy. "To fear that you have endangered your father...why would you do such a thing? I am trying to understand. Help me understand, Nicole."

"I don't know anything," Nicole whispered, her eyes full of tears. A lie. Lina felt it soak through the connection.

"Naturally, you had your reasons for doing what you have done. I just need to know those reasons, and I think you can help."

"No! I know nothing, Monsieur. Nothing!"

"Strange. Especially since your father tells us that you are a true patriot."

"I—?"

"Of course you are," Neils said, with that comforting, avuncular smile. "And I honor you for it. I believe the Reich will be good for France, but I cannot argue it will take time for her people to see that. I do not blame you for trying to help your country, misguided as your attempts may have been. And anyway, what did you do? Feed a few hungry men? Give them shelter for a night?"

"Yes," she said, her voice breaking on a sob. Lina felt a wave of relief break over the girl's mind as the secret she'd kept for so long came out. A series of rapid-fire images passed through Nicole's mind. Faces, weary, tired, scared. Mostly men, but two women stood out. One was a girl Lina didn't recognize, but she matched the description Neils had given of the girl seen leaving the Garreaus' house. The other...

A snarl of rage coiled within Lina's mind, like a serpent rising up to strike. She took a quick sip of air and withdrew all but the most tenuous of connections from Nicole's psyche, lest the girl feel her emotional reaction to the sight of the American psychic. She held up one finger where the prisoner couldn't see, to let Neils know she needed a minute. The intelligence operative didn't react, other than to turn to the tea service that had just arrived and to pour tea for all of them.

Calm, Lina told herself, speaking mostly to the writhing serpent of fury inside her skin. *Icy, clear, calm. Only thus will we find her. Only thus will we destroy everything she loves. Calm. Cold. Clear.*

Slowly, the serpent stilled, lulled back to somnolence by Lina's will and the promise of retribution to come. Lina took a deep breath, a sip of her tea, and met Neils' eyes. A slight curve of her lips (not a smile, not with the memory of *her* face so close...) told him that she was ready to resume. She extended her awareness back down the treacherous link to the girl's mind, and the interrogation resumed.

"So you are compassionate as well as patriotic. That is not such a large crime, now is it? How did they come to you, these men?" Neils asked casually, as he lifted his tea to take a sip. "Did someone give them your address?"

"I would pick them up," Nicole said. "But sometimes Deedee would bring them."

"And Deedee is?"

"My friend."

Another memory floated up to the surface of the girl's mind, and Lina reached out with the most delicate of touches to capture it. The train station, light streaming in through the windows. The young woman she'd seen, the other one, walking up, smiling. Her arm through that of a man who held himself stiffly, wariness in his eyes.

"And where would they go, when they left you?"

"I don't know," she said, but once again, her memory betrayed her. Lina got the image of waves crashing on the sand and a moon high in the sky. A beach? Which beach?

She hadn't actually articulated the thought to Nicole, but the girl must have felt the question on some kind of level, for another image came to the fore. A very famous painting of a short man wearing an ancient French uniform, surrounded by furnishings rich enough for a king. Or an emperor.

Bonaparte. Bonaparte Beach, just across the Channel to England. *They were going to try and escape to sea!*

This time, when Lina met Neils' eyes, she did smile. She lifted her tea and took another sip. She would relax and listen to the rest of the interrogation, but it didn't matter.

She had what she needed.

* * *

nother dawn, another safe house. Cosca brought them to a farmhouse just outside of a small village. He'd come to the top of a nearby hill and cut the engine and headlights, then coasted to a stop near the back of the house.

"Be silent," he warned Evelyn, who passed the admonition down through her connection to the men. She watched as Cosca eased out of the truck and closed his door carefully, so as not to make any tell-tale sounds. The tiny sliver of moon didn't provide much light, but enough that she could see him walking toward the house as it loomed in the darkness. Seconds ticked by with nothing to mark them but the call of some night bird and the distant roar of the ocean swells. She could smell salt on the breeze. They weren't far from the coast.

Moments later, Cosca reappeared out of the darkness next to her door. He opened it and helped her to step down out of the truck. Then he led her around to the back, where he gestured at the pile of hay. Evelyn gave him a questioning look, but he merely raised his eyebrows. With an inner sigh, she relented and reached down the lines of her net.

Time to come out, she said. *Be as silent as you can, and be careful. There's no light out here.*

There isn't much in here, either, Abram quipped, just before his head emerged from the noxious pile of hay. Cosca gave a soft grunt and reached up to help him out of the truck. Sean and Paul followed, thankfully without any more Abram-style witticisms. Once they all stood before him, Cosca made a gesture that Evelyn couldn't quite see and turned back toward the farmhouse.

He wants us to follow him, Paul said. He'd been standing closest to the old man.

Then let's go. But hang on to one another, Abram said. *Let's not trip or get lost in this darkness.*

Once again, Evelyn found Sean's fingers curling through hers. She looked up and gave him as much of a smile as she could summon. He squeezed her fingers in response.

They followed Cosca toward the building. As they drew close, Evelyn could begin to make out the outline of cellar doors similar to what she had seen growing up near the prairie. Cosca bent down and heaved one of the doors open, then gestured for them to proceed down the stairs inside. At least, Evelyn assumed there were stairs. It was hard to tell in the Stygian blackness.

Paul went first, followed by Abram, then Evelyn herself, then Sean. Cosca brought up the rear and closed the door behind them as soon as he'd descended the two steps necessary to allow the door to fully shut.

Almost immediately, a match flared in the darkness ahead. Evelyn jumped and felt her jolt of adrenaline ricochet through the minds of her three companions.

"Come, quickly," a soft voice said in French. The match dimmed, then the soft glow of an oil lamp replaced it, spreading light throughout the cellar. "Come in! I am Elise Bertrand, and you are very welcome here."

As they continued down the stairs, Evelyn got a look at Elise Bertrand. She seemed...soft. Fleshy. She was heavyset with steel gray hair and dark, penetrating eyes. Her smile, though, was warm and bright as she got a look at each of them. With expansive gestures, she shooed them each down the stairs and into a large room. Tall wooden racks lined the walls, and as Evelyn got closer, she could see a few dust-covered bottles here and there. A wine cellar, then, though it looked as if the contents had recently been pretty thoroughly looted. Evelyn supposed that was the way of things in an occupied country.

Madame Bertrand must have noticed Evelyn looking, for she carried the lamp over and gave a soft sigh.

"Ah, my poor cellar. The Boches, they take what they will. But we do not worry, my vines and me," she said with a knowing smile and a pat on Evelyn's shoulder. "We will get your men back into the fight, and they will water the soil with Boches' blood, no? What delicious wines my vines shall make then!"

Unsure how to answer this bloodthirsty declaration, Evelyn gave the woman a small smile. Madame Bertrand clucked and patted her face gently.

"Poor lamb. You look so tired. All of you are tired, I daresay. Come, here in the corner, I have a few mattresses and blankets. It is not much, but you can sleep for a few hours. I will wake you for dinner, and then we shall listen to the radio. If it is a good evening for my friend Alphonse, then it will be a good evening for us!"

Evelyn followed where their hostess led, and soon enough she lay wrapped in warm woolen blankets, curled between Sean and Paul, while Abram sat up for the first watch. They were probably safe here, but as always, it never hurt to be sure. Evelyn let her eyes fall closed, and sleep quickly rose to claim her.

The rest of the day passed in a combination of exhausted napping and punishing boredom for the four of them. The flickering light of their oil lamp served as both a source of illumination and a marker of time's passage. When the oil level had dropped to about half, Madame Bertrand returned, bringing water, bread, and cheese for them to eat.

"It is a good day," she said, her smile brighter than the lamplight. "Rainy and dreary. Perfect for your escape, though it will not be comfortable for you, I fear, poor lambs. But we shall see, we shall see. Will it be a good night for Alphonse? Only he can say." With this cryptic statement and a broad wink, Madame Bertrand left them, exiting through a door about halfway up the wall that presumably led into the farmhouse. The wooden stairs that led to the door creaked with each of her heavy-footed steps, and a tiny corner of Evelyn's mind wondered if the woman felt at all vulnerable, as if it might collapse. Evelyn certainly would have.

"Why does she keep talking about her friend Alphonse?" Sean asked as he began to spread cheese on a piece of bread. He handed the piece to Evelyn and then looked inquiringly up at the others.

"Beats me," Paul said.

"I think it's a code," Evelyn said. "She mentioned listening to the radio. I imagine 'Alphonse' is some kind of code word telling us whether our escape will be happening tonight or not. The BBC does those broadcasts, you know."

"That's right!" Abram said, his face lighting up. "And she mentioned it being a 'good night' or a 'good evening.' That's got to mean that we would go. Perhaps if we won't, it will be a bad night."

"I think you may be right."

They spoke aloud, in hushed tones, because it seemed to make the darkness outside their circle of lantern light less oppressive. After a while longer, Evelyn found herself dozing again, and she laid down once more. If nothing else, this experience had taught her the value of catching what sleep she could. She was vaguely aware of Madame Bertrand bringing water one more time before the motherly woman began shooing them all awake.

"Come, come!" she said, in that soft, yet intense voice. "It is nearly time for the broadcast. You must all come, to see if it will be a good night for Alphonse."

She accompanied this last with a giggle that seemed more suited to a small girl than a decidedly matronly farmwife. Clearly Elise Bertrand had an adventurous soul and found the idea of aiding allied airmen (and Evelyn, about whom she seemed determined to ask no questions) to be romantic and fun.

So they all trooped up the rickety wooden staircase to the less cavernous (but every bit as ancient-looking) ground floor of the farmhouse. They'd entered the kitchen, for on the far wall, a cavernous fireplace dominated the room. The thing looked big enough to spit an entire heifer and still have room on the side racks to bake a few pies. Nothing roasted or baked there now, though a fire had burnt down to radiant coals. Evelyn found herself wondering if all houses in France had those huge fireplaces.

She hadn't realized how damp and chill the basement had been until she stepped into the close warmth of the kitchen. Evelyn took a deep breath and smelled something baking, even if it wasn't apparent in the fireplace. A still-ancient iron stove stood in the corner between the hearth and the adjoining wall.

Whatever is baking must be inside that stove, she thought idly, more to cover the embarrassment of her stomach's sudden rumbling than anything else.

I hope it's for us, Abram said. *I have no idea how many hours have passed, but that bread and cheese seemed ages ago.*

"This way," Madame Bertrand said, as she stood in a doorway facing the stove and waved them forward. Evelyn felt a slight pang of regret as they filed past the vast wooden work table and out into another room.

Though not nearly as warm, this room also boasted a small fireplace with a cheery blaze, along with several mismatched chairs.

"Sit, sit!" Madame Bertrand said, and turned to bustle over to the large cabinet on the wall. Evelyn had just settled into the chair when she realized the French woman wasn't opening the cabinet, she was pushing it to one side.

Sean immediately leapt up to help her, but she waved him off with a clucking sound.

"I am fat, not weak!" she said in French, which Evelyn belatedly translated. "And anyway, it's on a mechanism. Isn't that clever?"

Sure enough, the cabinet, which looked as old and permanent as the kitchen hearth had done, slid to the side to reveal a shallow alcove. Inside this alcove stood a plain table, upon which sat a very modern-looking radio set. To the astonishment of the men, Madame Bertrand's fingers flew competently over the knobs and buttons. Before long, the tinny voice of the BBC radio announcer came through the small square speaker.

"Here we are now," Madame Bertrand said, and Evelyn felt a shock ricochet through her system, echoed and magnified by that of the men. The woman had spoken in crisp, British-accented English!

"Oh? This is a surprise? How delightful," Madame Bertrand went on, a twinkle in her eye. "I do so love surprising our allies. Yes, children, I am French by marriage, but I was born in Merry Olde England. Did you enjoy my 'eccentric French farmwife' performance? I suppose it's not strictly a performance, as I am all of those things."

"You're a spy?" Abram breathed. He seemed the most flabbergasted. Paul seemed to have a policy of never showing his surprise, even when it was clear to all in the net. Sean was a little more forth-coming, but he was usually quicker to roll with the punches.

"An agent, if you will. I work for MI-9. And that is all I shall tell any of you, in case the worst is to happen. Rest assured that if this house is ever raided, there are traps within traps to destroy my lovely radio and all of the other toys I have hidden around. This house has been here for a long time, my dears. And I daresay this is not the first time it's seen clandestine use in its history."

Fascinated, Evelyn began to ask more about that, but Madame Bertrand shushed her and turned up the volume dial on the radio set. The BBC announcer informed them they'd been listening to a program called "The French Speak to the French." There was a brief pause, and then he began to recite his litany of phrases which may, or may not, have meaning.

"Labrosse will bring his catch to the market in the morning... Dumais will meet his wife at the Shelburne hotel gala...The Cyclones have devastated the central plains...Yvonne always thinks of the happy occasion..."

Madame Bertrand let out a sigh and leaned forward to turn the dial down.

"Well," she said. "This is not such bad news, I suppose."

"It is not a good night for Alphonse?" Sean asked quietly. Madame Bertrand flashed him her quick smile.

"No, my dear child. But tomorrow night should be. We are delayed for twenty-four hours. So you might as well all get some dinner...and then more sleep, I think. Tomorrow will be a busy night."

* * *

So, in the end, they didn't go anywhere that night after all. Madame Bertrand fed them a kind of thick vegetable stew, with a pie made from preserved fruit for dessert. It was delicious and filling, and possibly the best thing Evelyn had eaten since...well, she wasn't sure when. Since they'd been picked up by the members of the Resistance in Belgium, the helpers had been incredibly generous to them. They'd been clothed, sheltered, cared for, and fed, and Evelyn had taken all of it with extreme gratitude. The men, too. After being on their own, a simple loaf of bread had seemed like ambrosia of the gods, and even the poorest of fare benefited from that most delectable of sauces: hunger.

That meal, on the other hand, needed no help. As the flavors and scents of honey and fruit and cream soaked through Evelyn's brain, she realized that among her many mysterious accomplishments, Elise Bertrand was also a gourmet, and quite possibly the finest pie-maker Evelyn had ever encountered.

"Madame," Evelyn asked in French, as the five of them worked to clean up the kitchen. "I hope I don't offend, but...may I have the recipe for your pie?"

Madame Bertrand looked over the basin of soapy water at Evelyn and gave a chuckle.

"Why on earth would that offend me, child?" she asked, responding in French. "Of course. I'll write it out for you when we're finished here. It may not survive the journey home, but at least we shall give a try, hey?"

"I would appreciate that very much, Madame."

"Oh, it would be my pleasure, child. I'm pleased you liked the pie. It *is* good, isn't it? My husband, God rest him, loved my pies when he lived. I would have had to have made two of them tonight!"

She gave a small smile and looked down at the work in her hands. Even linked in with the men and deliberately not reaching out, Evelyn could feel the sadness roll off of this remarkable woman.

"I am sorry for your loss, Madame," she said quietly.

"Oh, thank you," Madame Bertrand said, giving a mighty sniff and swiping at her eyes with her sleeve. "It is silly, but I miss him still. He's been gone for nearly ten years! But he was a good man. Such a sense of fun! He would have dearly loved all of this sneaking about."

"Forgive me," Evelyn said with a smile. "But I suspect he is not the only one."

"Yes, well," Madame Bertrand shrugged, the smile returning to her lips. "It *is* rather exciting, is it not? Staying one step ahead of the Boches, helping the young, desperate airmen...and you, of course. It helps me feel young again, I suppose."

"But you are safe, here? You do not worry you will be caught?" Evelyn thought of poor Nanette Cosca and her palpable fear of that very thing.

"None of us are ever safe, my dear child. Safety is an illusion. My beloved is dead, my children grown and gone. All I have left are my vines and this house...and whatever adventures I can conjure up for myself. If I am caught...well...I will count it my duty to both King and Republique to do the best I can to resist. And that shall be an adventure of its own, shall it not?"

Evelyn thought of her own brief time as a captive of the Germans, and the storm lurking in the depths of her mind began to rise up, howling. She swallowed hard and shoved it down, locked it away. She was here, now, with this woman and her men. Without conscious thought, she reached out to each of them as they went about their own cleaning chores.

Evie? Sean, of course.

I'm okay, she sent in a hurry. *I'm sorry, she just...something she said surprised me. I'm fine.*

All right, Sean sent slowly. Evelyn kept her eyes on the dishes, but she could feel him looking over at her, concerned. Abram and Paul, too, but they were quicker to accept her assurances. Sean worried.

Sean always worried about her.

And that was yet another thing Evelyn didn't want to think about, so she finished with the plate she was washing and quickly put it on the drying board before grabbing another.

Only to find Madame Bertrand looking closely at her as well.

"I am sorry," Evelyn said, giving a little laugh. "I did not mean to go off woolgathering. I was just...you are very brave, Madame. I do not know that I could be so brave."

"Ah, child, but you *are*," Madame Bertrand said, wisdom replacing the mischief in her smile. "You are exactly that brave. Courage is not the absence of fear, my girl. It is moving forward, even in the face of that fear. Never question your courage, American girl. You have it and to spare. I will go copy that recipe for you now."

And with that, she grabbed a dishtowel, dried her hands, and left. Evelyn blinked, her hands buried in soapy dishwater as she held the last of their dessert plates.

"She's right, you know," Paul said into the silence that followed. Whether he'd been actually listening, or just following through the link, Evelyn didn't know. "You are incredibly brave, Evie. I think you're the bravest woman I've ever known."

"Me too," Sean said.

"And me," Abram said. "None of us would have made it this far without you, Evie. I wish you'd believe in yourself the way you believe in us."

Whether it was the remarkable conversation she'd just had or the repetition of sentiments from her men, Evelyn didn't know. But for the first time in a long time, she didn't feel shy or ashamed at the praise. She'd never been daring or adventurous. Not like Mary. When she thought of courage, Mary's vivacious personality and vivid beauty came to mind. Either that or the brash bravado that men like her lost ball turret gunner, Logan Ayala, had displayed. It had never occurred to her that quiet perseverance could be brave in its own way. But then her mind flashed back to the calm voice of Carl as he ordered them to bail out, knowing he would probably not survive the crash that was coming. She'd known his fear...she'd felt it in the net. But he'd still forced his voice and his demeanor to be calm and collected. And he'd stayed at the controls in order to give them the best chance of survival. If that wasn't bravery...

Well. It *was* bravery. There was no question. None at all. So if Carl and Bob could be brave, knowing that they were facing their deaths...If Madame Bertrand could be brave when contemplating possible capture...maybe she, Evelyn Adamsen, could be brave in her own way, too.

They returned to the cellar after dinner and slept. The next day contained more of the same. The inaction began to chafe at the men, and even Evelyn felt the abrasion of ennui under her skin. It seemed forever before Madame Bertrand once again summoned them to sit around the fire and listen to the radio.

"This has been 'The French speak to the French,'" the BBC announcer said. Evelyn felt her own attention sharpen, and each of the men seemed to sit a little straighter in anticipation. "And now, a few words for our allies in occupied France. Jeanne prefers the red dress. Guillaume thinks his tea may be delayed. The brie, however, is right on time, and excellent. And a very good evening to those in the house of Alphonse. The winds are strong when a storm is coming..."

A very good evening to those in the house of Alphonse.

Evelyn looked up, feeling the electricity of the men's attention. Madame Bertrand met her eyes and smiled with that bright ferocity.

"So," their hostess said, "a good evening after all."

"What happens now?" Abram asked.

"Now, we must confirm. There will be another broadcast at nine o'clock. If it is still a good evening, then we will take the next steps and get you into position. But for now...shall we dine?"

They did, and just as well as the previous night. Given the news, everyone was in good spirits, so the meal was convivial and fun. They cleaned up as before and then settled down to listen one more time for the all-important phrase.

"...and a very good evening to those in the house of Alphonse..."

Looking back, Evelyn could never remember much of the details that came next. She knew they waited in the pitch black of the cellar for a long while. At a certain point, someone opened the outside cellar doors, and they climbed the steps out into the midnight air. The cold was quite biting, especially after three days of being inside.

Once again, they piled into a truck...though not the one driven by Monsieur Cosca. They took a short drive over a mercilessly rutted road and pulled up to a stone house perched on the edge of a cliff overlooking the tossing sea.

Evelyn felt the truck lurch to a stop, then felt the slam of the driver's door reverberate through the frame. A moment later and the silent man helped them each out of the bed of the truck and pointed toward the house. After the darkness of the farmhouse cellar, the sky seemed brightly lit, even though the tiny sliver of moon had to fight through a veil of clouds as it flung its light on the scene below. The roaring sound of the waves echoed up the cliff at them and left Evelyn with a shivery feeling. Whether it was excitement or fear, she couldn't have said.

In a single-file line, they trooped up the gravel drive. The stone house stood silhouetted against the cloud-laced sky. A door opened silently as they approached, and a thin-faced woman waved them in. Behind them, the truck roared to life again and pulled away. Evelyn could hear the crunch of gravel under its wheels.

"Inside, quickly," the woman said, her voice light. As they drew closer, it became apparent she was young and very pregnant. A feeling of awkwardness originated from one of the men and reverberated through the net. Evelyn thought it stemmed from Paul.

Are you all right? she asked through the net as she walked past the pregnant woman.

Why is she doing this? Paul asked. His discomfort surged through all of them again. Evelyn found herself trying to insulate Sean and Abram from it, with little success. They'd all four been linked together for so long, it had become near-impossible to separate their psyches one from the other.

A problem. But one for another day. First, they had to get back to friendly soil. Evelyn reminded herself that she was brave and pushed on.

What do you mean, Paul? she asked.

That girl! She's going to have a baby! This work is far too dangerous for her. What if she's caught with all of us in her house? The Germans would likely kill her and her child as well! How can she take that risk?

Evelyn paused, stymied. Of all of her men, Paul was by far the most practical. He'd killed three guards and not blinked an eye. She'd never have expected him to worry about something like this. But...

It's her choice, Abram said. *What kind of world do you think her baby will live in if the Nazis win? I can perfectly understand what she's doing.*

But there are others...It just isn't right.

It's not up to us, Paul.

But...

Enough. They're helping us. We're going home. Tonight. Let's not put them any more at risk by acting foolish, all right?

But...

Paul, Evelyn said. *Please. She has her reasons. And we can't do anything about it. Let's please just go home tonight.*

All right, Evie, he sent, finally. The tension he'd sent singing through the net slackened all of a sudden. *All right.*

The woman in question, their hostess, closed the door behind them before leading them through another doorway. In the room beyond, Evelyn came to a dead stop, surprise freezing her mid-step.

Nearly twenty men stared back at her. Men with hollow, hungry eyes. Men wearing ill-fitting clothes. Men with dirt smudged on their faces. Fugitive men, with a barely discernible hope burning in their gaze.

"We shall have quite a party on the beach tonight."

The voice spoke from behind them. Evelyn started as she recalled herself and stepped forward into the room in order to allow the speaker to follow her in.

He was a slight man of medium height and a wry smile. As he entered the room, she saw several of the men give him nods of recognition. More than one chuckled at his dry joke. He turned to Abram, who as usual had stepped forward to try and shield his own group, and offered his hand.

"I am Jerome Millet. Welcome to my home."

"Thank you," Abram said, taking the man's hand and shaking it. "We appreciate your hospitality, and that of your wife."

"Anceline. Yes. She tires easily, but she insists on doing what she can. She is tough, for someone so delicate and pretty," the man said, obviously bursting with pride in his young wife. "I am sorry for the cramped quarters, but we must wait until the moon sets. Around midnight, we will set out for the beach. I must ask you not to speak if you can help it. Sound unfortunately carries, and with so many of you here..."

"We understand," Abram said.

"Good. Make yourselves at home, then. I shall call for you in a few hours."

More waiting, Sean said. *Do we know any of these fellas?*

I don't, Evelyn said, probably needlessly. She and the other psychics had rarely had the opportunity to socialize with anyone other than their own crews. Their inclusion was, after all, classified.

Me neither, Paul said. He still seemed out of sorts about Anceline's condition, but he was dealing for the moment, so Evelyn left it alone.

Doesn't matter, Abram said. *We shouldn't talk anyway. Let's find someplace to sit down and get as much rest as we can. I get the feeling that our hike down to the beach ain't gonna be just a stroll along the sand.*

* * *

Unfortunately for all of the evaders in the so-called "house of Alphonse" that night, Abram's premonition turned out to be dead-on accurate.

Shortly after midnight, Jerome Millet announced that the moon had set and it was time for them to go.

"You will stay in groups of eight. Our people will guide you along the trail down the cliff. It is very treacherous, and while the rain is good for helping us not to be seen, it does make the cliffs more slippery."

Great, and it's raining, too? Abram groused silently.

At least it will be harder to see us, Evelyn reminded him. *And we're so close to going home.*

"There is some fog, as well," the Frenchman went on in his accented English. "So it will be very difficult to see. It will be necessary for each man to hold to the belt of the man in front of him as we climb down the cliff."

So, really hard to see us, Sean thought. He seemed rather determinedly cheerful about the whole thing. Paul, as usual, said nothing. But they could all feel his typical pessimism. Their bombardier expected things to go wrong so he was always prepared when they did.

"Once we reach the beach, you will hide among the rocks while we attempt to make contact with the British gunboat. Once we have positive contact with them, they will send out rowers. It will seem as if it takes forever, but the trip is only about ten minutes, I assure you. Then you will go in your groups of eight into the rowboats and out to the gunboat. If there are no questions, we will leave now."

Evelyn was relatively certain all of them, not just her crew, had many questions. But no one said anything. So at Millet's gesture, they all got to their feet and sorted themselves into groups of eight. She and her four men stayed together, of course, and they were joined by two Brits, a Canadian, and an American fighter pilot from Texas. They didn't dare exchange much more than a silent nod of hello as they were hustled out into the inky, wet darkness.

Not for the first time, Evelyn found herself thanking Providence for the skill of Doctor van Duren. Her ankle ached, but it was not so bad she couldn't push it to the back of her mind. They started down the steep, switchback trail (Trail?? This was more like a goat path! A *mountain* goat path!) that crisscrossed the sheer cliffs above a narrow strip of sand. Evelyn knew the ever-present ache was shortly going to become a full-on stabbing pain. That was, if she was lucky enough not to roll her foot under her.

Millet hadn't lied. The already slick path became even more threatening, thanks to the rain and the wet mist that seemed to cling to everything. Evelyn flexed her fingers around the cord that served as Sean's belt and fought to keep upright and close enough she didn't overbalance him in return.

Almost there, Sean sent after a few minutes. *Look, the fog is clearing; you can start to see the beach below.*

Forgive me, but I'm not looking down, Evelyn sent back, a bit tartly. *Let's just keep moving.*

Sean's silent laughter echoed through the net and intensified with humor from Abram and Paul both. They weren't laughing at Evelyn's refusal to look down so much as they were her tone with Sean. In fact, Evelyn found herself smiling, too. It was one of those moments that shouldn't have been funny...but manifestly was. And no one cared to explain why, even if they could.

Evelyn's foot slipped out from under her, sending a shower of pebbles down the slope to patter onto the heads of an earlier group.

She clutched hard at Sean's belt and felt Paul's strength straining to help keep her upright. Sure enough, pain lanced through her injured ankle, stabbing up toward her knee. She bit down hard on her lower lip in order to keep from crying out and tasted the metallic taint of her own blood.

It's okay, Evie. We've got you, Paul said, calm and cool as ever in a crisis.

I know, Evelyn said, reaching out along the lines of the net, borrowing their strength to steady her own nerves. *You always do.*

We always will, Abram said from his place behind Paul. *Keep going. We're almost there.*

At one point, they had to sit on the ground and let themselves slide on their rears down the unstable slope. Evelyn fervently prayed there weren't Nazi patrols waiting somewhere down on the beach, alerted by the avalanche of small rocks and dirt caused by their passage. By the time they reached the beach, Evelyn felt bruised from heels to crown, and her ankle throbbed its anger at this new abuse.

Their guide led them forward to a clutch of boulders near the base of the cliff and gestured for them to hunker down. This close to the base of the cliff, the roar-and-swish of the waves echoed deafeningly. So much so that Evelyn could barely hear their guide as he spoke into a device she'd never seen before. It was like some kind of radio handset, only the radio set itself was carried on the back of the second man.

I wonder where they got that, she sent to the men.

MI-9, no doubt, Abram theorized. *What I wonder is where they keep it so that the Nazis don't find it!*

Same places they kept us, Paul said dryly, causing humor to flow through the net from all corners once again.

"All right," their guide said in harsh, accented English. "The boat, he is coming. Wait here."

As if we could do anything else. That was Paul, naturally. Evelyn fought not to snort a laugh. Their combined impatience amped steadily up. They seemed so close to the end of this ordeal. To wait any longer seemed unbearable...

Light bloomed overhead, scattered by the fog. A moment later, the sound hit them like a truck as two shore batteries opened fire. The concussive booms echoed off of the sheer cliff that loomed above them. Evelyn couldn't hold back a cry as she slapped her hands over her ears. Someone (probably Sean) grabbed her and pulled her to the ground, sheltering her with their own body as hell itself seemed to open up in the sky above.

"Merde!" their guide swore before switching back to English. "The damned Boches! They're firing on the gunboat. They will be here any minute. Run! Scatter! Not the path up the cliff, you'll never make it. Down the beach...you may find another trail. Go!"

He reached down to haul Evie and her protector (It was Sean. Of course.) to their feet and shoved them out onto the sand.

Evie! Sean! Abram cried down the net. Evelyn looked around, lost in the confusion of male bodies, sand, and that horrible, concussive sound.

Here! Sean cried, as he reached out and grabbed Evelyn's hand, dragging her toward him.

We're at the base of the cliffs, heading south.

We'll meet you there. What just happened?

The shore batteries fired on the gunboat. Like they knew we'd be here.

Evelyn didn't know what it was that triggered her thought. Perhaps it was some subliminal clue. Perhaps it was simply paranoia. But for whatever reason, a dread certainty took shape in her mind. Sure enough, as soon as she thought about it, she became aware of a whisper-subtle probing around the edges of her psyche, and she couldn't help but share it with the men.

I think they did know. I think she's here. Lina, the psychic from the forest. At the thought of her, the tempest rose within. Evelyn squeezed Sean's hand, focusing on the slick, clammy feel of his skin. He squeezed back, even as they lumbered through the sand, and the howling storm in her mind receded.

Can't be! Abram said. *She's dead! We saw her body. There you are! I see you. Continue straight for the cliffs...*

We've got you, sir, Sean said, changing their angle slightly.

We don't know that she's dead, Evelyn insisted. *Did any of you check her body?*

...No. But Evie, we don't need to worry about that right now, do we?

We do if she's here! If she's searching for us! If she's trying to find me...

As if he knew (and maybe he did) Sean squeezed her hand again, helping her to anchor herself in the physical world. Helping her to fight off the storm within. Again.

I'm here. We're here, Sean said, and Evelyn felt the weight of Paul and Abram behind him. *We won't let you be taken again.*

A-All right, Evelyn said, and swallowed hard, forcing herself to focus on the here and now. She had to defeat the Nazi girl's delicate searching. She poured her strength into the borders of the net, reinforcing their connections and attempting to deflect any probes.

Paul found them a moment later and reached out to grab Evelyn's other hand. He caught the hitch in her step as her abused ankle protested, and without even pausing, he swung her up into his arms, as if she were a small child.

I'm sorry, she sent to him.

Shut up, he sent back, not unkindly. *Let's just get out of here.*

Sorry, Evie, Sean sent. *I should have gotten you off your ankle sooner.*

You shut up, too, Paul told the flight engineer. *You kept her safe in the initial panic. Keep moving!*

Behind them, Evelyn heard the sickening rat-tat-tat-tat of automatic weapons fire punctuating the ringing in her ears. She hadn't recognized the sound at first, but the men certainly had. Someone was shooting behind them, back where they'd hidden in the rocks. Fear and grief rocketed through her. Was someone dead? Who? Their guide? The silent Brits that had accompanied them down the cliff?

Don't think about it, Abram demanded. *Deal with it later.*

Paul hugged the dubious shelter of the rock face, with Abram and Sean close beside him as they ran south. Through the link, Evelyn could feel the searing effort in their legs as they fought through the loose, rocky sand. Every breath stabbed at them as their lungs burned. Paul's arms ached from holding her, but if she even thought about getting down, he'd hit her with a wordless negative that ended that line of thought.

Here! Abram cried triumphantly through the net. *I found a trailhead!*

Where does it go? Sean asked.

Who cares? Off the beach! Move!

And so they did. The "trail" was really nothing more than a game path that led up through a place where the cliff dipped down toward the sand. Scrubby, tough shore vegetation concealed the way, which was good, but made for slow going. They climbed up a steep trail that, while not as bad as their earlier descent, was still incredibly taxing.

You have to put me down, Paul, Evelyn said at one particularly diffi-cult point. *Otherwise we'll both fall. I can crawl up over this bit and then you can pick me up again if you insist.*

You shouldn't have to crawl, Evie.

This is survival, Paul, isn't that what you always say? I'm not proud. I just want to survive. Put me down.

Finally, he complied. The leaden exhaustion she could feel in his arms probably had something to do with it. Without a word or a thought, Sean skidded back down the trail to them and helped lower Evelyn to the ground. Something sharp dug into her palm, but she gritted her teeth and ignored it as she forced herself to climb up to-ward Abram's outstretched hand. Paul followed her, and Sean brought up the rear, though he'd already scaled that particular part once.

The climb seemed to take forever.

The whole time, Evelyn feared someone was watching them from afar, preparing to pick them off like crows sitting on a fence. She kept pouring her strength into the net, trying to mask the feel of them from the outside. Normally, this would be enough to defeat even the most strenuous of psychic searches. However, this was Lina, who had penetrated Evelyn's mind once before. Lina knew the flavor of her thoughts, and even though it was more difficult to link with a woman than it was to link with a man, Lina was more than powerful enough to do it. Their best hope was she didn't know for sure they were there...not until they had enough distance to make a difference.

So Evelyn kept pushing them on. Even when Paul stumbled twice, nearly dropping her. Even when Sean cut his arm open on a hidden branch. Even when Abram called a halt at the top of the cliffs and proposed they stop for a minute and come up with a plan.

No, we have to keep going. She can find us if we're too close.

Evie, the sun is about to come up. We have to go to ground. She'll definitely find us if we get picked up by some patrol, Abram said. *We're all exhausted, we need rest and a plan. Let's find a place to hole up. I don't want to go back to Madame Bertrand's safe house. It won't be safe, for us or her.*

All right, Evelyn acquiesced. Fear still hammered at her, but she could feel fatigue fraying the edges of her mind. That would diminish their psychic defenses, too, if Lina came looking. Despite the fiasco on the beach, Evelyn had to think they'd gotten lucky. If Lina had done more than just preliminary probing, she would have found them.

So maybe it wasn't Lina after all.

But that rang false in Evelyn's mind. She knew better. She'd felt that whisper light touch and recognized the iron strength behind it. Lina *had* been there...and somehow, she'd managed to escape her once again.

* * *

Fatigue and satisfaction tangled together in Lina's mind as she pulled her uniform straight. It had been a long night with a lot of physical activity, and she felt worn out. But for the first time since that hellish night in the forest, Lina felt an upwelling of joy within her breast.

She'd found her.

"Lina!" Neils said, opening up the door to his office and greeting her with a smile. "Back so soon! You must have news. One moment, my dear. Let me say farewell to our friend here."

He pushed the door slightly wider and Lina took a step backward to allow the other occupant to exit his office. The woman who emerged looked vaguely familiar. A singer or an actress or something. Someone fairly highly placed within Parisian society. Neils was working all angles, it seemed.

The woman passed Lina without making eye contact and sailed out the door without a single word. Lina looked after her for a moment, amused.

"What a bitch," Neils said softly. Lina looked at him, shocked. Neils wasn't usually the type to use such language about a woman.

"I am sorry, my dear, but she really is. These Parisians, they are so haughty. You would think they had conquered our country, rather than the other way 'round. Come in, please. You *do* have news?"

"I do," Lina said. She followed him into the now-familiar office and, at his gesture, sank down into one of his chairs with a sigh. "I apologize, Herr Sendler, but I've been up all night."

"I imagine you have! Here, let me get coffee, and then you can fill me in." He stepped out of the room long enough to have a short conversation and returned with a smile.

"Sophie will bring us coffee and some cake. You do look done in, dear Lina. So tell me, how did our operation go?" he asked as he seated himself at his desk.

"Decidedly well, Herr Sendler," Lina said, forcing herself to keep the exultation out of her voice. "The Garreau girl's information was invaluable."

"They were at Bonaparte Beach, then? And they were...what? Intending a rescue by sea?"

"It appears so. Our batteries fired upon a British gunship offshore, though with no confirmed hits. We did, however, prevent the extraction of any of the probably thirty airmen gathered on the beach."

"I'm sorry," Neils said, sitting up abruptly. "You said...thirty?"

Lina nodded and gave him a moment to let the number sink in.

"Our spotters said at least that number, probably more. The visibility was, as you can imagine, quite poor, what with the rain and the fog. But they led several groups down from the cliffs. I was surprised, too, but more and more of them just kept coming."

"And how many were captured?"

"Twelve enemy airmen and two collaborators. The wife of one of the collaborators is also in custody, though she insists that she knows nothing. She is also eight months gone with child."

"I see," he said. "I will ensure she is treated appropriately and given medical care for her confinement."

"I think that would be best. She is lying about not knowing anything, but I do not think she knows much. Certainly not as much as her husband."

"And do you think he knows enough to allow us to further break open this escape ring?"

"It is possible, Herr Sendler, but I have something better than that in mind," she said. Then she fell silent as someone tapped lightly on the door.

"Come!" Neils barked, impatience making him sound sharper than he normally did. Sophie opened the door, her eyes wide and worried.

"Ah, Sophie. The coffee. Thank you, my dear. Will you pour for Oberhelfer Sucherin?" he asked.

Sophie nodded silently, and put the tray down on the desk with tentative movements. Her hand trembled slightly as she poured Lina's coffee, causing the china to rattle just a bit. For just a moment, Lina considered reaching out, scanning to see why this normally placid woman was so nervous. But she was in Neils' employ. Certainly he must have vetted her. Scanning her would be impolite. Lina must really be tired if she was considering such a breach of etiquette. She looked up and met the girl's eyes with a smile. Sophie gave her a tiny smile back and handed her the cup of coffee.

Lina took a long drink. Partly, it was an excuse to allow Sophie to leave the room before she continued speaking, but partly it was because she needed the kick of the hot, savory beverage. When Sophie had closed the door behind herself, Lina looked up at Neils once again.

"You were saying?" he asked.

"Yes. Some of the fugitives on the beach...they are known to me. Because of this, I made the executive decision to allow them to escape the trap we set."

"I assume there is some reason for your...sympathy?"

Lina gave him her cold smile and set the cup down.

"It is not sympathy, Herr Sendler. Because they are known to me, I can more easily track them. I let them go as...beaters, perhaps. Or bait, if you don't mind a hunting metaphor. I am confident if we follow where they lead us, we will not only capture them in the end, but we will also uncover much more of their network."

"And you are confident you will be able to find them again?"

"Indeed, yes."

"Why?" Neils leaned forward as he asked the question, putting his elbows on the desk, his eyes dark and intense with interest. Lina drew a deep breath.

"Because, I have linked with them before. One of them, at least. The girl."

"What? A girl?"

"One of their number is an American psychic named Evelyn Adamsen. I and my escort of six Fallschirmjager captured her and two of her countrymen after they bailed out of their wounded bomber. Somehow, the Amis are using psychics to assist them in their bombing missions. I was not able to get to the details of why before she..." Lina stopped suddenly, as a fist of grief and pain constricted her throat. She couldn't speak of it. She couldn't breathe...She saw Neils' eyes go wide in alarm. She swallowed hard and looked down.

"My escorts were killed. I was nearly killed and left for dead. I must find her, Neils. She must answer for what she took from me."

"Lina," Neils breathed. "I knew this was personal for you...but this sounds like more than duty. This...a personal vendetta?"

"Yes," she said fiercely. "And I know it is wrong, but I do not care. Because I *can* use her to take down these enemies of the Reich. My work will not suffer...indeed, my emotional involvement only makes me stronger in this case. I have been inside her head! She cannot hide from me, not for long, and I will follow her at a distance, and we will snap up every traitor, every collaborator, every *enemy* that dares to give her aid or comfort!"

"Lina," Neils said again. "I understand what you are saying, but do you not see how this could be a danger to you?"

"No! What...how?"

"You are too close..."

"No! Did you not listen...?"

He cut her off with a sharp cutting motion of his hand.

"Yes, Oberhelfer, I did listen," he said, his voice stern. "And let me tell you what I heard. You are consumed with the thought of catching the woman who hurt you, and I cannot blame you. But neither can I risk you on a chase across Europe. I had misgivings about sending you out to Brittany last night, if I am honest. If I lost you, my operation would be severely degraded here. You are not a combat soldier, Lina. You are a highly-trained specialist, and you are too valuable to lose."

"You will not lose me, Herr Sendler," she said lowly. "I give you my word."

The head of the Paris office pursed his lips in thought, then took a deep breath.

"Convince me," he said. "I will not make any promises...but convince me you can do this with minimal risk to yourself. What is your plan?"

Lina drew in a long, shaky breath, and forced her agitation to calm. She must be in control if she were to win the right to go after the Ami girl. It had been a mistake to allow Neils to see her passion. He thought it made her weaker. In the depths of her mind, Lina knew he was wrong. The blazing hatred she felt could only make her stronger...but she would bank it, make it smolder. She was the most powerful psychic the Reich had ever trained; she could certainly control herself.

"I know her location to within a few kilometers," Lina started. "She must still be in the vicinity of Plouha."

"How do you know this?" Neils asked, interrupting. "She could have snuck out in the time it took you to travel back here."

"I had the local authorities impose a complete travel lock down. Unless she went cross country on foot, she has gone nowhere. And if she has gone cross country on foot...well. My range is very good, mein Herr. Especially because of the link I mentioned earlier. She cannot outrun me, even with this detour back to Paris."

"On what authority did you impose the lockdown?" he asked.

"Yours," she said, without a flinch or hesitation. "Even with our arrests, there are a number of fugitives from the beach for whom we have not accounted. The authorities did not question in the slightest."

He just looked at her.

"You sent me to do a job, Herr Sendler," she reminded him. "My personal motivations do not change that. I would have imposed the lockdown anyway, even if she had never been on Bonaparte beach."

Another long look and then a nod. She went on.

"I will return to Plouha and assist with the interrogations there. I will locate her, and when I do, the travel restrictions will be lifted. When she moves, I will follow in her wake. I will find who helps her, and I will funnel that information back to you."

"And how far will you follow her?"

"As far as she goes, Herr Sendler. Until she is close to slipping beyond our borders."

"And then?"

"And then," Lina said softly. "If you will help me, I will take her."

Neils steepled his fingers in front of his mouth and said nothing for a few moments. Lina sat unmoving under his gaze, imposing a kind of iron calm on herself. Her instinct was to be anything but calm. If he didn't allow her to do this, then she would have to find some way to chase the Amis on her own...

"Fine," he said, the word dropping like a stone into the stillness between them. "I am still concerned, but I have seen what you can do, Lina. I brought you here to bring down this network, and your plan will do it. One condition, however. I will accompany you every step of the way. To protect you. From yourself, if necessary."

And how do you plan to do that, mein Herr? She wanted to ask the question, but long ago Lina had learned discretion was the better part of valor, so she nodded and said nothing.

* * * * *

Chapter Sixteen

It was nearly three days before they could get out of the area.

They spent the first morning hiding in an abandoned barn. The structure wasn't entirely sound, and Evelyn feared that the weathered timbers might all come toppling down on them as they slept, but it was out of sight, and that was good enough for Abram. The four of them huddled together in a corner of the dilapidated structure, behind a pile of dirt and cast-off farm implements, and waited out the remainder of that wet, windy day. As the hours wore on, Evelyn's stomach began to cramp in hunger, and she thought longingly of Madame Bertrand's pies.

Perhaps we should go back to her house? Sean offered at one point as the afternoon sun slanted through a break in the clouds just before it set. *I think I could find the way.*

Too dangerous, Abram said. *For us and for her. We've been hungry before. We'll be all right for the day.*

Are we moving on tomorrow? Paul asked.

That's my thought. Unless Evie's not up to it.

I'm fine, Evelyn said firmly. *My ankle aches, but it's not as bad as it was. It's not even swollen...much.*

Right, then that's what we'll do. We'll wait until tonight, then we'll move on down the road. If we can get back to Guingamp, we can find that Cosca fellow again. I think he'd do better than Madame Bertrand.

After that exchange, Evelyn decided she'd better try to get some rest before they went out into the murky night. She composed herself for sleep, but uneasiness coated her mind. Though she kept it from the men, she remained certain Lina was out there, hunting them. She didn't know if the other girl would be able to find her or not...but she was not at all sanguine about her ability to evade detection. After all, it had always been easy to find Mary in a crowd, simply because they'd been linked so many times. She'd only linked with Lina once...but it had been an especially intimate link.

Nothing you can do about it now, Paul said, on the tight channel he knew how to use. So much for keeping her worries from the men.

She's out there, Paul. I know she is.

Maybe she is. And maybe she'll find us. And if she does, we'll fight. We'll protect you, Evie. You know that.

I know, Paul. But I don't know if you can protect me from her.

Why?

She's strong. She's so strong...I've never met anyone who could hold me inside my own mind like that.

Never?

No.

And yet, you defeated her once.

Evelyn froze, shock reverberating through her mind like ice water.

What?

You defeated her once, didn't you? She's so incredibly strong...but that makes you stronger.

I don't understand.

Paul was on watch, sitting a few feet away from where she lay curled between the sleeping forms of Sean and Abram. He shifted and turned to look directly at her, though his eyes were in shadow.

It's like this, Evie. You know how you stop being afraid of the monsters in the dark? You become the scariest monster out there. You took everything she threw at you...and you still destroyed her. Or very nearly. That makes you the most fearsome thing in the dark. She can't beat you, or she would have done it already. Remember that, Evie.

I...all right...

The corner of his mouth lifted in a slight smile, and he shifted so the last rays of the sun slanted through the barn-wood boards to light up his face.

Good. Now get some sleep.

* * *

Sometime after midnight, they vacated the barn and set out into the night. The soaking rain had finally passed, and the air felt cold and crystalline against Evelyn's face.

I smell snow, she told the men. *We'll want to get under cover before it starts.*

Well, you be sure and tell me when it's about to start, Evie, Abram said rather tartly. *I'll do my best.*

Hey, LT, ease up, will ya? Sean immediately leapt to Evelyn's defense as she recoiled, stung by the frustration and exasperation flowing from their leader.

I'm sorry, sir, Evelyn said. *I didn't mean anything by it. I was just trying to help.*

Evelyn felt Abram's mental sigh soaking through the lines of the net.

I'm sorry, too, he said after a moment. *I'm just frustrated.*

We all are, Paul said. *But it does nobody any good to sit and snipe at one another. Let's keep moving. The road to Guingamp is just ahead.*

Paul was right. Not quite an hour later, they came upon the small, narrow road Cosca had driven. Unfortunately, the road was blocked by a pair of trucks bearing the symbol of the Wehrmacht. They idled side by side, their headlights illuminating the dirt of the road from both directions. Evelyn counted four soldiers standing out in front of the trucks.

There are probably several more patrolling nearby, Paul added, in response to her thought. *I don't think we should go this way.*

Let's head west a ways, Paul decided. *They can't have every little road and cart track road blocked.*

But they did. At least, that was how it appeared. They found themselves creeping across winter-bare fields and through copses of trees, avoiding the Wehrmacht vehicles that seemed to be everywhere, roaming down every road, shining their headlights into every ditch, under every hedge.

Dawn found them hunkering under an ancient-looking culvert, mud smeared on their faces to make them less visible. Several times, they heard the voices of soldiers and the rumble of their vehicle engines as they passed overhead. Once, they heard men walking through the forest nearby.

Are they searching for us? Sean wanted to know.

If Lina is here, I'm afraid that they are, Evelyn replied, her mind grim.

You really think she survived? She was strangled!

We never checked her breathing. I think...I don't know, but I felt someone back on the beach, and my instincts tell me it was her.

Whoever it was, they're definitely searching, Paul put in. *We're going to have to get through this cordon somehow, or they will find us.* He didn't say more, but his thoughts held the flat practicality that they'd held when he thought about killing the Nazi guards. Despite her trust in the man, Evelyn couldn't help but feel a chill.

It may come to that, if they don't ease up tonight, Abram said. *We need a solid plan.*

If we could find a smaller roadblock, maybe just one vehicle, just a few men...we could neutralize the guards, then grab their uniforms and truck and make a run for it, Paul suggested. *I can show you what to do, to keep the noise down.*

Evelyn suppressed a shiver. Paul's cool practicality may be necessary, but it still unnerved her. Though when she thought about it, she couldn't see why it should. Weren't they all in the business of raining wholesale death and destruction down from the sky? Paul's criminal skills just brought things in a bit closer. Perhaps it was more honest that way.

Spooked by her own thoughts, Evelyn gave herself a mental shake and forced her mind back to the reality at hand. All the recent rain had made the ground under their culvert sodden and muddy. While this was excellent for camouflage, it also soaked through their clothes, leaving their skin clammy and uncomfortable. It would be worse when night fell, especially if there was any wind. Unfortunately, with so many Germans patrolling around, there was no way they could risk a fire. Not even one of Abram's dug out, shielded ones. At least if it snowed, they would have more water to drink. They'd made do with the small trickle under the culvert, thought it wasn't exactly appetizing. Filtering the mud through her once-lovely blue neck scarf helped some, but it still tasted of dirt.

Of course, if they didn't find something to eat soon, eating dirt might become more appealing. Evelyn's stomach twisted in hunger, and the dull, empty ache in her middle left her feeling listless and distracted...and irritable. Which was the case with all of them. Abram's snappy reply to her prediction of snow wasn't the only spark of temper that had flared between the four of them since the terrifying disappointment of the beach. Evelyn did her best to funnel the edge off of everyone's emotions, but as the situation steadily deteriorated, it was getting harder and harder to keep the net even and smooth.

She reached out a tendril of thought and ran along the lines that connected her psyche to her men. She drew the negative emotions away, as much as she was able, and laid down a soothing layer of calm. Contentment was a bit too much of a stretch, but she could at least strengthen the connections and try to keep tempers from flashing...

There it was again. That fluttering probe, like a the lightest of feather-tickles on the furthest extremities of her network. Evelyn caught her breath and held it as she began slowly, steadily reinforcing the strength of her defenses.

She's here again, Evelyn whispered, just the barest of thoughts. *She's trying to find us.*

In retrospect, she probably shouldn't have said anything. Sudden alarm flashed through their minds, which dumped emotional energy into the network. In effect, they lit up like a bonfire for whoever was searching for them.

Shit! Shit! Be calm, please! Evelyn swore, as she fought to dampen the emotions running hot along the lines of the net. *She'll find us all the quicker if we panic. Breathe deep, be calm, I'm hiding us as best I can!*

But calm was easier said than done. With her physical ears, Evelyn could hear the men shifting in the mud, and Sean's body radiated tension next to hers. The tickle at the far edge of her senses flared in triumph and then disappeared.

She'd spotted them. They had to move.

We're discovered, Evelyn said, her tone miserable and tense. *I'm sorry, it's my fault. I shouldn't have said anything.*

What does that mean? Abram asked, his tone short.

It means she has a location, or at least a direction. She'll probably have men here soon. We need to get moving.

Sun's just starting to go down, Sean put in. *We could try for one of the trucks, like the LT said.*

Abram thought for a moment. Evelyn could feel the bewildering array of possible scenarios as they flashed in his mind. The weight of leadership dragged at him, in the certain knowledge he was responsible for the safety of their group. She pushed support his way. Not subtle, but his mind accepted it, and he made a choice.

Fine, he said. *Let's follow this streambed to the northwest. We'll find another road and scout out a good roadblock. Evie, can you tell how soon they may be coming?*

Not without reaching out to her and giving her more information. Our best defense at this point is to move, quickly, and keep moving.

Roger, he said. *Paul, as we're going, you brief us on the best way to proceed quietly when we find a likely target.*

Got it.

All right, everyone. Stay low, stay quiet, and stay together. Let's go.

They crept out from under the culvert as the last rays of the afternoon sun slanted through the foliage overhead. Paul, in the lead, crouched low, folding his tall, lean body down to try and stay in the little creek's depression. Once again, the sodden ground worked in their favor, as the wet, spongy mud muffled their footsteps.

The sun continued to sink, and the temperature continued to drop. Evelyn felt the shivers begin at the base of her spine and radiate outward as the chill night air wrapped around her damp body. She sternly told herself to keep moving. It was her best and only defense against both the cold and Lina's searching malice.

Darkness stretched up from under the trees and bushes, and night consumed them fully before they came to another road crossing.

Best guess, we've gone maybe five miles, Paul reported back. *I think this might have what we're looking for, though.*

Right. We'll hole up while you scout for a roadblock. I'm betting it's behind that bend there to the South, Abram said.

I think you're right. Gimme just a minute.

The rest of them settled into a cramped hollow under a fallen log and watched through Paul's eyes as he crept south alongside the road. Sure enough, once he rounded a tight ninety-degree bend, two vehicles sat blocking the road, which faced north and south. One had its headlights pointed farther down the road to the south, and one pointed back toward the curve to the north.

Two vehicles, that's more than we want to tangle with, Abram said. Evelyn could feel his exhausted disappointment soaking through the net.

Maybe...but look, Paul said. *The way they're positioned, if we can disable the one truck and get into the other, we can just hit the gas and be on down the road.*

Yeah, but what about the uniforms?

We get them if we can, but if not, no big deal. We're headed to Cosca's right? We'll say we were hired to drive the truck there for some maintenance.

And you're going to say that in German, are you?

Evie can say it in French. Or teach me to. Hell, man, I'm just trying to get us out of here!

*No, I know. You're right. I'm just...*Abram scrubbed his hands over his face. *How many men do you see?*

Paul looked around slowly, knowing three other people were sharing his vision. The site had obviously been chosen because the road widened out after the turn. Trees crowded closely on either side, probably due to the stream they'd followed to get there. One driver sat facing them, looking at the curve of the road as he munched on cheese and bread. His headlights cast stark shadows on either side of the road. Which was sort of a good news/bad news type of situation. Those shadows could help them get very close undetected. They could also conceal more men.

Like the one that walked out from the trees on the opposite side of the road. Paul crouched slowly, careful not to move too suddenly and catch someone's eye as the German soldier whistled and zipped his fly as he walked. He shouted something toward the south-facing truck and then sauntered toward the nearer driver. They proceeded to carry on a conversation in a casual, unhurried manner. They both carried Mausers, but they carried them slung. Roadblock they may be, but it was clear that these men didn't expect to see anything of note anytime soon.

So like I said, we go in quick and quiet. I don't know where everyone else is, but they're not here, as far as I can tell. You guys come this way. I'm going to make my move, Paul said.

Evelyn felt a bit of startled resistance coming from Abram, but Paul was already in motion. He started creeping toward the truck, his knife out and ready. Abram breathed out a curse and motioned to them to follow the bombardier. They'd just started moving when Evelyn heard the voice of another man calling out between them and Paul. The two men in the truck called back in answer.

Before she could think better of it, Evelyn leapt to her feet and started running through the trees toward the road.

Keep moving, she told the men. *I'll distract them!*

Evie! Sean cried, but Abram took him by the wrist and dragged him forward toward the trucks. Evelyn felt the sting of a branch whipping across her face before she burst out onto the road, falling to her knees in front of a clearly very startled German soldier.

"Please," she cried in French, the sobs coming surprisingly easy to her as her eyes filled with tears. "Please help me!"

"Fraulein?" the German asked, confused. He reached down to take her by her arms and pull her gently to her feet. She let him do so, and then she struck, hard, with all the power she could muster. The power of the storm inside her psyche built, and for the first time since she'd escaped from Lina, Evelyn gave vent to the lashing, tossing, battering energy of her mind. She drove her consciousness in past his defenses, which were wide open with compassion and concern for her disheveled, distraught state. Her will slashed his conscious mind to pieces, fragmenting his psyche and causing pain to erupt in his brain. He gave a twitch, and blood began to flow from his nose as her onslaught caused the blood vessels in his brain to burst. He let out a breath of air and crumpled to the gravel at her feet.

The storm continued to rage, threatening to engulf her with its fury. But she was still linked with her men, though all three of them had frozen, stunned by the sudden violence of her actions. She pushed that away for the moment and focused on the three of them as her anchors: Abram and his leadership and responsibility. Paul and his practical, striking hands. Sean and his loving heart. Her links to each of them steadied her, allowed her to fight the storm back, to force the hurricane back into its bottle, to calm the raging seas of her mind.

Is he dead? Abram asked.

Yes, Evelyn said softly.

Get his uniform and get off the road, then.

Evelyn did as he said, biting her lip against the tears that threatened to fall. He was angry at her. She'd acted rashly and scared them. She'd used her abilities to destroy, and that was an evil thing. She withdrew as much as she could without breaking the net entirely and focused on the task at hand. It seemed she'd probably better pull the corpse off into the underbrush, but he was nearly twice her size and completely dead weight. So she settled for trying to strip him of his uniform.

A few moments into the tugging and pulling, Sean materialized beside her.

Let me help you, he said. *The others are taking care of the rest of them.*

And, indeed, in the back of her mind, Evelyn could feel the violence seeping from Abram and Paul as they slashed brake lines and cut throats in the darkness. If she concentrated, she could even hear a scuffling just around the bend. She wanted to reach out, to see if she could sense anyone else nearby, but she was afraid that to do so would only pinpoint their location again. She hadn't felt the tickling that meant that Lina was searching for her, not since the culvert.

We're done here. Come back this way, Abram ordered a few moments later. Evelyn and Sean hadn't made much progress at all, having just gotten the corpse out of the middle of the road.

We don't have the uniform yet, Sean sent back.

Leave it. None of the others will work, anyway. Better if we just get on the road. I have another idea.

And, indeed, he did. When they arrived back at the roadblock, they found Abram and Paul busy loading up the north-facing truck with the bodies of the three soldiers that they'd killed. Evelyn could see why the dead soldiers' uniforms wouldn't work: they were each covered in blood. Blood which left dark smears on the upholstery of the truck's cab as the three bodies were crammed inside.

Go get in the other truck, get it started. I'm going to start this one up and wedge the gas pedal. They'll go off the road at the curve and hit a tree. Hopefully there'll be a fire, and it'll confuse the evidence enough to buy us some time, Abram said. Sean nodded and took Evelyn by the hand, pulling her with him to the other truck. She climbed up into the seat, feeling miserable about it all, but trying to focus on only the tasks at hand. Sean followed her up and turned the key, letting the big engine roar to life. Behind them, they heard the other truck start up, and then Abram and Paul jumped into the truck bed with a couple of loud thumps that reverberated through the frame.

Go! Abram's mental shout whip-cracked through the net. Behind them, they heard a sickening crunch as the second truck impacted a large tree off to the side of the curve, followed by another crunch-bang as the truck turned over on its side. Sean stomped on the gas, and Evelyn felt herself pushed back into the seat as their truck leapt forward into the night.

* * *

They drove for about an hour, not totally sure where they were going. Sean knew that they had to head south and west toward Guingamp, but that was it. All they knew was that Cosca's garage lay along one of the main roads between Guingamp and Plouha. At least no one stopped them, though whether that was due to the lateness of the hour or the Wehrmacht markings on their truck, none of them cared to speculate.

Eventually, they found their way to one of the main highways and turned to follow the signs for the small town where they'd disembarked from the Paris train. It was only a few days ago, but to Evelyn, it seemed as if a lifetime had passed.

For once, it seemed that luck was on their side. After almost another hour, they caught site of a familiar house and outbuildings as Cosca's garage came into view. Sean turned into the rutted gravel drive and cut the engine. They coasted to a stop near the truck that had brought them to Plouha.

Now what? Sean asked. *Do we just go up to his door and knock?*

I suppose so, Abram said. *I can't think of a better idea. It's late. He should be home.*

He should be asleep, Sean put in. *He's probably not going to be real happy with us showing back up here.*

Probably not, but I still can't think of a better idea, Abram said. *So we knock.*

They trooped out of the Wehrmacht truck one by one and went up to the door that led to Cosca's kitchen. Abram looked at the darkened windows for a moment, then shrugged and knocked firmly on the door. The sound seemed really loud in the night silence. Abram raised his hand to knock again when a glow flared, then dimmed, then steadied inside the kitchen. Someone had lit a lamp.

The door handle turned, and it opened to reveal Cosca's weathered face. He looked at the four of them, his face inscrutable, and then pushed the door wider in invitation. Evelyn felt a surge of relief as they stepped over the threshold and into the kitchen.

"I heard about the beach," he said in French with no preamble. "I wondered if you were caught."

"Very nearly," Evelyn said. "We need to get out of France as soon as possible."

"It will be difficult," he said. "You will likely need to go south, to Marseilles, perhaps. Or over the Pyrenees to Spain. I have some contacts left that have not yet been swept up. I will see what I can do."

"Thank you, Monsieur Cosca."

Cosca's only reply was a grunt and a wave of his hand. With no more ceremony than this, he welcomed them in to his house for the second time. This time, he ushered them upstairs to an attic room where they could sleep. Evelyn didn't realize how tired she was until she caught sight of the old, narrow bed. Cosca left them in the room and returned a few moments later with an armful of blankets. Apparently, he was leaving the sleeping arrangements up to them. Without a wave or another word, he closed the attic door behind himself. They heard the stairs creak under his heavy tread as he returned to his own bed.

Evie gets the bed, Sean said quickly.

Naturally, Abram said.

*Someone else can have it...*Evelyn started to protest, only to have all three men look at her like she'd lost her mind. She stopped before the thought was fully articulated and gave an embarrassed shrug.

You're still a lady, Evie, Paul said on that tight channel that only she could hear. *It's important that we take care of you as one.*

Even when I do terrible things? she asked, and even her mental voice felt small and ashamed. To hide her face before she started crying, she turned and began making up the small bed. *I know that what I did to that soldier was wrong...but I was so afraid that he'd alert the others...*

Evie. You think we're worried about that?

Abram is. He was so short with me afterward.

That was because you scared him...not with what you did, but that you acted so quickly. We all felt terrified for you, that you would just rush into danger that way.

But I was the only one who had a chance of distracting him! If he'd seen any of you, he would have known for sure who we are. He wasn't expecting a crying woman.

Which is why it worked. But you did scare us. We all love you, Evie, even if we're not puppies like Sean about it. We couldn't make it if something happened to you. So just...keep that in mind, will ya?

I...all right, she said, humbled by his frank honesty and unsure what to do about it. They loved her?

Of course we do, Paul said. *We're all intertwined, you know that. To me, you're what my sister was. To Sean, you're his untouchable dream girl. To Abram, you're the muse, the reason we keep moving. Keep fighting. You're the heart of all of us, and you'll be the reason we make it home. Now lie down and get some rest. Who knows what tomorrow's going to be like?*

Perhaps it wasn't the most reassuring note on which to end their conversation, but it was uniquely Paul. And despite that (or maybe because of it), Evelyn felt comforted anyway. She finished smoothing the cover over the mattress and sat down on the bed to remove her boots and her outer coat. Abram and Sean lay rolled up in their separate blankets, not far away. Paul sat against the wall, watching her. She gave him a smile and laid down, pulling the blanket up to her ears.

You'll be the reason I make it home, too, she sent to him. *All of you will.*

That's the plan, he said.

* * *

Evelyn woke with the late morning sun slanting across her face. She blinked and opened her eyes. A steeply-slanting attic ceiling stretched above her. Midway up, a skylight with a broken shutter let the rays of light into the otherwise dim room. Her empty stomach rumbled loudly in the quiet, and she realized abruptly she was alone.

Hello? she said, reaching out along the lines of the net.

Evie! You're awake! Sean responded with his usual exuberant joy. Evelyn tried very hard not to think about what Paul had said about Sean's feelings for her and sat up in the bed as a distraction.

I am. Where are all of you?

Cosca put us to work, Abram replied. *I suppose he thinks we're hiding in plain sight.*

Or he just wants free labor, Paul said. *I swear, I'm the first one to sweep out this garage in decades.*

Is there food? Evelyn asked. On the one hand, she enjoyed their lighthearted responses after the ordeal of the last few days. But, on the other hand, it felt like her stomach was trying to eat itself.

In the kitchen, Abram said. *Cold meat and cheese, a loaf of bread. I guess it's for us, judging by Cosca's grunt when he put it out on the table this morning.*

Where is he? Evelyn asked. *I'll ask him.*

Gone, Abram replied. *Once he got us started on our various chores, he took the Jerry truck and left. Go. Eat. We all did, and he said nothing.*

All right, Evelyn said. She swung her feet to the floor and got up, marveling at how stiff she felt. All of her muscles ached, and her still-healing ankle throbbed a warning. She was careful not to put too much weight on it and hoped they'd be able to avoid walking for at least a day or so.

Downstairs, it was as the men had said. Bread and cheese and meat lay in covered dishes on the table. She took some of each and dove ravenously into the meal. The bread was dry and nearly stale. The cheese was warm and soft, and the meat greasy. It tasted amazing. She ate enough that her mother would have been embarrassed to watch her and then pushed back from the table. As she had done the last time she'd eaten in this kitchen, she began tidying up...then she began to deep clean. A few hours later, a glance out the kitchen window showed the sun lower in the afternoon sky than she would have expected. Apparently she'd awakened later than she'd originally thought, or she'd gotten so caught up in her task she lost track of the time. As she watched, elbows deep in soapy water, a truck pulled up the gravel drive, spraying dust up into the air in a brown haze.

Someone's here, she sent to everyone. *I hope it's Cosca, but in case it's not...I'll go see. Stay out of sight if you can.*

We're fine, Evie. You just be careful! Abram sent. Before her talk with Paul the previous night, Evelyn would have been tempted to quail at the tone of their leader's thoughts. All her life, she'd been taught it was the ultimate wrong to do as she'd done...twice now. Three times, if one counted the man in London. She must never, never use her abilities to harm anyone else. That maxim had been drummed into her by repetition since she was old enough to understand the words. And she had broken that most sacred of laws multiple times. She couldn't have blamed the men one iota if they abandoned her in fear and disgust...but they hadn't. Quite the opposite, in fact. By their simple acceptance of her, they'd shown they understood the necessity she'd perceived. They understood, and they supported her decisions...as long as her decisions kept them all safe and got them all home.

All truly was fair, she realized, when in love and war.

With these thoughts circling in her mind, she dried her hands and stepped out of the swinging kitchen door. She waited on the step for the truck to roll to a stop between her and the garage. As it did, she felt a flash of relief. That *was* Cosca in the driver's seat. And on the passenger side...

The door to the truck cab swung open, and the occupant tumbled out like a little cyclone.

"Evie!" Deedee cried, as she ran up and wrapped her arms around Evelyn in a surprisingly hard hug. "I'm so glad you're all right! We were so worried!"

"Deedee!" Evelyn gasped, as she hugged the other woman back. She'd forgotten just how much energy Deedee carried in her petite frame. "So were we!"

"Call the men, let us go inside, quickly. You must tell me everything, and then we will make further plans."

With that, the little cyclone swept her inside the house, where they were joined moments later by the men. Each of them received the same effusive greetings Evelyn had, which surprised Abram and Paul. Sean, however, took it in stride and gave Deedee a wide smile as he hugged her back. Something twisted in Evelyn as she watched, and it surprised her. She clamped down on the nasty, unpleasant feeling and shoved it away from the rest of the net, but Paul met her eyes with a knowing look.

"I am so pleased you are all safe...for now," Deedee was saying. Evelyn forced her mind back to the present moment and followed the other woman over to Cosca's table. Deedee and Evelyn sat, as did Abram. Paul and Sean stood close by, while Cosca moved with a sort of growly bustle to make some tea. "This was a heavy blow to our organization."

"I'm sure," Abram said. "How many were caught?"

"Many," Deedee said, all of her joy gone as she spoke the stark truth. "Both of your airmen and our helpers. The airmen, at least, will mostly be treated well as prisoners of war. Our helpers, however..." She spread her hands wide in a wordless gesture of helplessness.

"Deedee," Evelyn breathed. "I'm so sorry to have put you and your people at risk..."

"No!" Deedee said, her smile flashing back into being, though her eyes stayed sober and hard. "You must not regret. They have acted according to their conscience and have been incredibly brave. This was not your fault. None of you. You must *honor* them and keep fighting to get home."

"All right," Abram said, smiling slightly and making a "calm down" gesture with his hands. "So how do we proceed from here?"

"I think we must return to Paris," Deedee said. "It will be dangerous, but Paris is a large city. There are many ways to hide there, and...we have ears in certain places there. From Paris, you can take the train to Bayonne, to see my friend Madame Ballasdens. From there, we shall go south to the border and take you across the mountains."

She turned to give Evelyn a long look.

"It will be a difficult journey, I am afraid. The passage takes nearly twenty hours, and it is all climbing in the mountains. We will ford the Bidassoa River. Will you be able to keep up?"

"She'll keep up," Sean said quickly.

"Or we'll carry her," Paul added. "We've done it before."

Deedee shook her head in the negative.

"You will not be able to carry her on this journey, I am afraid. But I am willing to take you, Evie, if you are willing to go and give it your all."

"I am willing," Evelyn said softly. *I will keep up, I promise.*

We have no doubts, Evie, Abram said, and Evelyn could feel the strength of his confidence in her flowing down the lines of the net.

"Very well. We will board the train in the morning to Paris and then continue on to Bayonne overnight. It will be a chance for rest. It is good you brought Cosca a truck; he was able to sell it at his other garage and earn enough funds to pay for your tickets."

"How did you sell that truck?" Abram asked, swiveling in his chair to look at Cosca. "It had the Jerry Army's markings on the door."

"Parts," Cosca grunted. "Dumped the door, sold the parts back to the Boches."

"You sold the Jerry truck back to the Jerries?" Abram's eyes went wide at the old Frenchman's audacity.

Cosca just smiled and pulled the whistling kettle off of the stove. He poured them tea and then, without another word, walked out of the kitchen, back toward his bedroom.

"He is a very good man," Deedee said softly. "You are lucky."

"We know," Evelyn replied.

"I suppose you do," Deedee said. "I know it is early, but we should get some sleep. Our train leaves Guingamp an hour before dawn."

* * *

"Unfortunately, they disembarked in Paris and immediately boarded another train for Bayonne, rather than seeking refuge somewhere within the city. However, while we had hoped the Amis would lead us to further collaborators in Paris, we were at least able to positively identify the female escorting them. Her name is Diandra van Duren. She is a resident of Brussels, and we believe she, along with her father and possibly other members of her family, are at the very heart of the fugitive network," Lina reported. She sat at strict attention in Neils' office, conscious of the gaze of not only her friend, but his superior officer from Berlin.

"Who is the father?" Neils asked.

"A Belgian doctor by the name of Frederic van Duren. He may, in fact, be the mastermind behind the whole network, though I suspect otherwise. He does appear to be running the Belgian portion of the operation. He's been questioned before, but has always been able to explain his activities under the guise of his medical practice," Lina said.

"So who, then, is the mastermind?" the other man, Regierungs- und Kriminaldirektor Warren Smolenk asked, speaking for the first time since Lina had entered the room to give her report.

"I believe it is Diandra herself, Herr Smolenk," Lina said, addressing the man by his civilian title rather than his detective or SS rank. As he was dressed, like Neils, in plainclothes, this was the appropriate protocol. Though she rather got the impression he would have preferred otherwise.

"A woman? I hardly think that likely. A network of this size is incredibly complex. The female brain isn't capable of that kind of organization."

Lina fought to keep her face neutral.

"Regardless, mein Herr," Neils said smoothly. "It is clear this woman is deeply involved. You were saying, Oberhelfer, that we should continue to surveil her movements, I think?"

"Yes," Lina said, grateful for his tact. "She and the current group of fugitives boarded a train for Bayonne not an hour ago. If I may take a motorcar, we can beat the train down there and be in position to intercept and capture her, along with the American fugitives."

"That seems rather a waste of resources," Smolenk said. This time Lina couldn't help but raise her eyebrows.

"How so, mein Herr?" she asked, which earned her a sharp look from Smolenk and a warning one from Neils. After a moment, Smolenk deigned to respond.

"Because," he said, speaking with exaggerated slowness, as if talking to a child. "If we have the information on the father, what need have we to go chasing the daughter across France? Let us go pick up the man and interrogate him. We will decapitate this network of criminal dissidents and watch it fall into disarray. From there, it is just the mopping up of pieces. We can arrest the daughter at any time. The father is the key. Capture him."

Dread slammed into Lina's mind. Her eyes cut to Neils'. His look turned from a warning to a plea, as if he were beseeching her not to say anything. Though her instincts and desires screamed at her to defy this little-minded man who stood in the way of justice, Lina held herself perfectly still and trusted in her friend and mentor. After a brief moment, Neils gave her a barely perceptible nod.

"Very well, Herr Smolenk," Neils said, coming to his feet. Lina followed suit, as did Smolenk, slowly. "We will begin right away."

"Excellent," Smolenk said. "And be sure you take your pet witch to Brussels with you. I don't have to tell you how critical this interrogation will be. Let us ensure we do the job right the first time."

"Of course, mein Herr," Neils said. He stepped around his desk and gestured to Smolenk to precede him out of the room, leaving Lina standing forgotten in the middle of his office. She heard the pair of them walking down the hallway and the muffled sound of Neils' goodbyes as his superior left the office. She didn't move, not even when Neils walked back in and closed the door behind himself.

"I am sorry," he said quietly.

"You know I must go," she said, her voice low.

"Yes, I do. But you must come to Belgium, first. He said it again as we were walking out. To do otherwise is to court destruction,

Lina. You see how he feels about women. And he called you a witch. I am afraid, for your safety, we *must* obey."

"But if I lose them?" Lina asked, ice in her voice, ice in her veins.

"You will not. We will double the roadblocks in Bayonne. They will not make it out of the city."

"You do not know that."

"No," he admitted. "But perhaps you can follow them even so, as you said you could, yes?"

"Not from so far away as Brussels," she whispered. "I *must* get to Bayonne while they are still there."

"I will do everything that I can to see that you do, Lina. Again, you must trust me."

"I do," she whispered. Even though the ache of failure loomed.

No, she whispered to Josef's memory. *Even if I have to escape myself from Brussels, I will find her, and I will destroy her, my love. No matter how long it takes. Even if I must wait until the war is lost or won.*

"Lina?"

She blinked and focused on Neils' face.

"I trust you," she said. "Let us go."

* * * * *

Chapter Seventeen

The train from Paris to Bayonne took all night. Thanks to the funds that Cosca had handed Deedee, they were able to purchase a private luxury compartment. Inside, the five of them slept, hoarding their strength for what would be the most difficult, but hopefully last, leg of their journey. Evelyn found the rocking motion of the train to be soothing, but sleep didn't come easily to her. The end of their journey seemed incredibly far out of reach. Her mind kept drifting back to the other members of her crew. The lost pilots: Carl with his quiet assuredness and Bob with his eager arrogance. In the violence of her bailout, she hadn't felt them die, but she ached for them anyway. And what had become of the others? Logan with his irreverent grin and slightly inappropriate humor? Rico with his smooth Latin charm? Les with his rough exterior covering his golden heart, and John, their quiet radio man? Had any of them made it out of the aircraft alive? Had they survived the parachute landing? Had they, too, made their way into the welcoming arms of friendly resistance forces...or were they even now dying slowly in a Nazi prison camp?

Her mind circled these questions, doubling back on itself as she worried about her crew...and about the helpers who risked so much to get them home. Deedee hadn't told them who had been arrested. She refused, saying it was better they didn't know. But the quietly intense woman had a haunted look about her Evelyn didn't remember from before they'd left for Bonaparte Beach.

Haunted or not, Deedee was all business when they pulled into the station at Bayonne. She handed each of the men a beret and instructed them how to wear it flat, in the Basque style.

"You look very uncomfortable," she said as she eyed each of them critically. "Try to relax. We do not wish to draw attention. Follow me off the train, and we will meet up with my friend who will take us the next part of the way."

She says "relax" like it's going to be easy, Abram groused.

Hunch your shoulders, just a little bit. Don't avoid eye contact, but don't stare. Try to move at the same pace as the crowd around you. That's the best way to avoid notice. Blend in, Paul said.

What are you, an actor?

Paul turned to give Abram a look while Deedee fussed with Sean's beret a bit more.

No. But it works on cops, the bombardier said, and gave a little smile that didn't reach his eyes. The train came to a complete stop with a squeal and a slight bump, causing them to all rock back and forth in their seats.

"Good," Deedee said in French. "Now follow me."

They exited the compartment and made their way off the train and onto the platform outside. The morning light shone from the eastern sky, illuminating the throng of Bayonnais workers starting their days. Evelyn tried to follow Paul's advice and blend in as the group of them wound their way through the crowd and out through the main passenger terminal. Once outside, Deedee led them down the street for about a block, then turned into a small courtyard bordered by a low stone wall.

Inside the courtyard, a tall, strongly-built woman smiled and held out her arms to Deedee.

"Auntie," Deedee said, walking into the other woman's embrace. They kissed each other's cheeks, and Evelyn found herself smiling at the evident pleasure with which Deedee was received. Her aunt seemed to genuinely care.

"Everyone, this is my Auntie Sylvaine," Deedee said in French as she stepped away, leaving one arm wrapped around the other woman's waist. "Who is not truly a relation, except by affection. She will be our guide today."

"Yes," Sylvaine said, spreading her hands wide in a gesture of welcome. "Please, take a bicycle. I gathered several, for I did not know how tall any of you were...does everyone know how to ride?"

"We do," Evelyn said after mentally confirming with the men that this was the case.

"Good. It is not quite two hours to Urrugne, but there are some hills. We will go at a steady pace, so keep up." With this admonishment and another smile, Sylvaine took hold of the handlebars of the bicycle closest to her and swung her leg over. Evelyn could see the full skirt the woman wore was actually split, and she felt a quick stab of envy. Bicycling for two hours in her current dress would not be terribly comfortable.

Not that comfort was much of a consideration, she supposed.

It took a bit of doing, but they all eventually found bicycles that fit well enough, and one by one they pulled out onto the street. Thankfully, the day was unseasonably warm, almost spring-like.

Evelyn hadn't ridden a bicycle since she was a small girl. At first, she had a hard time keeping her balance, especially because her skirt kept getting caught on her pedal. She wobbled her way behind the others for a few hundred meters.

Evie! Are you all right? We don't want to get separated, Abram called back to her.

I...yes. It's just that I'm not used to this...and this skirt...

Ahead, Sean pulled himself out of the line and cycled back to her before stopping.

"Here," he said out loud as she stopped beside him. "Tuck your skirt up like this. You'll flash some leg, but it will help you balance better." As he spoke, the flight engineer reached out for her draping skirt and helped her to tuck it under her bottom on the seat.

"Thank you," Evelyn said, feeling her cheeks heat up.

"You're welcome. Now, do you think we can try to catch up?" he asked, looking forward to where the others had continued after Sylvaine. Abram was looking back at them, and Sean gave him a wave.

We're fine, he sent down the lines of the net. Evelyn looked back at him to see him watching her face. She gave him a small smile and a nod. *We'll catch up.*

And they did. Without the skirt problem, Evelyn found her balance and was able to establish a rhythm of pedaling that allowed her to pick up some speed. She and Sean started to push up the slight incline ahead of them just as the others disappeared over the top. A moment later, they reached the summit themselves. Sean looked over at her, one rusty eyebrow raised in a challenge. She laughed and pushed ahead, letting the bicycle accelerate as it coasted down the hill. A breeze lifted her hair, and the morning light felt like a benediction on her face. Behind her, she could hear Sean's answering chuckle over the whirr of her tires on the road.

They were still laughing when they joined the others, who had stopped on the side of the road.

"What's happening?" Evelyn asked Deedee in French, her voice still breathless and light with laughter. "Where's Sylvaine?"

"Up there," she said, pointing. Evelyn looked to see the tall, muscular Frenchwoman talking to someone through the window of a black sedan car. Deedee seemed calm, but something in the air put Evelyn very suddenly on edge.

Ahead, Sylvaine pushed her bicycle back and waved at the car. A hand appeared from the driver's side window and waved back, and the car accelerated toward a T-intersection ahead of them. The car turned to the right and soon disappeared behind a curve in the road. Sylvaine turned her bicycle and headed back to them, her face sober.

"The road to Urrugne is blocked," she said without preamble. "That was the head of the local police. He is friends with my husband. I told him we were out for a picnic on this lovely warm day. I think we must cut across country from here. This will add some time to our journey, but it is better to be safe, no?"

Without waiting for an answer, Sylvaine turned her bicycle to cross one of the fields that bordered the road. Evelyn and the others followed and continued when the field turned into woods, and it became apparent they were following some kind of game trail. It was rough going with branches crowding close on either side, threatening to stab an eye or whip across a cheek. Evelyn fell twice, once when her front tire slipped on some loose rock, and once when crossing a small stream. She didn't hurt herself, but she was muddy and wet, and all of her earlier joy in the day had disappeared.

It wasn't until the sun rode high in the noonday sky that they reached their destination. The village of Urrugne lay tucked between the mountains and the seashore.

It's lovely, she sent to the men as she looked around at the red tile roofs and bright white walls of the houses. Though the trees were winter-brown, there were enough mountain evergreens to give the place some color and that deliciously fresh scent. Evelyn felt a sudden twist of homesickness for the pine forests that covered the Black Hills of her home.

It is, Abram sent. *I bet Jerry thinks so, too.*

Evelyn blinked and looked through Abram's eyes. Sure enough, two men in German uniforms sat at an outdoor café a block or so away. Neither of them was currently looking in their direction, but unless their path changed, they'd be riding right by those men. She blinked back into her own eyes before she fell and tried not to let her sudden fear soak through the net.

Not that everyone wasn't feeling it.

Remember what I said, Paul sent. *Be nonchalant. They're busy talking, so they may not even look up at us. Just keep riding.*

But, of course, they did look up. And, as young men sometimes do when they see young women riding by, they called out.

"Ah! Mademoiselle! Did you fall? You are so muddy!" the first one said, with laughter in his voice. His tone was kind, if slightly mocking, and his smile held no malice.

"Yes, Monsieur," Evelyn answered, her heart in her throat. Her voice trembled, but she hoped he would just think she was breathless as she rode by. "I am not a skilled cyclist!"

"Come back! I will teach you!" the German cried, causing his companion to laugh as well.

"I am sorry, Monsieur, but we are late!" To lend credence to this claim, she pumped harder with her legs and inadvertently swerved when she pulled on her handlebars. She could hear the Germans' laughter fading behind her as they continued to pedal down the street. They turned into an alleyway, where a truck awaited them.

"Quickly now," Sylvaine said. "Off the bikes, put them in the back of the truck. That was well done, girl," she said to Evelyn.

"Better if they had not noticed us at all, but I think they will not be suspicious of a group with so many women," Deedee said. "And anyway, you could hardly avoid answering."

"If they ask, I shall say you are a friend of my daughter's from school," Sylvaine said as she lifted her own bicycle into the truck. "Good. Now, through that blue door there, you will find wine and some food. Rest for a bit. I shall return soon to collect you all."

The woman gave them a tight smile, hopped into the driver's seat of the truck, and pulled a men's hat down low over her head. She gave another wave and then the truck roared to life.

"Come," Deedee said. "We must get inside."

Inside the building, which turned out to be one of a row of narrow, tall houses, all was as Sylvaine had said. Evelyn took a moment to try and wipe most of the mud from her dress and wash her hands and face while the others poured the wine and parceled out the bread, cheese, and dried fruit that had been left for them. No one said much as they ate, for the ride had wearied them all.

"What is next?" Abram asked at one point.

"Next," Deedee said, after she swallowed the mouthful of fruit she had been chewing, "we will go up into the foothills, to my friend Neria's house. We will sleep there for the rest of the day and leave tomorrow night to cross the mountains."

"So this is it," he said, his lips curving in a smile. "We are that close?"

"We are close," Deedee answered, but her voice was grave with caution. "But this is the most difficult part. You must remain alert and avoid overconfidence."

"Sure. Of course. But we're close," he said, his smile growing. "That's not nothing."

"I suppose it is not," Deedee said, and returned her attention to the meal.

Perhaps half an hour later, Sylvaine returned in the truck. The bed had been emptied of the bicycles and covered over with a tarp. She entered through the same blue door they'd used and waved them over with impatient looking gestures.

"Come, hurry!" she said. "Men in the back. Evelyn, ride next to Deedee and me."

They left their plates on the table where they lay, assuming someone would come and clean them up soon. Sylvaine didn't appear nearly as concerned with tidiness as with speed, so Evelyn sent a silent apology to whomever had to clean their mess. Then she was out of the door and up into the truck.

Much to everyone's relief, Sylvaine didn't drive back through the middle of town. Instead, she took a narrow, dirt road that wound up into the foothills to the south. Again, Evelyn felt that twist of homesickness as more and more of the dark pines surrounded them.

You'll be home soon, Evie, Abram said. *We're close.*

She sent him back a wordless pulse of gratitude and warmth as the truck swung around another turn. A stone house came into view a few hundred meters farther up the track. It sat tucked down in a hollow between two ridges and looked out on the valley below. Sylvaine drove up to it and cut the engine.

"Lovely view," Abram said when they lifted the tarp and let the men out of the back. Evelyn felt a brief stab of pity as she watched them try to stretch out the kinks they'd gotten from riding up the long, winding, bumpy trail.

"It is," Deedee agreed. "Let us go inside, however. I do not like having you all in the open."

The farmhouse door was wide and wooden and looked as if it had been there since the late Stone Age. Deedee rapped her knuckles lightly upon it, and it swung instantly open. A figure stepped forward out of the gloom inside and crossed heavy-thewed arms over a barrel-like chest.

"Inigo," Deedee said with a smile. The man didn't return her smile at all, but simply opened his arms and welcomed her into a tight hug. Then he released her and waved them all inside.

"This is Inigo Zufiro," Deedee said, once the massive door had been closed and the windows un-shuttered so they had some light. "He is the best Basque mountain guide there is. He also speaks very little French and no English. But he will see us safely across the mountains. Tonight?" she asked, turning to look at the man.

"Tomorrow," he said in French. "Tonight storm."

"Ah, good. So...I will show you to some bedrooms, and you must all sleep as much as you can. We will leave as soon as it is dark tomorrow night."

* * *

Night came earlier in the mountains.

"Evelyn," Deedee whispered. Her voice pulled Evelyn from her napping dreams of pine forests and the Black Hills. Evelyn blinked and opened her eyes to find the Belgian woman holding a shielded lantern in the tiny bedroom they had shared. "It is time to go."

Evelyn sat up and rubbed her eyes. She had gone to bed shortly after the noon meal, hoping to rest up for the ordeal ahead. When she'd laid down, she had thought she wouldn't be able to sleep for nerves, but that turned out not to have been a problem at all. The creeping exhaustion of the previous days had overwhelmed any anxiety she had felt.

"Here, put these on your feet," Deedee said. "They will help you keep your footing in the mountains."

She held out a pair of canvas shoes with soles made of rope. Evelyn took these and turned them over. She'd never seen anything like that.

"Put them on," Deedee said again. "We need to go."

With the strange rope-soled shoes snug on her feet, Evelyn straightened the shirt and trousers she'd been given and braided her hair back out of her face. Deedee handed her a knit cap and then urged her downstairs. The men were there, with their own strange shoes on. Inigo, the big Basque, was checking their feet.

"They're called Espadrilles," Deedee said, in answer to Evelyn's obvious curiosity as they entered the kitchen. The fading sunlight was disappearing in the west as twilight rose around them. "They're the traditional Basque shoe. They're good for the mountains, as I said, and if they fit right, you should not get blisters. That is why Inigo will check your feet."

Which he did. Through gruff, peremptory gestures, he managed to indicate that he wanted her to sit in a chair near the kitchen fireplace. He then knelt before her and took her feet, one by one, in a surprisingly gentle grip while he tugged at the shoes to see if they would slip. He re-tied the long laces around each ankle and then grunted his satisfaction and got to his feet. He gave Deedee a nod and pulled a small bottle out of his bag and took a swig.

"Cognac," he said, and gave the group a tight smile. "Now we go."

"All right," Deedee said. "Here is what will happen. We must move in single file and in complete silence. Sound carries in the mountain air, and this passage is strictly forbidden. Stealth is our only chance. You must obey Inigo's instructions to the letter, without hesitation. This journey will take all night, but when it is over, you will be safe in British custody. Are you ready?"

"One hundred percent," Abram said, speaking for all of them. Evelyn could feel his determination echoing hers, and Sean's, and Paul's. Ready didn't begin to describe how they felt.

"Good, then let us go." She slung her small knapsack over her shoulder, while Inigo stowed his cognac in his own, larger ruck. He lifted and settled the pack on his back and then gestured for the rest of the party to follow him outside.

"Good luck!" called Neria, the lady of the house, as they went through the door one by one. Evelyn gave the quiet woman a smile and a wave.

They walked maybe fifteen meters away from the stone house, just enough to get into the trees, when Inigo stopped them beside a large pine.

"Sticks," he said, and bent to retrieve something from the forest floor. He straightened and handed Abram a stout stick, large enough to suit as a walking stick. The Basque had one for each of them, it seemed, even a slightly shorter one for Evelyn.

"Thank you," she said in French as he handed it to over. He gave her a nod and then pressed his finger to his lips. Right. Complete silence. No more thanks from here on out.

I suppose we can never thank them enough anyway, she thought to the men on the net.

Yes, we can. Cosca told us how, Abram replied. *You remember.*

Of course. Yes, I do remember, she said. *All right. Let it be so.*

Walking sticks in hand, they started up the path. The night was dry, thanks to the soft wind, and the temperature dropped rapidly. Evelyn was grateful for the woolen cap Deedee had given her, as it shielded her ears from the chill. Her nose and cheeks turned cold, and she imagined they were bright red. One by one, and then in groups and hundreds, the stars winked into existence. Evelyn's eyes adjusted to the darkness, and once again, her memory took her back to her mountain childhood. Only in the mountains did the stars shine with the icy brightness she saw overhead. Though the wind cut at them all, Evelyn felt the light of the stars like a benediction, and her spirits lifted as they climbed.

And climbed. And climbed some more. Inigo set a steady, distance-eating pace with his wide steps. He seemed to know this land as if it were an extension of his own skin. He led them up game paths that looked as if they'd never seen human feet, always with one wary eye on the nearby roads. Occasionally, he would stop at a certain tree, or behind a collection of boulders, and produce some treasure cached there. A bottle of cognac, once. Some dried meat another time. Once, another knitted hat, which he handed to Sean to use. And then he'd nod and turn without a word and start the climb again.

Some hours in (Evelyn had no idea how many), they were roughly halfway along the coast from their starting point when the strong beams of a lighthouse swung across their path. The light played over the hills, lighting the crests and casting the valleys into deeper shadow. In the distance, they could see clusters of lights hugging the coast. Irun, at the mouth of the Bidassoa River, lay just ahead. Farther along, San Sebastian stained the sky a kind of smoky orange color. Evelyn looked back over her shoulder. France, of course, lay mostly blacked out, due to the British and their night bombing raids.

That's the river down there, Abram said. *Just beyond that, and then we're nearly there. Nearly home free!*

It's starting to snow, Paul said. *This could get interesting.*

* * *

E velyn looked up. Sure enough, small white flakes were drifting here and there in the air. The mountain girl in her quailed at the thought of being caught out in the hills in a snowstorm, but their guide didn't look concerned. Neither did Deedee. She simply gestured to them to keep moving and walked tirelessly behind the big Basque man.

They started down into the stark shadow of the Bidassoa gorge. The snow started to stick to the rocks underfoot, reflecting back the starlight from above, but making everything slick and treacherous underfoot. Evelyn slipped once and fell heavily on her rear. Sean was beside her in an instant, offering a hand to help pull her up.

I'm all right, she told everyone. *It's just slippery.*

Place your steps carefully, Abram said. *And use your sticks.*

Despite this advice, Evelyn was not the only one to fall. Sean went down once, as did Abram himself. Only Paul, with his catlike grace, managed to stay upright for the entire path down into the gorge.

Gradually, Evelyn started to become aware of a distant rumbling, not terribly unlike the sound of a formation of Forts returning from a mission. It grew louder as they descended, the sound echoing off of the steep walls of the gorge. Here and there, through the trees, Evelyn could catch a glimpse of white water tumbling over the rocks below, racing west to the sea. Now and then, across the valley, they could see the gray gleam of the road that ran along the Spanish border. Just down the ridge from this road, a set of railroad tracks lay silent in the night.

They came to the bottom of the valley. Inigo held up his hand for silence and pointed west, downriver. Light gleamed against the sky, and Evelyn understood he was indicating they weren't far from a border checkpoint. She nodded her understanding and put her fingers over her lips as her men did the same. Inigo gave an answering nod and began removing his trousers. Deedee, too, stripped down and knotted her trousers around her neck, and though Evelyn could feel her cheeks heating up, she followed suit.

Gesturing to all of them to remain silent, Inigo stepped first into the torrent of water. Evelyn could see him reaching out, testing the depth and strength of the current. Evelyn saw him sink to his waist and then come back up to the bank. He held out his hand peremptorily, and Abram took it.

Evelyn felt the numbing shock of cold through the net as the water touched Abram's skin. He gasped silently, then gritted his teeth and followed Inigo farther into the water. They were about halfway across when Deedee reached out and took Evelyn's hand and pulled her gently to the edge of the water. Evelyn took a deep breath and followed the Belgian woman. The river bottom was even more treacherous than the mountain path had been, and Evelyn had a hard time keeping her footing. If not for Deedee's steady strength, she wasn't sure she would have managed to keep moving against the icy pain of the water. Numbness assaulted her feet and legs, reaching up to her waist as the water rushed against her, trying to push her westward, toward the lights and the danger of the border checkpoint.

Just when Evelyn didn't think she could resist the current's force, the bottom started to slope upward again, and the water level slid down her skin. The numbness, however, stayed as the cold wind whipped against her wet, chilled legs.

"Rest here," Deedee whispered in her ear as they exited the water into a grassy meadow. "Get dressed while we get the others."

Evelyn nodded, her teeth chattering too hard to speak. She limped over to where Abram lay already in the grass, his face pale and cold in the night. Without a word she sat down next to him and began pulling her trousers back on. They didn't go on easily, but she felt less like she was being flayed alive by ice knives afterward. Then she lay down next to the navigator. He put his arms around her and gave her a wan smile.

Seems like we've been here before, he said.

Only this time I'm not feverish.

True, thank goodness. Though a fever would probably feel pretty good right now. I don't think I've ever been that cold in my life. Ever.

Are you warming up? she asked.

Little by little. The feeling's coming back into my feet now. I wish it wouldn't. It feels like a thousand pins.

Here, let me help.

She sat back up and began chaffing his feet while tucking her own underneath herself to help them to warm faster. When Inigo and Deedee delivered Paul and Sean to the meadow, she did the same for them. As always, touch made the strength of their bond stronger, and that strength flowed through and bolstered her.

They rested long enough for everyone to get dry and warm. Inigo pulled some thin wool blankets from his ruck, and they used these to towel off and wrap around themselves as they regained their strength, for their ordeal was far from over. The hardest, most dangerous part lay directly ahead.

Inigo passed around his bottle of cognac and then got to his feet. This was, apparently, the signal to move on. They re-packed the blankets, replaced their Espadrilles, and crossed the meadow toward their next obstacle: the border road into Spain.

On the other side of the meadow, a rocky embankment led up to the railroad tracks. Though not as sheer as the cliffs above Bonaparte Beach, Evelyn quailed at the thought of climbing it, especially as tired as she felt after the river. At least the cold had kept her bad ankle from swelling up, for while it twinged at her in warning every once in a while, it was mostly not a problem.

Once again, Inigo showed them how to go. The embankment consisted of several large, piled boulders, and the Basque guide scrambled up over these with seemingly little effort. Once at the top, he reached down and helped the others to do the same. Only Deedee had the quiet strength to do it by herself.

I wonder how many times she's done this, Evelyn thought, not really expecting an answer, but needing to think about something other than her fear they'd be caught here at the end, so close to their goal. *It has to have been several. She's so calm and collected.*

I hope enough to get us through it safely, Paul said. They had crossed the railroad tracks one by one and taken shelter under the bushes that lined the Spanish highway. Inigo waited for a long moment, listening, and then darted out from undercover and crossed the road before diving back into the brush on the other side. They waited, hardly daring to breathe, until his face appeared again near the ground. He held up one finger and then made a beckoning gesture.

Here I go, Abram sent, and did his best to copy Inigo's movements. He wasn't as quick, or as oddly graceful as the Basque, but he made it before the sweeping headlights of a car sent them all face down, pressing noses into the dirt and hoping no one in the car saw them. Evelyn heard the whooshing sound of the tires on the pavement, and the change in pitch as the vehicle passed them without slowing. The night grew silent again before any of them lifted their heads.

Inigo says come now, Abram sent. *Paul.*

The bombardier got to his feet and crept across the road. He wasn't as fast as Inigo had been, but he was silent, and he moved so smoothly Evelyn could barely see him. She felt him though, through the net as he slid to his belly under a thorn bush on the far side.

I'm good, he sent.

Good. Evie, Abram said. *Quickly.*

Her turn. She pushed up on her hands and knees and carefully brought her feet underneath herself. One of her rope-soled shoes scuffed in the dirt, and she bit her lip in frustration. She rose to a crouch and glanced left and right along the road, just to be sure. It remained empty, so she took a deep breath and scurried across.

Once her feet touched dirt on the far side, she dropped to her knees and began crawling forward, feeling the scratchy boughs of the scrub catch at her hat, her hair, her clothing.

Good job, Evie, Abram sent. *Sean, you're next, then Deedee.*

The two of them made it across without incident as well, and Evelyn breathed a sigh of relief. There was still danger, and they still had a long way to go...but they were out of France and into Spain. And that, as Abram would say, was not nothing.

Beyond the road, they had yet another slope to climb, and this one was complicated. Once they got about ten feet above the road, they could see the frontier outpost that had been lighting up the sky. More importantly, if someone in the outpost were looking, there was a chance they could see *them.*

They crawled up the slope on their bellies, moving slowly, trying to use the brush and vegetation for what concealment it could offer. At one point, Evelyn looked over and saw a sentry patrolling a mere one hundred meters away, but with his back to them, looking down the road. She stiffened and put her face down and froze, not even daring to breathe for a ten count. Every instinct in her screamed at her to reach out and try to discern if the man had seen her...but if she did that, he *would* know she'd been there, and all would be for naught. So she let her breath out slowly, kept her head down in the mountain dirt, and continued her slow climb.

They topped the summit of that slope and went down over the back side. Once they were out of sight of the outpost, they were again able to stand up and go more quickly. No resting now, not so close to such a dangerous place. Though her legs and her back and her...well...everything, really, ached, Evelyn pushed herself forward, reminding herself she had promised she would keep up.

You can do it, Evie. You're doing great, Sean said now and again. Abram and Paul, too, encouraged her. Just as she encouraged them, bolstered their strength as they started to stumble on overtired, chilled, and sodden feet and legs.

They were back to climbing, heading up toward the triple-peaked landmark of the Trois Couronnes. At one point, Abram fell, dragged down by the internal weight of his heavy, tired legs. Evelyn felt the frustration they were all feeling surge through the net from him on a wave of pain from where he'd hit the ground.

Are you all right, sir? Evelyn asked.

Sir, Evie? Really? After all this? he shot back, his tone sharp as he used his walking stick to try and struggle back up to his feet. Pain twinged through his right knee and into her consciousness.

You're still an officer, and our senior ranking, she said, more to distract him from the knee than for any other reason. *I was trained to be professional under any circumstances.*

That got a pulse of humor from Paul and a following one from Sean. Abram got up and waved a hand at Deedee, who had stopped next to him to help.

"I'm all right," he told the Belgian woman in an undertone.

"Good," she said. "Keep going."

"How far? Until we rest?"

"Dos cien metros," Inigo said, from up ahead. Two hundred meters.

That's not far, Sean sent. *You can do this, sir.*

I know I can. We all can, Abram replied.

Paul said nothing, and Evelyn just sent a pulse of the confidence she felt in their leader down the lines of the net. She might have doubted her own strength, but she'd never doubt Abram's.

They didn't stop in two hundred meters, however. Nor after that. Inigo just kept walking forward and up with that steady, ground-eating pace. Evelyn began to struggle, and her ankle sent flashes of warning pain up her leg with every step. Abram asked Inigo one more time about taking a rest and received the same reply: dos cien metros. It was always dos cien metros, all the way to the top of the mountain.

Finally, with the dawn sky pinkening to the east, they lay down and caught their breath. Inigo handed his leather bottle of cognac around again and passed out some smoked fish and cheese he'd carried in his pack. Evelyn ate all she was given and licked her fingers free of the crumbs. When the cognac got to her, she took a tiny sip, savoring the burn of the liquor as it warmed her from within.

It wasn't much, but it refreshed them a little. Enough that they got back to their feet and followed Inigo back on the trail. They started back down, roughly following the outline of a road, but staying far enough off it they could fade into the surrounding woods and brush if necessary. At least, that was the theory. Despite their rest at the summit of the Trois Couronnes, Evelyn quickly felt as if her limbs were made of lead. Her steps dragged in the dirt, and she began to feel as if she existed only in a haze of fatigue and pain.

When the sun finally slipped over the horizon, the first rays of dawn found them hiking down a long slope into a meadow filled with wildflowers and waist-high grass. On the far side of the meadow, Evelyn could just make out the gray roof of a rambling house. They approached with great caution, keeping an eye out for police or other unfriendly beings. But no one was there, save the dark-eyed woman who opened the door with a grave smile.

"Welcome," she said in Spanish-accented French. "You have made it to Spain."

* * *

The woman's name was Estefania Irriarte. Like Neria Zubizarretta across the border, she welcomed the fugitives into her large, warm farmhouse and fed them bowls of steaming hot stew and milk. Evelyn was so tired she thought she might drop where she stood, but her stomach growled at the enticing scents of Estefania's kitchen so she forced herself to stay awake long enough to eat. She was halfway through her second bowl of stew when she noticed that, while Inigo sat beside them at the long trestle table, Deedee was nowhere to be found.

"She has gone to get a car," Senora Irriarte said when Abram asked her Evie's silent question. "You should sleep now, if you can."

"What happens now?" Abram asked, undeterred.

"You rest," Senora Irriarte said, with a smile that made her dark-eyed beauty shine. "And Deedee gets the car. She will be back to-night. Do not worry, my friends. You are nearly safe. But sleep. You must be exhausted after your journey."

Evelyn, at least, was. So for what felt like the thousandth time, she curled up in a bed that didn't belong to her and found her rest in the home of a stranger. She didn't even recall falling asleep and so was startled when Deedee called her name. She sat bolt upright in the bed, her head pounding.

"Oh! I am sorry to have startled you, my friend," the Belgian woman said with a soft smile. "I know you must be very tired, but you must wake up. It is time to go."

"More hiking?" Evelyn groaned. Deedee gave a little laugh.

"No," she said. "I have a car this time."

Only then did Evelyn remember the conversation at the trestle table in Senora Irriarte's kitchen. This, then, was whatever was to happen next.

She got to her feet and used the ancient-looking washstand to clean her hands and face as best she could. Her clothes were muddy and torn in places, but there wasn't much she could do about that. She re-braided her hair and handed the woolen cap back to Deedee. The other woman looked at her in confusion.

"For the next group you save," Evelyn said softly, and Deedee smiled as understanding dawned. She took the cap with a nod and tucked it into her knapsack. Evelyn took a moment to pull the blankets straight on her borrowed bed and then the two of them walked down the long hallway back to Senora Irriarte's kitchen. The men arrived from their own bedroom a moment later. Deedee gave their hostess a hug and ushered the rest of them out to the car.

It was a tight fit, but they managed to cram together. Evelyn and Inigo sat up front next to Deedee, who drove the gray sedan down the windy roads and into the town of San Sebastian proper. Evelyn looked around as they passed churches and banks and rows and rows of houses lit by streetlights. Compared to the destruction she'd seen in Brussels and Paris, San Sebastian looked like a peaceful seaside town. Though there were plenty of police, who certainly would have arrested them all if they'd known what they'd spent the previous night doing.

They drove through the downtown and out past the houses on the south side before turning off the main highway and onto a country lane. A few hundred meters up, a burgundy sedan idled by the side of the road, headlights off. Deedee let off the gas and coasted to a stop next to this vehicle, then cut the engine.

"All right," she said. "This is who I've brought you to see."

The rear door of the burgundy sedan opened, and a tall, thin man wearing a gray suit and looking rather quintessentially British stepped out. Evelyn felt something hard and tight constrict in her chest. She reached down and caught Deedee's free hand.

"Thank you," Evelyn whispered. "So very much. For everything."

Deedee smiled, and for the first time, Evelyn could see that she looked tired indeed.

"You are most welcome," she said. "Good luck."

With that, Inigo opened his door and slid out, leaving room for Evelyn to exit. He also opened the rear door, and Sean, Paul, and Abram all stepped out of the car. The man in the gray suit walked up to them and held out his hand.

"Orvin Broxton," he said. "British Consulate, at your service. If you please, the moment you get in the car is the moment you're safe. Diplomatic plates, you see. Can't touch you then."

Ladies first, Abram said. *Go on, Evie.*

Evelyn felt her eyes fill with tears as emotion overwhelmed her. She couldn't move, couldn't breathe. It didn't seem possible.

It's possible. You did it, Evie-girl, Sean said. *You got us safe. Now, let's get in the car and go home.*

Come with me? she whispered through the net.

Always and anywhere, Sean answered.

But let's start with home, Paul put in, and that did the trick. Between Abram's encouragement, Sean's devotion, and Paul's practicality, her men got her over the last hurdle. Evelyn Adamsen got in the car and started her journey home.

* * *

Lina sat rigidly, encased in ice, though flames licked at the corners of her mind.

"Well?" Smolenk asked, his supercilious gaze managing to convey both extreme disinterest and extreme impatience. "Did you find what you were looking for in Bayonne?"

"No, sir," Lina said, her voice clipped and very, very carefully blank. "My full report is on your desk. The abbreviated version is this: the information we received from my interrogation of Doctor van Duren turned out to be correct. His daughter was in Bayonne. We apprehended her along with a co-conspirator by the name of Sylvaine Ballasdens. I have not yet had the opportunity to fully interrogate these women, but it is clear there is more to both of them than was originally thought." *By you*, she added silently.

"What do you mean?" he asked. Across the room, Neils sent her a pleading look. Lina ignored it, just as her onetime friend had ignored her pleas for help leaving Brussels in time.

"It appears that Diandra van Duren is, at the very least, an incredibly knowledgeable guide and courier for the fugitive escape network," Lina said. "When we apprehended her, she had just completed a trip across the Pyrenees with four American fugitives."

"A woman? Crossing the Pyrenees? Impossible," Smolenk scoffed. Lina felt the anger building in her mind, felt its flames start licking the underside of her skin.

"Not at all, sir," she said. "I have touched her mind. I know she has done this. Many times, in fact."

"I don't believe it for one second, Fraulein Sucherin. Clearly she is delusional, and you have picked up on the fact she *believes* she has done this miraculous feat. If, in fact, you 'pick up' anything at all. You say the girl is involved in the escape network? Fine, I believe that, based on her father's position. But a courier? Across the mountains? Impossible."

Lina said nothing. Smolenk smiled thinly and stared at her.

"Fraulein Sucherin," he said after a moment, and Lina could tell he meant his voice to be kindly. "I believe this work is taking a toll on you. Intelligence work...police work...these are no place for a woman. Your mind is not designed for such harsh realities. I think it would be best if you transferred back to Berlin for some time. There is much record keeping work to be done there. Perhaps you might find yourself more...suited to a more traditionally feminine task."

Lina still said nothing. Smolenk's smile grew wider, his eyes sharper.

"Yes. I think that will be exactly the thing. Neils, have one of your people purchase a train ticket for her in the morning. I feel certain she will want to return as soon as possible. We thank you for your brave work here, Fraulein. It is not your fault it did not work out. Please do not think that in the slightest."

I don't, she thought, but still said nothing. Instead, she did something unforgivable. With the lightest of touches, the touch that even Evelyn Adamsen could barely detect, Lina reached out and pulled loose a single thread from the man's psyche. He felt it, of course, for she saw him twitch. But he didn't believe her psychic powers were real, so he could hardly accuse her of using them. His eyes went wide, and she finally gave him a smile.

"Good day, Herr Smolenk," she said and turned to leave without even acknowledging Neils' presence. He had refused to help her when she needed it most. He might as well be dead.

Behind her, she heard Smolenk start to say something and then stop, suddenly. Her lips started to curve in a smile. His psyche would start to unravel, slowly at first, but then faster and faster, like an old sweater. Nightmares, perhaps. Missing memories. Personality changes. All of these things were possible. She didn't know what form his madness would take, but she had no doubt it would come, slowly, and it would destroy his world.

Lina could be very patient where justice was concerned.

As Evelyn Adamsen would learn...one day.

* * * * *

Epilogue February 1944: Big Week

Colonel Ken Rizer stood in his office and watched out the window as the distant line of B-17 Flying Fortresses grew larger on the horizon. *Nineteen, twenty, twenty-one*...he counted as they dropped down out of the overhead cloud cover. On his desk, the telephone rang. He picked up the handset and brought it to his ear, his eyes never leaving the window.

"Rizer," he said.

"Ken," a voice said on the other end. "It's Chucky Bates. It's looking good, Ken. It's looking real good from where I sit!"

Colonel Charles "Chucky" Bates was the newly installed commander of the 364th Fighter Group over at RAF Honington. The 364th's newly arrived P-51B Mustang fighters had provided the much-anticipated long-range fighter escort for today's mission.

"Here too," Rizer said, and something in his chest eased as he counted three more Forts descending out of the cloud cover. Two of them were trailing smoke, but they'd made it home.

"I told you my boys would take care of yours, Ken," Bates said, laughter in his voice.

"That you did, Chucky. That you did. Next pint's on me."

"I'll hold you to it, Ken. I better head down to debrief my boys. Be seeing ya!"

"So long, Chucky," Rizer said and replaced the handset in its cradle. He shook his head with a tiny smile at the flamboyant fighter pilot and continued watching until the last Fort's wheels touched down on Ridgway's runway with a puff of smoke.

Only then did he turn back to the memorandum sitting on his desk.

To: Colonel Kenneth Rizer, Commander, 381st Bombardment Wing
From: Commander, 8th Air Force

Colonel Rizer, with the arrival of the P-51B long-range fighter, I have decided to stand down General Durant's secret WAC program. Please give my regards to your ladies and pass along my thanks and that of a grateful nation for the service they've rendered.

Effective immediately, all psychic aircrew technicians will be returned stateside and mustered out. Their program, however, remains classified, and they should be reminded of that fact.

Sincerely,
Harold Rayder, Brigadier General, USAAF

In the five months the WACs had been flying with his crews, Rizer had seen a remarkable uptick in mission effectiveness. However, of the twenty fresh-faced young women who had arrived back in October, only twelve remained. Seven of them hadn't returned from the war-savaged skies over Occupied Europe and were presumed to be dead.

That number had been eight, but the P-51B wasn't the only newly arrived miracle in England. Evelyn Adamsen, missing since just before Christmas of last year, had returned with three of her surviving crewmen aboard a British ship only a week ago. The four of them had been through hell and were still debriefing in London with MI-9, the British department responsible for recovering downed and evading allied airmen.

Rizer had talked very fast and pulled a little rank to do it, but he'd managed to bully his way in to check on his men and woman. What he'd found had surprised him and, frankly, made him slightly uneasy. Adamsen had apparently been linked to her three crewmen for so long she could no longer detach from them. There were additional extreme circumstances that had occurred, apparently, and he wasn't sure of all the details, but it was very clear that Adamsen would never lead a normal life. She appeared to be developing a relationship with the only surviving enlisted man on the crew, the flight engineer, Sean Carrol. Ordinarily, that would be a problem in and of itself, but it got even more complicated when one considered that she *also* appeared to be in a perpetual network with the other two survivors, navigator Abram Portman and bombardier Paul Rutherford.

He'd already made the decision the four of them would not fly another combat mission, not after what they'd been through. And truth be told, the cost of sending *any* of these women up with their precious gifts seemed extraordinarily high, even for the increase in mission success.

So General Rayder's order didn't shock him. It came as something of a relief. He could do what he'd wanted to do in his heart since the first time the women had come home from a mission. He could tell them they didn't have to go back out. He could keep them safe. He could protect them. He could send them home.

Rizer just hoped that would be enough. After what they'd seen...and from what he understood, having seen it through multiple minds amplified the psychological effects of war. He could look at any of the women and see the truth of that on their thin, tired faces and their huge, shadowed eyes.

Someone knocked twice on his door, jolting him from his reverie. It was time to head down to Operations. He grabbed the general's memo. He'd brief it this afternoon and begin preparations to send the WACs home in the morning. Their crews wouldn't like it, but unless he missed his guess, many of the men worried about their psychics just as much as he did.

War never changed: you always protected the man next to you. Even if that man happened to be a woman. Especially if that woman had also protected you.

Colonel Ken Rizer squared his shoulders and walked out of his office, head high, secure in the knowledge he could finally do the right thing.

<<<<>>>>

ABOUT THE AUTHOR

Kacey Ezell was born in South Dakota in 1977. Her parents joined the US Air Force in 1984, and she grew up around the world on various military bases. When she was seven, her mother gave her a copy of Anne McCaffrey's Dragondrums, and shortly thereafter, Kacey decided that she wanted to be a dragonrider when she grew up. In 1999, she followed her parents into the "family business" and graduated from the United States Air Force Academy before going to pilot training. As dragons were in short supply at the time, she reasoned that flying aircraft was the next best thing. She earned her wings in 2001, and has over 2500 hours in the UH-1N and Mi-17 helicopters.

From the time she was a small child, Kacey made up stories to tell to her friends and family. In 2009, while deployed to Iraq, she wrote the military-themed supernatural story "Light," which was accepted for publication in the Baen Books anthology Citizens. She was asked to consult on John Ringo's 2015 novel Strands of Sorrow, and wrote the cover story for the Black Tide Rising anthology set in Ringo's zombie apocalypse universe. That story, "Not in Vain" was selected for inclusion in the "Year's Best Military SF and Adventure Fiction" anthology produced by Baen Books.

Kacey writes science fiction, fantasy, horror, noir, romance...she writes fiction. She lives with her husband, two daughters, and two cats.

Connect with Kacey Ezell Online

Website: www.kaceyezell.net

Amazon: https://www.amazon.com/Kacey-Ezell/e/B0195040QU/

Facebook: https://www.facebook.com/AuthorKaceyEzell/

Twitter: @Sevillalost

The following is an
Excerpt from Book Two of The Psyche of War:

The World Asunder

Kacey Ezell

Available from Theogony Books

Summer, 2018

eBook, Paperback, and Audio

Chapter One

On a sticky summer day in June of 1948, Adalina Sucherin remembered who she was.

She'd been walking home from work, but she hadn't really been paying close attention to her route. There was no great reason for her to hurry home to her solitary flat. It contained only a creaky bed and the few meagre possessions she'd been able to scrounge after the war. Her neighbors, perhaps, might have looked for her, but they knew her habits, and it wasn't unusual for her to walk for hours each night. There was solace in movement, in the illusion of action that exercise provided. Standing still provided the horror an opportunity to creep in, and so Lina preferred to walk.

It was the sound that did it. She would remember that, later. That deep rumble, just at the edge of her hearing. It started in her chest and built to an audible roar...but distant. A sudden flash of fear brought her head up from her unseeing study of the broken concrete road. Bombers? An air raid?

No. Stupid, stupid, she chastised herself. The war had been over for three years. Three years since the Reich had fallen, taking with it all of her illusions, all of her fire. Three years since the Soviet soldiers came ravening through the streets of Berlin, looting and raping everything in their path. Three years since she'd last torn a man's psyche apart, watching him bleed from his eyes and nose as his brain hemorrhaged in response. Three years since she'd killed to keep herself and three little girls safe, then locked her power away behind shields thicker than concrete, stronger than steel. Three long, uncertain, fear-tainted years.

Those weren't bombers after all.

She glanced around, looking for the hand-lettered signs that sometimes indicated the names of streets in this corpse of a once-great city. Wilhemstraße. She hadn't realized she'd come so far south. She was next to the border of the American zone, just north of the airport. A glance at the sky showed her a line of aircraft darkening the horizon. She watched them as she continued walking.

"I'm sorry, miss. You can't go any further without a pass."

Lina blinked and focused on the man who spoke in harshly-accented German. She pressed her lips together and fought not to recoil in revulsion. A Soviet soldier, standing next to one of the borderlines the so-called allies had set up when they drew and quartered Berlin after the armistice. She gave him a nod (one must be polite, else one invited more attention!) and started to walk away, when a thought stopped her. These "allies" *did* have men with guns stationed on the borders of their claimed territories. That didn't seem like a particularly warm alliance to her.

"Sir," she asked. "Why are there so many aircraft?"

He gave her a smile, a sweet one. It made him look young.

"Do not be frightened, miss," he said. "The war has not begun again. The British and Americans are flying supplies into the other sectors of Berlin in an attempt to bribe the population with their decadence and corruption. But it won't work. No ground transportation from the west is permitted into Berlin at all. No one has ever supplied a city this size by air alone. It cannot be done! The city will be reunited under the rightful rule of the workers soon enough. Have no fear."

"Thank you," she murmured and stepped away. He touched the fingers of his free hand (the one not holding his rifle) to the brim of his cap and gave her another smile. She barely noticed, as thoughts began to tumble one over the other in her brain while she resumed her walk home.

Berlin was cut off from the west. The Soviets were trying to starve the population of the British and American sectors out.

The British and Americans were airlifting in supplies. Why? Did they know what kind of hell the Soviet occupation of Berlin had been?

If they knew, why did they ally with such monsters?

Lina did not like the British. The Americans were worse. During the war, the Americans had bombed her hometown and killed her family. Then, just when love had ignited in her life amidst the dreariness of war, another American, a woman, had destroyed everything she held dear. Lina had carried that woman's name in her heart as a talisman against fear and as fuel for the fires of hatred she nurtured inside. One day, she promised herself, one day, Evelyn Adamsen would pay for what she had done...

And then the world had ended, and the Soviets had come.

Amid the fires and the screams, Lina had hidden with her neighbor's three daughters in a cellar under a bombed out building. They had heard the cries and laughter, the crashing of glass, the sharp coughs of rifle fire, and the distant booming of the field guns. For three days and three nights, she'd hidden with those girls, drinking water from a leaky pipe, eating the crumbs from an old crust of bread. Until the night when a group of soldiers crashed drunkenly through the hidden cellar door.

For the first time in three years, Lina didn't flinch from the memory. She forced herself, instead, to examine it. To replay it in her head, just as it had happened.

Something heavy hit the door. It cracked near the hinges, along the lock. Something hit it again, and it slammed open, banging against the far wall. The girls screamed and fled for the corner behind Lina. So young, all of them. Nine, seven, and barely three. Mere babies.

Lina interposed her body between the girls and the soldier. He reeked of alcohol, sweat, and gunpowder. He leered at her, craned his neck to see behind her, his pig-like eyes glinting in the light of their single lantern. Behind him, two more crowded in, then stopped, drunk and confused.

"Take the woman," the first soldier slurred. Lina was fluent in Russian, and she barely understood him. "I'll take the girls."

"No," Lina said, her voice cracking like a whip.

"Shut up, cunt," he said with a laugh, "You're too old and ugly, especially when there are pretty little girls--"

Lina heard no more. She took two steps forward and jabbed her fingers into the man's throat before he could marshal his drunken reflexes to react. The moment her skin touched his, she reached out with her mind, in the way she'd been taught by the Reich's best scientists and theorists, and she ripped his natural, latent psychic shields away. And then she, the most powerful student to ever graduate from the Reichschule, stabbed her power deep into his brain.

His cranial capillaries exploded. All of them. At once. Blood flowed from his eyes, ears, and nose. She watched him stumble toward her a step and then crumple to the ground. Then she turned and looked at the other men in the room. One raised his rifle halfway to his shoulder. She stared at him, wondering if he would do it.

He didn't. Neither did his partner. They just turned and left. The corpse of their friend stayed crumpled in a heap on the cellar floor.

Lina blinked away the memory and looked skyward once more. She didn't like the British, or the Americans. But they were crazy enough to try and airlift supplies to her city rather than see it fall into the hands of the Soviets. Evelyn Adamsen had been an American aircrew woman. Perhaps...perhaps there was hope.

For the first time in three years, Lina felt a spark of interest ignite in her mind, and the coals of her burning need for revenge began to smolder once again.

# # # # #

The following is an

Excerpt from Book One of the Revelations Cycle:

Cartwright's Cavaliers

Mark Wandrey

Available Now Seventh Seal Press

eBook, Paperback, and Audio Book

The last two operational tanks were trapped on their chosen path. Faced with destroyed vehicles front and back, they cut sideways to the edge of the dry river bed they'd been moving along and found several large boulders to maneuver around that allowed them to present a hull-down defensive position. Their troopers rallied on that position. It was starting to look like they'd dig in when *Phoenix 1* screamed over and strafed them with dual streams of railgun rounds. A split second later, *Phoenix 2* followed on a parallel path. Jim was just cheering the air attack when he saw it. The sixth damned tank, and it was a heavy.

"I got that last tank," Jim said over the command net.

"Observe and stand by," Murdock said.

"We'll have these in hand shortly," Buddha agreed, his transmission interspersed with the thudding of his CASPer firing its magnetic accelerator cannon. "We can be there in a few minutes."

Jim examined his battlespace. The tank was massive. It had to be one of the fusion-powered beasts he'd read about. Which meant shields and energy weapons. It was heading down the same gap the APC had taken, so it was heading right towards the APC and Second Squad, and fast.

"Shit," he said.

"Jim," Hargrave said, "we're in position. What are you doing?"

"Leading," Jim said as he jumped out from the rock wall.

# # # # #

425